Hugh closed his eyes and breathed deeply. He could smell Catherine's skin where her face hovered above his. Opening his eyes again, he found himself drowning in the green depths of her eyes. Warm, gentle, trusting eyes that smiled down upon him like an angel's.

"Hugh?" Catherine breathed quietly. The palm of his hand cupped her face, feeling the softness of her. Slowly, gently, he drew his face against her neck, breathing in the essence of her. He felt her pulse throb against his lips. Gently, he pressed a kiss there, letting his lips linger.

Another kiss. Slow and perfect, savored like a sweet drop of water after a long, hot day in the desert. Catherine sighed, and the sound vibrated against his mouth. He kissed her again moving along an imaginary line that drew him like a moth to flame, his lips traced a line up her neck.

His hand twined through the thick curls of copper and he drew her lips to his even as he rose to meet them.

A sudden jolt of heat coursed through him at their touch. Hot and liquid. Like wine set to flame, it seared to his very core. She met his kiss with a fervor of her own. He felt her arms encircle him, her fingers caressing the muscles that crisscrossed his shoulders.

And from the back of her throat, he heard the sound of her soft moan as she molded herself to him.

ELAINE KANE

TEMPTED

ZEBRA BOOKS
KENSINGTON PUBLISHING CORP.

For Alex and Heidi
who have given me so much support and love

ZEBRA BOOKS are published by

Kensington Publishing Corp.
475 Park Avenue South
New York, NY 10016

Zebra and the Z logo Reg. U.S. Pat. & TM Off. Heartfire Romance and the Heartfire Romance logo are trademarks of Kensington Publishing Corp.

First Printing: May, 1994

Printed in the United States of America

One

Catherine de Tralle leaned out between two of the massive limestone blocks which crowned the castle parapet, hoping to catch a better view of the horsemen climbing the narrow, winding road far below. Despite the carefully plaited braids that crowned her head, she sported a halo of unruly curls—the eternal bane of her young existence. Not only were they curls that refused to stay where she put them, but they were the golden red of a cloudless dawn besides. And try as she might to keep the willful mass at bay, her life seemed a constant battle to tame her stubborn tresses. Pushing a stray tendril off her face, Catherine wedged the toe of her slipper into the castle wall and scooted farther out over the edge.

"Well?" her brother Jean asked impatiently from behind her. He chose to let Catherine inch over the wall rather than do it himself. But then, he was only ten—two years younger than Catherine—and possessed of a far less adventuresome nature than his sister.

"I think they are only travelers," she replied
wistfully. Catherine continued to watch the party
despite her assessment. She had been so certain
that at last Crusaders were arriving. Regardless
of the fact that the sea-bound route the Crusaders took passed close to Avignon, none had yet
bothered to seek lodging at the intimidating castle of Bernard de Tralle. The castle perched on
unforgiving cliffs above the Rhône, and though
its white stone sparkled invitingly in the sunlight
of southern France, travelers came infrequently.

"Climb down now, Catherine. If they are only
travelers there is nothing more to see. I'd rather
visit my hawks in the mews than watch some old
pilgrims climb the hillside."

"Don't pout, Jean," Catherine reprimanded
gently as she unsnagged her kirtle from a limestone protrusion. "It's a gorgeous day to be outside, and besides I haven't had a really good look
at them yet. Oh, see!" she exclaimed, pointing.
"They are just now coming out of the trees!"

Unable to wait for her to describe the entourage, Jean braved a look, hoisting himself into
the next archer's slit. Catherine squinted against
the bright spring sun as the party progressed
slowly up the hillside. It was a small group. She
counted twenty men in all. Ten rode chargers,
five on smaller palfreys and the others on foot.
Though they rarely had unexpected visitors, she
had seen enough pilgrims while hawking in the
forests to know that they traveled in much larger

groups and always with a following of women and livestock.

From his perch, Jean gave a whoop of glee. "They *are* knights!" he cried. "At last!" he shouted in excitement. "Our first real Crusaders!"

Excitement blossomed in the pit of Catherine's stomach at the thought that these must, indeed, be Crusaders. They were nearly at the portcullis directly below them now, and she could see clearly the two men who led the group. They sat astride gigantic chargers draped in white with the Holy Crucifix emblazoned on the haunches of each tremendous beast.

"Come on, come on!" Jean called, jumping back down to the battlement. "I cannot wait to hear their tales, Catherine. Just think! They are going to Jerusalem to fight the Saracens!"

Jean was swallowed up in the darkness of the center tower, but Catherine remained fixed in her spot pleased to be able to observe the knights from her secret cubby. A brisk wind, common atop the cliffs, blew a fistful of hair across her face, and she shoved the wayward tresses up into her braid in exasperation. When they were at last in place Catherine looked down to find one of the Crusaders watching her, his attention caught by her sudden movement. Embarrassed at being seen spying, Catherine quickly pressed herself back against the wall. But a moment later her embarrassment gave way to curiosity and she peeked out over the edge again. The knight was still looking at her, and as her chin appeared above the stone wall, he gave her a broad smile and a courtly nod. Nonplussed, Catherine could think of nothing to do except stick out her tongue, which was precisely what she did before bolting—mortified—to her chambers.

"What are you looking at?" Terrence followed his brother's gaze to the top of the center tower in concern. "Certainly you do not fear treachery. We were assured that Bernard de Tralle is a man of good faith."

"No treachery, brother," Hugh Vougnet chuckled. "Merely a child, possessed, I fear, of a spoilt nature. Surely one of the count's children. Wasn't it said he has a handful of them?"

"Indeed," Terrence agreed. "And 'twas also said that they are a wayward bunch. Schooled overmuch and disciplined little."

"Schooled?" Hugh commented in surprise. "Are all de Tralle's brood destined for service to God?"

Terrence shrugged. "I have no idea what possesses a man to educate children otherwise. Had our father not intended such a path for me, I would be as dull as an ax handle."

Hugh winced at his brother's words. "Fortune smiles upon you, Terrence. You have your letters and your calling. Those of us without such tools have cause to envy a man like you."

"You jest, of course. There isn't a man in all of France possessed of your skills with a broadsword and lance. What stronger sign can you wish of our Lord?"

"Yes, I know. I'm good at fighting. But I do not feel a calling." Hugh dropped his head in despair. "I just do not."

The younger man eyed his brother with chagrin. "You let Adele's words torment you."

"Only the truth of them."

Terrence didn't respond. It was no use. If not for Adele's convictions, he and his brother would not be ten days' ride from their home, bound for Constantinople and, from there, Jerusalem. It was Adele who had made the taking of Edessa a cause. Adele who had been so certain it would put his brother's heart at ease and cool the raging doubts that burnt there. But Terrence saw this entire expedition as nothing but a useless romp across the Continent. It wasn't a lack of faith which hindered Hugh, it was a lack of love.

Hugh waited patiently for the iron gate to be lifted and then urged his charger into the bailey. There was a large gathering waiting to greet them, but among the assembled group he did not see the redheaded imp who'd so impertinently greeted him from overhead. Bernard de Tralle came into the courtyard to meet them himself, and Hugh found the Count of Avignon precisely as he had been described. Wiry and spry, he carried the necessary airs of dignity about him and yet possessed a certain twinkle of the eye. More than merriment, it was a spark of wisdom that surrounded him, and it was demonstrated in every cranny of the castle he ruled. As Bernard de Tralle gave orders that the

mounts and servants be seen to, he led Hugh
and Terrence into the Great Hall of the keep.
Though it was much like every other hall in design, it was by far the cleanest Hugh had ever
stepped foot in. Brighter because of the white
limestone walls, the flagged-stone floor was covered with fresh rushes. Atop them, spring flowers had been strewn everywhere, giving off a
sweet odor mixed with the tang of clover from
nearby fields as they were crushed underfoot.
Gay banners hung from intricately carved rafters
and even the long wooden trestle tables and
benches smelled of pine soap.

"You must stay as long as you like," the count
urged. "It has been far too long since Marguerite
and I have had a chance to entertain. It is the
only thing I curse about this majestic place," he
continued, crossing to the enormous hearth
where a fire burned brightly all the year round.
"All too often travelers are unwilling to venture
the mountainside. Ah!" de Tralle said with satisfaction as they reached the hearth. "Here is the
countess and my children."

The assembled group could have been a small
army unto itself, Hugh noted as each was named
and bobbed respectfully at the two brothers. The
eldest appeared about fourteen and the young-
est just a babe. Hugh counted eight in all, but
de Tralle added two when he mentioned that his
eldest sons were now accolades and, of course,
living with the knights they served. None had
red hair, however, and Hugh was just beginning

to wonder if the sun and the long ride had been playing tricks on his brain when the scurry of feet announced a late arrival.

"And this," the count announced in a disapproving tone, "is my eldest daughter, Catherine. She will assist you with your bath."

Hugh watched the child's jaw drop and then snap shut before anyone else could notice her surprise. He hid an amused grin behind a cough and dropped to his knee, pulling her small hand to his bent forehead before she could think to snatch it away. "I am honored to accept your attentions." When he looked up again, her face was as scarlet as her hair, but the countess was looking quite pleased to see her daughter treated with such chivalry.

"Monsieur Vougnet," Marguerite de Tralle urged. "We have been remiss and kept you overlong in introductions. Let Catherine and I assist you and your brother. Surely the mail and chauses you wear are burdensome. A bath and some refreshment will no doubt do you well."

Hugh nodded in agreement. "We are indeed tired and hungry, my lady. We would be ever grateful for your attentions."

Catherine's mother did not speak another word, but merely nodded and then, folding her hands serenely in front of her, swept from the Great Hall leaving Catherine little choice but to follow her.

As Catherine walked behind her mother up the curving stairway to the second story, she caught snippets of the two knights' words excusing themselves from her father's presence.

Though her mother headed for their duties as though it was the most natural of events, Catherine was not nearly so calm. Certainly she had been trained in such things, but at the time, her lessons had been merely theoretical. Since visitors of any sort, much less of this magnitude, rarely came to Avignon, knowing the arts of bathing and serving a knight had been a simple thing in Catherine's mind—something vague and distant. No one, however, was so well aware of the sudden sharpening reality of those lessons as was Catherine at this very moment.

From the gallery above the hall, she dared to sneak a glance over her shoulder. Indeed, the two knights were barely twenty paces behind her. The larger of the two—the one, in fact, that had seen her on the parapet and kissed her hand— again caught her eye. He cocked a brow in mock question when her glance met his for the shortest minute, and Catherine jerked her head around to front, trying this once not to blush.

She hastily caught up to her mother. Silver-and-beryl brocaded drapes hung from the huge canopied oak bed and the colors were repeated on tapestried wall hangings that gave an air of richness and comfort to the large room. The room boasted a large paned window which had been put in at great expense before Catherine's older brothers had been born. Though rarely

used, the apartment was kept as fresh and cared
for as the rest of the keep.

Now the room was lit by a dozen thick candles
and three torches blazed in sconces on the walls.
A fire crackled in the large hearth and a brass
bathing tub had been brought in and placed in
the center of the room.

As Catherine stood in the doorway, her mother
cleared her throat and nodded at her. "My dear,
beware behind you."

Stepping quickly out of the way, she watched
two servants carry in four huge buckets of water
on yokes slung across their shoulders.

"I will see to the elder Lord Vougnet. You,
Catherine, must see to the needs of the younger
knight."

"Which is that?"

Her mother smiled gently and shook her head
at her daughter's sometimes inattentive nature.
"He is slighter in build and with hair shaded
more brown than blond. Lord Terrence."

Catherine nodded and bit her lip uncertainly.
"I hope I do as well as you, Mother."

"I have no fear that you will do less than see
me proud, my dear. You never have."

Catherine smiled gratefully at her mother just
as the two guests entered the room.

"Lord Terrence," Marguerite directed calmly.
"If you will but follow my daughter, she will
show you to a room and see to your needs."

Hugh watched Terrence and the sprightly redhead disappear from his room. Although it was

an honor for her to do so, he was surprisingly disappointed that Marguerite de Tralle had chosen to see to his bathing herself. He'd wanted to engage the young girl in a conversation, for she peaked his interest. The children he encountered were usually so similar in nature, docile and quiet things who put all their efforts into either the arts of chivalry or needlework, depending upon their gender. But the little redhead was clearly busy with other things. Things such as spying over parapets and other activities that made her frequently late and often irreverent of rules and orders and obedience.

Marguerite de Tralle soon had Hugh stripped of his surcoat, armor, and chauses. The linen surcoat was sent for cleaning and mending and the mail delivered to his own armorer to be checked and rechecked for weak links. Although she was far from the court of Louis VII, the countess knew the finer points of her duties, and Hugh appreciated each one. While the mistress of any keep knew the basic rules of decorum for a visiting knight, few made him feel at ease. Marguerite de Tralle neither ignored the care a knight required, nor thought to throw herself upon his male attentions. It was a refreshing change after weeks of nights spent as a visitor under strange roofs where one never knew what to expect from the lady of the keep.

He had just stepped into the steaming tub, easing his tired muscles into the balsam-scented water, when a horrific bellow blasted from down the hall. Hugh jumped up, reaching for his broadsword while still standing calf-deep in bathwater. The countess dropped the tights she had been unpacking for him and raced for the doorway. A flash of red-gold hair in the door frame stopped the countess who drew herself up with the grace of a queen and gave her clearly distraught daughter a questioning look.

"Quickly, Mother," Catherine pleaded, wringing her hands in despair. "The most terrible accident has occurred."

Hearing the word 'accident', Hugh leapt from the tub. "What has happened to my brother?" he demanded.

Catherine turned to respond, but instead found herself completely speechless. Staring at the giant before her, her overactive imagination combined with the distress of the moment to create the vision of a being more fable than man.

Seeing the look on her face, Hugh scowled and grabbed the towel that lay warming by the fire. "By God's word, girl, if any harm has come to my brother, I will take you over my lap myself and see to your penance."

For a moment, he thought his words would bring her to tears, and he regretted them. But instead, he watched the child draw herself up with dignity and face him straight on, reminding him more of a falcon who, having missed a kill, prepares to go back and find a better prize than a recalcitrant little girl.

"In my inexperience, I saw fit to have Lord

Terrence set himself in the tub so that I could pour the buckets of water over him. I am afraid I did not check the temperature of the water, for when I poured it over him, he became scalded."

Her mother gasped, and fled down the hall to assist Lord Terrence, but Catherine finished her explanation to Hugh. "It was not so hot that he has lost his flesh," she continued apologetically. "Only that his skin is quite red and he has made some complaint about remaining forever childless."

Hugh burst out laughing. The mixture of relief, admiration for the child who so fairly faced his anger, and the sheer comic tone of the picture Catherine painted, touched his humor. Setting his broadsword back on the oak table, he crossed his arms before him and peered down at Catherine de Tralle. "Since your mother is caring for my brother, will it be you who will assist me with the rest of my bath?"

"If you wish, my lord."

"I wish to finish my bath, and since you appear to be the only other woman here, I will accept your assistance."

Catherine nodded. "I think it best for me to test the water now, before you reenter the tub."

A smile crept across Hugh's face. "Indeed."

Bowing her head in determination, Catherine set about testing the water, which had cooled far too much for Monsieur Vougnet to enjoy. She ordered new water brought and busied herself making his bath ready.

Hugh watched with interest. He would have thought, given the calamity that had occurred moments ago with Terrence, that the girl would prove inept at preparing the bath. To his surprise, she carried on much as her mother had. Though young and still coltish in many ways, she comported herself with pride, and he watched her confidence grow as she fell into her task.

"My lord," she said turning to him at last, "your bath is ready. I shall reassure you myself that you will not suffer your brother's fate at my hand." As means of a demonstration, she plunged her own arm up to the elbow into the waiting bathwater.

Hugh chuckled as he rose and crossed to the tub. "I am greatly relieved. Tell me, Mademoiselle de Tralle, are you planning to help with the meal preparation? I might require a food tester if you do."

"Ah," Catherine admonished, joining his game. "I can see you are wise indeed, sir. But so is my father, which is why I am not permitted in the kitchens."

It was quite enjoyable to talk to the knight, Catherine thought. As he stepped into the tub, she noted that Hugh did not drop the towel he had modestly wrapped around his waist until he could slide quickly into the water. She must have looked somewhat a fool, she realized, staring at him as she had when she'd first run into the room. But standing there dripping water and soap, his sword held at the ready and the glow of the blazing fire lighting him from behind, he'd seemed a mythological beast of ages past, and every other thought had vanished from her mind. Even now as she stood ready to assist him should he need his back soaped or hair washed, she could not help looking at his body.

She often saw her father's retainers and the vassals in the fields stripped to the waist. Every day but the Sabbath, retainers practiced their weaponry and warfare in the bailey of the castle or serfs worked their crops in fields at the base of the mountain. But there was not one among the hundreds of them who looked like Hugh Vougnet.

His shoulders were as broad as two table planks. Beneath his bronzed, wet skin, thickly corded muscles rippled with the gracefulness of the Rhône flowing below them. His chest was also deeply muscled and golden fur made a light covering which glistened in the firelight. The hair of his head was golden, too, and his eyes were blue. Not a cold, hard blue, but warm and inviting in their depths. He was indeed like a mythological being, she thought, though heaven help her if Father Godfried was ever able to read her mind.

Although she offered her help, Hugh saw to the washing of his own hair and asked not about his back. So Catherine kept him company with light banter about the castle and her family. It was a task that demanded immense self-control, for her tongue burned with a thousand questions about the new Crusade and his travels thus far. She knew it would be impolite to ask such things, though, so she carried on about herself. Catherine thought he must be bored to distraction for so little seemed to happen in Avignon, but Hugh listened attentively, nodding often and smiling quietly over certain things she said.

"I have heard that you and your brothers have learned to cipher as well as read. Is it true?" Hugh asked as Catherine's endless conversation began to wind down. His bath had become quite cool by now, but he had remained in the chill liquid because he did not want to break the moment. Such a chattering little thing she was: unassuming and with a wit that had him often holding back his laughter for fear of embarrassing her.

"Father feels quite strongly about that," she replied. "At the age of five, each of us began our studies. Latin and ciphers, scripture, of course, and also for the girls medicinal knowledge."

Hugh was not quite certain he believed her. It was just too unusual. De Tralle was an unusual man, Hugh had seen that already, and he had heard rumors that the children were all educated. But to teach them all Latin—only those entering service to God were to learn Latin, else how were the Scriptures to be protected and kept from misinterpretation by the serfs? That is what

Adele said. Terrence had studied Latin because as the third son he would take up the religious life upon his return from Jerusalem. He was accompanying Hugh in order to enhance his esteem with the bishop, a man who felt Terrence had his mind a bit too much on the earthly for the good of his calling. And Giles, as the eldest son, knew only enough to use for the management of the duchy. Would Bernard de Tralle really educate all his children?

Goose flesh popped out along the whole of Hugh's right leg from sitting overly long in the cold bathwater and he hoisted himself from the tub. Catherine was quick with his towel, and as he reached to take it from her, he noticed the brooch pinned at her shoulder.

"You wear a lovely ornament," he commented, nodding to the piece of jewelry.

Catherine fingered it gently. "It is my favorite. Thank you."

"A gift from an admirer?"

Catherine blushed. "No, sir. Who visits Avignon to admire me? Besides, I have not any looks to admire."

"What!" Hugh looked at her in mock surprise. "Perhaps you are yet too young to see it, but I think there will be many admirers for you, Catherine de Tralle." Hugh immediately wondered why he had said that. The girl was not ugly, but neither was she of the coloring or look that minstrels sang praises. The women of song were inevitably fair-haired with downcast eyes and demure bow-shaped mouths. This impish girl was none of those. Yet there was something about her which held the promise of beauty yet fully formed and a sparkling vivacity that already could take many a man's breath away.

Catherine had not answered his question about the brooch. Instead, she had turned away to busy herself while Hugh pulled on aubergine-colored hose and a woolen tunic trimmed with the prized white fur of a vair. As he buckled a heavy gold belt at his waist, he inquired again, more gently, "Then from whom is the brooch you wear? It is quite unusual and you have said you prize it."

Catherine turned back, shy in the face of his compliments. "It was a gift from my parents upon my tenth birthday."

"May I see it more closely?"

Catherine nodded, moving to stand before the hearth where he could view it in the light. Hugh bent over her, but the warmth of his breath on her neck and the bare flesh of her young breasts made her uneasy. "Here," she said stepping away. "Let me remove it for you. It is best to see it close to the fire." Quickly unpinning it, she handed the brooch to Hugh.

Holding to the firelight, Hugh realized it was a stunning piece of great value. In the center was a cabochon sapphire which Hugh knew must be worth a small fortune by itself. The sapphire was surrounded by a rich oval frame set with pearls, aquamarine, and amethyst.

"It is quite beautiful," he commented, handing it back to her.

"What is most beautiful is not on the front," she explained. She turned the brooch over in his hand. On the back of the frame was a script.

"Very nice."

"I like that it is French rather than Latin."

"Oh?"

Catherine tilted her head to one side and looked at him. "Do you like what it says?"

Hugh looked at her and then looked away, staring into the flames. "I do not know what it says."

"You don't know how to read, my lord?"

Hugh pursed his lips before turning back to the young girl who suddenly seemed much older than a little twelve-year-old. "My older brother, Giles, was trained to become duke. My younger brother, Terrence, has studied Latin as preparation for the religious life. I am the second son, therefore my training was as a knight. There was no need for me to study other than the crafts of war."

"Everyone can benefit from reading and numbers, even the lowest villein. I help in the teaching of my younger brothers and sisters. I can teach you."

The room became intensely quiet. The silence of Hugh's response becoming louder and louder in his own ears. His whole life he had felt less than his brothers because he alone had not been taught in scholarly subjects. Giles knew less than

Terrence, but he could read missives and understand the books kept by his steward.

Hugh could not read a word.

He had spent frustrating hours hidden away
in his father's home with Terrence's rare book
or two and parchment records from the chapel,
but he could not read one letter or one word or
one number. And he had always felt stupid because of it. He was nothing but a brawny war-
monger. If not protecting someone, he was of
no use at all. Certainly of no use to himself.

"I am a grown man," he said. "My brother
and I shall only stay in Avignon a few days. What
can I learn in a handful of days?"

"You shall see, my lord. And no one shall
know I am teaching you. We shall meet just at
vespers each day until you depart. At least you
can learn a few things. You will see. It is fun to
learn."

Hugh nodded. "We can try."

Catherine gave him a brilliant smile. "Let us
start with this," she said, nodding to the brooch
which still lay in his hand.

"What does it say?"

"Vous estes ma ioy mondeine," she read slowly,
then turned expectantly to him.

Hugh looked down into the child's young, confident face and repeated the words. "You are my
earthly joy."

She nodded. "Tomorrow I shall bring parchment and a quill and you will begin to copy the
letters. That is how we will begin. Now, if there

is no other way I may be of service to you, I must change for supper."

"Thank you, Catherine."

She turned in the doorway and curtsied to him. "You are most welcome, my lord."

Two

Two steeds clattered over the drawbridge and entered the bailey of Avignon Keep amid the bustling activity of the late-spring afternoon. Snorting and blowing, they pawed at the cobbled yard while their riders held them in check. Catherine kept a firm hand on her little roan-colored mare as she and Hugh shared their enjoyment of the day's hunt just ended and waited for Thomas to collect the hawks which rode on their gloved fists.

" 'Twas a fine kill your bird made, Catherine. Thomas tells me you trained him yourself."

Catherine blushed proudly at Hugh's compliment. "Thomas gives much credit where little is due. But I did help raise him."

"He hunts well. A bird twice his size could have done no better. Your merlin downed four partridge in as many hours."

"He does well for a small falcon," she agreed. Catherine was pleased that Hugh so admired her bird. It was no small compliment. The art of falconry was esteemed above all other talents in the forest. Lords and ladies alike preened over their birds, keeping them with them at meals and devoting lavish attention to a prized bird. Her merlin was small, as befit her age, but he was handsome with his slate-blue bands striping his tail. He had never lost a kill. Once in his pursuit of a small dove, he'd shot like an arrow into a bramble thicket and Catherine had been certain she'd lost her little merlin forever. But he had not only emerged unscathed from the thicket, he had brought the dove with him, and Catherine had rewarded him richly from her falconer's purse.

"He aims to please you, Catherine," Hugh commented as he dismounted. Nearly three weeks had passed since his arrival at Avignon, though it seemed to Hugh a mere day or two, the time had flown so. Bernard de Tralle was the consummate host, filling each day with hunting and armory practice. Evenings were spent on more genteel activities. Pantomimes, poetry, and games of "dames" and chess before the great fire led far into the evening. There was such joy at Avignon. It made Hugh long to linger.

He took the reins of Catherine's horse as she hopped down from her saddle. The happy little redhead had become his shadow. It seemed she appeared at his elbow at daybreak and managed to make herself indispensable until her eyes could no longer hold up their lids at night. She hunted well, and her horsemanship could naught but be admired. But it was her way with the children that he truly cherished, he thought as a group of them flocked to her. As always, there were sweets in the purse she'd secured to her belt and she let the serfs' children help themselves while she held the merlin high over their heads.

The small falcon screeched in protest at this intrusion, but, hooded, he remained steady on Catherine's gloved hand. "That's enough!" she cried in mock protest as the passel of small hands searched her purse for more sweetmeats and almond confections. "You can't find what is not there!"

"But my lady," the smallest among them whined, "I've had none. The others' arms are longer and there is never a treat left by the time I reach your purse."

Catherine chucked him beneath his chin. "Then you must go to the kitchens and tell Cook that I've said you are to have a dozen pastries packed in a basket to take home tonight."

The child's eyes grew round as coins. "A dozen, my lady! Ho! How large my belly shall be then!" he cried in delight.

"They are to be shared with your brothers and sisters as well as your mother and father," Catherine reprimanded, pulling the little boy back by the collar of his jerkin as he turned to scurry for the kitchens. "And not more than two for you or your mother will curse me for keeping her up all night with a sick child."

He nodded obediently, and the moment Catherine released him, he bolted in the direction of the keep's massive kitchens.

Handing the reins back to Catherine, Hugh headed for the stables chuckling as he went. "You will have as many children as your mother, I think. Already your adopted family numbers far beyond the scope of all your digits."

"I *hope* to have many children," Catherine agreed. "And I pray that my husband will join me in enjoying their company, although I have heard that his people are somewhat cold in temperament and care less for a large family."

"And who are his people, Catherine?"

"I have been promised to a baron in the area of Strasbourg since I was a babe."

Hugh contemplated this news without much relish. He didn't think Catherine would be at all well suited to the temperament of a man from that area. He had met many at the king's court. They tended to be a cold people and he could not picture Catherine's glowing enthusiasm at ease in a household where everyone hid behind shielded eyes. He felt a melancholy creep into his heart at the thought of this bright child doomed to a life of restraint in a damp, drafty castle somewhere far north and east of the sunny south of France. How unfair that would be. As unfair as . . .

Hugh shook the thought from his head. That was wrong, to think such things. He shook himself mentally and caught a glimpse of Catherine looking at him oddly from where she walked beside him. He grimaced and closed his eyes for a moment. He didn't want Catherine seeing his moods. She needn't know that side of him.

"I think the stag you downed will feed the castle for a fortnight," Catherine commented quietly. She hoped that changing the subject to something Hugh would have more interest in than her future husband might sweep away the air of sadness that had descended upon him as suddenly as a spring shower could dance across the valley below.

"I doubt it will last even a week," Hugh laughed. "Your family has the most ravenous appetites I've ever encountered."

" 'Tis true," Catherine agreed. "Still, he was a magnificent beast and he gave good chase. None but you could keep up with him. If not for your skill and your charger, he would still be free in the forest." She reached out to pat the thick neck of Hugh's stallion. "Even I thought your steed would not be nimble-footed enough to follow the stag through the woods. A horse his size has no right to be so agile."

Hugh was proud of Cepheus. Though he usually rode one of the other horses for hunting, Cepheus hadn't gotten enough exercise since they'd arrived at Avignon, and Hugh had chosen to ride the charger knowing they'd both receive a good workout. Cepheus was a giant and yet he could sidestep a lady's kerchief on the battlefield. And battlefields he'd seen aplenty, for Hugh served Louis VII and none had been called more frequently to the king's side over the past two years than Hugh Vougnet.

"He's no different than your falcon," Hugh replied. "Like you, I raised him from the day he was born. He knows me well and has never refused me."

"But he knows you will never ask the impossible of him," Catherine replied sagely. She handed her mare over to the stable boy and followed Hugh and Cepheus down the wide stable corridor beneath its peaked roof of thatch.

"I have asked the impossible of him often, I'm afraid. But I have never asked what I do not think him capable of doing." Cross-tying the enormous charger, he loosened the girth and lifted the saddle off his back. There were more than enough hands to take care of the knight's steed, but Hugh preferred to see to the warhorse's care himself. Cepheus was too important to his trade for Hugh to chance the stallion's health to anyone but his most trusted grooms. Even then, it was a chore he enjoyed, and more often than not it was Hugh who assured that Cepheus went to his stall only after every inch of the steed had been inspected, cuts tended, and the smith called to repair any signs of a loose shoe.

Catherine settled herself comfortably on a wooden bin nearby as Hugh set to his task. "When you have conquered Edessa again, what will you do?"

It was an ongoing conversation—the unraveling of Hugh's life history. She had already extracted from him information about most of his childhood and the years of service he had given to Louis. She knew everything there seemed to be to know right up until his decision to ride on this second crusade to the Holy Land. Then had come the lengthy discussions of exactly what was to be done in Edessa once he and Terrence arrived—although Hugh himself was not entirely certain what the retaking of Edessa from the Saracens would entail—and now she was determined to know his plans once the brilliant battle was won and he returned a victorious knight of the Crusades.

Hugh picked up a burlap rag and began to rub the sweat marks from Cepheus's sides. Seemingly engrossed in his work, he tried to think of a fair answer, for he was not at all certain he had one. Catherine cleared her throat impatiently.

Hugh smiled to himself at her impetuous restiveness. "I shall return to France, of course."

"And?"

Hugh did not answer immediately. He focused on a distant point over the stallion's withers and felt the fingers of gloom thread their way back into the pit of his stomach. Thinking about his return home was the thing he tried hardest not to do. What would happen when he came back from the Holy Land? He was supposed to return a Knight Templar. Victorious in the work of God. It was expected that when he returned to Anet he would be different. Holier. Dedicated to the ideals of service to God and family. Would he be? Would he be any different than he was now?

It wasn't that Hugh didn't believe in those ideals or practice them. He desired a family. And he was never blasphemous of God, considering himself a faithful servant of the Lord. But it was Adele. She wanted so many things that Hugh just wasn't. He didn't know exactly where he had gone wrong in Adele's eyes. How he could change to become the man his betrothed would want? He was just himself. And although Adele always asserted that she indeed loved him, he never seemed to be enough. There was always something he was lacking.

She wanted a man with a religious fervor that Hugh did not feel. She thought that joining Pope Eugene's call to the aid of those in Edessa would light the fire of zeal in Hugh.

He prayed that it would, and that with that zeal would also come the flames of desire and love for Adele de Pisan. If this didn't change him, Hugh was afraid that nothing ever would.

Turning back to his stallion, Hugh again pushed his doubts away and carefully formulated his reply to Catherine's question. "I will return to Anet. There I shall help Giles with the estates." He shrugged. "Perhaps I will again be called to King Louis's service."

Catherine pondered this quietly for a moment. "Then you will definitely come back through Avignon?"

Hugh smiled. "Yes, mite. I will come back to Avignon and fill your head with a hundred bloody stories of the battle and the victory."

Catherine nodded, quite content for the moment with his answer. "How long will it be then?"

"For what?"

"Until you return here."

Hugh shrugged. "I don't know. Two years. Possibly three. Jerusalem and Edessa fell to our cause in a matter of days during the first Crusade. Our knights overran the Saracens and regained passage to the Holy City easily.

"This time there are already several thousand Christians living in the two cities. They know the people and their ways. They know their style of warfare as well. Everywhere we have stayed so far we are assured of a swift victory."

Indeed, based on the information and tales they had heard so far along their way, Hugh imagined he and Terrence would hardly see battle.

Catherine contemplated Hugh's comments while he completed his ministrations and put Cepheus in his stall. When he returned, she was still deep in thought. Silently coming up behind her, Hugh's fingers shot to her ribs and he tickled her just to see her jump. She did exactly as he had hoped, giving a pixie screech as she leapt from the bin.

"Has a mouse scampered up your leg?" he inquired blithely.

" 'Twas no mouse, sir!" she cried. "You tickled me!"

"Certainly you're not ticklish, Catherine. A girl who rides and hunts and studies mathematics." He looked incredulous. "It cannot be!" Hugh took a step toward her and Catherine jumped back.

"Nay," she warned, shaking a finger at him. "Someone has told you that I am ticklish. I shall have Jean's neck for this! You have been solicited by my brother to join his buffoonery. I warn you, my lord, it will come to no good for you. Jean is a trickster, and a knight of your standing should have nothing to do with his antics."

Hugh grinned broadly. "Do not blame your brother, Catherine. Perhaps it was a little chipmunk with a taste for sweets who whispered such a clue in my ear."

"Mickal! And I've just sent him off for a dozen pastries, the little scamp!"

Hugh took another step toward her, his fingers curled in mock threat.

Grabbing a three-pronged hay fork from against the wall, Catherine hoisted it menacingly in Hugh's direction. "There will be no tickling, my lord knight," she commanded, all the while her green eyes sparkling with mirth. " 'Tis an unfair advantage you have, for you know my weakness while I know none of yours."

Hugh threw up his arms in mock surrender. "Put down your weapon, Catherine. I don't care to meet my end on the prongs of your pitch fork."

"No tickling?" she queried suspiciously.

"None."

She began to lower the tines of the fork, then stopped, eyeing him carefully. "Have I your word as a knight?"

Hugh nodded and ceremoniously dropped on to one knee before her. "You have my word."

Relieved, Catherine set down her weapon, but when the man before her remained on his knee, she became self-conscious. He was so handsome. So powerful and possessed of an air of ease. Standing beside him Catherine felt the awkward child, all freckles and long limbs that somehow never did as she wished or directed. She imagined him on bended knee before ladies of the court who were dazzling in their beauty, not here on the dirt floor of the stable before her. Dusting her riding kirtle with her hands, Catherine attempted to hide her sudden embarrassment. Having this giant man on his knee before her made her feel so strange, and she hid her uncertainty behind a facade of business.

"I must change before our lesson. Vespers will be no more than two hours from now and we will be rushed to study anything at all." She looked at Cepheus's saddle still set against the wall and noticed a thousand cobwebs amid the rafters as her eyes darted about the stable looking at anything except the knight who knelt before her.

At last, Hugh rose quietly from the wooden stable floor until he once again towered over her. "I have a few things to attend to myself."

Catherine nodded, relieved to have their game over yet unaccountably sad, as if a shadow had passed over them at that moment. "Then I shall meet you in the vestibule of the chapel in an hour's time?"

"That will be fine."

Catherine eyed Hugh with chagrin. The sadness seemed to have settled over him again, and, as always, she wondered at it.

"What vexes you, Catherine?" he asked, for he was always unusually attuned to her moods. "Is it me?"

"No, not you, my lord. Only that I forget to be a lady when I am with you."

Recalling her pixie face peering down at him from the parapets the day of his arrival at Avignon, Hugh could not suppress a hearty chuckle. "Oh, Cay. I don't think you can blame me for your antics. I think they were quite a part of you long before I arrived at Avignon. Now, off to change or we'll have no time for a lesson at all and I was up half the night copying the script you gave me. Go!" he commanded.

Catherine turned on her heels and scampered halfway out of the stables before catching herself. From where he watched, Hugh saw her suddenly stop, straighten her kirtle once more and walk regally out into the bailey. But even her coltish antics did little to lighten the cloak of remorse that had begun to settle on him once more.

Since his arrival at Avignon he had been able to push thoughts of home aside. He had let the enthusiasm of this place and these people carry him along with it. But he had other things to think of, primarily the purpose toward which he had set himself. He was not destined for the Holy Land simply to win back the city of Edessa. Nor was he going at the behest of the pope to do God's work. Hugh was bound for Constantinople and then Edessa for one purpose alone—to prove to the woman he was to marry that he was worthy. A true, heart-bound Christian. A man devoted to God's purpose. His broad shoulders stooped under the weight of what he feared was an impossible task.

In her room, Catherine asked that a copper tub be brought. She bathed quickly and then donned a moss-green kirtle. A yellow tunic trimmed in gold followed and then soft leather slippers. She plaited her hair into a long single braid, added a velvet cap to the crown of her head, and attached a small, sheer wimple to the center, allowing it to hang midway down her back. Satisfied that she was acceptably dressed for vespers and the evening meal, she seated herself in the small chair in her room and placed the writing table in her lap. Before she took up the poem she had left off copying the day before, her thoughts returned to Hugh.

'Twas no use to ask about his moods, she knew. She had tried before and learned that such questions were the only ones that received no answers. But she wondered about them. What made him so sad? Whatever it was, it was a heavy burden to carry, for it weighed visibly upon his soul. She had seen its power sweep the joy from his face in the blink of an eye as it had today. It rendered all else in life useless to him. But mostly, it made *her* sad. She thought of Hugh Vougnet as the most wonderful being God had ever created. To Catherine, he was perfect in every way. Everything he said, every gesture he made, was to her liking. She hoped quite sincerely that her affianced baron would be exactly like him.

Pursing her lips, she turned back to the poem in her lap. It was a motley ditty about a hunter who pursued a doe into the forest. But rather than shoot the doe, the hunter became entranced by the doe, following her into the forest never to return again. Catherine thought it a good poem for Hugh. She had worked hard to find works that would interest him. The childish verses she had learned upon certainly weren't appropriate for a grown man. So she'd found verses and poems, letters of instruction, and whatever else it seemed to her might be of interest to a knight and sportsman.

Completing her transcription, Catherine glanced at the hourglass which stood on a small table by her chair. It was later than she'd thought. Quickly gathering up her papers and quills, Catherine started for the chapel. It was a perfect place for them to work. They studied in the small vestibule that connected the chapel and the cleric's quarters. Friar Godfried was always preparing for vespers at this time and there was little chance he would see them. Not being seen was very important. Catherine knew instinctively that Hugh was too proud to let anyone discover he was learning to read and write from a mere girl of twelve. It was also quiet in the small room, and there were plenty of candles as well as a large window of mottled glass which shed a good deal of light for them.

As she stepped into the vestibule Catherine expected to see Hugh's large frame bent over the transcription she'd asked him to complete yesterday. To her surprise, the room was empty. Still, she went about setting her papers neatly on the table, anticipating his arrival at any moment. She lit tapers and opened the inkwell she'd left the day before. When all was arranged, Catherine stood back glancing at the door. Where was Hugh? It was unlike him to be late. A few minutes more passed. Suddenly she was struck by the possibility that Friar Godfried had come across Hugh and waylaid him. She would peek into the chapel to see if perhaps Hugh had been called to assist in the preparations for vespers.

Quietly opening the door, she slid into the chapel. The candles and torches had not yet been lit for evening prayers and the room was shrouded in shadow. There was no sign of the friar, but she had found Hugh. Her pupil was kneeling before the small altar deep in prayer.

Catherine slid silently behind a pillar, watching the proud knight intently. He murmured his prayers with a quiet strength, and his bowed head seemed to her to almost hang in shame of some terrible wrong he had committed. What was it Hugh had done to feel so abased before God?

Minutes passed and she began to feel as though she was intruding on some private torture. Hugh seemed not to gather strength from his prayer but to become more abject and lost with each passing minute. Ashamed that she was privy to his exposure, Catherine began to tiptoe silently from the chapel. She reached the vestibule door and opened it only wide enough to slip her small form through. As the door closed behind her it gave a small squeak of protest, but she continued on without looking back. The noisy hinges must have told Hugh of her presence, for she had barely collected a small book from the supplies she had set out when he appeared in the doorway.

"I'm late," he said quietly.

"You were busy."

Hugh didn't acknowledge her comment. Instead, he reached into his tunic and extracted the verses she'd assigned him to transcribe the day before.

Catherine glanced up at him as he handed the

paper to her, but while he did not meet her gaze neither did he turn away from her. They talked about everything else, Catherine thought. Why then would he not even acknowledge that he had been at prayer? What was it, she wondered, that was so terrible it must be hidden even between friends?

The lesson was short. The chapel began to fill for vespers soon after they began to review his work from the day before. Hugh was distracted, and three times Catherine had to whisper his name, nudging him from some netherworld of thought. They struggled through the recitation and then she unfolded the poem she had so painstakingly transcribed for him and laid it on the writing tablet in his lap.

Hugh sighed and ran his fingers through his hair. "It is no use, mite. I cannot concentrate today. My mind is occupied with other things."

Catherine nodded silently. Her feelings were injured by his inattentiveness just as they had been by his refusal to confide in her. She had thought they were friends, yet he was so far away from her at this minute she wasn't certain that she knew him at all. "We can do more tomorrow."

Hugh twisted the quill between his fingers and pursed his lips, neither acknowledging nor denying her statement. "You should go to vespers," he said at last.

Catherine nodded and rose, waiting for him to come also.

"I am not going today, Catherine. I have things I must see attended."

The twelve-year-old withdrew to the chapel door, turning once more to see if her friend would change his mind. But there was no response from Hugh. He strode from the vestibule without a backward glance and Catherine slipped quietly into the chapel where vespers had already begun.

Three

That night the rafters of the Great Hall shivered with echoes of laughter rising from below as the hunters celebrated their success. The haunch of Hugh's enormous stag was served as the center of the meal surrounded by beds of tender spring fiddleheads, young carrots and sweet onions scented by the first sprigs of thyme. Steaming bowls of wild duck stew accompanied the venison as well as several brace of hare caught during the day. Platters carried other roasted birds, plucked and stuffed with vegetables and herbs then cooked and arrayed once more in their feathers to make their appearance before the Lord of Avignon. For dessert there were dates and sugared almonds from the Holy Land, a special treat secured by the Crusaders' control of the cities there. It was a wonderful feast with plenty of ale and wine to quench the thirsts of all in attendance.

But not everyone was in attendance, for neither Hugh nor his brother appeared for the evening meal.

It seemed to Catherine that she alone noticed

their absence, for there wasn't a single comment made about the two men not appearing for the evening meal. Not wishing to be presumptuous, Catherine didn't ask where the knights were, but her confusion over the events of the day only grew as she pondered this new turn of events. She managed her way silently through the meal, moving her food around on the trencher without relish and making no attempt at all to taste the feast.

At last Jean elbowed her in the ribs. "You look as though you've swallowed a bowl of lard and your belly has turned sour," he hissed.

Catherine ignored her brother and pushed the wing of roasted swan before her away. "I've eaten nothing foul, Jean. 'Tis you and Marc who make sport of eating anything you can set your hands upon and then keep Mother up all night with your groans, not I."

Jean made a face at her. "François says you are moon-faced over your Crusader."

The thought of Hugh made her feel worse still and Catherine thought it best to simply ignore the pest at her side.

"I see François is right," Jean continued, undaunted in the face of his sister's silence. He made another face. "You are pickle-brained, Catherine. He is on his way to the Crusade! What would he do with you? Anyway, they leave on the morrow."

"What?" Catherine jerked forward on the

bench she occupied beside her brothers and sisters. "What do you mean they are leaving?"

"As I said, you goose! Why do you think they are not here to sup with us and celebrate? Sir Hugh spoke with Father not an hour ago. They will leave at dawn."

Taking in her stricken look, Jean repented his taunting tone a bit. "Don't look so, Catherine. They have been at Avignon nearly a month. If they are to meet with the other knights and form a force to attack the Saracens, they must arrive in Constantinople on time. You heard them say so themselves."

Catherine said nothing at all, and with a final disgusted look, Jean returned to his meal.

As soon as it was possible to be excused without raising questions from her parents, Catherine left the Great Hall. She climbed the stairs to the gallery above without a backward glance to the merriment below. In the hallway upstairs, she turned in the opposite direction from her room, walking instead toward her knight's room. As she approached she heard the sounds of men deep in discussion. Catherine stopped herself two rooms from Hugh's. What was it she intended to do here? Beg him to stay? What would these warriors think of her? They would only laugh, of course. As well they should.

Jean was right, she thought. They must get themselves to Constantinople. Hugh and his brother had lingered long enough in Avignon.

Perhaps that was what had bothered Hugh so today. It would explain his somber moods, for there was much to think about, much to pray about for a successful journey to the Holy Lands and a victorious campaign once there. The holy cities must be secured for all Christian pilgrims, of course.

Standing in the darkness of the upper hall, Catherine listened to the muted voices coming from Hugh's room. The torch flames danced in their sconces along the wall as a breeze through a crack in the thick wall prophesied a coming change in the weather. Quietly, she turned and walked in the direction of her own bedroom. He was a knight. He must go to the Holy Land. Catherine understood that well. She wished he would have told her he was leaving, though. That was the one thing her child's heart still could not understand. Perhaps he was not really the friend she'd thought him to be.

But what did it matter?

On the morrow he would be gone, and despite his words earlier in the day to the contrary, she did not believe he would come back to Avignon. Their lives were not meant to touch again. That Hugh Vougnet had passed through Avignon at all was no more than a chance occurrence. With that strangely adult thought in her brain, Catherine turned back toward her own rooms and quietly put herself to bed.

* * *

The world was wrapped in a gray fog when she awoke. For a moment Catherine did nothing other than roll onto her side, snuggling deeper into the spring quilts that covered her bed. Then suddenly she remembered. Her eyes flew open and she leapt from bed. Running to her small window, she peered through the thick panes of glass that let in light, but little else. In the courtyard below she could make out black shapes milling about in last-minute preparations for their leave-taking. Some she knew were horses, others wagons, and still others were cooks and vassals in Hugh's entourage.

Never in her life had Catherine dressed so quickly. She yanked her kirtle on over her sleeping gown and dispensed completely with tunic, undergarments, hose, and shoes. Grabbing a bright blue cloak from the top of her chest, Catherine darted through the door and down the hallway.

She had no idea the sight she made when she burst from the keep's doorway moments later.

Hugh stood beside Cepheus in the misting rain. It was not a good omen for this next leg of their journey and he wished now that he had not acted quite so impulsively in setting their departure.

"The ten vassals of Bernard's who wish to join us?" he asked Terrence. "Have they weapons and horses, or are they serfs who will walk?"

Terrence didn't answer. Instead, he stared over Hugh's shoulder as though seeing an apparition. Impatiently, Hugh followed his brother's gaping stare. What he saw made him whirl on his heels. Emerging from a cloud of fog on the far side of the bailey came a princess-waif. Yard-long strands of gold-red hair streamed from beneath her velvet hood and her cloak billowed in the breeze behind her like strange blue wings. She was barefoot and her face was as pale as moonstone in the predawn light. As she reached them, Hugh stepped forward, catching a velvet-encased arm in his gloved hand.

"What are you doing, Catherine?" he asked quietly.

"Were you going to leave without saying good-bye?"

"Nay, mite. I was not. Your father has my good-bye for you. Ask him and he will give it to you."

"Will you . . ." The words "come back" stuck in her throat. It was a childish attachment she had to him, and he was a knight. She could not be so foolish as to ask.

"Yes, Cay. I shall return. And I will have all my gruesome tales to tell you of how snakes grow from the heads of the Saracens in place of hair and the way men in trances walk across beds of hot embers." He grinned, and then his grin faded and he looked directly into her eyes until she could not miss the sincerity of his words. "I will not forget."

Releasing her arm, Hugh gathered up Cepheus's reins and swung into his saddle.

Catherine looked up at him trying to remember exactly how he looked. He was again as he had been when he arrived. Dressed in his white hauberk, the red cross of the Crusades emblazoned on his breast. Hugh looked down at her and smiled. There was something special there that made her heart leap in her chest. She nodded. "God go with you, sir knight."

"Thank you, Catherine."

He turned Cepheus on his haunches and rode to the drawbridge gate where her father waited. Catherine watched him pay his respects and give his thanks for the shelter and hospitality of Avignon, and then he rode out, his brother and their vassals following after him. The rain came harder as soon as they were out of sight, turning mean and vicious with the dawn.

Catherine's mother came up behind her and wrapped a slender arm about her shoulders. "He is a fine knight, Catherine. Your own baron will be like Hugh Vougnet, I'm certain of that."

"He said he left my good-bye with Father," Catherine replied.

"Indeed he did. Come inside, child."

Together, Catherine and her mother returned to the keep. Only when her toes sunk into the wet rushes did Catherine realize that her feet stung with the cold.

"Go by the fire and warm yourself, Catherine," her mother told her.

"But the thing Hugh gave to Father . . ."

"It's there." Her mother nodded to a chest just inside the door.

A scroll lay where Catherine looked. It was tied

with a red ribbon that seemed the exact hue of the red cross on Hugh's hauberk. She picked it up and carried it to a chair beside the crackling fire in the hearth of the Great Hall. Sitting down, she slowly pulled the ends of the neatly tied bow and slowly unrolled the parchment to reveal Hugh's special gift for her. And it *was* special. Catherine knew it would have taken Hugh a good part of the night to create his good-bye.

> *Dear Catherine,*
> *I am afraid I had almost forgotten my purpose in making this journey and the reason I came to Avignon, which I cannot do. For it is God's purpose. But I must continu the lessins you began for me. So I will write to you all my adventures and you may correct my errors and send them back to me in Constantinople. This way, your work wil not have benn for naught. And when I return, I shall challenge you to a test. Which I shall win.*
>
> *Hugh Vougnet*

The cold and rain seemed to dissipate from Catherine's heart and she smiled an impish twelve-year-old smile. "Of course you shall not win, my lord."

Four

The blistering Jerusalem sun beat merciless, unbroken heat upon the city—even upon the sacred places. There was no escaping it except within the thick stone walls of the Crusaders' castles. Hugh stepped gratefully into the cool darkness and breathed a deep, exhausted sigh. His throat was parched and sand gritted between his teeth. Dust lay like a fine webbing across every inch of his battle-weary body. It did not matter that he was clothed from head to foot in linen and mail. The dust was so fine that it found its way to every crevice of skin where it rubbed and chafed until raw sores grew. Now he wanted only to ease the ulcers of their fetid ooze and caked blood. A bath. How he longed for a bath.

Hugh dropped his iron helmet on the trencher table just inside the castle. The long nose guard thudded dully against the cypress wood, followed immediately by the sound of his mail gloves thrown down beside it. He ran his forearm across his brow, wiping away the dripping sweat.

"All peaceful in the city and beyond?"

Hugh looked up to see Terrence walking toward him from the darkness of the Great Hall. No fire burned in this hearth. It was coolness that the knights sought—escape from the unending heat. "For now. Tomorrow I leave for Damascus. We have word that a group of pilgrims wait there for safe passage."

Terrence shook his head slowly. "Of course, we know there is no such thing. But you will offer your services anyway."

"They have a right to make their pilgrimage, Terrence."

"And you have sworn to uphold that right."

"Yes. That is my oath as a Templar." Hugh led the way back to the room Terrence had come from, but his brother stopped him.

"Let us go to my apartments," he urged. "I grow weary of the talk in the Hall. They do nothing but brag of their growing wealth."

Hugh turned toward the stairs following Terrence's suggestion, but not letting his brother see the grimace that crossed his face. Terrence's apartments were far more luxurious than Hugh's. Though Terrence, too, was a member of the Knights Templar, he belonged to the sect which cared for the day-to-day business of the order. Unlike the knights, who called a chaste cell their room, Terrence had a large apartment in the castle complemented by a fireplace, luxurious furnishings, and a garderobe of its own.

As soon as the door was closed behind them, Hugh dropped into a high-backed carved chair beside the darkened hearth. His legs sprawling before him, he heaved another sigh, exhausted beyond the point of caring that the mail armor added forty pounds to his load. God in heaven, he was tired. So tired. He didn't want to ask the question that hung in the air. Didn't want to care if Terrence's comment about the other knights had been true or not.

He had taken an oath two years ago, pledging his allegiance to the Grand Master of Jerusalem. As part of that oath, he sported the cropped hair and untrimmed beard that all Templars wore. He ate his two meals a day in silence and wore no adornments at all on his person. He protected the pilgrim roads between Damascus and Jerusalem, offering his protection to the innocent Christian pilgrims coming to the Holy Land. He had done exactly what he had come to do. Why was it then, that he felt as bleak and devoid of hope as ever?

He watched Terrence who stood silently on the raised dais surrounding his bed and looked down at Hugh as though he were the older of the two.

"Let's go home, Hugh."

Hugh sat forward, resting his arms upon hose-encased knees as he massaged his temples. "Terrence . . ."

"You know that there is nothing left here. We came for a cause, but that cause is dissipating in the wind!"

"We came to do God's work. We are under the special protection of His Holiness the Pope. To say the cause is dead is . . ."

"Blasphemy?" The word was spoken so softly, Hugh might not even have heard it if it wasn't the exact word that hung unspoken in his mind.

His shoulders hunched. He felt his back bow with tension. "Isn't it?" he asked quietly.

"We are not asked to stay here for the rest of our lives. Baldwin knows the degree of your dedication, Hugh. You are his finest knight. You have done more for the cause of the Templars than any other ten men, and Louis has rewarded you with the castle of Pontoise and all its holdings. There isn't a more prime piece of land to be had in all of France. You will be within a day's ride of court, on the cusp of vineyard lands. I can think of no more certain way for Baldwin to have proven your worth to him."

"Which is why I cannot go. Edessa is lost, the Saracens daily increase their strongholds and we lose ours. The Holy Land is not safe for our pilgrims. There is no safe haven here for our people to come and worship."

"There will *never* be safe haven in Jerusalem, Hugh. You know that as well as I. That is why we are here in my rooms talking and not down with the other knights. We know the truth. And it is not a good truth."

Hugh said nothing. He squeezed his eyes shut and concentrated on banishing the voices in his head. But they would not leave. They never left. Why could he not be like other men? The knights gathering in the Great Hall below them didn't care that the cause was lost. They cared nothing that the true reason they were here was to gain a fortune by winning the gratitude of the king, the pope, and Baldwin—reigning King of Jerusalem. They lived in his castle, ate his food, and fought his wars against a people who had lived in these lands for ten thousand years. And they cared not at all, so long as their coffers were filled with gold.

But Hugh could not live with what he was. He had come to the Holy Land answering the pope's call to save Edessa from the Saracens. He had heard Bernard of Clairvaux speak at the king's table, beseeching every able man to gather at Constantinople. He had spent long nights listening to Adele's arguments that the Crusade was the answer to his lack of faith, that to be a Templar was his calling. And he had come, dragging Terrence along with him. But he had not found what they had told him he would find.

The campaign to recapture Edessa failed. Hugh had become a Templar only to discover that he was no more than a hired sword. They all were. But they were worse because they hid their gluttony behind a mask of poverty, chastity, and humility. To the world outside they were warrior monks. But within the walls of Baldwin's castle, they were simply mercenaries. Hugh stared into the gaping blackness of the stone fireplace.

"Don't turn your face from the truth, Hugh," Terrence said after a long silence.

"What do you want me to do?"

It was Terrence's turn to sigh. "I'll send the Moor up with a bath for you." He started for the door, stopping only when his hand was upon the haft of the latch. "Think about it, Hugh. If you choose to stay, then so be it. But I have decided to return to Anet. I will leave at month's end."

Hugh looked up at him and after a moment nodded slowly.

"Oh, and there is something of yours on my chest," he added, nodding in the direction of the leather travel case that stood at the end of his bed. Without another word, Terrence left, closing the door behind him.

Hugh stared at the thick door as it closed. Home. A picture of green forests alive with game of every size and shape conjured itself in his brain. He envisioned a cool dawn with tendrils of mist hanging in the air and the smell of freshly mown fields filling his nostrils. He closed his eyes and could almost feel the texture of thick, wet dauber mud between his fingers. As he let his mind wander, Hugh realized for the first time that he had not really believed he would ever go home. Somewhere in his soul he had come to believe he would die in this hot, dry world far from France. Because he did not deserve to return to a world he loved.

A knock at the door awoke him from his strange reverie. Barking an annoyed order for the Moorish slave to enter, Hugh jumped up from the chair and paced across the room. As the bath was filled, the Moor helped Hugh out of his mail, chausses, and surcoat. Piece by piece the weight was lifted from him and he was again struck by his exhaustion. His craving to be rid of the dust and dirt returned, and he grew impatient to be in the healing water. When at last his braies were stripped away, he wordlessly dismissed the Moor and climbed into the copper tub.

Tiny cedar chips floated on the surface, releasing a restorative scent, and Hugh inhaled it deeply as he relaxed against the tub's high back. He tried to concentrate on tomorrow's work. There was much still to be discussed with Baldwin before he left with a small army of men for Damascus. But it was as if a floodgate had been opened in his mind. Images of France tumbled one after another from his memory. The forests, the fields, the villages. But mostly he imagined the cool and the wet. To see a raging river rather than the lame trickles of moisture they called by that name here—that would truly be a gift from God. Or to experience the power of a waterfall or hear the joyous laughter of a brook bubbling over rocks with moss clinging along the dark black earth beside it.

To hear laughter.

Just to hear laughter again. Genuine laughter. Not the raucous barks of the knights he called his brothers with God. But the soft gentle laughter of a woman. Someone warm and happy who smelled of cloves and spice and a bit of apple blossoms. Someone with hair like soft clouds tinted by the sunrise and eyes the aqua of deep pools.

Someone like Catherine de Tralle.

Hugh's eyes closed and he sunk deeper into the water. This once he let his mind wander down a path his vow of chastity forbade him. It wasn't really a violation to think of Catherine. She was no more than a girl. Young and full of spirit, she was his own personal angel. An unreachable thought, and therefore a safe one. His *aimée de plume*. His little tutor. She would be proud of how talented he had become with his reading and writing. The letters he sent her did not let her know that he was now fluent in Arabic and Latin as well as the vernacular French she had begun to teach him.

He sat up in the tub and searched the bottom for the cake of soap. Slowly he washed away the imbedded grime and sweat. What was it Terrence had mentioned as he left? Hugh looked over to the chest and immediately saw the leather pouch lying there. A slow smile spread across his face, reaching all the way to the single deep dimple in his left cheek. Carefully drying his hands, he reached the pouch easily with a swipe of his long arm.

The scroll inside was of a fine parchment. He held it to his nose, inhaling the vague scent of apple blossoms and spice that clung there. He unrolled the paper slowly, savoring every bit of this moment. Then, after he had run his fingers over the crisp edges and crushed the velvet ribbon that tied the scroll between his fingers, he began to read. His eyes flowed over the fine, pointed script so like the seven other letters he had from Catherine.

My dearest Sir Knight,

I write to you as Christmastide comes to a close. The weather for the merry holiday has been fine and crisp with just a touch of chill to the air. My brother Jean was crowned the Lord of Misrule this year. Ma mère created a costume of such whimsy there was not a person who did not cry tears of laughter. And, of course, Jean is still a trickster even now at fifteen years. His jests and buffoonery spared no one, least of all myself. I believe he has never forgiven me for keeping our only visiting Crusader to myself so many years ago.

The mummers arrived after the Christmas feast with many songs and dances—some rather bawdy. But good fun was had by all.

I think of you especially on such holidays. I wonder how it is to celebrate Christ's birth right there upon the soil he walked. Are there celebrations such as you remember from France? Or do the Knights and other Christians in Jerusalem celebrate in another way?

You said that it was just beginning the Autumn Solstice when last you wrote, and so I know it took more than year for your letter to reach me. You told me of King Baldwin's castle where you live now, and of the city of Jerusalem. Please describe to me the people you call the Poulins? You said there is much bickering between them and those who arrived with you from Edessa, yet you describe these Poulins as Christians. You must tell me more. You assume we know more of that place than we do. We hear so little of the Crusades. You have become our most reliable source and my family loves to gather by the hearth in the Great Hall and debate over the information you send in your correspondence.

I hope you are well, Hugh Vougnet. I am, of course, the same. But a little sad. It will not be so long before I leave my family for Strasbourg. It is still more than a year away, but I feel the time slipping by. I have only known this home and Avignon. While I am anxious for the adventure and to learn to call another place home, I shall always miss this one. And, then, too, I will not be here when you, Sir Knight, return from your quest. You remain in my prayers.

Catherine

He read and reread the letter until the bath-water turned from warm to tepid and at last to chilled. Each word created a picture in his mind—Christmastide with the wassail bowl and yule log burning in the hearth. Catherine's huge, boisterous family gathered in the Great Hall, laughing and arguing—alive and full of happiness. And Catherine, moving to Strasbourg to be married. Was it possible? Had so many years passed that the little redheaded imp he pictured was really a grown woman?

Hugh climbed out of his bath and wrapped a Turkish towel around his waist. Bracing his arms against the wall, he bent his head between his shoulders and stared down at the stone floor. His beard dripped water, patterning the gray stone between his feet. It suddenly seemed an eternity that he had been in this land, fighting an enemy he had grown to respect.

But Hugh also dreaded what waited for him in France. If he returned much would be different, but much more would be the same. Hugh was no longer an unlanded second son. But Adele still waited for him. Still expected a changed man upon his return.

All his shortcomings rose up before him like ugly specters from a dark box. He was still, at heart, only a knight. Hugh raised a fisted hand and pounded it against the solid granite of the wall. It didn't matter. He was going home.

He lifted his head, a smile tilting across the flat planes of his rigid face. He *was* going home.

Five

Avignon, France, 1152

Catherine placed stitch after painstaking stitch in the vestment edging and tried to block out the droning whine that filled the solar. Her Aunt Mathilde's silver needle flew in and out of the tapestry she worked with the same speed as her tongue. Mathilde's objective appeared to Catherine to be nothing short of discussing every conceivable subject under God's heaven, and all of it this very afternoon.

"You can't imagine what a good influence the king's court will be on Catherine, Marguerite," she announced changing topics without so much as a pause for breath.

Catherine stabbed her needle into the linen and grit her teeth. There was only one thing worse than Aunt Mathilde's never-ending litanies, and that was when the subject of those one-sided conversations became herself.

"She's had absolutely no exposure to people of such noble blood, you know," Mathilde continued, launching into her subject with zeal.

"And she desperately needs to develop her social and womanly skills, dear." Mathilde leaned over to pat Catherine's leg and took a convenient peek at Catherine's handwork. Pursing her full lips together she gave a little cluck of dismay. "Catherine dear," she chastened. "You must take your stitches half again as small as these you've done. All the powers of the blessed saints won't prevent snags if you leave those gigantic stitches in the bishop's vestments."

Catherine nodded silently, all the while squelching the retort that hung on the very tip of her tongue. She let her needle dangle and reached for the small silver scissor tucked into the purse which hung from her waist. Carefully, she began to snip out the stitches which represented nearly two hours of her day.

"If only you'd insisted that Catherine practice her needlework rather than allowing Bernard to ruin her hand with such nonsense as ciphers and script."

"I trust Bernard's decisions, Mathilde," Marguerite replied with quiet dignity. "And need I remind you, Sister dear, that Bernard is Louis's cousin. We may not be in the domain of the king's rule as we rule our own here in Avignon, but Catherine's blood has enough royalty to more than equal anyone you might find at the king's court."

Mathilde tittered and pressed her broad face into a fleshy smile that reflected no warmth at all. "I certainly didn't mean to imply that Catherine or any of your brood aren't nobles of the highest order. But there *is* a difference. Even you, Marguerite, cannot deny that. Your children have grown up with only the barest semblance of society. And Catherine will soon be on her way to Strasbourg. She will be expected to be conversant in a courtly setting."

"Yes, there is a difference. But not one that Catherine won't be able to overcome easily," Marguerite stated simply. She smiled lovingly at her eldest daughter. "She will make us all very proud in Strasbourg, and the baron as well. I have no fears otherwise."

Catherine lifted the vestments to the tip of her nose, seeming to inspect a minute problem in order to hide her smile as her aunt harumphed and shifted her overly generous figure noisily on the tufted bench where she worked. Aunt Mathilde's silence lasted a bare moment before her need to fill the silence in conversation won the day and she launched into another subject.

"You know, I heard just before leaving Paris that Strasbourg was having some problems. Ever since King Conrad left with Louis for the Holy Lands there have been continuous uprisings. The fighting among the barons and lords has decimated the noble population and their serfs as well." As if the thought had just at that moment occurred to her, Mathilde turned and stared at Catherine. "My goodness, dear. I certainly hope nothing untoward has come of your baron."

"I hope not as well, Aunt," Catherine agreed. She threaded her needle with a rich crimson thread. As she knotted the end, Catherine rolled the silk between her fingers. It was the perfect color for a Crusader's cross, and her thoughts turned down a familiar path. A path she thought of often. Too often, her mother said. Still, she made no attempt to confine her thoughts, letting her handwork sit untouched in her lap.

Conrad was on his way back from Jerusalem, or so it was rumored. Louis VII had just returned himself a year ago, having stopped at Avignon to visit his cousin and inspect the newly completed bridge over the Rhône. But Hugh was still there. Still fighting. Catherine had gone so far as to ask the king about him. And though her mother had reprimanded her later for being so forward, Catherine had found his answer pleasing. Hugh was a success in Jerusalem, and knowing that he was realizing his hopes made Catherine happy. But the king had said nothing about Hugh's return, or even if there was ever to be one.

Her reverie was broken by a knock at the solar door. A moment later Michel entered.

"Madame de Tralle," he announced with a sheepish duck of his graying head, "Crusaders approach."

Catherine watched her mother calmly set aside her needlework. She never seemed to take a quickened breath, while Catherine was a constant tempest of emotions. Though she tried valiantly to be like her mother, gliding from day to day on a cloud of serenity, Catherine could not. Her emotions flitted from high to low, peace to fury, calm to catastrophe—all within any given week or month. She, too, calmly put down her handiwork, rising to sweep serenely from the room. Within, however, she was a maelstrom.

With her mother and Aunt Mathilde leading the way and her sister, Aneelene, following behind, Catherine traversed the passageway from the solar to the Great Hall and from there to the bailey. The entire distance her heart pounded like a war drum. She told herself this was no different than a hundred other times Michel had made such an announcement. But despite the logic of her arguments, as with every other time, Catherine's soul believed that this time it was Hugh.

The women entered the bailey and were immediately accosted by a brisk autumn wind that blew a claret blush to Catherine's cheeks and tossed her red-gold tresses into her eyes. Sweeping the masses of hair from her face, Catherine turned her attentions to the knights who stood dismounted from their destriers and ready to receive the welcome of the lady of the keep. It took only seconds for her heart to sink, for she saw immediately that not one of the men was of Hugh's stature. These knights, while well kept and clearly noblemen, were slightly built. One sported locks the color of pitch and two others dark-brown hair and eyes to match.

While her mother received them, Catherine's gaze caught the eye of one brown-haired knight. He smiled pleasantly at her and Catherine returned the compliment.

"Catherine," her mother called gently. "Sir Jeffrey must needs his mail cleaned and a comforting bath prepared. Would you please see to it?"

Catherine nodded and gave the young knight a second smile. "Sir Jeffrey, if you will but follow me, I will see to it that you receive every comfort while you stay at Avignon."

"Ah, Lady de Tralle, how I will relish every moment of such attentions if they but come from you."

"Of course, my lord." Catherine directed the knight into the keep and upstairs to one of the apartments which had become the common residence of visiting knights. Much had changed in the four years since Hugh and Terrence had breached the portcullis at Avignon. Then, they had been the first knights to pass through Avignon in nearly two years. Now, however, with the construction of the Avignon bridge and a letter last year from the pope stating that he hoped to build a cathedral here, the arrival of Crusaders was an everyday occurrence.

They came by the dozens. Sometimes by the hundreds. If they arrived with an entourage of pilgrims who traveled with a knight and his retinue for protection, they might fill an entire field and need food and water for several weeks. More often they arrived as this group had, half a dozen knights with horses, mail, and a few servants. Often they brought heathens with them. Slaves who for one reason or another had reason to feel that remaining in the Holy Lands would only bring them death. She had seen them arrive weekly. All of them returning home. And every time, no matter how often the word came that Crusaders awaited within the bailey, Catherine hoped that it would be Hugh Vougnet.

But once again it was not.

Catherine and the young knight entered one of the smaller suites at the end of the upper balcony.

"I plead with you, dear lady, permit me the right to be your champion," the young man announced as soon as they were inside the closed room. "My heart has been, upon the moment I first saw you, smitten with a pure and total love I have never felt before."

Catherine smiled quietly to herself and moved about the room assembling various necessities for his bath. "It is so kind of you, sir. However, I am spoken for and leave within the season to meet my betrothed."

"It cannot be!" Jeffrey Winfrey cried, clutching his left breast as though his heart would leap from his very chest at her words. "Mayhap I can at least persuade you to hear a poem I have written. It reflects quite truly my love for you."

Catherine smiled indulgently, but she continued with her duties quite unaffected by the young knight's declarations. How very much things had changed in the past four years, she thought to herself.

"Sir," she inquired, deftly changing the subject. "Were you impressed with the Avignon Bridge?"

Happy to have any reaction at all from the stunning beauty attending him, he again put his hand to his heart and nearly swooned with his emotion-laden praise. "Lady de Tralle, I have seen the likes of such a bridge only in Constantinople itself. Your bridge is a wonder in this part of the world."

Catherine nodded in agreement. "It was designed by a Constantine."

"Ah, then that explains the wonder of seeing something so Eastern here in France."

Adding a fistful of balsam chips and several drops of skin-soothing oil of chamomile, Catherine indicated that the knight should place himself in the bath.

"It has changed our lives here," she explained, reaching for a sea sponge and a cake of soap. "Before the bridge was built we saw few visitors. But in the past year they have come in droves. Some from the North come just to see the bridge, and to watch for knights such as yourself who are returning from the Holy Wars. But mostly we see Crusaders. Whether they come over the land routes from Constantinople or by sea, they must needs cross the Rhône here rather than forging it farther north. I believe we have become a popular resting place."

"But of course," Sir Jeffrey replied enthusiastically. "When our route was being planned, the beauties of Avignon were mentioned often."

"The beauties of Avignon?" Catherine inquired as she poured rinse water over the knight's head. "The bridge I know is one, but what other beauty do you speak of?"

"Surely you are not ignorant of the stories that circulate about you?"

Catherine drew her brows together in perplexity. "About us at Avignon?"

The young knight twisted in the brass tub to face Catherine and enthusiastically pulled her hand into his. Clutching her palm to his wet chest, he stared purposefully into her eyes.

"Not Avignon, dear lady. Nor the bridge. Nor this breathtaking castle crested upon these cliffs," he declared breathlessly. He stared into her face, clutching her hand against him as he spoke. "But you, sweet lady. 'Tis you the minstrels sing praise of and you they describe as the wonder of Avignon."

"Me?" Catherine stared doubtfully at the young man dripping water on her arm and shook her head with a laugh. "I cannot imagine what silly, half-blind minstrel saw fit to play such a trick."

"A trick!" he cried. "I daresay the only trick was that he did not describe your beauty in glowing enough terms."

The knight was half out of the tub such was his enthusiasm for his subject. He pulled Catherine closer. "Dear lady, they describe you as a ruby sparkling in the sun, but you are far more beautiful than that. Only hear the love poem I have etched in my heart as I traveled here, and allow me to become your champion."

Catherine tactfully extracted her hand from the knight's grasp, and cleared her throat in embarrassment as she reached for a Turkish towel. "Sir," she said carefully. "I am touched by your dedication to become my champion, but . . ."

"Do you have another champion already, my lady?"

She smiled. "None."

"Then I shall pursue my cause until your heart softens, and you relent."

"I suppose I cannot prevent you from trying, sir."

He grinned like a child at this small victory and climbed enthusiastically from the water.

"Were you long in Constantinople?" Catherine inquired, changing the subject to one less personal.

"One year and a half."

"And how long in the Holy Lands? Did you fight for Edessa?" As Catherine arranged his hose and tunic on the bed, her questions began to tumble out. "Have you heard of a knight by the name of Hugh Vougnet?"

Pleased to have suddenly attracted her attentions, Jeffrey furthered his cause by impressing her with his knowledge. "Of course I know of Vougnet. His is a legend, the greatest of the Templars."

"Then you know him?"

"No. I could not know him, for he lives in Jerusalem and I did not go beyond Constantinople."

Catherine covered her disappointment with feigned interest in the young knight's escapades. But if he had not met Hugh, could not tell her if her knight was safe, her interest in his stories waned. Still she listened politely to Sir Jeffrey's stories, adding what she could to her store of knowledge about the route to the Holy Lands and the world which Hugh had described to her in his letters.

The afternoon drew to a close, and by the time she emerged from the knight's apartments, the keep was alive with preparations for the evening meal. As Catherine walked along the corridor, the smell of roasting meats wafted through the air. She was hungry. But there was her own dressing to attend to and probably well over an hour before her family and their guests began assembling for supper. Catherine returned to her own rooms where she laid out an indigo kirtle with matching leather slippers. Over this she donned a silver-threaded tunic heavily embroidered along its edges with blue-and-green scenes of the hunt.

She pulled her hair back from the sides of her face, twisting the thick mass into twin coils that crowned her head before clasping it in the back with a silver clip fashioned with emerald and sapphire cabochons. The rest of her hair she left free to froth about her shoulders and fall in a wild cascade of curls to her waist. She thought for a moment about donning a velvet chaplet and veil which matched her kirtle, but could not bear to put on the hateful accessory and its long wimple. Instead, she went to the velvet case that sat on her bedside table and lifted the heavy gold chain which bore her pendant over her head. The rope of gold settled against the back of her neck with welcome familiarity. At last feeling that she was ready for the evening, Catherine headed down to relieve her grumbling stomach.

Her mother had ordered an extravagant meal to welcome their visitors. There was ale and mead aplenty, a joint of roast beef, wild duck, fresh fish, and a dozen tiny songbirds roasted on a spit. Served with the meats were treasures brought by the knights from Constantinople and given as gifts in return for the de Tralles' hospitality. Dates and sugared almonds glistened from beds of freshly picked pears. There were steaming bowls of rice spiced with ginger and dark, pungent cloves and loaves of bread fresh from the kitchen ovens.

Individual cakes flavored with cinnamon and wine were served for dessert when the minstrel appeared to entertain. He began with one comic ditty after another, punctuating his songs and quips with acrobatic tricks and feats of juggling.

But as the hour grew late, he strummed his mandolin more slowly and his subjects became the heroes of the Crusades. He sang of the beauty of Constantinople and the strange barren silence of the Holy Lands. He sang of the fight, and of the cause, and of men dying far from all they knew and loved.

Catherine stared silently into her silver goblet watching the dark mead reflect the dancing lights cast by the resin torches high on the walls of the Great Hall. Beside her sat Sir Jeffrey, watching her every motion like a moon-eyed, lovesick swain. But Catherine was lost in the sad tenor of the minstrel and his song.

> *Upon the cracked and scorning land,*
> *Do I bid my troth,*
> *Knight bold, and true to God's fine hand,*
> *my fate will ere be tossed.*
>
> *Dare dream I of your face again*
> *Sweet damsel I once knew?*
> *Beneath this cross I wear with pride*
> *My heart beats but for you.*

Sir Jeffrey leaned close to her, his fingers reaching for hers, another declaration of love nearly visible there upon his lips. But Catherine did not wait to hear the precise words which would issue forth from the knight. She rose quickly, turning away as she spoke so that the words were barely more than a whisper.

"I fear I have eaten more than my fill this night. I must beg your forgiveness, kind knight, if I feel it necessary to excuse myself."

Jeffrey leapt to his feet, heavy concern creasing his unlined forehead. "Lady Catherine, if you are unwell you must allow me to escort you to your rooms. Women swoon so easily. I fear I have been remiss in some way. I should have overseen your appetite with more concern for your welfare."

"No, no." Catherine shook her head. "You are too kind, sir. I assure you I will be fine. It is only that it has been a very eventful day. I think a night's rest will restore me." Before he could protest more, Catherine extricated the hand he had clasped between his own and moved briskly to the stair. Keeping one eye cocked in the direction of her empty place on the long wooden bench to assure herself that the lovesick knight was not, indeed, going to dog her to her apartments, Catherine made her way up the stairs. But once she was in the darkened hallways beyond the Great Hall, she turned in the direction opposite her rooms.

Without thinking where she was headed, her feet carried her until she stood outside, high on the parapets of the keep. The night was crisp and sharply scented with the smells of the autumnal equinox. Catherine wrapped her arms about herself for warmth and tilted her head back, letting the breeze run its cold fingers across her high cheekbones and down her neck.

Above her, a waning moon hung low in the harvest sky.

She walked to the archer's slit and leaned out onto her elbows. The Rhône ran like a silver ribbon through the pine forest. She watched its progress, slow and steady after the long, dry summer, and wondered at how different this river was from the wild, frothing thing she saw each spring. Yet they were one and the same.

Very soon, she would be different. She would leave her home, travel to a new place, marry, bear children, become as her mother was—serene. And yet, Catherine somehow sensed that, like the river below her, she, too, would remain essentially unchanged. Different, yes. But the same. How strange that they could all be so unchanging despite a world of changes. As she pondered these things, a glimmer of lightness broke the black shadows of the forest.

Catherine watched, then dismissed the strange occurrence as a trick of the moonlight upon her vision. But a moment later, it was there again. In among the trees she saw the flash of moonlight upon something light. A wolf perhaps? Some night predator exposed by the bright moonlight for all his prey to see?

She waited, watching for another glimpse. It came but a second later. But it was no wolf she saw in the moonlight. A man rode hard, the white of his hauberk flashing like a series of lightning bolts as he galloped his destrier up the road to the keep. He came on through the forest, first here in blinding brightness—then gone, back into the shadows. When he broke from the trees, crossing the cleared expanse surrounding the moat and thick walls of the keep, Catherine stared. She leaned farther out over the edge of the parapet, never daring to remove her attention lest this apparition disappear forever.

In the moonlight, his hair shined like silver, flowing to broad square shoulders. Catherine watched him, not breathing, not daring, but watching every move he made no matter how small. His horse appeared black as pitch in the night, although he could be any dark color, Catherine reminded herself. The horse and rider halted at the moat, and the lone rider cupped one gloved hand around his mouth calling for entry. He waited a moment, then called again. From the courtyard below came nary a reply. Frustrated, the knight circled his war horse and the animal, sensing his master's impatience, pawed at the ground beneath his hooves.

The rider called a third time, then running his gloved fingers through his hair, the knight dropped his head back and looked up at the sky above him. For a moment, he didn't see her, for Catherine was frozen in her place. And then his eyes focused on the parapet directly above the portcullis. For a moment, there seemed, suspended in the cold night air between them, something powerful. A knowledge without knowledge. A certainty without reason for certainty.

And then she saw the flash of a broad, bright smile caught in the moon's glow and a gloved hand lowered ever so slowly to the pommel of the saddle as the world grew still.

"Are you still spying on people, Catherine?" It was a deep voice which she knew without having heard for year upon year. "I fear you are no better at it now than you were. Come down, mite, and let me in. I need your help. Terrence is deathly sick and I fear for his life."

Six

Catherine burst through the battlement door and into the castle hallway. To her parents, on their way to their apartments, she appeared more an ancient berserker than their well-bred child. Twisted askew from leaning out over the battlement, her tunic was wrinkled and stained by damp soot. Her hair had been blown loose by the wind atop the portcullis and it frothed about her head with a life all its own adding a wild cast to her wide green eyes and the bright blush of her skin. But it was the shortness of her breath and the way she raced past them as if they did not exist that sent Bernard and Marguerite de Tralle in pursuit of their daughter as she disappeared around a dark corner.

"Catherine!" Her father's voice came from the top of the stairs as she jumped the final three steps. "Stop this moment."

It was a command, and one that no matter what Catherine's destination, she could not disobey.

Breathlessly, she whirled to face them. Poised on her toes with a handful of heavy skirt in each fist, Catherine took a deep breath and looked up at them with a brilliant smile.

"He's back." It was a quiet, simply made statement and she said no more, as if those two words explained all.

Bernard gave his wife a perplexed look. "Who's back?" he asked impatiently.

Marguerite only cocked a thin eyebrow and gave her husband a mysteriously circumspect glance.

It was Catherine who replied. "Hugh."

"Hugh Vougnet?" A grin split Bernard's face. "Well!" he harumphed. "If it's true, he's taken Job's own time getting here! Let's get the gates open and give our old friend aid."

"We haven't a moment to lose, Father," Catherine agreed, turning back toward the door as she spoke. "Terrence is injured or sick."

"Sick? How? Where is he?" Bernard barked out a plethora of questions, but they fell unheeded on the empty hall.

Catherine was already unbolting the heavy oaken door of the keep. As she slipped through the door, she collided with something as solid as a rock on the stone step just outside the doorway. Thick, mailed arms wrapped themselves around her and for a moment her head reeled with the smell of warm sweat and a tangy maleness that seemed to permeate her senses. Her hands were wedged against a rock-hard chest, a small and ineffectual shield between two bodies.

Catherine looked up. Up past the red cross set

on white linen, past the broad shoulders, up past the mail hood that had been shoved back off his head. Her gazed traveled over the thickly corded neck and then she was looking into his face. For a moment she could do no more than stare. In the passing of a second she drank in everything about him. The stubble of a day's growth of beard, a scar on his cheek which she knew was recent, the crinkled lines that radiated from the outer corners of his eyes and bespoke long hours in the sun. And the blue depths of his eyes.

He was the same. And he was different. But her heart knew him well. It was her knight come back as he had promised. Her friend. It was Hugh.

His face broke into a smile. "Hello, mite."

"Vougnet!" Bernard's bellow echoed through the hall. Hugh broke his gaze from Catherine and stepped away from her, turning his attention to her parents. In three long strides he was before Bernard and Marguerite. He dropped to one knee, placed his gloved hand to his chest, and bowed his head in salute.

"Get up, man! There's no need for such formality here. We're just damned glad to see you safe and well."

"You've been in our prayers, Hugh," Marguerite added warmly.

"My thanks for that, my lady. There have been more times than I care to recall when I've needed those prayers."

"Well, you're well beyond the grasp of those heathen Saracens now," Bernard concluded.

"It's not always the Saracens which pose the greatest threat."

"Indeed," Bernard agreed. "And your brother, how fares he? My daughter speaks of some illness."

Hugh grew grave, his eyes piercing in their intensity as he bowed his head. "Bernard, I need your help. Terrence lays on a litter just at the bottom of the hillside below. I tried my best to reach your keep, but the pain has become too great for him. I fear it will kill him if I move him another inch."

Hugh felt the air stir beside him and, looking down, he found Catherine at his elbow.

"We will go down to him," she stated calmly. "What is it that sickens him?"

"It is too long a story to tell now, but he is wounded and the wound festers. He burns with fever." Hugh turned back to Marguerite. "You must send someone to him."

"We will send men to carry the litter up here. He needs to be where it is warm and dry. It will cause him less suffering than being pulled behind a horse. And Catherine will go with you. She can give him a tonic to numb his pain."

Hugh glanced at Catherine, surprised that Marguerite would put such responsibility in the hands of one so young, but he nodded in agreement. "Then get a cloak, mite. Every minute he comes closer to death."

While Catherine raced for her cloak, Hugh and Bernard went back into the bailey, where orders were quickly issued for horses and men to be readied. The courtyard had already come alive with Hugh's arrival, and by the time Catherine returned, dressed for the cold and carrying a satchel of herbs and medicines, her mount was waiting and both Hugh and her father were ready to depart. They galloped from the walled castle with an entourage of ten men, and raced down the road following the pace set by Hugh.

Catherine rode close to Hugh, thinking only of Terrence and of reaching him with the medicinals which she knew would ease his discomfort. They must get him to the castle at all costs whatever his injury. She had treated enough serfs who had accidentally sliced off a hand with a sickle or maimed a foot in the fields to know that a wound, no matter how small, could kill a man within hours if it became diseased.

The forest closed in around them, blocking out the moonlight except for an occasional patch of silver that filtered through the thick canopy of leaves overhead. The road before them was black as pitch, and although the men behind them carried torches, Catherine could see nothing but darkness ahead of them. Hugh seemed not to need the light, however. His steed stretched out at a full gallop down the steep hillside and neither horse nor rider hesitated in the blackness. Determined not to fall behind, Catherine kept her horse's nose on the tail of Hugh's stallion. She felt as though they were plunging headlong into a black pit, but still she stayed with Hugh. At last Hugh began to pull his stallion back, slowing their wild pace.

At a bend at the bottom of the mountain, he drew to a halt. Not waiting a moment he swung down and strode into the thick underbrush along a trail of broken branches and flattened undergrowth that marked where Terrence's litter had traveled. Fifty feet into the woods, they emerged into a small clearing.

Hugh stopped dead at the edge of the trees. "Terrence?" he called quietly.

For a moment there was nothing, and Catherine's heart leapt into her throat in fear. What if they were too late? But then a faint moan came from the darkness, and Bernard's men came into the clearing, their torches lighting the night. Catherine heard a horse nicker and then made out the quiet form laying on the litter on the far side of the clearing. Without thinking, she started toward him. A gloved hand on her arm stopped her.

Hugh looked down at her dubiously. "Do you know what you are about, Catherine?"

She nodded silently. "I won't hurt him more than he hurts now, Hugh. I know well what I do. And I know his pain. Although I have never felt it myself, I have seen it before, and treated it. Once I have ministered him, you and the other men will be able to take him to the castle. There we can treat his wound. For now, all I will do is give him something to block out the pain. It will still be there, but he will not feel it."

Hugh nodded, releasing her arm and falling in step behind her as she crossed to Terrence. Signaling for a torch, Catherine knelt beside the litter and untied the satchel from her waist. In the yellow light of the flare, Catherine saw how very sick Terrence was. His cheeks were gaunt and sweat ran in rivulets along the sides of his face. His clothing was soaked with the sweat of his fever, and a fetid odor issued from the pallet.

Catherine did not even attempt to look at his wound. She knew already that he was very, very sick. Not wasting a moment, she loosened the leather cord from the neck of her bag and extracted a small phial. With sure hands, Catherine removed the stopper and gently slid her palm beneath his neck. His skin was scorching. An almost imperceptible moan came from between his parched lips and she whispered gentle words of encouragement. Carefully, she put the phial to his mouth.

"Drink, Terrence. Drink so we can take you to safety."

She poured a tiny measure of the medicine between his lips. The liquid began to run from the corner of his mouth, and she tilted his head back, forcing it down his throat. He swallowed, and after a moment she tipped another thimbleful between his lips. It was several minutes before Terrence drank the full measure of medicine,

but almost immediately it began to take effect.
She felt his head become heavier as a deep
numbing took over, temporarily chasing the pain
from him. Laying his head back on the litter,
Catherine looked up at Hugh who had watched
every move intently.

"You can take him now," she said quietly.

Hugh looked from her to his brother and back
again. Then with a single nod, he took over. Six
men moved quickly to take the pallet, but Hugh
waved one away and took one end of the branch
which fashioned the poles himself. Carefully,
they hoisted the sick man and began the long,
slow walk up to the castle.

It was an arduous, silent journey back to the
castle. Not a man spoke; even the forest around
them was still. When they were at last within
sight of the keep, Catherine urged her horse
around the litter.

"I will ride ahead to help my mother with the
preparations," she whispered as she passed
Hugh. They were out of the forest now, and in
the moonlight she could see the concern that lay
like an iron cast upon his face. Without waiting
for a reply, Catherine rode to the gates and on
into the keep.

By the time Hugh and her father reached the
castle, Catherine and her mother were ready.
Terrence was carried to his rooms and carefully

lifted from the litter onto a bed. The men left—
all but Hugh who hovered over his brother.

"Hugh," Marguerite admonished gently. "You
are exhausted. Let me have a meal brought to
you so that you may sleep. There is nothing you
can do here. You have done all there is for him
already."

Hugh shook his head. "I will stay."

Catherine, the sleeves of her kirtle rolled up to
her elbows as she helped her mother bathe the
sweat from Terrence, glanced at Hugh with understanding. In his letters, Hugh had written at
length about his brother. She knew he felt responsible for his younger sibling, felt that he had
dragged Terrence to Jerusalem when he would
have happily stayed in France. Often he had
hinted that Terrence was restless and unhappy
with the Templars. That he had been wrong to
bring Terrence with him.

Turning back to the younger man who lay pale
and feverish on the bed, she evaluated Terrence's
wound. It was to his right forearm and it was
clear that the muscles had been sliced to the
bone.

"How many days has it been since this injury?"
Marguerite asked as she lay a steaming poultice
over the gangrenous tissue.

Hugh sighed in anguish and ran his fingers
through his hair, his head bent in misery. "It was
on our way to Constantinople. Terrence wanted
to return to France, and had made plans to depart for the city a month before. But at the last

minute I decided to go with him and asked that he stay until I could prepare for the journey. Because of me, we arrived at Nicaea on the day a band of Saracens attacked the town.

"We could have gone around the town. We could have turned back. We could have been weeks in Constantinople, but no. Terrence had waited for me. And I had to fight. We were Templars. Such was my duty. I went to the aid of the Nicaeans, and Terrence followed. It was a Saracen's scimitar that cut his arm to the bone."

"But that must have been months ago," Catherine said.

"Yes. The Saracens rode back into the desert at last, and two days later we were able to travel to Constantinople. There we stayed for nearly a month. Terrence was healing well; the emperor's bleeders and surgeons had served my brother skillfully. A ship headed for Marseilles was anchored at the mouth of the Bosporus, and I thought Terrence healed enough for the journey. I had become anxious to see France again, and weary of the East."

Hugh closed his eyes in self-torment. "But it was a selfish choice. The trip across the Mediterranean was hard and wet. His wound became infected and I did not know how to nurse him."

Marguerite removed the poultice, pulling away infected skin with it and Terrence jerked reflexively through his drugged haze. Hugh stared at his brother, his eyes burning with guilt as he watched Marguerite begin to cut away the rotted flesh and muscle. When Terrence cried out, Hugh jumped up from his chair like a man stung. He hovered over the bed, clenching and unclenching his fists in helpless frustration.

When Marguerite collided with Hugh for the fourth time, Catherine knew she could be of more aid by distracting him. She laid a hand on his arm and smiled gently up at him.

"You will do Terrence little good if you yourself become ill."

"I cannot rest while my brother fights death. I will stay."

"The wound must be cleaned deeply. He will cry out like this and his body will move as if in pain, but I promise you, Hugh, he feels it not in his mind. You torture yourself by watching. Please. You can do naught for him now. But when the wound is cleaned and resewn, then will come the pain. At that time he will need your strength and your comfort. You must be ready."

He stared blindly across the room into the darkened corners, but did not move. Gently, Catherine put her small hand into his broad one and without a word she led him from the sick-room.

Hugh leaned back in the oaken armchair, his eyes closed, every muscle in his body held rigid. He felt the muscle in his left cheek jump once, then again. The warmth from the fire radiated against his left side, but it gave him no comfort.

His hands clenched the carved lion's-claw arms of his seat until his knuckles burned white-hot from the strain. Across the room he could hear the soft sounds of Catherine moving calmly from the hearth to the tub and back again. Slowly, he opened his eyes.

In the glow of torchlight that bathed the room her hair gleamed like burnished copper threads. Still untouched since she'd peered down at him from the battlements, it billowed like sea froth down her back. Curling wisps about her face accentuated her high cheekbones and the small chin that ended in the slightest dimple. Her mouth was not overly generous, nor tight and small, and it broke into a soft smile each time she looked at him. Her brows arched over a set of long dark lashes which in turn fringed enormous aqua eyes. She was beautiful.

What had happened to the twelve-year-old who wore a braid down her back and played blind man's buff in the courtyard? In the four years he had been gone, Hugh thought he had changed very little. But Catherine had grown from child to woman. He watched her bend over a ewer of wine, pouring it into a silver mazer.

She was petite and slender, yet she moved with a grace that bespoke supple strength garnered from years of riding and hunting. How could this beauty be the wide-eyed innocent who had taught him to read and write? Hugh thought of her letters, each one carefully wrapped in oil-cloth and packed with his most precious possessions. Each read over and over until the parchment edges had become supple with the oil from his hands. He knew that Catherine so well. But this gentle, perfect woman—did he know *her*?

Catherine came to him, handing him the goblet of warmed wine. "Drink this, it will help you sleep."

"You have drugged my wine?"

She laughed as she settled onto the boarskin that lay at the foot of Hugh's chair. "I have only sprinkled it with the essence of dried berries and herbs. They are safe, and if you do not drink it, you will never sleep."

"When did you become an alchemist?"

"I did not become one. I have only learned from my mother what her mother passed on to her and hers before that. Such knowledge is vital to the welfare of our serfs. Our people are in our care, and care for them we must." Catherine turned her attention to the fire that burned in the hearth, and her voice softened. "When I go to Germany, I will be expected to have such knowledge. I cannot fulfill my duties as mistress of a barony if I have no knowledge of healing."

"When do you go to Germany?"

"Drink!" Catherine demanded, ignoring his question.

Hugh shook his head. "I must be alert for Terrence."

"You must rest or you are of no use to him. One way or another, you will rest. I have put the herbs in your food as well."

"Then I will not eat."

Catherine smiled at him. "Oh, I think you will eat."

As if to punctuate her statement, a soft knock sounded at the door. Catherine left her place at his feet and gave entry to a line of servants bearing silver-coffered platters. The room was immediately filled with smells that set Hugh's mouth to watering. He had not realized how hungry he was. When had he last eaten? He'd broken fast very early, while Terrence lay sleepless on the litter beside him. It had been more a show of bravado than hunger then. He'd determinedly gnawed on his dried crust of bread and cured meat, hoping to instill in his brother a will to live. But Terrence had been little interested, and Hugh's concern had deepened. It was then, before the sun was up, that Hugh had realized he must reach Avignon at all costs tonight—for Terrence was dying.

Two serfs set a small table before him and covered it with a linen cloth richly embroidered with autumn fruits and oak leaves in golds and russets. Then a trencher and knife were laid in place. Catherine took a seat on the opposite side of the table and nodded silently for the first course to be presented. With a bow, a young boy lifted the first silver dome, revealing a roasted peacock, fully dressed in iridescent feathers, sitting in a nest of braised cress, sage, and fennel. Another platter revealed succulent fox served with a savory bread pudding studded with raisins. Groaning, Hugh succumbed to his hunger and soon his trencher was heaping with meats and pudding and sauces.

Catherine watched him devour three trenchers of food. A serving boy stood at attention in one corner of the room, and repeatedly Catherine nodded for him to refill Hugh's plate. His mazer as well was refilled time and again with warm, spiced wine which he used to wash down the quantities of food. When he reached for the plump peacock breast, Catherine sat back in her chair and cocked a dubious brow at the knight.

"What?" Hugh demanded, the meat midway to his mouth.

"I believe the boy fears that in your hunger you may mistake his own arm for some tasty morsel and he'll be devoured whole."

Hugh pondered the possibilities, then licked his lips ominously. "Lad, come here into the light."

A panicked hiccup issued from the far corner of the room. There was a shuffling of feet and then a small voice squeaked, "My lord, the platters are empty. Let me go to the kitchens and see if the cook has something else for you. 'Tis only a few hours till the dawn and mayhap he is baking some fine loaves of bread." The boy did not wait for a reply. He flew from the room, empty platters clutched in his arms.

Catherine pressed the back of her hand to her lips, but it was no use. Laughter burst from her in long peals.

Hugh grinned at her from across the table. "Do you think there's any chance at all that he'll return with bread?"

She shook her head, dabbing at the tears of mirth that threatened in the corners of her eyes. "I fear you've quite sabotaged yourself. He took every last morsel of your supper with him."

"Nay," Hugh replied, snatching a golden pear from the bowl in the center of the table. "Besides, the boy hadn't an ounce of decent meat on him."

"Ah, then he was right to flee. You were ogling him for your next course," responded Catherine blithely. Their eyes met and he smiled again. Catherine felt her heart catch in her throat. It was the first true smile she'd seen. Any others he had worn on the surface, but this reached down to his soul and radiated, like glowing embers of light from his ice-blue eyes.

Hugh bit into the pear and closed his eyes in sheer pleasure. "Ah, Cay, how I have missed the smallest things. A cool breeze. The sound of rain. The taste of a pear in autumn." His eyes opened again and he grinned. "You were right. I was hungry."

She nodded sagely.

"But I'm not tired. Your potions did not work."

"Ah, but they did, my lord. The herbs were not intended to put you to sleep, merely to relax you."

He leaned back in his chair, tilting it backward

as he stretched his long legs before him. "That it has done. Or something has done." The smile stayed on his face and Catherine smiled back.

"Then you are ready for a bath, sire?"

"Nay, I must see how Terrence fares."

"If all was not well, my mother would certainly have sent for you. He rests now. There will be time enough on the morrow. Now, I think, you must see to your own needs." Catherine leaned forward and turned a sly, sidelong gaze on him. "If your humor is this much improved by a little food, it does not bear imagining your good nature should you be clean."

Hugh scowled, all the while thinking that a warm bath would be incomparable. Reading his thoughts, Catherine rose to see to the final preparations. Hours ago she'd had a tub set up. Now she quickly ordered hot water, then came to assist him in removing his clothes.

Hugh finished his pear in two bites and washed it down with the rest of the wine in his mazer. He could not recall the last time he had felt so peaceful. The muscle in his cheek had even ceased its twitching and his fingers felt strangely numb. It must be the herbs, he decided. Smiling, he held up his foot so that Catherine could remove his boot. As she skillfully slid off first one, then the other, serving maids arrived with horsehair buckets of steaming water.

Catherine directed them with quiet aplomb, and when they had departed she returned to his side. Hugh chuckled as he stripped off his chausses, hauberk, and tunic.

"Do you recall, Cay, that this is much like the first day we met?" He watched closely as a tawny blush crept across her face. "You scalded my brother. Then came in here and proceeded to tell me that everyone should know how to read and write, and you would be pleased to teach me how."

Catherine dunked a cake of soap into the bath-water as Hugh settled himself into the tub. "They should," she replied simply.

"I know." Hugh felt her fingers splay across his chest as she rubbed the scented soap in slow circles over his body. She leaned over his shoulder and his nostrils were assailed by her scent. It was fresh and spicy and far more enticing than all of the smells of his supper combined. "I speak, read, and write three languages now."

Catherine's eyes lit up. "How wonderful! French, Latin, and . . . ?"

"Arabic."

"The language of the Saracens?" she asked in surprise.

"They are people, too, Catherine. I learned much from them."

"That's good, Hugh."

He turned in the tub to face her. "Do you think so?"

"Of course."

Hugh nodded and settled back against the tub. Catherine scrubbed his back and neck, then his hair. Her rhythmic motions set his scalp to tingling, and a deep groan of pleasure escaped him.

"Now rinse, please." Catherine ordered, gently prodding him with a finger.

Hugh slid down in the water until his head disappeared beneath the surface. When he emerged he turned to face Catherine, mischief twinkling in his eyes.

"Are you ready to get out?" she inquired.

In response, Hugh spit a stream of water directly at the center of her kirtle.

Catherine shrieked, and for a moment she did nothing but stare at the dark water stain on her dress. For one instant Hugh feared she would stomp from the room indignant. Then he saw a playful spark light in her eye and a moment later she grabbed a bucket, scooped it full of bathwater, and dumped the entire thing over his head, bucket and all.

Hugh grabbed the bucket off his head and dunked it into the tub.

Now Catherine cried out in earnest. "Hugh Vougnet! Don't you dare to even think of drenching me with your bathwater!"

"Argh!" he protested in mock disgust. "You've become an old crone, Catherine! You used to be *fun!*"

"An old crone!" The cake of soap catapulted into the bath, hitting Hugh squarely in the chest. "I'll have you know I'm still the best hawker in all of Avignon!"

Hugh rolled his eyes. "You expect me to believe that?"

Catherine marched over to the tub with saucily swinging hips, and bent close to his face. "Nay, sir knight. You need not believe it! I shall prove it to you. The moment Terrence is well enough for us to venture away from him for a day, we will go hawking. Then you will see."

Catherine leaned mere inches from Hugh's face, her brows drawn low over eyes that threatened mock thunderstorms. She pursed her lips into a challenge. Hugh stared at her mouth, mesmerized by the perfection of its form, the pliant softness of lips that seemed to him to be exactly the golden red that marked the skin of a peach waiting to be bitten into. A golden red that held the promise of sweet, succulent treasure awaiting within. Dragging his gaze from those lips, it locked on her eyes. Aqua. Pure sea-green orbs with nary a fleck of brown or blue or any other color to lessen the impact of their unsullied depths. He had remembered all of this, but in the form of a child. And here was that child, changed now into a woman of rare beauty and a soul as kind and loving as he had remembered. His cherished Catherine.

Catherine balanced her weight over the copper tub, unable somehow to pull herself away from the trance that tied her to Hugh. She smiled hesitantly at him trying to break the strange catalepsy that spun out between them like an invisible thread. But Hugh did not smile back.

His gaze locked on hers, reaching through her eyes into another, deeper part of herself. The game was done. There was nothing playful about him anymore. His visage had changed. The smile faded from his mouth, replaced by another, deeply intense emotion. For long seconds he stared at her, never moving.

He was so close. Her knight. Catherine's senses were assailed by all of him. She heard his breath like a roar in her ears even as she felt the heat of his gaze on her skin. Her nostrils filled with the scent of soap mingled with his warm skin. In the darkened room, the firelight licked across his bronzed skin creating an ever-changing pattern of gold that lit his face and outlined its rugged planes. Even the scent of the spiced wine on his breath drew her, making her mouth water. The silence stretched out, broken only by the hiss of the fire and she was captive to the penetrating absoluteness of his presence.

Slowly, as if in a dream, she felt Hugh's fingers wrap around her arm drawing her closer. As he pulled her to him, he came to meet her and somewhere, halfway between the inches that had separated them, they met. Instinctively, Catherine's lips parted as the warmth of his mouth touched hers. Her eyes closed and his lips moved against hers. Warmth. Gentle warmth. Need. Desire. From behind a haze, Catherine absorbed each message that crossed between their lips.

The tip of his tongue caressed the moist inside of her lower lip sending rivulets of heat spiraling outward through her every limb until her very fingertips tingled. As his mouth moved against hers, urging greater entrance between her lips, the nubble of his unshaven face brushed the tip of her nose and she inhaled the smell of him. She felt the tip of his tongue, moist and warm, run along the inner wall of her lip and it was like nothing Catherine had ever experienced before. Her stomach lurched and softened, like butter in the sun. Her arms became leaden. A sigh escaped from somewhere deep within her, as though the door to her soul had swung wide on unused hinges for the first time in her life.

Suddenly she felt exposed. As though a cool forewarning of a storm had suddenly blown across her heart. Awkwardly, Catherine pulled away. She cleared her throat and stepped back, not meeting his gaze. "The water must be chilly."

Hugh said nothing. For a moment more he gazed at her, then silently, he nodded. Catherine handed him a linen towel and self-consciously turned away, busying herself with some small project as he stepped from the tub and dried himself.

"I must check on my brother," he told her quietly.

"I shall," she quickly offered. "It will be faster. You still need to be dressed." It was as good an excuse as any to escape the sudden quiet of the room and Catherine needed escape. Like the serving boy fleeing earlier, Catherine felt the sudden need to put a great deal of space between herself and Hugh Vougnet. Without waiting for his reply, she slipped out of the room not letting her gaze meet his as she fled.

Seven

Catherine forgot her promise to check on Terrence and instead went straight to her room. But one look at her bed told her she would find no rest there tonight. Instead, she paced nervously before the hearth trying to resolve the spinning, off-balance feeling that enveloped her. For four years she'd thought of Hugh day and night. He was in her prayers at Mass, and in the words she penned as her quill skimmed across the parchment each night recording the events of her life, her musings, and her hopes. For four years she had pictured Hugh much as the hero of a minstrel's song. He had been as she'd always thought of him—mythical. The man-beast with a gentle, hidden heart that only she had seen and understood. But now—nay, ever since he'd come through the door tonight—she had seen him differently.

Why had he kissed her? One moment they had been playing just as though he'd never left Avignon. So easy. So joyous and simple. Then his eyes had suddenly turned smokey and a tightness had taken possession of his mouth. She hadn't known that he was going to kiss her. It was nothing like the time the visiting squire's son had kissed her down by the river two years ago. Nor had Sir Jeffrey's pecks on her hand in the least resembled Hugh's kiss. No, Hugh's kiss had been like a hand reaching deep within her. It pulled forth something she had never felt before. And it had frightened her more than a little.

What was she to think now? She was betrothed. And Hugh, as well, was promised to another. Catherine was suddenly beset by an uncontrollable curiosity about Adele. Terrence used to speak of Adele as one would a cur, and Hugh had always changed the subject whenever Catherine had asked about his fiancé. Was he no longer betrothed to Adele? Had he perhaps received word that she had taken ill and died?

Catherine contemplated this thought with growing shock. If it was true, then Hugh was free to marry anyone. Would he want to marry her? The very thought of marrying Hugh Vougnet sent Catherine's emotions careening wildly out of control. Oh, to be married to her knight! For a moment she let herself imagine it. Endless days of shared laughter. Long evenings before the hearth in their own Great Hall discussing projects for their serfs, improvements to the land and the keep.

Abruptly, Catherine shook her head. No matter if Adele was dead and Hugh free to choose another bride. *She* was not free. In fact, she was only days away leaving for the first part of her journey to Strasbourg. In less than a fortnight she would journey to the Abbaye de Royaumont. Her father had made arrangements for her to stay there for six months while she completed her knowledge in medicinals. She would also learn the fine arts she would need to carry out her duties as the wife of a baron and mistress of a manor. Ever since she was a child, she'd been preparing for this marriage, and it would not be changed. Not even for Hugh.

But Catherine wondered about Adele. It would explain Hugh's kiss if, indeed, the course of his future had changed. Terrence would know. Catherine chewed at her lip in worry. She had promised Hugh that she would check on his brother, but then it might be hours or even days before Terrence was well enough to talk at all, and it did not bear thinking that she might disturb Terrence to discuss such a frivolous subject. Still . . . Catherine paced once more from one side of the room to the other. She *should* check on Terrence.

Deciding that she would peek in on Hugh's brother and then be done with her speculations, Catherine headed down the passageway. In the Great Hall below, the first signs of the day's activity were beginning. The hounds stirred from their beds beside the hearth and three serving girls had begun to sweep away yesterday's rushes, to be replaced with freshly sickled grasses. While the harvest lasted, they would change the rushes every day, but in winter, the rushes would remain for no less than two weeks and as long as a month.

Catherine knocked gently at Terrence's door. There was no reply, so she let herself quietly into the room. Within, all was still as death. The torches had been set to burn low because Catherine's mother believed it was better to keep a sickroom free of their acrid smoke, but the room was warm to keep the chill, and its dangers, at bay.

Catherine crossed quietly to Terrence's bed. She touched his forehead with the back of her hand. She smiled. He was cooler now. The worst of the fever had passed. It would only be a matter of time before he would recover. Though there were still dangers, she knew that in her mother's care, Terrence would soon be beyond the grasp of death. Still, he was gaunt and drawn. It would do him well to eat heartily while he was here.

Her gaze dropped to his arm. All seemed well. The bandages were still fresh and there was no telltale odor to indicate that the infection lingered. Catherine noticed that the bandage her mother had wrapped around his arm was enormous. It covered his forearm from wrist to elbow and completely encased the lower half of his arm.

Someone, probably her mother, had pulled a heavy oaken chair beside his bed, and now Catherine sank into it, resting her chin on her hand as she watched Hugh's brother sleep. He slept well, which pleased Catherine even though it meant there would be no chance to query Terrence about the possibility of Adele's demise. There would be time for that later. For now, she simply wanted to rest a moment herself. She'd been up all night, and between the feast for Sir Jeffrey and his group, riding down to find Terrence, and supping with Hugh, she realized suddenly that she was completely exhausted. Her eyelids grew heavy at the very thought of how long she had been up this day, and she yawned a great yawn.

Dreamily, she wondered again about Adele. No matter, she thought, she was going to Strasbourg and there was no use thinking about something that could not possibly be. But nearly a fortnight lay between then and now. She mentally laid out her plans for the next fourteen days. Between now and then, she promised herself languorously, she would simply enjoy Hugh's company. He and Terrence had stayed nearly a month when they first came to Avignon. And she had carried those memories for four years. These next two weeks would have to last her a very long time. Much longer than the four years she'd waited. But she would have her fortnight with Hugh.

As the netherworld of sleep engulfed her, Catherine made herself a promise. During these weeks she would not think about the baron who waited to engulf the rest of her life. She would pretend that all that existed was Hugh and Terrence and Avignon. And with that fine thought Catherine fell quite soundly asleep.

Hugh awoke to the sound of a sharp rap at his door. For a moment he thought he was in Jerusalem, but as his head began to clear he realized that the bed on which he sprawled facedown was far too soft to be his Templar's pallet, and the smell of oak logs burning in the hearth could not possibly belong to Jerusalem. The rapping came again, more insistent this time, and Hugh rolled onto his back. He shook his head violently to rid himself of the fog that enveloped it. It must be Catherine's damned herbs, he thought, swinging his legs over the side of the bed and sitting up. The knock at the door repeated.

"Come in!" Hugh cried irritably.

The door creaked on its leather hinges and the youth who'd served his supper last night entered. He seemed to hug the walls of the room as he inched his way toward the temporary table which had been set there the night before. Hugh gave him a sidelong stare. Running his fingers through his hair, he watched the young serf. The boy was still terrified.

"I see you've finally returned with some food for me. Let me see," he commented dryly as he stood and stretched. "Of course, it has been, what, four hours . . ."

The boy ducked his head and with shaking

hands laid the silver platter he bore upon the small table. "Six hours, sire."

"Six hours? Then certainly you had to wake the cook and require of him that he create some culinary delight for my enjoyment. Such dedication is quite notable. But in the meantime, I have become nearly starved. Next time a simple crust or two of bread will suffice."

"Yes, sire." The lad bobbed his head at Hugh, then hesitated for a minute before plunging on. "But the cook has prepared much more than a crust of bread for you today. The lady has given strict orders that you and Sir Terrence are to be stuffed like two pheasants upon the platter."

Hugh eyed him doubtfully. "Is that what Lady Marguerite said?"

"No, sire. Those were Lady Catherine's words."

"Lady Catherine?" Hugh asked.

"The same."

Hugh crossed to the table and lifted the silver dome that encased his breakfast. The most wonderful smells issued from the platter, and Hugh's mouth began to water. There was quail sauced in quince and apples, a loaf of freshly baked bread, a bowl filled to overflowing with an assortment of filberts, black walnuts, and chestnuts, and a tall tankard of perry. Suddenly starved, Hugh drained the tankard of fermented pear juice in a single gulp and tossed down a handful of nuts.

"And where is Lady Catherine now?" he inquired.

The lad shrugged. "Asleep, I should think, my lord." The boy stopped with a pitcher of fresh milk held in midair and let a grin split his long, narrow face. "My mother says the castle hasn't seen a night like this in a hundred years! Everyone up all night, men riding out into the pitch of night, and Crusaders appearing in the moonlight like wraiths from the dead." As if realizing he might have offended the knight, the serving boy stopped long enough to give Hugh a sidelong glance. Then, seemingly reassured, he took a deep breath and prepared to plunge on with his description.

Hugh interjected before the lad could get a second wind. "I'm sure Father Godfried will be anxious to hear about the wraiths."

The boy's eyes grew to twice their size and he clamped his mouth shut, sidling toward the doorway. "Shall I return to clear away your breakfast in an hour, sire?"

Hugh gave the boy a preoccupied nod as he made his escape. Cutting a thick slice of the freshly baked bread, he applied a dollop of honey to it and proceeded to devour the delicious meal quickly. Now that he was back in France, Hugh seemed unable to get enough of the foods he had been deprived of in the Holy Lands. Wiping his mouth, he strode to the chest at the end of his bed. Hugh pulled a leather jerkin and woolen hose from the small leather traveling case which he always carried behind his saddle. Donning these, he then settled a wide leather belt about his waist and pulled on high black boots. Hugh ran his fingers through his hair as a means of putting it in some semblance of order then left his apartment and headed in the direction of Terrence's rooms.

As he strode down the long corridors toward the opposite wing of the keep, his thoughts drifted to the night before. Momentarily closing his eyes, Hugh let regret and shame wash over him. Why did he always do the thing he should not? There was no reason, certainly no excuse, for kissing Catherine. He was a Knight Templar. And his vow of chastity precluded any intimacies with a woman. Of course, when he returned home, he would be released from his vows, for he would no longer be in the service of Baldwin of Jerusalem and he would marry Adele. That was as it should be.

But to have kissed Catherine. An innocent. A young woman with whom he shared a friendship, and friendship alone. Hugh knew his actions were reprehensible in the eyes of God, and in the eyes of those he owed allegiance to—and that was Adele. His mouth flattened into a thin line of remorse. By all that was holy, had he spent four years away from his home, traveling from one end of the world to another only to return having learned nothing?

Hugh still remembered why he had left. Adele had demanded that he cleanse his soul, that he purge from his thoughts and actions all pride, all selfish need—everything except the calling of

God. Only then would he be fit to begin a life with her. And Hugh believed he had.

He'd fought hard and well. Hundreds of pilgrims still lived solely because Hugh Vougnet had been there to defend them from the ruthless attacks of the Saracens. He had lived for three full years under the edicts of the Templars, practicing chastity, abstinence, and prayer. And he had believed he was changed. Believed that he was ready to come home and serve Adele as a husband should. But he had been in Avignon less than a day, and already he had allowed himself to be sullied by temptations of the flesh. He shook his head and then set his face with determination.

He would stay away from Catherine. The little mite was affianced to her German baron. Hugh could offer Catherine nothing. He had pledged himself to Adele, and she had the rights to everything Hugh had to give. No, he told himself, he must keep away from Catherine. He would go to the chapel this very day and renew his vows. And he would tell Catherine that he had made a mistake. It would be a simple matter.

Hugh reached out for the latch of Terrence's door. He didn't bother to knock, he had never in his entire life knocked before letting himself in Terrence's rooms. But the moment he was in the door, he stopped, frozen by the unexpected sight before him. Terrence was sleeping soundly in his bed, but beside the bed was a sight that caused Hugh's heart to lurch like a man drunk on too much ale.

Catherine lay curled like a sleeping kitten in the large wooden chair beside the bed. She still wore the kirtle and tunic she'd ridden to the glade in, making it clear that she'd never gone to her rooms at all. Her breath came in long, even measures and a peacefulness seemed to light her being from deep within, as though a small flame burned inside her and lit the space all around her. Dark shadows lay in crescents beneath her long, red-gold lashes and her skin was pale as the pearly inside of a shell.

Hugh stood transfixed in the doorway. Catherine seemed, at that moment, incredibly vulnerable. He was struck by an overwhelming desire to protect her, to shelter her from all harm, whatever it might be. He took a single step forward, drawn by a force that was stronger than all his resolves.

But he stopped himself. Giving his head a hard shake, he stepped back into the hallway and turned his head away from the door.

What had he almost done? Hadn't he *just* made a vow to stay away from Catherine? And yet, within the span of a moment, he had come within a hairbreadth of completely disregarding that vow. Hugh clenched his hands into fists. He wanted to walk away. Go off into the forests below Avignon Keep and put as much distance between himself and Catherine de Tralle as he could. But that would be admitting to an inability to resist her, and that was a weakness he would not allow himself. There would be hundreds of women within his reach for the rest of his life, and if he was to return to Anet, his home, and Adele in victory, he would learn now to resist these temptations.

But as a knight who lived under the codes of chivalry, he could not leave her there, curled up in the chair. It was his duty to move her to comfort. She hadn't slept all night. She had done as much or more than her mother to save his brother's life. She deserved better than to be left with a chair for a bed.

The sound of footsteps coming from the far hall drew Hugh's attention. A moment later the same serving boy who'd fled from Hugh twice in a single day rounded the corner and nearly crashed into Hugh's chest. The boy gasped in Hugh's face and then, as quickly as he had come, spun on his heels intent upon a third escape.

But this time Hugh called out to him with deadly intent.

"Halt!" The lad froze midstride. "What's your name, boy?"

"Avril, sire."

Hugh nodded. "Avril, I must get Lady Catherine to her rooms. And you will help me."

Avril nodded silently.

Eyeing him, Hugh waited for the lad to bolt, but he didn't. And Hugh couldn't help liking the boy for his determination.

"I will carry her," Hugh continued at last.

"But you must carry a torch, for the corridors are dark and deserted, and when we arrive at her rooms, you will open the door and turn down the bedding for her.

Again, Hugh received a mute nod in reply.

An assistant recruited, Hugh turned back to Terrence's room. He crossed the room in six long strides and, without a pause, gently lifted Catherine into his arms. In a moment he was back in the hallway and following Avril toward the north tower of the keep. Avril carried out his duties to perfection, shushing maids at their work before Hugh passed by with Catherine. And though his jaw remained determinedly set, he realized with each passing moment that he was far from unaffected by the warm being in his arms.

She was as soft as a tiny fawn, warm and trusting, and as easily injured. He carried her as he would a holy, illuminated manuscript. With a sense of the reverent. Red-gold curls tickled the skin of his neck where her head lay in exhausted slumber. And her scent filled his nostrils, sending a sublime smoke rising into his brain.

"Lord," he muttered to himself as Catherine shifted in his arms and he felt her cheek burrow into the hollow below his shoulder, "I pray that you do not tempt me in this way. I am not strong when I am with Catherine. Since the first day I saw her so many years ago, she has tugged at my heart. I can only hurt her with this weakness.

And of all the people in this world, the one I should least wish to hurt is Catherine.''

It was a walk of eternity before Avril preceded them into Catherine's rooms and made haste to turn down the fur throws.

"Avril," Hugh directed as he entered the room. "Build up the fire. The day is gray and damp and Lady Catherine will wake too soon if she should become cold."

The boy jumped to obey while Hugh bent over the draped canopy bed and gently set Catherine against the pillows. The moment she was out of his arms he felt a strange sense of loss settle over him, but he refused to give the sensation quarter. He pulled a coverlet and two fine ermine blankets up to her chin and then with a wisp of straw lit the thick candle on its wrought-iron stand by the bedside. Satisfied that the logs Avril had set in the hearth were burning well and would warm the room for several hours, Hugh nodded for the boy to depart.

Alone in the room, Hugh gazed down at Catherine. Her hair was spread like a coppery mist across the pillows. One finely boned hand lay across its path and her fingertips brushed against the delicate line of her jaw. In sleep her lips were parted just enough to afford the slightest glimpse of moist, pearly-hued teeth. And the fine line of her slender neck curved gracefully until it was interrupted by edge of the white fur throw. But even its solid weight could not help Hugh forget the full swell of her breasts against his chest as he'd carried her, or the hypnotic rhythm of her breathing.

For a long moment Hugh did nothing but watch Catherine sleep. Then, taking a long breath, he bowed his head. "They are not good, Catherine, these feelings. Forgive me, mite, for while I would stay a month and spend every hour of it with you, to do so could only bode ill for you. You have changed and I have changed. And we cannot be friends again as we were. Not ever again." Turning, Hugh walked from Catherine's room and headed for the stables. He needed the cold, fresh air to clear his head. He needed to clear the scent of Catherine de Tralle from every crevice of his mind forever.

It took Hugh no time at all to find Cepheus. He applied a brush to his coat with more vigor than the stallion was accustomed and the steed brayed at Hugh irritably over the mistreatment.

"I'm glad to see it's your own charger you're mistreating and not one of mine." Bernard patted the stallion's muzzle as he came around to where Hugh had worked Cepheus's coat to a near-blinding sheen.

"Bernard, I can't wait for Terrence to recover. I can never thank you for all you and your family have done for me, and for my brother. And a man with so much debt to one family should not ask more, but it is vital that I return to my family home as soon as possible."

Bernard nodded in agreement. "You've been away for a long, long time, Hugh. I'm sure they need you there. And, you have Pontoise now as well, have you not?"

One brow came down over his smokey blue eyes as Hugh digested this bit of information. "How did you hear about Pontoise?"

"My sister, Mathilde, is visiting. She spends much of her time at court. Too much time, I fear. And she has a tongue that wags without rest from dawn till dusk. It would try the patience of anyone, but by the time she's ready to return to Louis's court, there is very little left to know about the goings-on among the nobility.

"Even so, the news that Louis bestowed the Duchy of Pontoise upon you in reward for your services in the Holy Crusade is well known. Even for a place as removed from activities of court as Avignon, it did not take Mathilde coming for us to hear about his gift. You must be anxious to visit your lands and castle. And for my part, I am very pleased. I cannot think of a knight more deserving of reward."

Hugh said nothing. Did everyone, then, know that he was returning to France not as a mere knight? Not simply as a second son and brother to the Count of Anet, but as a duke in his own right, complete with one of the largest duchies in all of France and a castle rumored to be nearly as splendid as Louis's castle?

Hugh had pictured himself returning home to tell his family himself. But if Bernard de Tralle knew, then certainly everyone at court knew. And that would include Giles. And Adele.

Hugh looked up to find Bernard watching him carefully.

"It's a perfect day to hunt," he stated casually. "You've brushed that poor stallion until he's more fit as a mare with silk ribbons twined through his mane than a war horse. My mastiffs are anxious for blood, and the huntsman tells me he's spotted fresh boar tracks the past three days.

"Get your spear, Lord Vougnet. A day of hunting will do us both some good. Afterward, as we rest by the hearth with a tankard of mulled wine, we'll make the arrangements for your departure."

They rode far into the greenwood that day. The overcast sky turned dark and ugly as the afternoon passed, but Hugh welcomed the cold and wet. While they still tracked the boar, the heavens opened up and rain came down in sheets. Even the thick canopy of forest overhead did little to shield the group of hunters from the deluge. The other men, including Bernard, pulled the collars of their jerkins close around their faces and hunched over their mounts, warding off as much of the wetness as possible. But Hugh turned his face toward the sky. His skin soaked up the wetness like a sun-parched field. His mouth tasted ecstasy in raindrops devoid of sand. He breathed in the scent of wet pine woodlands, and the sound of Cepheus's hooves sliding in the slick mud as they tramped over twigs and golden leaves was like music to his ears.

It was dark by the time the group of hunters returned empty-handed to the keep. The moment he was in the door of the castle, Hugh took the stairs two at a time and bounded to his rooms. He had stripped off his soaked jerkin and leather leggings before the door to his room was even shut. The day's cold had felt good, but as night descended around them, the rain had turned into a pelting sleet. Now he was frozen down to the bone and the joints of his hands creaked painfully.

A steaming tub waited before the hearth and Hugh plunged into it, enjoying the sting that replaced the numbness in his fingers and toes. He dunked his head into the water and the icy coating of sleet melted off his hair. His earlobes burned. Even his nose dripped. Finally settling against the back of the tub, he closed his eyes and let the warmth of the water seep deep into his muscles.

He had ridden hard today, intentionally working both himself and Cepheus until not a thimbleful of energy remained. His goal had been a state of exhaustion, the point at which he could think of nothing but rest. He didn't want to think anymore. He wished simply to exist in this perfect little world on the Rhône.

In Jerusalem he had been exhausted all the time, and his fatigue had allowed him not to think too deeply about what was going on around him. But despite the aching fatigue that wrapped his body tonight, his thoughts would not cooperate. The moment Hugh relaxed, his mind refocused on the one person he wanted to keep out of his mind.

Just last night, in the same tub and the same room, he had been kissing Catherine. The memory of that kiss had haunted him all day. When he'd carried her to her room and laid her gently upon her bed, the memory of their kiss had throbbed like his heartbeat beneath her cheek. When he'd scrubbed at Cepheus's coat, trying to eradicate the feel of her from his soul, he only tasted the warm sweetness of her lips more completely. Even as he'd scoured the brambles and undergrowth of the forest, willing her memory from his mind, her image had grown stronger. Until now the memory invaded his very soul.

But it was a memory he must forget.

It was a growing need that he must defeat before it became stronger still. Hugh climbed from the bath and dried off quickly as he contemplated his inexplicable obsession. He donned a clean white shirt, tunic, and hose and was just pulling on a pair of comfortable, dry boots when a knock at the door broke his torturous battle. Crossing the room, he pulled open the door to find Bernard there.

"I thought I'd join you," Bernard explained, hoisting a large pitcher of ale and two tankards. "The hall is smokey tonight, and I have a matter to discuss with you."

Hugh made way for Bernard to enter and grinned in mock surprise. "A host who brings the ale to my room! It must be your guilt over dragging me through the coldest, wettest forest in all France today."

Bernard laughed. "I feel no remorse in the least. And do not be deceived by the joint of beef I have ordered to be sent up for us, either. Indeed, I am about to make quite the opposite suggestion—that for so fine a day of hunting you will be indebted to me."

The serious note in Bernard's voice caught Hugh's attention. "Bernard," he said, coming to stand before the older man. "Never doubt the debt I owe you. Twice now you have sheltered my brother and I as we traveled, and last night your family saved Terrence's life. I owe you much. Whatever I can do to repay the smallest portion of that debt shall be done."

Bernard's dark, twinkling eyes met Hugh's and he nodded in acceptance of Hugh's words. "Then I have a favor to ask of you."

Hugh took a seat by the fire opposite the one Bernard had settled into. Leaning forward, he rested his forearms on his thighs and waited intently to hear Bernard's request. Whatever it was, Hugh knew he would do it without question. Bernard de Tralle had become as good a friend as Hugh possessed.

There were not many men he put his trust in, but from the first Hugh had liked the Count of Avignon. Hugh found him intelligent and honest, two traits he had come to realize were more rare among men than gold. Among the Templars it had been those men who most represented the things which should be wise and honest who were the least so. And his experiences had tainted his view of the world. But for Bernard de Tralle, he would do whatever was within his power.

Bernard set the two tankards on the table and poured a full measure of ale into each. Nodding for Hugh to take the one closest to him, Bernard helped himself to the other. He took a long drink before meeting Hugh's gaze again.

"I know you are anxious to return home, and we are happy to have Terrence here until he is well enough to travel. But we have need of an escort to Paris, and I was hoping you would agree to act as such in our behalf."

Hugh nodded easily.

"I will provide a group of men to go with you, naturally. But you are a knight, and as such offer better protection."

Again Hugh nodded without hesitation. "Bernard, I will certainly escort anyone you wish to Paris. As you know, Anet is less than a day's ride from Louis's court and Pontoise closer still."

"Isn't Chantilly also on the way to Pontoise?"

"Actually, it is a bit beyond. One can easily reach it in half a day's ride, I believe. But what is in Chantilly that interests you?"

"The Abbaye de Royaumont. We have made

arrangements for Catherine to stay there for six months before she goes on to Strasbourg."

"Catherine?!"

Bernard eyed Hugh quizzically and nodded. "The arrangements were made several months ago."

"Her marriage . . ."

"The sisters there will help my little red-haired hellion grow up a little," Bernard continued, seemingly unaware of Hugh's nonplussed stare. "I'm afraid Mathilde has been right all these years in her odious warnings and gripes. I've let Catherine run a bit wild. She is far too accustomed to spending her days racing about in the forests or with her nose in the accounts of my small fief."

Bernard twirled the ale in his tankard thoughtfully and watched the amber liquid lick at the rim of his cup. "I hope I'm doing what is best for her." Again he paused, contemplating his drink as though in hopes that some answer would rise from its depths. "The marriage contract was made so long ago. She is my first daughter, Hugh, and she knows only Avignon."

Bernard looked up. "But that is why her stay at the Abbaye de Royaumont is essential. She will have some time to curb her headstrong tendencies, and she will learn how to be a good wife to the baron."

Hugh rubbed his battle-scarred hands through his hair and tried not to frown. This was *not* what he had intended by leaving Avignon. If he carried out Bernard's wish, he would only leave to take the very thing he wished to escape with him. "This," he thought to himself, "is God's punishment for the kiss I stole. I must now spend every hour of the day for two weeks with the very thing that tempts me." He let loose a great sigh.

"Hugh, if you do not wish to do this . . ."

"Nay, Bernard," Hugh responded with a resigned wave of his hand. "I told you I would do whatever was in my power. And it is no great thing for me to take Catherine to the Abbaye. As I said myself, it is so close as to be very nearly on my way." He sat back in his chair and drained his tankard.

Bernard reached out to refill it. "I will send six men with you and a page as well. Has the young boy attending you now done well?"

"Avril?" Hugh smiled at the mention of the boy's name. "Yes, when he does not think I am about to devour him."

Bernard gave him another strange look, and Hugh laughed. "It is too long a story to explain, Bernard. Catherine . . ." Hugh caught the words back and the smile disappeared suddenly from his face. He didn't want to recall anything about Catherine. Not her teasing, nor the laughter. He did not wish to recall any part of their evening together. He needed to blot such things from his mind, else he would not be able to carry out this request of Bernard's. He would take Catherine safely to Chantilly, but he had to create a distance between them. A chasm which would be too wide to be crossed.

The arrival of their supper interrupted Hugh's thoughts, and the smell of roasted beef brought his gnawing hunger to the forefront of his mind. Both Hugh and Bernard attacked the meal like a pair of starved wolves. They heaped their trenchers to overflowing, fitting the discussion of their plans for the journey between bites of meat and quaffs of ale. And as the night drew long, Hugh did not think of Catherine's kiss again. Forcefully, he curbed his mind to his will, pushing aside the soft, gentle feelings that seeing Catherine once more breathed life into.

Long ago Hugh had realized that feelings were not good. They only caused chaos, and a knight could ill afford such a thing. So instead, he turned his mind to more controllable things. He discussed the upcoming journey as he would have a campaign into the desert. He and Bernard planned, and organized, and discussed. It was familiar ground for Hugh. In Jerusalem he learned to function as a commander. Each day was spent either laying out a strategy, or executing that plan. He has become inured in the tactics of war, and planning was key to success. He had ceased to feel, almost to think, because it was better that way. A Knight Templar could not survive if he had a conscience or a heart. There was only the mission. And the mission was to provide safe conduct to Christian pilgrims. To live a life in keeping with the tenets of the order. To perform.

Methodically, as the fire burned down and the shadows lengthened, Hugh shut away the impossible. It didn't matter what he felt. There was only duty. Honor. Responsibility. He made Catherine just another pilgrim to protect. He closed every door on his heart, every crevice through which emotion might seep out. When at last Bernard left and Hugh's head came to rest on his bed, a mask of control had dropped over him obliterating any sign of the man within.

Eight

Amaranth screeched irritably from beneath his hood and Catherine smoothed a gloved hand down his ruffled feathers to calm him.

"Quiet now," she crooned softly. "Soon enough you'll have a chance to fly."

Riding beside her, Jean shielded his eyes from the afternoon sun and again scanned the grasses for movement. " 'Tis too nice a day, Catherine. Not a single hare is moving about. They are all sunning themselves on some rock barely breathing enough to stir the air. We'll never spot them."

Catherine kept her eyes on the horizon and shrugged. "As you said, 'tis too nice a day. If we never spot a hare the only one who will be upset is Amaranth. He needs a reason to fly. As for me, I'm happy just to be out in the day."

"There aren't many of these days left for you, I suppose."

Catherine glanced at her brother and then returned to scanning the skyline. Jean was fifteen now. Tall and lanky, he often seemed to Catherine like a badly fitted suit of mail. But that was to be expected. She'd seen her older brothers go through this age. Like Jean now, their voices had cracked and their arms seemed always to have a life apart from the rest of their body. But she knew that these were simply signs of impending manhood, and soon Jean would be grown as well. Of all her brothers, she had always been closest to Jean. Her baby sisters were far too young to be companions for her, but Jean had always been the one who would gladly take up after her and follow her out for a day's hawking or join her in exploring the forests of Avignon. Like today, she had but to suggest and he would join her.

"I'll miss you, Jean," she said quietly.

"And what will you miss about me?" he snorted derisively.

"Having a friend," she told him simply.

"You'll be traveling with Hugh, Catherine! What more could you want? Since the day you met him, you've pined to spend every moment of the day with him. I think you are about to come as close to heaven as you've ever been."

Catherine watched the tall field grass part around her mare's chest as they rode. She hid the grimace that pulled down the corners of her mouth beneath her guise of concentration. "I think not, Jean." She hesitated, tugging at her lower lip with her teeth. She hadn't spoken to anyone about Hugh's strange behavior. But ever since her father announced that Hugh would take her to Chantilly, Hugh had been acting strangely.

It was worse than even that. He was as cold and distant as a person could be. When they gathered in the Great Hall, he sat at the other end of the room, absorbed in conversations with her father and the other knights. He spent an entire afternoon with Sir Jeffrey, an event Catherine could not fathom at all. The two men had nothing in common. Jeffrey spoke of the Crusades as though they were great victories and the highlight of his young life. What little Hugh had said of the Holy Wars was far, far different. And yet, Hugh sat night after night drinking and listening to tales of Constantinople from the other men. He visited Terrence little, spent the days from dawn to dusk hunting alone in the forest, and when Catherine did manage to cross his path, he looked through her as though she didn't even exist. He paid more attention to Avril than he did to her.

With each day that passed it bewildered her more. On the morrow they would leave for Paris. There would be long hours on horseback with only a handful of men, Hugh, and herself. How was she to bear being treated as though she was a leper? And why? What had she done to so completely change his treatment of her? Catherine simply did not understand.

Whatever the reason, she could not imagine making the trip this way. "I don't know, Jean," she admitted. "Hugh has been strange these last days."

Her brother tossed his head impatiently. "Of

course he has! He has planning and organizing to do. Do you think a journey to Paris is made without a thought? He and Father have spent hours selecting men. There are horses to ready, cases to be packed, food . . . Catherine, you act as though you are the only thing in the world Hugh should attend to!"

Catherine's frown deepened. Was Jean right? While Hugh was spending all of his day every day planning for her safe transport to Chantilly, had she been selfishly expecting him to attend to her needs? Ashamed, she pushed her worries and hurt aside.

"It *is* wonderful that Hugh agreed to take me," she concurred quietly. But why then did she feel so miserable about it? she wondered. When he'd first arrived, it was as though not even a day had passed since his last visit to Avignon. They had immediately fallen into the closeness, the easy give and take, which had always been theirs. He had even kissed her. But since then Hugh had treated her as though he barely knew her. As though she was a stranger. Was she being overly sensitive?

Amaranth screeched and spread his wings wide. Catherine absently slid off his hood while keeping a tight hold of the leather thongs tied to his legs. Again her little merlin screamed. Jean pointed to a movement in the grass at the edge of the forest. Both Jean and Catherine released their birds. Amaranth fairly leapt from her hand. The two hawks took to the sky and

Catherine watched her hawk beat his way toward the setting afternoon sun. Higher and higher he climbed, until, if Catherine had not known her bird so well, she would have thought he was never coming back.

The merlin circled once, twice, and then, without hesitation or warning of any kind, he folded his wings and dropped straight for the earth.

When he again came into sight he carried a fat, young partridge in his talons. The merlin returned immediately to Catherine, who praised him lavishly and rewarded him with two chunks of meat from the pouch that hung from the belt of her tunic. Jean bagged the partridge with a scowl.

"That hawk of yours is old and decrepit. Why he beats every hawk and falcon in the mews, I cannot understand. Even Father's new gyrfalcon is no match for that old merlin of yours."

Catherine couldn't help laughing at Jean's frustrated tirade. "You haven't been saying your prayers to Saint Hubert of Liege, Jean. Mayhap you should direct your requests to him at vespers this eventide."

Her brother made a face that their mother would have beat him for. "A thousand hours of prayer wouldn't explain how that old bag of bones and feathers does it." A brisk wind blew his words into the forest and Jean twisted in his saddle to scan the horizon to the west. "I think the weather is about to change, Catherine. One partridge will have to be enough for today."

Catherine wheeled her mare toward the keep and urged her into a canter as another gust whipped across the field. Pulling her cloak around her, she set the mare on a course directly for home. Pulling even with Jean, she called to him. "Do you think it's rain?"

Jean shook his head and, seeing the concern on her face, his own split into a broad grin. "I think you will be heading for Paris in the middle of a snowfall, Catherine."

Snow! Catherine let Jean's horse pull away from her. She turned back to scrutinize the clouds that had formed in the distance. They were heavy and gray as snow clouds would be, and it was, after all, October. Snow was not unheard of at this time of year. Still, she didn't relish the thought of riding in cold weather. And as for Hugh and his strange mood—tomorrow the planning and organizing would be over. Then it would be just the two of them really. And there would be plenty of time to enjoy each other's company. Smiling, Catherine turned away from the approaching clouds and headed for home.

Her conviction that all was well lasted only as long as it took Catherine to return to the keep, bathe, and dress for the evening. It was late, vespers were over, and the hall had long ago filled with hungry guests and family members ready to fill growling bellies with the special feast that had been prepared in honor of Catherine's departure by the time she left her rooms and headed for the Great Hall.

She had taken extra care with her appearance tonight. First, because the feast and revelry of the evening ahead were primarily intended for her. But also because she hoped to get some reaction, no matter how small, from Hugh. She needed some acknowledgment that she had not imagined all that had passed between them over the past five years. Her packet of letters from the Holy Lands was packed carefully in her trunks along with the last poem she had copied for him from his reading lessons when she had been only twelve. But tonight she needed a more tangible reassurance that she was—in some small way—a part of Hugh's life.

High above the other guests, Hugh sat comfortably on a raised dais at the head table just in front of the huge hearth. He had been placed at Bernard de Tralle's left hand in a place of great honor while the other visiting knights enjoyed the evening from the long oaken tables set below them. He quaffed the spiced wine in his goblet and leaned back in his chair taking in for the last time the warmth that was Avignon Keep.

A serving maid passed behind him and he stopped her, reaching for one of the tiny sparrow breasts that were piled like a small mountain on the trencher she carried. The morsel was gone in a single bite. Carefully licking the juice from his fingers, Hugh glanced toward the second-story gallery. Despite the haze of smoke that hung in the room, his gaze locked on the figure poised at the top of the stairs.

Catherine.

She didn't see him watching her, and he took the opportunity to soak in every detail of her appearance. It was only when she was engrossed in something else that he had allowed himself to look at her these past two weeks. And every time it was a sublime sort of self-torture, for she seemed only to become more beautiful with each passing hour. But tonight, as she stood regally at the top of the stairs, she took his breath away.

She wore a fine bisque gown richly trimmed in gold. The sleeves of her dress touched her delicate wrists and the satin cuffs fell to the hem of her dress, nearly sweeping the stone floor. The bodice was fitted close to her, outlining the full, rounded shape of young breasts, then narrowed to a shapely waist. The deliciously proportioned curve of her hips was clearly defined by the close-fitting fabric and a gold-linked belt that lay across her hips and then dipped into a V just below her firm belly. A golden claw that held a glittering ruby marked the end of the belt and nestled in the deep folds of her skirt. Between her breasts lay the fine pendant that seemed always to be around her neck.

Her hair was braided on either side of her head and then left to cascade in soft curls that fell to her waist. In the firelight, its color reminded him of cinnabar he'd seen in Jerusalem marketplaces. Her skin was as fine as alabaster and her eyes were soft, green, and warm. He could not think of anything finer in all the world at that moment than Catherine de Tralle.

As always happened, she felt his gaze upon her and turned to look for its source. But before she could follow its heat to him, Hugh looked away, concentrating his attentions on the table of knights below him.

Catherine stared down at Hugh seated beside her father. Was her imagination again playing tricks on her? She had been certain someone was watching her, and when she'd turned her head she had looked directly at Hugh. But he was nodding to Lance de Monteville, one of the knights traveling with Sir Jeffrey and seemed not even to know she was anywhere about. For a moment, Catherine's gaze remained on Hugh. In the entire length of the Great Hall, there wasn't another man to compare with him. His shoulders were as broad by twice as those of any of her brothers, and even the fine cut of his tunic could not hide the well-defined chest muscles beneath the spruce-hued linen. The sleeves of his shirt, as well, drew taut as he bent his elbow to take a long sip of wine revealing arms that could wield a battle-ax or broadsword with deadly power.

Most knights were battle-scarred and maimed. Many had passed through Avignon whom Catherine had barely been able to look upon so fearsome was their appearance. She had little doubt that Hugh bore many a scar as well, but he possessed a face so finely sculpted that it took her breath away just to watch him.

His forehead was broad and strong, possessed of fine golden brows that were thick, yet did not meet in the center of his face to form one long line as did many a man's. His nose was straight, his cheeks flat and strong, his jaw strongly carved and bold. And his eyes. Oh, his eyes. The room was smokey and Catherine stood far away, but she did not have to be close to know his eyes. They were etched in her mind and her soul. She had simply to close her own to see his.

They were deep-set and clear. When he was thoughtful, they were gentle. When he laughed— rare as that was—they sparkled with light. But always they were a blue like no other. They were as blue as God's sky. As blue as sapphire. As blue as the rushing waters of the Rhône. At the head table sat a lone empty chair. She was to be seated beside Hugh, yet he seemed not even to be aware that the guest of honor was absent. Catherine's mouth dropped into a flat line of hurt. Why didn't he care anymore? What had she done to deserve his indifference? How could he be so heartless? She had ridden into the night to save the life of his brother. She had plied him with good company and care, and tended his needs well. Yet he couldn't give her so much as a nod these last two weeks.

Catherine squared her shoulders and tilted her chin stubbornly. She didn't understand why, but this was her night and she would not let anyone tarnish the importance of the evening. Determinedly she took a rigid grip on the railing and descended the stairs.

Tossing his head back to roar with laughter over a saucy ballad being sung by the troubadour, Bernard spied his eldest daughter making her way into the hall. Setting his wine on the table, he pushed back his chair and stood up. With a loud clap of his hands, he called for the attention of everyone in the hall. "My good friends. Give me your eyes and ears. Tonight we celebrate my daughter, Catherine. So for the rest of the evening let us turn our attentions to her. And let not a moment go by that she is not well attended, for we will miss her sorely."

As he stopped for a breath, Catherine reached the dais and stepped up beside her father. He took her hand in his and smiled at her. His expression grew soft, and when he spoke again it was in a voice quiet and filled with emotion. "I, especially, shall miss her."

Catherine smiled gently in response as Bernard pressed a fatherly kiss against her forehead.

"Now!" he declared, clearing his voice gruffly. "Let the true revelry commence!"

The great hall reverberated with the hearty roar of the guests. Her father handed her into her chair and a serving girl appeared with a pitcher of mulled wine to fill her goblet. One by one her brothers planted kisses on her brow and mumbled words of affection to her. Even her little sisters, just five and three years old, planted soft baby kisses on Catherine's cheek. But from the man beside her, there was no acknowledgment at all.

Servants poured from the covered walk that connected the kitchens to the main keep. Silver platters so large they required two men to carry them were brought until the long tables groaned under the weight of the feast. Five whole suckling pigs were presented, pheasant and wild duck, a joint of roasted black bear, and fresh trout caught just hours before in the river below. There were countless loaves of bread, and honey cakes studded with almonds and raisins. Fine molded puddings accompanied them as well as platters of autumn fruits dressed in a sugar glaze that glistened in the torchlight. And into every mazer and goblet flowed ale and hard cider, and warm, spiced wine.

A serving boy appeared between Catherine and Hugh bearing a fine bronze aquaemanale fancifully hammered into the likeness of a griffin and filled with rose water. Both Catherine and Hugh turned to dip their hands into the basin. For a moment Catherine hesitated. Then she carefully washed her fingers and took the proffered towel to dry her hands. But she made no attempt to draw Hugh's attention.

"You are not enjoying your party, Catherine?" Hugh asked with disinterest as he followed suit.

Catherine flashed him an overly bright smile. "Quite the contrary, my lord. I am delighted with it. The entertainments are myriad and my feet fairly itch to dance. My family has gathered around me with affection. On the morrow I begin a great new adventure in my life." She cocked one brow at him in query. "What more could a woman wish for, sir?"

"Truly nothing," Hugh responded. Catherine examined the staghorn handle of her knife with a carefree air, determined not to let Hugh see the hurt he had inflicted upon her. "There is nothing more you could want, Cay."

The shock of hearing him use the pet name he'd bestowed on her five years ago rocked her. Why would he ignore her so completely and then use a name only they shared? Her question about to fly from her lips, she turned to Hugh. But he had turned away. Once again he was engrossed in some other interest. He laughed at a ribald jest made by one of her brothers and paid no further heed to Catherine until they were served half a pheasant and pudding. Hugh dug hungrily into the meal they were to share.

But Catherine had no taste for food. She toyed with her wine, dipping the tip of her finger into the warm liquid and then running the wet digit around the rim of her bronze goblet.

"You are not hungry, Catherine?"

"Oh, I am too excited to think about eating," she responded lightly.

"I see." Hugh paused a moment before continuing. "It is over a week's ride to Chantilly, and there is not one among the men we are taking who professes to have any skills at all in the kitchen. I have heard that the meals at the *abbaye* are sparse and somewhat limited in appeal. You might try just a little to get down a few morsels of this wonderful meal. You are not likely to have another such as this for many months."

"Oh, I am not concerned," she said blithely. "I will only be at the *abbaye* a few months before I go on to Strasbourg. There, I have heard, the baron serves such feasts daily. He is very wealthy, you know. His keep is twice the size of Avignon, and his fief is ten leagues by twenty."

Hugh nodded slowly. "I'm sure it will be a wonderful life for you, Catherine." Without another word he returned to his meal.

Miserable, Catherine stared out over the crowded hall. They had talked, but it was more a set of parries than the easy conversations she missed so much. The night was turning out to be wretched, and she was certain now that the journey to Chantilly would be equally dismal.

The minstrels began to tune their mandoras and harps. The room quieted in anticipation of good ballads and songs. First came the Chansons de Geste about good King Charlemagne and Arthur, the Welsh king of old. Then the minstrels strummed a long tune that wound around the great battles of the Holy Wars. Settled back in her chair, Catherine watched Hugh from the corner of one eye. He seemed almost to wince as the troubadour mournfully sung about the long journey from Constantinople to Jerusalem. She glanced down at Sir Jeffrey. The knight caught her eye and smiled at her as though they shared a secret affection.

Catherine smiled back, and from the corner of her eye she thought she detected Hugh's brow tightening into a dark scowl.

"Sir Jeffrey is a very intriguing knight, don't you think, Hugh?" Catherine asked blithely.

"Do you think so?"

"Why, yes. He has been to the Holy Wars and returned unscathed. He is young and handsome and landed. If I were not betrothed, I would find him quite irresistible, I think."

Hugh carefully set his goblet on the table and leaned close to Catherine. "He is a sop."

"A sop?" she repeated in feigned shock. "Hugh, how can you say such a thing of a fellow knight."

"Did you not read even one of my letters?" he asked irritably. "You, of all people, should recognize a boy who is playing at being a knight!"

Looking away, Catherine cleared her throat in order to hide her smile. When she turned back to Hugh, her countenance was set in a mold of disbelief. "Nay. I think he is quite wonderful. Why, before you arrived, we spent many hours together. He told me such wonderful tales about the emperor's palace on the Bosporus and—"

"Catherine." Hugh abruptly cut short her breathless litany. "You are betrothed to be married. You have no quarter to speak of another man in such ways."

"It is harmless to—" She did not have a chance to finish her thought. Sir Jeffrey bent solicitously over her shoulder.

"They have begun a dance," he said as he placed his hand over hers. "Will you allow me? After all you *are* the guest of honor and your father has charged us with keeping you entertained."

Catherine did not want to dance. She wanted to talk to Hugh. She wanted to find out why he was acting so strangely. One minute he ignored her, the next he was reprimanding her for having a conversation with another man. Instead, she looked into the young knight's face and smiled prettily. "I cannot think of anything I would enjoy more, sir." She let him lead her to the far end of the room where the tables and benches had been cleared away to make room for the dancers. Catherine stepped into place in the inner circle of women and Sir Jeffrey took the spot beside her in the outer ring.

"My fair lady, do I ask over much that you call me by my Christian name? We will be spending so much time together these next weeks. My heart would be gladdened to know we were friends enough to be familiar."

Catherine looked at him in confusion as the musicians began the dance and she followed suit as the other dancers moved around the circle. "What do you mean? I leave on the morrow and I think our paths shall not likely cross again."

The two faced each other. Catherine curtsied and the knight bowed. Looking up, he gave her the broad grin of a little boy who has hoodwinked the lord of the castle. "Hugh Vougnet had need of men to make the journey north. I am one of those who will have the honor of accompanying you to Paris."

The dancers moved again. This time, though, the two circles moved in opposite directions, giving Catherine a few minutes to absorb Jeffrey's news. She had envisioned long days on horseback with Hugh and hours of quiet conversation. Now that vision had been wiped away in a single stroke. Jeffrey Winfrey and heaven only knew who else would be traveling with them. The circle brought her back to where Sir Jeffrey waited.

"So," he asked, bowing again to her curtsey. "Will you call me simply Jeffrey?"

"Yes," Catherine replied in defeat as the knight's cheeks flushed red with pleasure.

"Lady Catherine, I cannot find the words to express my joy at your response." He reached for her hand, but Catherine drew it away, suddenly tired of the game she had begun.

"Sir, Jeffrey," she corrected. "You know I am to be married."

He nodded and reaching for her hand led her

away from the dancers. "But it is my duty as a knight to protect the weak and pledge my loyalty and fealty. It is not wrong for you to accept my attentions. I am honor bound to see you safely on the first leg of your journey to your fiancé. As I pledged, so shall I do. But, my lady, a dalliance between us would be a delight. No one would be harmed."

Catherine stopped in her tracks. "I think—"

Quickly, he put his finger to her lips, stopping the words she was about to utter. "It is quite common at court and across the countryside. Sophisticated lords and ladies understand the natural order of such things."

Catherine hesitated. She knew that Jeffrey was right. Aunt Mathilde spoke openly about ladies who took a knight as a lover while their husband was away at war or fighting in Jerusalem for the pope. It was often years before their husband returned, and accepting the "protection" of a knight was often deemed quite acceptable. But Catherine had not been raised at court. She thought of her own parents, who were so completely dedicated to each other. Looking up at the head table, she saw her father lay a gentle hand over her mother's, who turned to smile up at him.

Catherine did not want a dalliance. She did not want to go to her German baron deflowered and sullied. Unbidden, the image of Hugh came into her head. Would he approve of such a thing?

Was she just being childish to feel that such an alliance was a sign of a poor marriage?

Still only halfway to the table, Jeffrey hovered attentively beside her. She knew he expected some sort of answer, but she had none to give him. Uncomfortable, Catherine dug the toe of her leather slipper into the rushes. When she looked up again, she found Hugh bearing down on them with a thunderous scowl on his face. He was beside her before she could so much as utter a warning to Jeffrey.

"Sir Jeffrey," he barked in a tone that tolerated no breach of his command. "We leave before dawn tomorrow. Don't you think you should check your horse and armor? You do have armor, don't you?"

Blanching, Jeffrey Winfrey opened his mouth to respond, but Hugh cut him short. "Go to the stables and check every animal thoroughly. Be sure none is lame, nor any shoes loose. If need be, wake up the blacksmith. I am holding you personally responsible for the good condition of every steed tomorrow."

Afraid to countermand a great Knight of the Templars, especially the most famous of them all, Sir Jeffrey turned to leave. But not without one parting attempt to secure Catherine as his own. "Will you allow me to escort you tomorrow, Catherine?"

"Jeffrey, I—"

"Go!" Hugh ground out the word with an authority that was absolute, cutting off Catherine's reply. Jeffrey jumped visibly and was gone without another attempt against his adversary.

Exasperated, Catherine set her fisted hands on either hip. "What right have you to command us!"

Hugh gave her a dark look. Taking her by the elbow, he steered her to the stairwell. But instead of releasing her there, they passed the stair. Glancing over his shoulder to see if anyone noticed them, he took one long stride behind the stairs and pulled Catherine into the shadows with him.

"What are you doing?" she demanded. Never in her life had she seen Hugh Vougnet act like this.

"What are *you* doing is a better question."

"I was returning to my chair."

Hugh glowered at her for a moment before responding. "Stay away from Jeffrey Winfrey."

"And if I do, then who will I ride with tomorrow and the next day and the next?"

"Ride alone."

Catherine stared at him. "What is wrong with you? You kiss me, then you ignore me, then you tell me to ride alone all the way to Paris." Hugh opened his mouth to speak, but Catherine plunged on, stabbing her finger against his tunic as she finally allowed her frustration to escape. "You used to be the person I liked most in all the world. Now I don't even know who you are. I've realized tonight, though, that it matters not at all. We have to travel to Chantilly together, but we do not have to be friends anymore. I will ride alone. I will do whatever you command until we reach the *abbaye*. But I will not try to be your friend." Catherine spun on her heels and marched from the shadows. Lifting her skirts, she mounted the stairs at twice her normal speed, leaving Hugh to stare angrily out into the crowded center of the Great Hall.

Nine

Jean had been right. The night had brought a hand's depth of snow, transforming Avignon into an iced confection. The wet autumn snow clung to every branch, wall, and rock, etching everything in sparkling whiteness. The puddles in the courtyard were glazed over with a fine layer of ice, and the last of the fallen leaves bore glistening crystals that outlined their spidery veins. Catherine stepped into the wonderland and clapped her fur-lined gloves together in excitement. The cold nipped at her nose and ears, but she had donned a tunic of the finest Flemish wool over her kirtle, and it did much to keep the chill away. Her feet were encased in boots lined with wolf fur to match the hood of her long woolen mantle and the edging on her mitted gloves.

The thick wolf fur tickled her cheeks and she brushed it aside as her mother came to stand beside her. "Are you excited?"

Catherine turned a glowing face toward her. "Oh, yes! It is going to be such an adventure! There is so much to see on the way there, and

I look forward to my stay in Chantilly. Aunt Mathilde speaks so well of the prioress and the work they do there. I'm hoping to help teach some of the children they have taken in."

"You are there to learn how to run a castle, Catherine. Remember that."

"But you have already taught me everything I need to know, Mother."

Marguerite smiled warmly and patted Catherine's cheek. "There is still much you don't know. But I fear you will not learn it at the *abbaye.*"

"It will be good for me," Catherine concluded contentedly. Her father spotted the two women from across the bailey and headed toward them. Clapping his bare hands together and stomping his boots to rid them of snow, he smiled warmly at Catherine.

"You are my eldest daughter and you have never been a disappointment to me."

"Not even when you caught me wading barefoot in the river?" she teased.

"Least of all then. Catherine, we are not sending you to Chantilly to change you. We live away from court by choice. Your mother and I have never cared for the ways of those people. There are some who are worth their weight, but most have too little to do and cause only havoc."

Catherine thought of Jeffrey Winfrey's words last night. He accepted the ways of King Louis's court as the right way and expected all to conduct themselves in the same manner. But there were different ways. Her family was far from typical. Too often she had seen the strange looks visitors bestowed on her parents when they learned that Catherine could read, write and cipher. But she was glad that her father had felt such things were important.

"Be good, Catherine," her father continued, drawing her thoughts from Jeffrey Winfrey. "And trust Hugh. He is a good man. Like us, he does not always choose the way of most, but he sees well the right way."

Catherine nodded even though she knew her father was talking about the old Hugh Vougnet, not the one who had returned from the Crusades. She glanced over to where Hugh sat high upon Cepheus's back directing the final preparations for the journey. Imposing and powerful, he towered over everyone else. Gone was the quiet, caring man whose return she'd waited for. This man was cold and hard. Even his eyes seemed flat and emotionless to her.

"Here." Bernard thrust something into her hand and Catherine looked down to find herself holding a scramasax sheathed in a finely etched scabbard.

"But . . ."

"Thieves are everywhere. And though I trust Hugh to protect you, there will be times when you will be alone in the forest. It is best that you have some protection. I taught you many years ago how to handle a dagger. Use it if you have to, Catherine. No matter what the target."

Catherine met her father's gaze evenly and

nodded. For the first time she felt the weight of the journey she was about to begin. There would be no return for her. Not really. Perhaps she would come to visit someday, bringing with her a brood of children and an entourage of servants. But she would never return to Avignon as her home. It suddenly seemed immensely final. The fine dagger weighed heavy across the palm of her hand and she made haste to slip the knife and its covering into the belt of her tunic.

A warm arm wrapped around her shoulders and pulled her close. Instinctively, she recognized Terrence's presence. "I cannot believe you and Hugh are leaving me here," he informed her with companionable humor.

Catherine bestowed her warmest smile on her patient. "You know you can't make such a journey yet. Besides, you have become invaluable to my father."

"Well, I'm less than certain of that; however, I do need a bit more practice on that half-dead beast your father puts me on before I'm ready to tackle real riding again."

Bernard smiled good-naturedly. "It won't be but another week and you'll be handling any stallion in my stables."

Terrence looked down at the misshapen curve of his right hand. "It may be a fortnight, Bernard," he commented wryly. "But I *will* be able to do it."

"It is as we said," Bernard agreed. "You're too fine a rider not to easily regain your skills."

"I am so grateful to have the limb still attached to my body that it matters little whether this appendage is of any use ever again," Terrence agreed.

Since the night Hugh and Terrence arrived in Avignon, Terrence had healed well. Less than a fortnight ago he'd stood on the very lip of death. But on this snowy morning he was happy simply to be alive. Marguerite and Catherine's ministrations had saved his life. And the only visible sign of his brush with death was an arm that hung useless by his side. He felt nothing from his elbow to the tips of his fingers. The gangrenous tissues Marguerite had cut out of his arm had included over half of the muscles. When the wound healed, his hand had curved into a tight ball that no amount of determination could alter. Terrence counted himself lucky.

What was more, he was happy to complete his recovery in Avignon, even though that meant having Hugh and Catherine go on to Anet without him. At Avignon, his injury was barely given a glance, but Paris, he knew, would be another story all together. Louis was as likely as not to forbid him from ever setting foot in the city again. The king liked his men perfect.

When the time came for Terrence to return home, his two brothers' titles and the influence of the family would help, but he had already decided that he would stay in Anet. He had no desire to face the scorn of men he knew well, nor dodge the repulsed looks of women who had hitherto found him most appealing.

"Catherine," he said. "You must do me a favor."

Catherine patted his cheek affectionately. "Of course, Terrence."

"Keep an eye on Hugh."

Catherine blanched visibly thinking of last night and the treatment she'd received at Hugh's hand. She could not picture herself trying to care for Hugh after that. She started to speak, then choked on her words.

Terrence held up a finger for patience. "Walk with me for a bit."

Skeptically, Catherine did as he asked. Unlike Hugh, Terrence had continued to be exactly as she'd known him before. Her affection for Terrence was like that she felt for her brothers. And if he wanted her to listen to him, she would.

"I've seen the rift between you and my brother, Catherine. And I know that Hugh is the one who has brought this on."

Catherine gave a short nod of agreement and jutted a stubborn chin before her as she walked on in silence.

Terrence sighed. "Don't judge him too soon, Catherine. You have always had a special ability to see the part of him that he hides."

"He didn't use to hide it," Catherine protested.

"He did. His entire life he has hidden it. But not from you. When he came here he found in you someone he trusted. You understood him. You saw him not as a warrior, invincible and hard, but as something else."

"A warm man." The softness in her voice turned bitter as she remembered Hugh then. Tossing her head in frustration, Catherine turned fiery eyes on Terrence. "What have I done to deserve his loss of that trust? Tell me, Terrence, for I am confounded by that question. I sent him letters faithfully for five years. I followed him into the forest to help you. I entertained him. I talked to him. I offered whatever solace I could. How could these things have altered that trust?"

They had reached the wall of the stables and Catherine stopped to face Terrence. Her sense of the injustice Hugh had settled upon her brought twin blossoms of pink to her cheeks and set her lips to trembling. "Tell me, Terrence. What have I done to deserve the contempt he treats me with?"

Terrence's face held a sad, helplessness as he slowly shook his head. "Catherine, it is nothing you have done, and yet, I believe, it is everything you have done."

"I have never heard anything so silly."

"Yet it is the truth." He sighed and reached out to take Catherine's hand in his as any of her brothers would have. "Listen to me, Catherine. And try, for a moment, not to think of the last few days. You are going on a wonderful journey. You are going into the future. But for my brother, this is a journey into the past. A past he was trying to escape in the Holy Wars. He is returning to a prison, and although he will not admit so, he knows it is true.

"Watch him. My fear is that the closer he gets to Anet, the greater will be his anxieties."

"Then why is he going back?" she asked.

"Because he believes he must."

"But Terrence, I cannot help him. He will barely speak to me. And the words he has spoken these past days I wish I hadn't heard."

"You are the light for him, Catherine."

She opened her mouth to protest, but Terrence shook his head. "Sometimes we run from the light. Other times we run to it. Just think about what I've told you. No matter what he has said or done these past days, he needs you."

Without another word, Terrence signaled to Avril who had been waiting with her mare. At Terrence's sign, he led the roan to where they stood.

"Take care, Catherine. I shall come to visit you on my way home." Terrence gave her a warm smile and patted the mare on its rump. "And don't let that abbess touch your hair," he added, wagging a finger of his good hand at her. "Now, I've got to find that brother of mine," he muttered and headed toward the assembled group of men in the center of the bailey.

Catherine watched him leave with a mix of emotions. There was much she still wanted to talk about. Terrence's last words had been so very strange. She didn't understand at all what he meant. He was quite mistaken if he thought she was any sort of light for Hugh. And, her mind protested, she was nigh well sick to death of men who told her what they wanted to say and then walked away leaving her without an opportunity to voice her opinion.

Beside her, Avril cleared his throat nervously. "My lady, Sir Hugh asks that you say your good-byes, for the sun rises high and we must be on our away."

Catherine pinned the boy with a glare that would have melted beeswax in an instant. "Truly?"

The boy nodded warily.

"Well then, I had best hasten to do his bidding."

Avril didn't dare speak, for though the words sounded right, the flare of his lady's nostrils and the angle of her brows reminded him of nothing so much as a filly about to heave her rider to the heavens.

Without another word, Catherine marched back to her parents, leaving Avril no choice but to lead her mare after her. But by the time she reached Marguerite and Bernard, Catherine had calmed herself. This was her leavetaking from her parents. And she refused to let Hugh or anyone interfere with her good-bye. Marguerite was waiting with open arms. And Catherine slid into her arms, hugging her tightly. "I'll miss you so, *ma mère.*"

"It shall not be the same here without you, my dear," her mother replied, her voice cracking with emotion as she squeezed Catherine in return.

Her father waited patiently, and when the two women had broken their embrace, he reached out to pull Catherine into his arms. "God go with you, Catherine."

Unable to speak for the heavy knot that blocked her throat, Catherine turned to her mount. Avril offered his knee, and though normally Catherine would have refused—being fully capable of mounting on her own—this morning she accepted the assistance. At that moment her heart felt as though it would indeed break into a thousand tiny shards.

And so, to make the parting no more sorrowful than need be, she did not look back, but turned her horse's head to the portcullis leading away from Avignon and the life she had known until now.

Urging her mare into a canter, she rode past Hugh without giving him so much as a glance. But she heard the men on horseback fall in line behind her as though she was the one leading them. Out through the portcullis and across the wooden drawbridge Catherine led the group. She knew the forest road as well as she did her own palm and the steep slope didn't slow her pace in the least. In fact, she urged her steed faster. She needed the feel of the wind against her face. She needed the smell of the pines to invade her. But more than anything she needed to put miles between herself and Avignon, else she would haul back on the reins and turn back.

Faster she rode, down the winding road. She knew she shouldn't, that it would hurt her mare's legs, but she couldn't make herself care. She needed to put more space between herself and her home. With the wind singing in her ears, she didn't hear the sound of hoofbeats approaching until they were nearly upon her.

Hugh reached across her horse's neck to take the reins and drag Catherine's mare to a halt. "Whatever it is you think you're doing, it's going to get someone's neck broken," he bit out.

Catherine jumped in her saddle. She could only stare at him in disbelief as both horses came to a stop. "I've ridden this road more times than I could ever count. How dare you tell me I can't," she declared, wrestling the reins from him. Catherine heard the words she spoke as they issued from her lips, but they didn't seem to be hers. Who was this person who was so angry? How had the wonderful friendship she shared with Hugh come to this?

Still, the bitter, hurtful words poured out of her and she could do nothing to prevent them. "*Lord* Vougnet, Duke of Pontoise, faithful servant of Louis VII and Knight Templar extraordinaire! I'm sure I forget myself to wish to *breathe* without your express permission! How absurd of me! Here," she said, tossing the reins she had just toiled to take away back at him. "Lead me to Chantilly. You can come into Paris leading me as a spoils of war! Won't that look fine. I'm sure Louis will be mightily impressed." She glared at him mutinously. Her breathing was coming in short, angry gasps and her insides were quivering like a flan pudding. She had never in her life been so angry.

Hugh pressed his mouth into a thin line and drew his brows low over his eyes as he watched Catherine. "Are you finished with your tirade?" he asked.

Catherine's eyes flashed ominously and she opened her mouth to continue, but Hugh cut her short.

"You *are* done," he announced as his eyes narrowed into fine blue points of brightness in his face.

"I won't have you acting like a spoilt child in front of the men. You're riding with me now, Catherine. We are not on our way out for a light afternoon of hunting. Hundreds of miles lie ahead of us and many days of hard riding. Besides which, I'm responsible for these men. They'll do as I do, and if I have to ride after you like I'm being chased by a band of Saracen assassins, then they'll follow me. I am responsible for their lives as well as yours. You may care nothing for yours, but give a care for theirs." Dropping her reins, he wheeled Cepheus around and galloped on ahead of her.

Catherine slumped in her saddle. The truth of his words sapped away any fight that was left in her. Hugh was simply doing his job. He commanded these men, and at least he did so with a conscience. She recalled letters she'd received from him which spoke of commanders with a different view. Men who sent their troops into hopeless battles and watched them be massacred. The men came up behind her and, as they passed, they nodded politely. Some she knew well as men who served her father, others had arrived with the group of knights from Constantinople. She was ashamed of her thoughtlessness. Mortified by her selfishness.

Sir Jeffrey pulled his charger to a halt beside her. "Lady Catherine, allow me the honor of riding with you."

Catherine nodded and urged her mare into a walk beside him thinking it was the least she could do to make up for her imprudence. Immediately, he launched into inane chatter about last night's dinner. Catherine paid little attention to his conversation, nodding occasionally to give the appearance of participation while her own thoughts went elsewhere. She looked carefully at Jeffrey Winfrey. He had brown hair, and eyes that were pleasant but ordinary. He was muscular and his physique was well attended, but not noticeably different from that of other knights. The full suit of mail he wore was of good design, but she noticed that here and there the links were rusted or missing and his hauberk needed repair. There was nothing really to complain of in him, but she did not particularly like him. She hoped the baron was not like Sir Jeffrey Winfrey.

". . . to ride a mare so ill-trained is a danger to a woman of your delicate beauty," Jeffrey finished with a smile that seemed watery and shallow to Catherine.

"Your pardon, Jeffrey, I did not fully hear that last."

"I was saying that we must secure a better horse for you for the remainder of the journey. You should ride a mild little pony."

Catherine bit back the words that sprang to mind. "I am told I am a very competent rider. You needn't fear for me on this excursion."

"But Catherine," he explained, giving her a look she could only describe as condescending, "a *lady* should ride a quieter mount."

Catherine cocked a single brow at him and smiled sweetly. "It seems to me that you define a lady rather narrowly."

Sir Jeffrey smiled knowingly. "A lady always knows her place."

"And does a lady's place include reading and writing, or merely a good hand with a needle and a fine voice for song."

"Really, Catherine, what need does a woman who is well cared for have of numbers and letters? I myself have no need for such mundane skills. Such things are left to my banker."

"And how do you know that your banker has not cheated you?"

"I would know," Jeffrey told her with supreme confidence.

"I see," Catherine replied. She rode on in silence for the rest of the morning. Jeffrey seemed to have an endless number of dull subjects with which to charm her and Catherine simply nodded where required or made an appropriate gasp when called for in his stories. But so far as she was concerned, there was nothing at all in Jeffrey's conversation that interested her.

They stopped along the Rhône to take a light meal and then continued on. But she managed to avoid a boring afternoon of Sir Jeffrey's discourses by catching Avril's attention.

"Ride with me, Avril."

Avril's response was an enthusiastic nod. He dug his heels into the ribs of the small gelding Hugh had given him to ride and trotted up beside her. "My lady, isn't this a grand day!" he spouted enthusiastically. "I never thought to travel beyond the woods of Avignon and the fiefdom, and now I'm on my way to Paris!"

Catherine smiled at his excitement. "If you do very well as a page to Sir Hugh, mayhap he will take you to court with him."

"I might see the king himself!"

Chuckling, Catherine agreed. " 'Tis a fine opportunity you've been given. Rarely does a young man do so well for himself. You must make the most of this, Avril."

Avril nodded seriously. "I will never let my lord down. I will be at his beck and call at all times, and he will see that he chose well. He can depend on me.''

Catherine smiled, pleased. Hugh had done a good thing to choose a serving boy as his page. Avril was smart and eager. And while he probably could do no better than to be a knight's page, he would see a great deal. Perhaps if he stayed in Hugh's service he would see a better life than he would have otherwise.

Avril was one of the youths who Catherine had taught to read. For many years it had been her pet project. She loved the children of her father's villeins and had filled her time with teaching rather than sitting in the solar pricking her fingers over some piece of handiwork. She would gather up those who were too young to work in the fields and spend an hour a day making games of reciting letters and numbers. For many of the children it would serve them little. But perhaps Avril would see some benefit. That would please her very much.

Her afternoon went by considerably faster than the morning. Avril entertained her well. He was two years younger than her brother, Jean, and seemed much the same in his ways as Jean had then.

"I'm told we'll make camp before darkness falls," he commented, eyeing the sky hours later. "It will be sunset soon. I should see if my lord has need of me."

"Of course," Catherine agreed. "Thank you so much for your company, Avril."

" 'Tis my pleasure, Lady Catherine. But you have so many others to entertain you," he said, indicating the entourage of knights.

"If they are of the same mind as Sir Jeffrey, I would be bored to distraction. I'd rather ride alone and enjoy the views than have my ears talked off with chatter about a particularly rousing game of dames or tables played a year ago," she said, speaking plainly.

Avril rolled his eyes. "Thanks to God that I don't have a lord like that. Sir Hugh is a knight a page can be proud to serve. He's not like those others." Seeing Hugh riding back toward the group, Avril gave Catherine a quick bow and rode to meet him.

As Avril had expected, it was less than an hour before they stopped in a copse along the river for the night. The men were all experienced travelers and Catherine was amazed at how quickly tents were pitched for the knights, horses rubbed down, and fires started. Everyone had something to do except for her. Seated on a log she'd found off to one side of the encampment, she watched the men work. Their boots crunched as the snow packed down beneath their constant tracking across the ground, and they used it as melt water for the horses. It was interesting and she watched closely, but after a while it became clear that she was expected to fend for herself until all was ready. Thinking that this was a good opportunity to relieve herself and wash a bit of the day's grime from her face and hands, she made her way to the case she had packed for use during the trip. She extracted a small cake of soap and a linen towel and struck out for the river.

The riverbank was steep and she had to walk along the river several minutes before finding a slope that was not covered with tangled brambles. She was glad to have her wolf-lined boots and cloak, for the snow was deep in spots, coming over her ankles. And the air was cooling quickly now that the sun was nothing more than a faint light on the horizon. At last she found a small deer trail leading to the water's edge. Eyeing the narrow path that led down the steep embankment, Catherine tucked the cake of soap and towel into her belt. Then, snatching a great handful of skirt in one hand, she took hold of a low hanging branch with the other and started down. Twice she slipped on the snowy slope, but her hold on either a branch or root kept her from tumbling head first all the way to the Rhône. And the last bit, she simply slid down.

By the time Catherine reached her destination, she was dirtier than ever, and desperately in need of a cleaning. Stripping off her mitted gloves, she shrugged off her cloak and laid it on a stone by the water. She knelt on her cloak and breathed in the fresh scent of briskly running water. She plunged her hands into the ice-cold river and quickly splashed her face. Using the soap, she cleaned her face and hands, then pushed up the sleeves of her kirtle as far as they would go and scrubbed her arms. She considered pulling off her boots and stockings to wash her feet and legs but thought better of it. It was too cold, and, besides, darkness had settled in completely. She needed to get back.

Bending down again, she cupped her hands and took a long drink of the river water. It was icy fresh, so much better than the water from skins they'd had all day. She drank her fill thirstily.

When at last she was ready, Catherine turned back toward the embankment, but it looked quite different from this angle. The root she'd held on to for the bottom half of the trip down was a third of the way up the slope and out of reach. Catherine searched around for a way to start up, but the snow had hidden any rocks or handhold. Finally, she decided she would simply have to go up, regardless of handhold or rocks to use as stepping-stones. But determination alone would not get her up the embankment. Three times she tackled the slope to no avail.

"I suppose I need sharp little hooves for this," she muttered to herself when the fourth attempt got her only half as far as the others. Realizing she could not return the way she came, Catherine decided she would have to walk along the river in the direction of the camp until she could find a way up. It occurred to her that she might have to go beyond the camp because all the way along her route she'd seen nothing that looked vaguely transversible.

The way along the river was much harder

walking than it had been up above. Here the ground was uneven and full of underbrush that grew right to the edge of the water. She was forced to step high over bushes and tall grasses that scratched at her stockinged legs and caught her cloak and kirtle. Over and over she had to stop to loosen her clothing from nettles and thorns. It was dark now, and colder. Catherine wondered if she was tired because she had walked a long way, or because it was so much harder to walk down here. There was no moon to light the snow for her, and she could only see the barest bit in front of her. Was she near the camp? Every few meters she stopped to inspect the slope for any place where she might be able to climb to higher ground. But she could no longer even make out the top of the slope, and so she was unsure of how high the slope was, or if there was a way up. She listened for sounds of horses or men. Anything to indicate where she was.

Catherine's trek came to a sudden halt. There was nowhere left to go. The riverbed widened in front of her and the slope became a short cliff where the soil had given way completely leaving no way for her to continue. Frustrated, Catherine stared at the rolling black river before her. She could not remember if this was beyond the camp or still before it. She hadn't paid attention as she'd walked. She stood very still, straining her ears for any sound at all. But there was nothing. She turned to look behind her. Blackness.

Closing her eyes, she forced herself to think. She was lost. Well, not truly lost, but in the darkness she could not find her way up the slope. She was not too far from camp, but far enough that she could not hear them, nor smell the campfires. If she began walking back the way she had come, she would still not be able to see. She was tired. The hem of her kirtle and cloak were wet and getting heavier by the moment. Walking back would only tire her more, and she didn't know for certain that she had passed the camp. It might still be ahead of her, in which case there was no use in going back.

Her mind made up, Catherine opened her eyes and looked around in the darkness for some form of shelter. She would sleep here tonight, and with first light, she'd be able to find a way up the slope. A stone's throw from where she stood she spotted a large bush that appeared to have a hollow within. She headed for the bush and found that some animal must have used it to rest. Peering beneath the branches, she found that there was no snow there and whatever had used it for a home, had left it clean and well swept. The center was hollowed and the earth smoothed. Crawling in, Catherine pulled her cloak about her. She curled her legs up close to her chin and pulled her hood close over her face. It was a little hard, but not so cold as it had been outside. Running her fingers along her belt, Catherine felt the reassuring outline of the little dagger her father had given her. She had thought it an unnecessary accoutrement then, but she was dearly glad for its small comfort now.

She wondered if Hugh would wait tomorrow, or go on without her. She imagined him so furious that he didn't even bother to leave her mare behind. The old Hugh—for that is how she thought of the man she'd liked so well—would have known her well enough to know she needed his help. But Hugh Vougnet, Knight Templar and Lord of Pontoise, would accuse her of purposely causing him trouble. He would point his finger and call her childish and warn her not to try his patience with such antics again. Catherine gave a great sigh. The new Hugh wouldn't understand at all.

Ten

When Avril told Hugh that Catherine wasn't to be found anywhere in the camp, Hugh could barely contain his fury. The *last* thing he needed was to chase after Catherine once again. But as the hours passed, his anger turned to worry. And his worry slowly became ice-cold fear.

He had spent the day doing everything in his power to ignore Catherine, but no matter who he rode with, or what he used to divert his thoughts, he had remained keenly aware of everything she did. When she rode with Jeffrey Winfrey, Hugh had become so sickened by the knight's drooling and fawning over Catherine that he would have sent the man back to Avignon on some pointless mission if the noon meal had not presented an opportunity to disrupt his activities. Hugh had been more at ease when he saw her select his page as her riding partner for the afternoon. But four hours of listening to the two of them laughing and chattering like two jaybirds had only created a deepening anger over the fact that they could possibly have so much to discuss. By the time they stopped for the evening, Hugh had been so tense that he threw himself into the work of overseeing the setting up of the encampment.

But now he realized with sickening clarity that he was to blame for Catherine's disappearance. He hadn't assigned a man to watch her, nor had he warned her about going off on her own. The blame lay squarely on his shoulders. Catherine had never traveled away from home. She knew nothing other than the safety of Avignon and her father's lands. How could she understand the dangers of a strange forest or a well-traveled road?

Supper passed, but Hugh had no taste for food. He kept the news of her disappearance from the other men. He didn't want or need a massive search. A trampling brigade of men would only alert thieves if there were any about and if they had Catherine captive.

Hugh had his own way of doing things, and that was alone. As the night turned late, Jeffrey Winfrey came over to inquire about Catherine. Hugh informed him in a tone that brooked no further questions that she was asleep. And the explanation seemed to suit the man's needs, for he retired without another word. Hugh could only shake his head at the man as he walked away. *He* would never have settled for such an answer. If he had wanted to know where Catherine was, he would have seen for himself. And if what he saw did not satisfy him, he would have gone on until he found the answers he desired.

But Jeffrey Winfrey was a far different man than he.

Hugh and Avril sat and counted the hours as the night stretched out interminably. The men rolled into their cloaks and went to sleep. The fires burned low. As he sat staring into the darkness, willing Catherine to appear from the woods, Hugh contemplated the endless number of tragedies which might have befallen her. The later the hour became the more Hugh knew with a certainty that Catherine was in trouble.

At last he could wait no longer. "Keep this fire burning brightly, boy," he growled in a low tone as he jumped up from the stump he had moved close to the fire and stared into the darkness.

Avril jumped to his feet as well, his head bobbing a staccato nod. "What are you going to do?" he asked breathlessly.

"I'm going to find her, for God's sake. If she hasn't got the brains to come in out of the freezing night, somebody has to make sure she does."

"Lady Catherine isn't out for a midnight stroll! She's brave and smart and she wouldn't do a thing such as that!" Avril cried, leaping to his lady's defense. "She could be hurt. Her leg broken, or her arm. She might have come upon a bear. Or worse!" he cried. Hugh could see the boy's gawky limbs shake with his anger. "Wherever she is, she's cold and alone and, knight or no, my liege lord, you've no right to say otherwise."

Hugh sighed and took the young page by the shoulders. "Avril, I'll find her. Wherever she is, I'll find her and bring her back to safety. Now, get my mantle, my broadsword and my ax." Avril swallowed hard, but after giving Hugh one more look that Hugh could only have described as a warning, he headed for the tent.

Hugh pressed his mouth into a thin line of concern as he checked his belt for his dagger by the light of the fire. Avril's words had hit to the very core of his own fears. Fears he'd hidden beneath a cloak of anger. There were too many things that could have happened to Catherine and there was not one among them for which he would ever forgive himself if it had occurred.

Behind him he heard the sound of Avril's approach. Grimly, he took the sword and ax. The handle of his ax fit smoothly into the palm of his hand and the blade of his sword seemed to glow golden in the reflected flames of the fire, giving it an eerie life of its own. How many heads had he severed from their necks with these tools of his trade? How many times had he wielded them with deadly intent in the name of God? Was it really God's will that all Muslims die? Was the Lord's intent truly to pit man against man for the cause of *property*? And how could it be God's will that Catherine should be lost in the forest on her first night away from her home? That the brilliant light within her should be extinguished and the world be left that much darker?

"My lord?"

At the sound of Avril's voice, Hugh's mesmerized gaze broke away from the shining blades. The boy stood before him with his scabbard and belt ready. Hugh lifted his arms and let the page cinch them around his waist. He sheathed his broadsword and slipped the ax handle into his belt on the other side. Taking the mantle Avril held out, he flung the long, heavy garment over his shoulders in one swift movement. Avril stood silently before him, and without saying a word, the boy's expression said much to Hugh.

"I'll bring her back, Avril. Make her tent ready for her."

The snow and the desert sand were not so different when a man was tracking someone. Hugh's initial guess was that she'd headed for the river and he easily confirmed his intuition when he found her footprints not three rods from the point where he began to head north. He followed them along the lip of the embankment wondering where it was she had intended to go, but when the trail turned and her footprints went sliding down the embankment to the river, Hugh became alarmed. He leapt easily to the bottom of the ridge, but all he found there were more tracks. It appeared that she had fallen by the river's edge, a fact that concerned him. Even if she had not injured herself in the fall, she would be wet. The night was cold as it was, and a crisp breeze blew through the forest. A second set of tracks, which could only be hers, led along the water's edge back in the direction of the camp. The measured steps of someone walking on two good legs let him breathe easier; at least she wasn't hurt and she could not be far away, he thought. But Catherine had walked a long way and he tracked her a good distance before coming to a dead end. When the river broadened, her tracks ended suddenly. In front of him stood tall cliffs that only an experienced climber might scale. Fear once again clutched at his heart.

Hugh stared along the river in front of him. It would have been impossible for someone of Catherine's build to scale the sheer cliffs before him, yet her tracks led straight to them. Even if she were not dressed in a kirtle and heavy cloak, it would have been impossible for her to accomplish. Yet, if she had started back in the direction she had come, he would have seen her.

Where was she?

Hugh refused to look at the swiftly flowing river beside him. The Rhône was wide, and deep, and icy cold. A single false step and a woman would be swept into the boiling breach without a chance of survival. He would not believe that had happened. Until he held her lifeless body himself, he would not believe it. Instead, he concentrated on the ground nearby. Retracing the small footprints in the snow, Hugh strode back in the direction he had

come. But the trail ended abruptly after twenty
paces and Hugh was left once again to stare into
the blackness before him with no idea as to where
Catherine might have gone.

Bemused, Hugh turned in a slow circle inspect-
ing every piece of ground for some indication,
some sign that would tell him what he needed to
know. A stand of fir trees lined the embankment.
The ground beneath them was strewn with small
stones nestled deep in pine needles. Just on the
edge of the trees some small beast had beaten a
trail to a warm den beneath the snow-laden
branches of a set of shrubs. Across from that, a
large boulder had long ago come to rest. But there
was no sign of Catherine. Carefully, Hugh moved
in the half circle that encompassed Catherine's
two sets of footprints. Bit by bit, he examined the
ground, the rocks, the bushes, looking for a clue
that would unravel this mystery.

She had to be here. His mind refused to consider anything else. It was only luck that he noticed the small footprint among the animal tracks
leading to the little bramble bush. He didn't
know what made him look down exactly as he
did and find the footprint among the muddled
animal tracks. He only knew that in the moonless
night he'd never have seen her sleeping there
otherwise.

Catherine didn't know whether she'd slept for
one hour or four hours, but suddenly she was

awake and she didn't know why. Her heart was beating like a sparrow frightened by the nearness of a footfall.

Just outside her shelter a twig snapped.

Then she heard the creak of snow underfoot. So close! Wide-eyed, Catherine lay motionless, her breath caught in her throat. A branch overhead moved and a black shadow fell over her. Catherine opened her mouth to scream.

"Cay?"

Catherine felt a hard lump of tears knot her throat at the sound of his voice so close. "Hugh!" She tried to scramble out from her small haven, but her legs had become tangled in her kirtle and cloak and she could not move.

Hugh didn't bother waiting for Catherine to come out from the cub hole she'd found; he climbed into her little shelter and pulled her into his arms, breathing in her essence as he gathered her close to his heart. "My God, Catherine, you could have frozen to death. Here." Pulling his cloak open, he pressed her body against his own and wrapped them both in the lengths of his own mantle. "Get warm." He tucked her head beneath his chin trying to envelop every inch of her in his own heat. As he encased her, he willed the warmth of his body into hers.

"Hugh," she breathed against his chest. "I didn't mean to get lost. Everyone was busy. I just thought to . . ."

"Nay, mite. Never mind how you got here. I'm just so glad I found you." They lay very still.

Hugh felt the warmth of her breath against his neck and he closed his arms more tightly around her.

"I'm cold," she whispered quietly.

"You've been laying still," Hugh said softly. "If you're lost in the forest, you must always stay awake and keep moving. Too often when the cold makes a man sleepy, he lays down for nap and never awakens."

"I didn't know."

"How could you?" Hugh smiled to himself as he lay with Catherine curled against him in the small shelter. "You managed to find a unique spot, mite. I shouldn't have worried about thieves, they'd never find you here."

Catherine smiled, please to have any compliment from him, then a frown creased her pretty face. "Thieves?"

"I hope the owner of this little den doesn't come home tonight," Hugh continued, moving away from the subject of the numerous robbers who roamed the countryside between Avignon and Paris.

"It can't be too large an animal, Hugh," Catherine reasoned. "It's only a small place."

"I think it might well belong to a wolf," Hugh informed her with a sly grin. "But nary a worry, Cay. With his cousin's hide on your mantle and boots, he's sure to take a liking to you."

Catherine looked up at him with a startled expression and Hugh chuckled.

"Should we go?" she asked.

"Nay." Hugh wrapped his arms more closely around her. "We'll warm you more. It's a fair walk back to our camp." But in truth, Hugh didn't want to leave the bramble enclosure. All his promises and prayers, all his intentions to stay away from her were gone like so many leaves in the rushing current of the river beside them. He had not felt so at peace since the night he arrived in Avignon. Not since he had touched Catherine's lips with his in the quiet of his rooms. Instead, he had been tortured night and day by the shackles he had placed upon himself. He had watched others talk with her, laugh with her, and dance with her when all the while all he had desired was to be the one living those moments with her.

Gently, he pushed his hand inside the hood of her cloak. His fingers stroked her hair and he reveled in the satiny texture of it. "Stay close to me, Cay," he whispered.

Catherine lifted her head and looked up at him. Her eyes were so soft, the green orbs almost luminous in the darkness of the enclosure. For a moment she looked at him, searching his gaze for something. "But you told me to leave you alone," she said quietly. "You said . . ."

"I was wrong." Hugh closed his eyes, and when he opened them again, he pressed the palm of his hand around the curve of her cheek. "I want you to ride with me tomorrow and the next day and the next."

"I will be a burden to you."

"You will be my friend and my companion and a joy to have beside me." Hugh took a deep breath. He had treated her terribly all because he did not want to be tempted by her. He had been afraid of that temptation, for he felt it as surely as he breathed. Catherine was beautiful. She sparkled with life and vitality. He could spend an hour or a day or a year in her company and never be bored. Of that he was certain. It had been that way when she was just a mite. Why had he believed for even a moment it would be any other way when he returned to find her grown?

Yes, she was his temptation. And sweet temptation it was to be happy. To laugh, to talk, to hear and be heard. For the past three weeks he had taken the one person in all the world who filled his life with joy and treated her with contempt. Yet when she looked at any other man, he became consumed with jealousy.

Catherine smiled tremulously at him. "You're back."

Hugh knit his brow and shook his head. "I never left. You're the one who went wandering off."

"No," she responded quietly. "You went off to the Crusades and when you returned you were— different. Terrence told me that you were still here somewhere, but I didn't believe it. I only saw that you treated me like a stranger, and strangers as though they were your friends. I felt the hurt of your coldness to me. The ache of seeing you ignore me. It made me want to hurt you in return. Make you think someone—any-one—else was important to me in the way you are. Make you feel the pain I did at the changes I saw in you."

Hugh pressed his mouth into a grim line. "Mayhap you're right, mite. Perhaps I did change."

Catherine searched his face. Her fingers reached up to touch his brow gently. "But you are back. The man I wrote letters to and talked to in the silence of the night for five years. You're back."

And then, before he knew what had hap-pened, her lips brushed lightly against his cheek. "I am so glad. Please don't ever change, Hugh. There is no one I like better than you."

Hugh was glad for the darkness. It hid the sud-den wetness that swamped his eyes and the hard lump that lodged in his throat. He couldn't re-member a time when anyone had said that they liked him. So often he was found wanting. Oh, they praised him for his prowess as a warrior. But Hugh had never been misled by such words. As a man of war he was useful to many. But as a man, as the person he was—who had ever liked him?

Terrence. His mother, mayhap. But she had died during his baby sister's stillbirth when Hugh was too small to remember. And what was he returning to? Would Adele speak such words to him? He did not think so.

He closed his eyes and breathed deeply. He could smell Catherine's skin where her face hovered above his only a hairbreadth away. Opening his eyes again, he found himself drowning in the green depths of her eyes. Warm, gentle, trusting eyes that smiled down upon him like a benevolent angel. All thought of Adele fled from his mind as he drank in the nearness of her. She was all the things he desired—for she was like him. She marveled at the beauty of the world, enjoying every dewy morning, breathless in her admiration of the painted sunset.

It had been her letters that allowed him to stay sane in Jerusalem. And more than her letters, it had been the memory of her. Of the impish, laughing little girl who shone like a bright light in his world of darkness. He knew the truth now. He hadn't come back for Adele. He had come back for Catherine.

"Hugh?" Catherine breathed quietly. The palm of his hand cupped her face, feeling the softness of her. Slowly, gently, he drew his face against her neck, breathing in the essence of her. He felt her pulse throb against his lips. Gently, he pressed a kiss there, letting his lips linger. She was so warm and soft. So soft.

Another kiss. Slow and perfect, savored like a sweet drop of water after a long, hot day in the desert. Catherine sighed, and the sound vibrated against his mouth. He kissed her again. Moving along an imaginary line that drew him like a moth to flame, his lips traced a line up her neck.

The curve of her jaw was like fine wine to him; the lobe of her ear like a succulent date, savored, tasted, adored. The taste of her was unique. In all the world, there could be no equal.

"Catherine." Her name escaped unbidden from his soul. It was like a drop of fine mist in a dry desert night wind. She turned her face to his, her eyes reaching for him. Her lips parted. He stared into her soul through those eyes, and lost himself within them. His hand twined through the thick curls of copper and he drew her lips to his even as he rose to meet them.

A sudden jolt of heat coursed through him at their touch. Hot and liquid. Like wine set to flame it seared to his very core. She met his kiss with a fervor of her own. He felt her arms encircle him, her fingers caressing the muscles that crisscrossed his shoulders. And from the back of her throat, he heard the sound of her soft moan as she molded herself to him.

Like a bulwark breaking beneath the unceasing attack of a battering ram, Hugh felt his desires overrun him. He pulled her closer, pressing the length of her petite frame against him. His tongue caressed the line where her lips met and they parted, giving entry. Her mouth was warm, and as his tongue delved inward, Hugh felt the tip of her tongue touch his; shyly at first, then with more boldness. Exploring. Learning. Seeking out.

Gently, Hugh set Catherine away from him. Still holding her in his arms, he tucked her head

against his shoulder. She was quiet, her breath
a soft whisper against his chest while his own
came ragged from within him. Hugh wrapped
his arms around her. He wished that he could
draw her into himself. Create a oneness that the
king or pope or the world could not look upon
with judgment. For he loved Catherine. Loved
her as no one he had ever known before or since.
But she was not his. Not his to love. Not his to
shelter. Not his to care for and protect, *and love*.

He drew her against him so close that his arms
ached. "Come on, mite," he said at last. "Let's
get you back to a warm bed and a fire."

But Catherine did not want to go. The weight
of Hugh's arms around her felt too peaceful.
When she'd kissed him, it had been everything
she remembered. A pure expression of his care
for her. This could not be wrong. This need.
This caring. They could share this and still be
true to their own lives. There was so little time
now. Only days. Then she would be at the *abbaye*
and Hugh would go on with his life. But this
journey they could make theirs alone.

Catherine felt Hugh's arms tighten around her
once more as though he read her very thoughts.
Then, gently, he urged her to rise. "But the
bank," Catherine told Hugh as he handed her
out into the night. "I can't get up it."

"Come here," Hugh said, smiling.

Catherine obeyed, and a moment later found
herself lifted off the ground and slung unecere-
moniously over Hugh's broad shoulder. "My

brothers always said I was half goat. Although I can't say if that was from stubbornness or my ability to climb anything in front of me." Hugh headed straight up the slope, and in no time at all he was setting Catherine down on the ground again, but this time she was ten rods above the riverbed.

"Try that in a kirtle sometime," she told him.

"Nay, Cay. I don't envy you your drapings. Although I can't imagine you in hose and a tunic."

Catherine laughed at the thought and Hugh grinned broadly at his jest. Wrapping an arm around her, they walked toward the camp.

Avril jumped up from where he sat bundled in a woolen blanket. "My lady, thank God you are safe!" he said, dropping his blanket in his dash to reach them. "And you, my lord Hugh. You took your time. I was sitting here thinking how I was going to have to rescue the both of you. Me and my little pony!"

Hugh grinned. "You grow too big for your own good, lad. But my thanks for your help and company tonight." Avril turned a near shade of purple with pride at Hugh's words. "Now," Hugh continued, "get some sleep. Dawn is far too near for all of us."

"And, Avril," Catherine added gently. "Please. Not a word to anyone about tonight." Avril gave her a sharp nod, and without a backward glance marched off.

Hugh walked her to a small tent set up next to his. "This is where you were meant to sleep.

Although I think perhaps your little bramble cave may have been the cozier of the two."

"I shall be happy to be in this." Catherine smiled. "Thank you, Hugh."

"It's just a small tent—"

"No," she interrupted gently. "For coming to find me."

Hugh reached out and gently chucked her beneath her chin. "I could not have done otherwise."

Eleven

Catherine emerged from her tent the next morning to find the camp a bustle of activity. The sun had at last emerged from the heavy cover of clouds that had screened out its warmth all the day before and had created the pitch night. A series of trails crisscrossed the snowy earth around the camp, some leading to the horses and pack animals, others marking the routes taken to and from the campfire. The trees were still heavily laden with the snow now becoming wet and heavy. Here and there clumps fell to the ground making soft plops as they landed on the forest floor.

Catherine crossed to the campfire and settled herself quietly on a stump. "Good morning," she said to one of the knights as she held her hands out to the warmth of the flames.

"Good morning, Lady Catherine," the knight responded politely as he continued eating the contents of the bowl he held in his hand.

"Where would I get something to eat?" she inquired politely. The knight stopped shoveling the food into his mouth long enough to nod in the direction of a black kettle sitting at the edge of the fire. Catherine moved to the pot. The contents looked somewhat questionable—a combination of large, ill-formed lumps and a brown sauce that sported glistening pools of grease on the surface. Catherine glanced back at the knight. He was engrossed in his own meal and seemed to take no heed of her. Deciding he would be of little assistance, Catherine cast about for some sort of trencher and spoon. But she could find nothing.

The camp was clearly breaking as preparations for their departure were made. Knights, serfs from her father's fief, and pages strode purposefully in all directions, but nary a one gave Catherine so much as a passing glance.

"Ah, my dear Catherine, there you are." Catherine looked up to find Jeffrey standing on the other side of the fire. "You slept well, I trust, for you retired early and slept rather late."

Unsure of how to respond, Catherine just smiled at him.

"Ah, but 'twas not a purposeless sleep," he continued, "for your sparkle outshines the snowscape that surrounds you."

"You are too kind, Sir Jeffrey," Catherine responded, unable to think of anything more to say.

He smiled as though he fully agreed with her. "I sought you out last eventide, hoping we could have shared a stroll in the moonlit wood, but you were already abed." He gave her a secretive smile. "Would that I was sharing it with you . . . but if you will acquiesce to ride with me today, my injured heart will not ache quite so much."

"Unfortunately, she is riding with me today."

Catherine turned in surprise and found Hugh approaching in long, purposeful strides from the area where the horses were being saddled. Nodding, Catherine confirmed Hugh's statement. "I'm so sorry, Jeffrey. But you *did* ride with me all of yesterday morning."

"Then you will share your noon meal with me."

"I'm afraid not," Hugh stated plainly. "And the afternoon ride will be spent with me as well."

"I see." Jeffrey Winfrey's jaw tightened noticeably and a wave of tension spread in the surrounding air.

"Do you have any questions, Sir Jeffrey?" Hugh asked, breaching the challenge that hung between the two men.

The younger man's eyes slid away from Hugh's direct look. "No."

"Then I think there is much yet to be done and the morning is getting old while we stand here and talk."

Without another word, Jeffrey stepped across Catherine and Hugh's path. He did not look Hugh in the eye again, but as he passed before her, he shot Catherine a spiteful glare.

Taking a deep breath, Catherine looked up at Hugh. "I fear I am making an enemy of Sir Jeffrey."

"I do not think it is you who is becoming his enemy, nor I. A man such as Jeffrey Winfrey has few interests other than those which suit his own needs. When he finds that you are not available to him, he will lose interest. You may be surprised at how quickly you are replaced in his affections by any available woman."

"I have already told him I am betrothed, but that did nothing to cool his interests."

"Your baron is far away and Jeffrey's interests are immediate. Knowing that you are not available to him now or ever will cause him to lose interest. Unfortunately, many women are available to men like Jeffrey Winfrey. Their husbands have been gone for years and they are open to dalliances."

Catherine's mouth turned upward into a dimpled smile. "And am I not available to him?"

"You are not."

Catherine smiled. "Good."

For a moment, Hugh stared down at her, and Catherine felt as though she was being consumed by his gaze. His eyes did more than look at her. They touched her—a touch that reached far deeper than her skin to some secret place within her that was vulnerable and open only to him.

"Collect your belongings, Cay. We have a long way to travel today." Turning his attention to the campfire, Hugh began to kick snow onto the glowing embers. Catherine turned back to her tent and in a few minutes was ready to mount her horse. Avril arrived to pull down the tent that only hours before he had so carefully prepared for her safe return. Stomping the ground like an irritated colt, the page yanked the stakes from the frozen ground and rolled up ropes, all the while grumbling under his breath.

"Avril, have I done something to anger you?" Catherine asked at last.

"Nay, my lady!" he assured her emphatically. Then with a scowl, he added, " 'Tis Sir Jeffrey. I have no great love for that man."

"I'm sure he means well."

"Humpff!" Avril snorted in disbelief. "Here we are, working at our hardest to move on for the day and all he wants is the attention of every page in the camp. 'Do this for me. Do that for me. Where is my sword? Who has my spurs?' "

"Does Jeffrey not have a page of his own?" Catherine asked.

"Indeed. But he has sent his page off on some errand of the utmost importance, leaving us to do his bidding!"

"I'm sure you do not mind, Avril," Catherine said with an understanding smile. "You could be at home preparing the fields for the winter wheat."

Avril tucked the last rope into place behind his pony's saddle and sighed. "I am not ungrateful, my lady. You know that. And I will do whatever I can for Lord Hugh and any of the men who ride with him. But I do not have to *like* every knight."

"That is true," Catherine agreed. "But keep

it only between you and I that you hold no affection for Jeffrey. It can only cause problems,
and he is far, far more powerful a man than you,
Avril. You must remember that."

Even as he nodded, Avril grumbled again beneath his breath. "This being a page is not so
perfect as I thought when I was just the kitchen
boy at Avignon."

Catherine laughed aloud at him. "So little in
life is ever as we imagine it."

The day went far too quickly for Catherine.
But unlike her comment to Avril, it passed exactly as she had dreamed it would. The sun's
rays grew stronger as it rose in the sky, melting
away much of the snow and warming her till she
could ride without her cloak. Hugh rode with
her, ate with her, talked with her, and laughed
with her the entire time. They discussed horses,
hunting, and Paris. He described Louis's court
to her and told her endless stories of the battles
he had fought and won for the king. There was
an air of ease and comfort between them that
she had thought was gone forever. And it washed
over her like the warm sunlight.

She learned much about Hugh that she had
never known before. Catherine had learned from
his letters that he was a Knight Templar. And
though Hugh spoke not at all of the power and
fame he won for his victories, she had heard it
from other sources. Now, however, she learned

that before he had even arrived at Avignon those many years ago, he had been famous for his prowess in battle. It wasn't so much that Hugh actually said he was the king's most trusted knight. It was simply the conversations with the king that he described to her. It was the requests and commands that he spoke of the king giving to him. It all expressed eloquently the trust his sovereign placed in him. Catherine's pride in Hugh grew with each hour. He was the finest knight in all of France, of that Catherine was certain. But it was the fact that he said nothing about the power such trust gave him that so pleased her. It was the way Hugh remained an unassuming, honest, and dedicated man despite it.

The only bit of darkness in her day was the change that came over Hugh when she had asked about his home. What was Anet like? she had asked. And Hugh had suddenly become shuttered and quiet. It seemed that in that, at least, nothing had changed over the past five years. Terrence had told her little about their childhood home, only that the castle and fief were the property of their older brother, Giles. And that Hugh had not lived there for many years.

Catherine had hoped that Hugh would tell her about Anet, as he had Paris. And that through their discussion of his ancestral home, she would learn something about Adele. Despite her intentions to speak to Terrence about her, Catherine had never had the opportunity. Preparations for the journey had been too harried, and Terrence had remained too sick for more than the shortest of conversations. She had learned only that Adele de Pisan lived in the neighboring fief, just on the other side of the river that marked the boundary between the two lands. The betrothal, like her own, had been made long, long ago. Hugh had known since the age of eight that he would wed Adele de Pisan.

Catherine wondered why they were not already married. Adele had been, according to Terrence, only six years younger than Hugh. If such were true, it would have made sense for Adele and Hugh to have been wed when Adele turned sixteen or seventeen, just as Catherine herself was about to do. Hugh was in his twenty-eighth year. Which would have made Adele seventeen the year he left for the Crusade. Why had he gone? Why had he not wed Adele then?

All these things created an aura of mystery around Adele. But what Catherine wanted to know most of all was whether or not Adele was truly dead. Catherine had come to think of her so ever since the night Hugh and Terrence had returned to Avignon. It was the one question that plagued Catherine. Although she was not free to wed him, she could not believe that Hugh would act so possessively toward her if he was on a journey back to the woman he would marry. He was not like Jeffrey Winfrey, who thought nothing of dalliances.

Hugh was a different kind of man entirely.

But there was so much unanswered, so many questions in her mind, questions that Catherine wanted to understand. They had only a few days together. Possibly a few months, if Hugh came to visit her at the *abbaye,* which she hoped he would. She wanted to know everything. She wanted to imprint him in her mind forever. She had known him only a few weeks when he left for Jerusalem, yet the strength of her impression had carried her through five years. Now it would have to carry her through a lifetime, and she needed to know all there was to know of Hugh Vougnet.

Except for that one blemish, Catherine's day was near to perfect. The day's ride was longer than the first. Hugh pushed them on past sunset, for he had told Catherine there was a keep which they might stay at and he wished to reach it to-night. Catherine was glad for that news. She had missed breakfast and was certain Hugh could hear her stomach grumbling by the time they stopped to eat again. But one bite of their repast at noon had convinced her that she was fortunate to have missed breakfast. The stew Hugh presented her with looked much like the strange concoction she'd examined in the cookpot that morning and it tasted mostly of grease and flour. A few bites had served to sour her stomach completely. The thought of dining in a keep with a cook who knew something of fresh meat and the application of herbs to season the food made her mouth water. Nor would she mind a soft bed to sleep in or a tub of steaming water in which to soak.

By the time they reached the keep, they were riding by torchlight. Their approach had been heralded by trumpets sounding at the turrets of the castle and a sentry rode to greet them while they were still on the lowlands surrounding the keep.

"Do you know the owner of this castle?" Catherine inquired of Hugh as the sentry galloped toward them.

"No. Terrence and I did not bother to stop when we were traveling to the Holy Lands. We rode hard and slept on the ground when we needed rest. Avignon was our only stop and I think we would not even have stopped there had Terrence not heard that your father was very familiar with many of the ship merchants in Florence."

"Then how do we know . . ."

"One never knows." Hugh finished for her. The sentry pulled his horse up before Hugh and bowed courteously.

"You are on the lands of the Duke de Neville, Lord of Bueil and vassal to Louis VII, sovereign of all France. State your business, please."

Catherine watched as Hugh gave a courteous nod. "I am Hugh Vougnet. I travel with an entourage of knights of Louis's court and of the army of His Holiness the Pope. We have returned from the Holy Lands and seek nothing more than a night's shelter, food, and lodging for our horses."

The sentry nodded sharply. "My lord welcomes all who have fought in the Holy Wars. The things you request shall be yours." Turning, the sentry led the way toward the imposing castle. It was larger than her family's keep, though not nearly so lovely to look at, Catherine thought as they rode in silence. The stone structure was a darkish brown in color and stood on a small rise rather than the high hilltop of Avignon. She counted ten turrets in the thick wall surrounding the keep itself—twice the number at Avignon.

"I shall have to write my father," Catherine whispered in muted tones to Hugh. "He must secure a sentry to ride out and inspect everyone who wishes to approach Avignon."

"Do not make fun, Catherine," Hugh admonished. "The closer we get to Paris, the greater is the threat of thieves and impostors. Every lord must protect his vassals and serfs as best he can. To simply open your gates to every stranger who passes by may be a sign of welcome in Avignon, but here it is a sign of a foolhardy lord."

Catherine looked at him in surprise. "Is it so in Pontoise as well?"

Hugh raised an eyebrow and shrugged. "I don't know. I have yet to see my new home and its surroundings. I hope I shall not have to resort to such things, but if I deem it necessary, than I will do whatever is required to create safe lands for my people."

They rode into the courtyard and were immediately greeted by the blaze of what Catherine thought must surely be ten thousand torches. As they pulled their horses to a halt before a tall wooden platform, the Duke de Neville stepped forward. He was dressed in a long brocade tunic that reached to the ground. A thick, gold-linked belt studded with enormous cabochon stones in each circlet hung from his girth. His shoes were of fine velvet and the mantle that lay across his shoulders was trimmed in ermine. Upon each finger he wore a ring. Some even sported two rings. Each was gold and set with precious gems of every conceivable color. But his clothing could not disguise the pinched look to his thin, pointed face with its hooked nose, nor the pasty pallor of his skin.

Hugh dismounted and bowed before the duke. "My lord. I come to you for food, shelter, and the goodness of your hospitality. I return from Jerusalem just this past month."

"You are Vougnet?"

Hugh nodded.

"I have heard of you. They say the Saracens run at the very mention of your name. Is this true?"

Catherine sat on her mare listening to the conversation. Beside her, Avril leaned over to whisper in her ear, "I don't like the Duke de Neville, either," he commented. Catherine didn't care for the duke herself. Who made an entire group of knights on horseback sit outside in the cold night air while he chattered on about the Saracens? Just then Jeffrey pushed his destrier between Catherine and Avril.

"The great warrior of the Holy Lands may be good with a broadsword, but he will never be known for his social skills," he muttered to Catherine as he passed. Without another word, Jeffrey rode to a stop side by side with Hugh. The Duke de Neville glanced at Jeffrey, turned his attention back to Hugh, and then turned to stare back at Jeffrey.

A smile, as much as it could be called one, creased the duke's face suddenly. "My good friend!"

Confused, Hugh snapped his head around to find Jeffrey beside him.

"My lordship. You do me a great honor to remember me."

The duke smiled his thin, watery smile. "But of course. How could one forget such a guest as yourself Sir Jeffrey. Indeed, the guests I have entertained here have all lacked greatly since your departure."

Jeffrey laughed. Catherine listened intently, for Jeffrey's laugh had suddenly changed. It was a laugh infused with the sound of power. Where before he had simply slunk away when confronted and appeared to Catherine to be little more than a puppet, his voice now held a completely different tone to it. "I am pleased to be back, my lord."

Post haste they were ushered into the keep. As

opulently as the duke had dressed, the keep was even more opulent. Every wall was hung and double hung with tapestries. Though the rushes seemed overly used to Catherine and the air within the keep smelled acrid and stale, the tables were set with the finest goblets she had ever seen. She found herself escorted to a spacious guest room with a large canopied bed and a warm fire set in the hearth.

Two hours later, she emerged from her rooms ready for the evening meal. She had bathed and changed into a kirtle and tunic in two shades of teal brocade that were trimmed in silver shot braiding to match her slippers. Her hair washed and brushed dry, she had wound half of it into a knot at the back of her head and let the rest of it fall in long, glistening waves down her back. At the top of the stairs she met Hugh, who had also bathed. His face was clean-shaven and he had donned a burgundy tunic over fine gray hose and soft gray boots.

"You look beautiful tonight, Catherine," he told her as he came to stand beside her.

She smiled up at him. "I am much refreshed after a bath. I'm afraid I am not the outdoorswoman I imagined myself to be."

"Nay," he replied. "You are a fine hunter and rider, but a journey is always difficult. One must make do without the simplest of amenities."

"Such as food," Catherine said more to herself

than to Hugh as her growling stomach caught the aroma of grilling meat wafting through the great hall.

Hugh cocked his brow. "What did you say?"

"Nothing," Catherine responded lightly. "Come, Hugh. Jeffrey is already at the table."

Hugh looked down to the table of honor set at the end of the hall. Jeffrey Winfrey sat at the duke's right hand, relaxed and seemingly very at home as he helped himself to a trencher of sweetmeats. There was something here that bothered Hugh. Although he had not said so to Catherine, it was indeed somewhat strange that they had been approached by the sentry today. And if Jeffrey knew the duke so well, why had he said nothing at all until they were in the castle walls? When he *had* come forward, he had carried an air quite different from that of the man Hugh had seen in Avignon and thus far on their trip.

Hugh reached out to take Catherine's hand as they descended the stairs. He saw Jeffrey glance up at them and then lean over to say something into the duke's ear. The duke glanced up at Catherine and gave Jeffrey an iniquitous smile that settled like a piece of steel blade into Hugh's back. There was another muffled exchange between the two men as Hugh approached with Catherine on his arm.

"How lovely you look, my dear," the duke wheezed from between thin lips as they reached the table. "You must do me the honor of sitting beside me tonight. I so infrequently entertain a woman of your beauty.''

Catherine gave him a guarded smile and began to take the seat to his left when the duke rose and indicated that she take the seat he had vacated. It was as smooth an action as Hugh had ever seen. Catherine was now seated between the duke and Jeffrey Winfrey and Hugh was left to take the seat by the duke's other side, which would rightfully place him in a seat of honor as the visiting nobleman.

"You must make yourself at home," the duke commented, giving Hugh a single watery smile. Then he turned his attentions to Catherine.

Leaning back in his chair, Hugh watched the wolfish dance the two men performed on Catherine as the meal progressed. With each course the duke leaned closer. But it seemed to Hugh that his actions were meant solely to push Catherine closer and closer to Jeffrey Winfrey—an objective which he was accomplishing handily. The closer he pressed along Catherine's shoulder the more she leaned toward Jeffrey, affording the knight a fine view of her finely bared neck and softly rounded shoulders. Hugh sipped his spiced wine. It had been liberally fortified with brandy, and was being poured far more freely than was normal for a simple dinner.

Hugh sat back and watched. Every fiber of his being was drawn like a tightly drawn bowstring, waiting for the moment when the two men at the table with him would make their move. For there was no doubt in his mind that they would indeed make a move. The entire evening was too perfectly orchestrated. Something was going to happen. The only thing that bothered Hugh was that he did not know what. So he sat back and watched, taking note of every movement, primed and ready for whatever it was the duke and Jeffrey had planned. But whatever their intent, he knew with a certainty that there was only one thing they had not planned for, and that was him.

A cake, studded with candied fruits and soaked in brandy, was served for dessert. When it was cleared away, the little performance still went on. On the other side of the duke, Jeffrey rested his arm on the back of Catherine's chair and bent over her solicitously as she leaned closer and closer to his chest. The other men were either deep in conversation with their mazers of ale or had retired for the night. In a far corner, Hugh felt a pair of eyes pinion him and he glanced over to find Avril glaring meaningfully at him.

Of one thing Hugh was eminently positive. Avril was loyal to him, but only to the extent that he looked out for Catherine. There was not a minute of their journey that the boy had not kept a careful eye on her. When he was satisfied that she was safe, he was somewhat more relaxed, but the moment he sensed even the smallest threat to his lady, he became like a wolfhound prowling about in search of the smell of danger.

Hugh wondered if Bernard had suggested

Avril as his page intentionally and had given the boy orders to see to her safety at all costs. Whatever the reason, the skinny little page was making it known that he was not pleased with the activities at the head table. Nor was he pleased with Hugh's lack of initiative to put an end to the leering, lecherous attention being lavished on Catherine.

But Hugh waited. It could not be long now.

The Duke de Neville turned to Hugh, suddenly taking an interest in the guest he had pointedly ignored all night. "Sir Hugh," he began. "I have heard your name many times. Even here the fame of Hugh Vougnet is well known."

Hugh smiled and leaned a bit farther back in his chair. He sipped his wine and said nothing. The duke tried again.

"Is it true that you are the new lord of Pontoise? I have heard it is an enormous property. Quite a gift from the king." Hugh cocked a non-committal brow and took another sip of his wine. The duke looked over to the serving maid and nodded for her to fill his goblet. He waited in silence until the wench arrived, then indicated that she should fill Hugh's as well. Hugh watched the maid pour the wine. When she was gone, the duke leaned forward, all artifice suddenly gone. The broad smile that creased his face was flagrantly base. He leaned over to Hugh and intentionally licked his lips.

"She is too gorgeous to bear, isn't she," he said, referring to Catherine. "And she looks so lovely on your arm." He took a long drink of his wine and continued in a casual tone. "I couldn't help noticing how you watch her. And Jeffrey, the dear man, has told me that you have become rather possessive of her. It's a shame," he said carefully putting emphasis on each word, "that you will be wed as soon as you reach Paris."

Hugh's muscles tensed across his back as though an arrow shaft had suddenly impaled itself there. The duke continued his one-sided conversation as though Hugh hadn't reacted at all. "Lady Adele has waited so long for your return. She has spent a fair fortune of your money making improvements to Pontoise since the king granted you the title. All in preparation for your return. And I heard—my sources are quite reliable, you know—that Louis swore to her that the day you returned, the two of you would be wed. Now, how many days ride is it to Paris?" The duke tapped his forehead dramatically. "Two days more." He gave Hugh a sad shake of his head. "So soon."

"I'm sure you've told sweet Catherine all about the Lady Adele, of course," he continued. "It's so good of her, so like her very generous nature, to wish you well. But such a shame. The two of you wed to other people. And I understand your attraction to Catherine. After all, I've met Adele de Pisan. She's nothing like Lady Catherine, is she?

"So pious and good. It makes up for her plain features, doesn't it? And none of this fine lady's fire and sparkle. She'll be so pleased to have her

God-loving knight back. So proud of all the Saracen blood you've spilt."

Hugh's fingers had tightened around the bowl of his goblet till his knuckles stood out white against the jewel-studded gold. "How do you know all this to be true?" he demanded.

"Oh, I know," the duke replied. "You see, I've made you somewhat of a hobby."

"You have an overaffection for men?" Hugh said as he took another sip of wine. "You must visit Jerusalem. It is a common practice among the infidels."

The duke's nostrils flared in angered afrontery. "Quite the opposite, my dear *knight,*" he said, emphasizing Hugh's lesser title. "Women are a preoccupation of mine. You don't remember me, do you?" It was almost a challenge, and Hugh looked at him carefully, taken by surprise at his inference that he *should* know him.

"No, I didn't think you did. But I remember you. As soon as my guards spotted your banner marching toward my castle, I knew who was coming to grace my humble castle." His smile grew tight and hard and his eyes glistened with cold hatred as he spoke. "It was in Paris. I had spent months there acting as Louis's personal doormat. Ingratiating myself to the king. And for what? Only one thing. This castle. This land that I inherited from my father is so damned far away from everything! Oh, it's fine and grand and I have the money to fill it with objects that please me. But who ever comes here? Passing travelers?

Beggars? Pilgrims on their way to Jerusalem or merchants going to Florence and Genoa? But ladies? Noblemen? Never!

"I was in Paris to curry Louis's favor. There was a castle that I wanted. And I wanted it badly. It is grand and imperial and *close!* So close to Paris and court. Why, the nobility pass by it everyday. Everyone loves it. Everyone knows it. Oh!" he said, and his voice cracked with his feverish desire. "I wanted Pontoise! And it was almost mine! Louis had mentioned it just the night before. Told me he wanted me closer to Paris. Mentioned that perhaps it would be better if I had land nearby. I could feel it. I could smell it. Pontoise was mine, and with it, all the prestige. My castle would be filled with women. And they would see my gold, my jewels. They would fall at my feet. I could have any one of them I desired.

"But, no. You arrived. Fresh from the battlefield and full of good news for the king. You'd routed Gilbert Cahuzac. Destroyed the troops he'd rallied to break with Louis. The king's lands were secure. Gilbert Cahuzac was dead. The land to the north was safe.

"What did you say to Louis that night?" he demanded, slamming his goblet on the table. Wine slopped over the rim and soaked the arm of his bejeweled sleeve, but the Duke de Neville didn't notice. "Did you tell him that you desired Pontoise? And did he tell you he would give it to you?

"You stole my castle from me! He sent me back here, to this isolated hell. Because of you."

Hugh looked at the flushed, thin face of the duke. He was the worst kind of man. A dangerous man. Not because he was cunning or determined. Hugh had fought a lifetime of men like that and they were men he respected. This man was small and petty and he would use any trickery or thievery to inflict injury on anything or anyone that Hugh's life touched. Normally that would not have bothered Hugh in the least. He knew many men such as the Duke de Neville. Men who lusted after Hugh's successes. And until now, he had never given them a moment's thought, for they held no threat to him.

But the Duke de Neville had found a chink in Hugh's armor. And he had made it clear that if he could not hurt Hugh, he would hurt someone else.

He would hurt Catherine.

Twelve

Catherine shifted uneasily in her chair as the knight beside her leaned solicitously over her. His arm had cupped itself around her shoulders and one stubby, nail-bitten finger trailed a path from the base of her neck to her earlobe and back again with an irksome repetition. Before, when the duke had been breathing down her dress and outright caressed her thigh twice, she had chosen what she felt was the lesser of two evils. However Jeffrey's "protection," as he had so accommodatingly offered to her, had not diminished in the least since the duke had turned his attentions to Hugh. In fact, it continued to increase, and Catherine was not in the least deceived that his intentions were for her protection at all.

"Sir Jeffrey," Catherine said, swatting at an imaginary insect in the vicinity of his hand. "You are a good friend of the duke's, are you not?"

"Indeed. He is indebted to me."

Catherine smiled sweetly at him. "Do you think, then, that you could use that influence to convince him to change the rushes here? I have been plagued all night by some bothersome bug creeping up and down my neck, and it has become so vexing to me that I'm afraid I must retire for the evening ere I am forced to jump from my seat and kill the meddlesome creature forthwith!"

The finger on her neck came to a sudden and complete halt. Jeffrey Winfrey cleared his throat and helped himself to a long draught of ale. "I should be more than happy to speak to him."

"Oh, thank you so much. Now, I'm afraid I must retire. It has been such a *long* day, and Hugh has told me that tomorrow will be equally as long."

"You must allow me to escort you to your rooms," Jeffrey insisted.

"No, you have been too kind already this evening. I'll be fine," Catherine assured him, rising quickly. It was her plan to move as quickly as possible, hoping that Jeffrey had imbibed enough of the wine and ale to make him slow. But her plan did not work as she had hoped. Jeffrey was on his feet in a moment. Leaning close, he bent to whisper in her ear, but his words carried a steel edge to them.

"I insist, dear Catherine. There may be *bugs.*"

Catherine gave a panicky glance in Hugh's direction, but found him staring, blind-eyed, across the room as though he did not even know where he was. She looked to the far corner of the room where she'd last seen Avril whittling a twig, but he had disappeared. Before she could muster some sort of attention in the Great Hall, Jeffrey took her firmly by the elbow and propelled her toward the stairs. As they climbed toward the upper level leading to the bedchambers, he pulled her close against him. She could hear his rasping breath in her ear and feel its rancid heat against the sensitive skin of her neck.

"Really, Jeffrey, this isn't necessary," Catherine said as they moved down the dark corridor. "You have been overly kind this evening."

"Then surely you would not begrudge me the smallest of rewards, my dearest Catherine."

"I can't imagine . . ."

"Oh, I think you can. Or do you save all your kisses only for Hugh Vougnet?" Taken by surprise, Catherine reacted sharply to his words. "I see my guess was right. You deny me the sweetness of your affections, but give them freely to Vougnet. It isn't quite as you told me then, is it, sweet Catherine? That you cannot share your favors because you are betrothed."

"I *am* betrothed!" Catherine told him as her panic mounted. They were nearly at her door and the hallway was dark, lit only by the infrequent torch in its iron sleeve along the cold stone walls.

"Ah, but so many are betrothed. Or married! It matters not, my dear. I learned long ago that the vows of matrimony matter only to the pope and his clergymen. I have soothed the needs of many wives and fiancés. I am the most proficient of lovers. Vougnet cannot be half the lover I am."

"Hugh is *not* my lover!" Catherine insisted. She stopped where she was in the hallway. She would not go on. She would not allow Jeffrey Winfrey to take her one step closer to her rooms. "You may well entice lonely widows of the wars, Jeffrey. But I am not one of them. I am betrothed and I will go to my husband-to-be a virgin. I will love him and be faithful to him always."

Even as she said the words she knew the lie of them.

She had never before thought of her marriage that way. She would stand before a priest and promise her fidelity, but it would not be true because she loved Hugh. She had loved him from the moment she'd met him. Loved him year in and year out while he was in Jerusalem. Loved him even more when he had returned. Loved him now.

Jeffrey Winfrey felt the falseness of her words as well and a smile of triumph lit his eyes. "You see, Catherine, we are all the same. We promise to be one thing, but we never are. We take vows, we speak words, but we will never live them. The flesh is so weak!

"I said I would go to the Holy Lands, but why would I go to such a godforsaken place when I could eat succulent sweets in the emperor's palace on the Bosporus and satiate my body on the flesh of doe-eyed women who were there for my taking? And now I return to France a hero! A victor! A Crusader! I am no worse than any other man. I am better, because I admit the truth. It

is all falseness, what we are. We say we will reach
for the goals of godliness and goodness, but we
are prisoners of our base needs." He gave her a
resigned smile and lifted his shoulder in a gesture of the inevitable. "What is worse, Catherine? To admit the truth, or to hide it?"

Catherine shook her head in denial of his
words. All the world was not as he described it.
There was love and honesty. There were noble
causes and men who lived them. Hugh was such
a man. And perhaps a man such as Jeffrey Winfrey could not see the sterling qualities in men
like Hugh. Perhaps that was why they glared with
hatred at them when they were not looking, or
cast about for ways to thwart them at every turn.
Catherine did not know, nor did she care. She
did not believe what he was saying. If she was
weak, if she loved a man she could not have,
then that was her weakness. It did not reflect on
Hugh. And she would go to Strasbourg. She
would marry the baron there and be a faithful
and good wife. And if on some lonely nights she
thought of Hugh, if she included him in her
prayers, then that was her own cross to bear.

"So kiss me, Catherine." In the darkened hallway, Jeffrey pulled her to him. His lips were
upon hers. Wet and hot they pressed down upon
her mouth. His tongue forced its way into her
mouth violating her in a way that made her feel
ill with revulsion.

Catherine wedged her hands against his shoulders and pushed with all her might, but Jeffrey

had waited too long, plotted too carefully, and was too certain of his victory. He had not lost before when he chose to pursue a lady. If they resisted, he was always bigger than they. Stronger. And although Catherine was the finest prey he had ever dared to hunt, he did not consider defeat. He understood a woman's frailties too well. He knew their darkest side, the needs that drove them, that could make them succumb to his control. They might say no, they might shove and cry and declare that they wanted none of it. But their cries always turned to moans. The clawing to keep him away turned to grasping nails that pulled him closer. He knew how to make them writhe and beg. He knew what it was they liked. He knew how to make them pay. His mother had taught him well.

Catherine shoved harder, but Jeffrey only pulled her closer. His tongue plundered her mouth like something thrust forcefully into a foreign place. Her neck ached from the force of his assault and she heard the sound of fabric ripping and felt cold air rush down her belly as he rent her clothing. His dry, calloused hand scraped across one breast and he moaned into her mouth as he squeezed the tender flesh.

Tears sprang into her eyes as she fought to get him away. This could not happen, her mind screamed. This could not happen. Jeffrey lifted her from the ground and, with his tongue still plunged into her mouth, began to drag her toward her chambers. Catherine bit down hard on the member that was gagging her. Jeffrey yanked his mouth away from hers, and for a moment Catherine gulped down air with relief. But her respite was short-lived.

"So you like for it to hurt, do you?" he said with a cold glint in his eyes. "I know how to do that, too." In one swift movement he dug his fingers into her scalp and snapped her head back with such force that she thought her neck was surely broken. Bending over her, he began to suckle at her breast. Then with vicious intent, he bit her.

Catherine would have screamed if her throat had not been stretched to the breaking point. Jeffrey's face came back into view before her. His mouth was just inches away. "Do you like it, Catherine? You must, for I did not hear you scream in pain. That's good. I'll make you quiver with agony. I'll hear you beg me to go on. You will never have a lover like me, Catherine. And lovers we will be.

"I will come to visit you at your *abbaye*. That will be even more exciting, won't it? The abbess and all her pious little nuns will be teaching you to be the devoutest of wives and beneath their very roof I will be teaching you how to lust after pain." Pulling back, he eyed her sadly. "I think I will miss you when it's time for you to go to your decrepit old man in Germany. Even in Constantinople I never saw a woman the equal of you. You are incomparable, Catherine. Incomparable. But if you are smart," he added "you'll show your baron what I teach you. It will make him a very happy man, I promise you."

"Jeffrey, don't do this," Catherine begged. "Hugh has vowed to protect me. He would be bound to kill you," she reasoned, trying somehow to create a tiny doubt in his consciousness. In an instant his fingers closed around her neck, cutting off her breath until she began to hear the very throbbing of her lifeblood slowing in her ears.

"Hugh will never know, will he?" he whispered in her ear. "Will he, Catherine?" It took all the strength she had to move her head back and forth once. He released her throat and life flowed into her once more. "Now," he said quietly. "Invite me into your chambers."

Catherine knew she couldn't do it. She would rather die here in the dark hallway of this strange castle than willingly let this madman use her. She opened her mouth to tell him so, but the rush of wind just inches above her head stopped her as an arrow imbedded itself in the cross-timber not a hairbreadth from Jeffrey's ear.

The knight released her like she was some forgotten plaything, his head jerking around to stare down the hall stupefied. "What—"

Avril stood less than two rods from them. In his hands he held a drawn crossbow, aimed at Jeffrey Winfrey's heart. "Get away from her!" he commanded in a voice that shook.

"Why, you snot-nosed little knave," Jeffrey breathed. "I'll break every bone in your spindly body." He turned on the page, every ounce of power in his knight's body emanating fury.

"Don't come a step closer, Sir Winfrey!" Avril warned. He pulled back another inch on the crossbow, but the weapon shook in his hand, the arrowhead unsteady on its target.

"You think you scare me, *boy*? A knight of the Crusades?" He took another step closer. Avril backed up.

"You didn't go to the Crusades!" Avril shot back.

A maniacal laugh came from Jeffrey. "And you think that makes you a match for me?" He advanced on the page again.

"Don't. I warn you, sir. You have threatened my mistress and I will kill you if you do not turn now and leave. I am giving you this chance, Sir Jeffrey, to save your life."

Jeffrey roared and threw himself at the twelve-year-old page. Catherine screamed, at last able to find her voice as he landed on Avril and the two rolled to the rushes. In the darkness, she heard a gurgling groan. Sir Jeffrey rolled onto his side, revealing the arrow that had impaled itself in his chest.

Catherine ran to Avril, pulling the boy up by his tunic. "Are you all right?" she demanded frantically. The boy could only nod dazedly. Beside them, Jeffrey groaned again. Blood dripped from his mouth and blended with the oozing redness that poured from his bosom. "I am going to die!" he cried in disbelief. "I am going

to die because of you and your stupid chivalry,
boy!

"Don't you know, boy? Don't you know she's
no different than any other woman? She's giving
it away to that pious, lying dolt you think is so
God-fearing and noble. Giving it away! Do you
hear me? And you're killing me because I
wanted a little taste of her, too." He laughed—a
wheezing laugh that used his last breath and
then he lay still.

Catherine and Avril sat in the hallway staring
at the dead man beside them. A chilly draft
passed down the hall and Catherine gathered the
torn bodice of her kirtle and tunic into some
semblance of modesty. Despite her efforts, she
was suddenly cold. Her skin began to crawl and
her limbs to shake uncontrollably. Avril, as well,
was shaking. Catherine pulled him against her.
"You are a fool," she told him and then she began to cry. "He would have killed you."

"No," Avril responded quietly. "I knew I was
going to kill him."

"What shall we do now?" Catherine asked after a long silence. "If we tell anyone that Jeffrey
is dead, the duke . . ."

"We can't tell anyone," Avril concluded. "He
was the duke's friend and we are on his land.
He could have us killed, for he would not believe
that we had a reason."

Catherine nodded. Pulling herself up onto her
knees and then her feet, she dragged Avril up
with her. "I can burn the rushes that have his

blood on them, and you can put the crossbow back from wherever you got it. But neither of us is strong enough to carry him away. And where would we put him?" Catherine stared down at the corpse in futility. "There's no use, Avril. Any minute someone will come down the hall and find us here."

"No," the young page stated emphatically. "I know two of the other pages who hold no love for Sir Jeffrey. I trust them. Can you wait here while I go to wake them?" Catherine did not know what else to do, so she nodded. "I will be back in an instant," Avril called back to her in a loud whisper as he began running down the hall.

Catherine stood dazed in the middle of the hall for several minutes. Her mind could not take in all that had occurred. Was it hours ago that she had tried to leave the Great Hall or merely moments? She could not think how much time had passed, only what had occurred here. She felt dirty and violated, and the more she stared at the stiffening body of Jeffrey Winfrey, the less real it all seemed to her. Yet here she stood beside the dead body of a man she had spent the evening talking with. If someone was to approach now, she would, no doubt, be stoned to death in the courtyard of the Duke de Neville's castle.

The sound of scurrying footsteps jerked her from her daydreams. Her heart began to pound in fear, yet she stood rooted to her place, unable to run from her discoverers.

Avril and two other pages appeared in the torchlight. While Avril inquired about Catherine, the two other boys stared gape-mouthed at the man by their feet. "By all that's holy, Avril. You've killed a knight of King Louis's!"

Impatiently, Avril brushed their awe away, creating an even greater awe in his friends. "Are you with me? Will you help my lady in her distress?" Both boys nodded vigorously. "Then grab a leg," Avril ordered.

The two did as ordered, then one, a bit older than the other, straightened and shook his head. "Nay, Avril. This will not work. What are we to do? Drag him bumping and thumping down the front stairs and through the Great Hall?"

"Do you have another plan?" Catherine asked.

He nodded. "We're not far from one of the turrets. If we can get him out there we can toss him over the wall into the moat. It will be days before they find him, if they ever do."

"There's a good plan," the other page agreed. Each one taking a booted leg, they turned Jeffrey around and began pulling him farther down the hall. Avril hauled on both arms at once, but Catherine could not stand there helpless while these three young boys chanced certain death over the deed they were committing. Brushing Avril away from one arm, she began to pull along with the rest of them. Between the four of them, it took only a few minutes to pull the knight out onto the walkway between two turrets. Propping him up against the wall, they worked first one leg and then the other over the lip of the wall until, at last, the bulk of his weight took him over the edge. There was a loud splash and they all held their breath waiting for a sentry to call attention to the noise. But it was late and the castle guards were used to little danger coming to the keep, for no one called an alarm at the noise.

Catherine ran back into the hall and gathered up the bloodied rushes. Thrusting them into the fire in her room, she watched the last vestiges of Jeffrey Winfrey curl into smoke. When there was not a single piece of straw left in the hearth, she went back into the hall. The pages had spread other rushes in the place where Jeffrey had died, and there was no sign at all that the man had ever been there. Avril had taken the crossbow. Catherine did not ask him where it came from, nor did she wish to know. She wanted to forget everything about this night. She wanted to imagine that it had never, ever occurred. She did not know what they would say about Jeffrey's disappearance tomorrow. She would simply say she didn't know. Avril had protected her. She would protect him, no matter what the cost.

Thirteen

"By all that is holy," Hugh swore under his breath. "When I *do* find Winfrey, I'll hang him by his toes like a game bird!" He was in a black mood this morning. First, two horses had come up lame, making it necessary for them to delay an early departure. And now Jeffrey Winfrey had disappeared.

"Avril!" he barked.

"My lord?"

"Where is Lady Catherine?"

"In the chapel, sir, attending Mass before we depart. The services are just starting if you wish to go."

Hugh shook his head. He had not attended Mass since returning to France, and he had no desire to do so now. There was much he didn't want to say in confession. "By the way," he added. "What happened last night."

Avril could feel his hair stand on end. "Last night, my lord? What do you mean?"

Hugh shot him a look of deep frustration. "I saw you follow Catherine and Sir Jeffrey out last night. I assume you saw to it that she made it safely to her rooms."

Relieved, Avril nodded vigorously. "I did, my lord."

"And you haven't seen him since then?"

"No, sir."

Hugh glared at him. "What is wrong with you?" he demanded. "You're usually so full of things to say—remonstrations and who knows what. And today you're acting like the cat has gotten your tongue! I wouldn't be surprised if there wasn't a full moon tonight," he grumbled to himself. "The whole place is acting bewitched."

Avril shrugged. "May I return to my work, my lord? I have much to accomplish."

"Yes, go!" Hugh muttered irritably. "And get Catherine on her horse the moment the Mass is ended."

"I think that will be easily accomplished," Avril stated quietly as he walked in the direction of the stables.

Hugh stared after him. "Now, what did that mean?" he wondered aloud. But he didn't have time to think about the curious statement, for out of the corner of one eye he spotted the Duke de Neville approaching.

"I pray you slept well?" the duke inquired, coming to stand beside him. It was a sickeningly sweet query, the kind Hugh had learned many years before was not sincere.

"Very well, thank you."

The duke looked up, examining the clear blue sky with exaggerated interest. "A grand day for a journey, don't you agree?" Hugh made no comment. "Especially back into the arms of the woman you are to wed . . ." He didn't bother to look at Hugh as he spoke, choosing, instead, to gaze in interest at the activities in the bailey as he stood beside Hugh, his hands clasped behind his back. "I was so pleased that we had a chance to talk last night. I feel that much was accomplished, don't you, Sir Hugh?"

"If you are implying that based on your interests in Pontoise, you believe I might go to Louis and tell him I do not want the estate and the title that goes with it," Hugh stated calmly, "you have misinterpreted our discussion."

The duke's posture stiffened visibly. "Then you have not thought out all of the possible ramifications, Monsieur Vougnet. My influences are substantial, and my desire to have Pontoise ardent."

Hugh turned to the duke. His face was as unreadable as stone and his manner deadly calm. "I, too, have spheres of influence. Or have I neglected to mention that fact? But that is of no matter, because threats have never impressed me. I have dealt with them often and I find them, inevitably, to be far less of a hazard than the events that come without warning. Pontoise is mine, Lord Bueil. Make no mistake. And I protect what is mine at any cost." Not waiting for a reply, Hugh walked away from the duke, leaving him to stew in his fury.

Staring after Hugh's broad, unyielding back, the duke's anger rose to a new pitch. He had given up all hope of owning Pontoise until Jeffrey Winfrey had planted the seed of a plot in his fertile mind. He was not going to lose what should have been his again. There were many ways to achieve his end, many indeed. And Hugh Vougnet was a fool if he thought that a rude refusal would suffice to stop his plans.

Spinning on his heels, the duke nearly collided with a serving boy in his haste to return to the keep. "Get out of my way, you stupid oaf!" he bellowed, backhanding the boy in the side of the head. The lad sputtered an apology and made haste to get out of the duke's reach. "On second thought, come back here! Find me Sir Jeffrey Winfrey and bring him to me at once in my chambers."

The boy scampered off to do as directed while the duke continued into the keep, calling for his scribe as soon as he was inside the hall. "Take a message," he ordered.

"And to whom shall your message be delivered?" inquired the scribe.

"To Lady Adele de Pisan. She is in residence at the castle in Pontoise."

Hugh did not have the patience to wait any longer. Wherever Sir Jeffrey had gone, he had not bothered to tell anyone. As the morning had wasted away in the search for the self-absorbed knight, Hugh had learned that he had sent his page off on some unknown errand the day before. And now Jeffrey had disappeared himself with nary a word to anyone about where he was going or when he might rejoin them.

"Avril, leave word with Lord Bueil that Sir Jeffrey can either meet us farther along the route to Paris or return to his home, as he chooses." Seeing his page hasten to do as he bid, Hugh swung around in his saddle searching for Catherine who waved to him from atop her mare. Galloping over to her side, he signaled to the men that they were making their departure.

As they clattered over the drawbridge, Catherine felt the palms of her hands go damp and the hairs on her neck stand on end. She dared not look into the muddy waters of the moat below them for fear she would see the blank, deadman's stare of Sir Jeffrey gaping up at her.

Like the day before, the sky was clear and bright, and with each mile that fell between them and the duke's castle, she was able to breathe a little easier. Still, the events of the previous night weighed on her emotions and she rode in silence all through the morning.

At noon they stopped to eat a light repast. There was little time for a fire and warm food, for they had time to make up for the earlier delays. The men did not even bother to sit down, but pulled dried beef and hard crusts of bread from their packs which they washed down with warm ale that they carried in animal skins. Seated in a patch of sunlight upon the small coverlet Hugh had laid for her, Catherine watched them as they gnawed on the desiccated meat and her appetite dwindled.

"Are you ready to eat?" Hugh asked, coming up behind her.

"I don't really think I'm hungry today."

"Not hungry? This from the maiden who near to bowled me over at the mere smell of food last night?"

Catherine couldn't help but laugh at the thought. "I'm afraid my tastes run to the succulent and toothsome with a sprinkling of sweets included. Not the fare of travelers," she explained somewhat sheepishly. "Although I do not mind at all, Hugh."

"Then let me entice you."

Catherine turned to look at him in bewilderment and discovered a repast fit, if not for a queen—then surely a princess, spread out before her. Upon the head of his battle-ax Hugh had arranged a miniature wheel of fine, buttery cheese and a cluster of red grapes still fresh from the harvest. Beside them were a pair of soft, freshly baked rolls and a tiny crock of butter blended with thyme and parsley as well as a comb of honey that had begun to run in the warm sunlight.

"Hugh!" she cried in delight. "Where did you get such a feast?"

" 'Twas a small thing to bribe Bueil's cook into packing something delectable for a lovely lady," he replied, smiling over her obvious pleasure at his surprise.

Catherine dipped a slender finger into the honey and licked the sweetness away. She closed her eyes and turned her face heavenward, savoring this unique moment as much as the taste of the sweet. The sun was shining and she was with Hugh. Catherine could not think of any other thing that she truly desired in all the world.

The image of Jeffrey Winfrey's corpse intruded on her peace, and Catherine forced it from her mind. If only she could keep the world at bay for a few more days, she thought. Just until they reached Chantilly. *Let me have these hours,* she prayed silently. *Just these few hours to make up for a lifetime without him.* She opened her eyes to find Hugh staring down at her. Slowly, he dropped to bended knee and bent beside her. She thought he would kiss her again, as he had in the forest and, before then, in Avignon. But he did not. He reached across her to slice a wedge of cheese for her. Ripping open a roll, he spread the cheese across the fine crumb and handed it to her.

"For my lady," he said softly.

"Am I indeed your lady?" she asked.

But Hugh's only reply was, "Eat well, it will be another long ride to the next fiefdom."

Catherine bit her lip anxiously. "Must we stay

at another keep? I think the fresh night air is so
much more appealing."

Hugh eyed her in disbelief. "You would rather
sleep on the ground, in a tent, than in a warm
bed beneath a featherquilt?" He shook his head.
"Even if that were true, I have seen that you
would rather starve than eat cured beef and
warm ale."

Catherine cast about for some explanation
and, at last, decided that the truth was best told.
"Hugh, I did not care for the Duke de Neville.
I'm sorry to be blunt, but the man behaved no
better than a lecher last night. I know not all
keeps are the abode of men such as he, but, in
truth, I don't care to discover that the next one—
or the one after that—are. You said to me yourself that one never knows who abides in the fiefs
when you stop."

Hugh seemed to consider Catherine's words
carefully, and at last he nodded. "Lord Bueil was,
indeed, a strange host—though I have seen my
share," he added. "If it was my choice, I would
always spend my nights beneath the heavens, and
if you are telling me that such is your preference
as well, then so be it."

Catherine breathed a sigh of relief. "Thank
you, Hugh."

Reaching out, he took her hand in his and
kissed the back of it gently. "It is the least I can
do for my lady."

Catherine's heart leapt with joy at his words.
She knew that they would each go their sepa-

rate ways soon, but knowing that she loved him, it was her fervent desire that she should hear him say that he loved her in return. Glancing toward the group of knights gathered ten rods away, Catherine's brow creased with a frown. "Do they think our friendship unseemly?" she asked Hugh.

"They have only seen us ride together and share a meal or two. I do not think such things would be considered untoward," he replied.

"And you?"

"I?" Hugh responded benignly.

"Yes," Catherine said softly. "Do you think it unseemly that we spend so much time together when I am betrothed to another man?"

Hugh picked up a twig and slowly twirled it between his fingers in silence as Catherine waited for his reply. She had not been able to banish the image of Jeffrey Winfrey all day and neither had she been able to purge from her thoughts the fact that he believed she and Hugh were lovers. Had he believed so because such were the workings of his twisted mind, or because her feelings toward Hugh were so plain for all to see? She needed to know if Hugh believed others thought as Jeffrey had.

Catherine waited as the silence spun out into a long thread and Hugh's lack of a response became like a growing ache in her side.

"There is no reason for them to think so," he told her at last. "They know you are on your way to the *abbaye* and from there to Strasbourg, where you will be wed. I would not be overly concerned."

Catherine nodded and asked nothing more, but Hugh's reply left her uneasy. They shared the meal Hugh had packed for her and wiled away the afternoon ride talking about inane, unimportant things. While the sun was still high on the horizon a few hours later, Hugh gave orders for camp to be made.

"I thought we would ride till well after dark," she told Hugh in surprise at his decision. "Did we make up so much time this afternoon?"

Hugh shook his head. "Nay, we are a little behind schedule. But if we arrive a day late, the nuns will not be overly concerned. It is common for journeyers to be delayed. Besides, it will be good to have some fresh meat tonight. I intend to take Baston and Grier with me and see if between the three of us, we can't find a fine buck. You wouldn't turn down a venison dinner, would you?" he inquired with a wink.

Catherine laughed in return. "Nay, my lord. As you know, I have the appetite of an overgrown sow."

Hugh looked her up and down and shook his head. "But where are you putting all this food, Cay? You are as tiny as a sparrow."

"Ah, but I am as solid as a boulder to carry," she quipped.

"I shall be the judge of that." Swinging down from Cepheus's back, Hugh reached up to lift Catherine down from her saddle. Her waist was tiny, for his fingers touched when he encircled it. He could have carried her with one hand, had he chosen. There was nothing about Catherine that was not perfect, he thought as she slid to the ground beside him. She was as finely boned as a bird and equally as light. Her eyes were intensely green, like a mountain lion's, and her skin was the tone and texture of fresh cream. Red-gold curls spilled down her back, glistening in the sunlight. If he could, he would have pulled her against him. He would have crushed the fine silk of her locks in his hand and wooed her with gentle kisses showered over every inch of her sweet self. He yearned to tell her that simply being near her lifted every fiber within him to a fevered pitch that left him aching with need. Yet he did none of those things.

Hugh set her gently on the ground. They stood inches apart, not touching. "You are as light as a feather," he said softly. Without another word, he turned and walked away.

Moments later Avril appeared at Catherine's side. "I'll pitch your tent, but it will take a bit. Shall I build a fire for you in the meanwhile?"

"Nay, Avril," Catherine asserted. "You treat me as though I were incapable of fending for myself! Go about your work and don't worry about me."

"Lady Catherine?" Avril queried in a low voice. "Are you all right? I mean, with everything that happened last night . . ." His voice trailed off.

"Are you?" she asked.

Avril squared his shoulders and gave her a sharp, decisive nod. "I would do it again."

Catherine smiled at him. "I know you would, Avril. Thank you."

Gladmoore, a hulking man who had been in her father's service for as long as Catherine could remember, strode toward her. His over-sized head hung between his shoulders as though he was trying to make himself inconspicuous and his face bore an expression of self-conscious discomfort. "Lady Catherine," he said, ducking his head sheepishly, "might I have the pleasure of your company in a game of dames?"

Catherine gave the vassal a sidelong glance. "You have a set of dames pieces here, in the middle of nowhere?" she asked, referring to the checkered boardgame that was a popular pastime.

"I do, milady. I enjoy playing when I have the chance. It comes rarely enough, you know."

"And among all the men we are traveling with, there isn't a single one who would play with you?"

Kicking a stray rock with his boot, Gladmoore wrung his hands like an errant boy and shrugged. " 'Twould be an honor to play with you, milady."

"I should be delighted, Gladmoore. Will you confess why you asked me."

" 'Tis better if we all spend a bit of time with

you, Lady Catherine. The others and I have been talking," he said, the confession coming in a burst at last. "Who's to say where Sir Jeffrey has gotten to. And he made much yesterday of your friendship with Lord Hugh. If he comes back we can say, in truth, that we all spent time with you."

Catherine nodded silently. "Then you are concerned for my reputation?"

"Nay, milady!" he declared, blushing crimson. "Lord Hugh is trusted by all. We don't believe that pack of lies! But it would be better for you to play a little game of dames with me. You are the only woman among us. It is always best to make it difficult for tongues to wag."

When Hugh, Baston, and Grier returned after dark with a freshly killed stag in hand, it was to round upon round of raucous laughter sprinkled with roars of approval and a few colorful curses. Riding up to the campfire where the group of vassals had crowded around the firelight, Hugh nudged Wesley du Fonte's shoulder with his toe. "Who wins at dice?" he asked.

Wesley looked up at him and grinned. " 'Tis not dice, Hugh. Lady Catherine has roundly trounced Gladmoore thrice in dames, and he's the best dames player in all Avignon! Ha!" he crowed. " 'Tis a fine comeuppance for him!"

Dismounting, Hugh stepped into the circle of watchers as Catherine jumped Gladmoore's last king.

"Crown me, please," she said with a gleam of victory in her eye.

"Mademoiselle," Gladstone protested. "How have you won *again*? 'Tis some unfair advantage you have."

Laughing good-naturedly, Catherine winked at him. "You did not ask me the level of my skill at the game before you so kindly asked me to play. I did not know that losing was a prerequisite of playing with you. The men hooted boisterously at Gladstone's obvious embarrassment and slapped him amiably on the back. "Shall we play again?" she asked. "A good winner always offers a chance for her opponent to redeem himself."

"Nay, my lady," Gladstone said, rising from his stump. Perhaps some other unsuspecting dolt would like a chance."

"You play against her, my lord." Avril gave Hugh a quick jab in the ribs.

"Yes, Hugh," Catherine called. "Come play."

Hugh opened his mouth to say no, but the sight of Catherine's shining face smiling happily up at him changed his mind. Taking Gladstone's place at the makeshift table, Hugh settled his elbow on one knee and watched Catherine set the game up. The group of men quieted in anticipation of a challenging game.

"You have replaced the loser, therefore you may make the first move," Catherine told him.

Hugh cocked one thick eyebrow at her as he

reached for his man. " 'Tis a leniency you shall regret, Cay."

The game progressed with the players carefully contemplating their moves. Each turn was greeted by grunts of approval or doubt from the gathered men as Hugh and Catherine proceeded to match each other move for move. When at last Hugh took her last king, he thought he had her beat, but in a sly move, she used her last remaining men to defeat him.

"Hugh, you never told me you were such a skilled player!" Catherine commented with a warm smile. "You must play often."

Hugh looked down at the game board, remembering how Adele had implored him to give up the vice. That had been over six years ago, and since that time he had never sat down to any game—be it dames, dice, tables, or chess. He looked at the affable faces of the men around him and across the board at Catherine. What was the evil in a game? He had never understood, but Adele would quote verses to him and speak to the priest about his lack of devoutness. And so, like so much else, he had acquiesced at last. Now he could feel the presence of Adele's disapproval like a palatable poison in the night air. Every day he came closer and closer to Adele and it was as though he could feel her watching him. As though he could hear her disapprovals and condemnations. All that he wasn't. All that he should be. Everything that was wrong with Hugh Vougnet.

"Here." Hugh reached into the purse threaded to his belt and pulled out a gold coin. "The winner must have a reward." Tossing the coin onto the game board, he stood and walked away. The men parted to let him through and Hugh continued past the tents and horses and out into the darkness.

Catherine stared down at the gold sovereign that still spun on the board before her. Her cheeks burned crimson in embarrassment.

"Milady, he meant nothing by it," Du Fonte assured her gently.

" 'Tis just a jest on his part," averred Baston Sutony.

Grabbing the coin, Catherine ran out into the darkness after him.

"Hugh!" she cried, breathless from her pursuit. He strode over the rough ground of the frozen field without looking back. But that only made Catherine run faster. Grabbing up a handful of her kirtle, she chased him with long-legged strides, the coin clutched in her palm. "Hugh! Stop!" she called.

"Go back, Catherine." His words were cold and hard and edged with some other emotion that Catherine could not quite identify. But she was not going back, not until she had said what she had come to say.

"Your coin, Lord Vougnet," she said, holding out the gold piece as if it was animal dung she touched. Hugh just looked at it without making any move to take it. "Then let it rot in the ground," she told him. She let the coin drop onto the uneven grass between them. "Tell me, Hugh, what did I do to warrant such a betrayal? You entered into the game of free will. No one said you must. And you played of your free will. Was it because I won that anger replaced your good humor? I don't think so.

"Was it because I was enjoying myself? Or, perhaps, was it because *you* were enjoying yourself? Why is it so wrong to enjoy life? Who told you that it was? Over and over again I have seen you laugh loudly, seen happiness emerge from within your soul. But you always snatch it away, as if you don't deserve it. As if it is somehow wrong to be joyous.

"Let me say something to you, Hugh. So that you know. So that for all time you know this one thing. You bring me joy. You make my heart fill to near bursting with pleasure and joy whenever I am with you. I know we cannot be together. I know I am betrothed and that we will part and never see each other again, but it does not change the fact that I love you."

Hugh's head, which had hung in shame as she spoke, snapped up. " 'Tis true, Hugh," she continued, her voice softening as green-eyed and blue-eyed gazes locked. "I love you."

As though they had a will of their own, a will separate and distinct from the one he struggled to force upon himself, Hugh's hands reached out for her. *Dear God,* he prayed even as he pulled her into his arms, *forgive me.* He crushed her to him. She was as soft as velvet, as warm as fire, as live, and sensual and real as anything he had ever known.

Her arms curled around his shoulders and he felt the soft movement of her fingers twining in his hair. She turned her face up to him willingly and his gaze met hers. Hugh felt himself drowning in emerald pools that spoke to him of acceptance and warmth. He plunged his face into her neck, breathing in the scent of her—fresh and sweet and warm. His lips tasted the subtle saltiness of her skin, caressed its warmth.

"Catherine." It was a moan torn from his soul. Never had he needed anything as he needed her. She was the realization of dreams he had long ago stopped believing in. He heard her whisper his name and he pulled her closer against him, molding their bodies together. Creating one being from two. His mouth covered hers and he felt her lips part, offering him welcome. It was like paradise. Warm and soft as nothing else could possibly be. His tongue ran along the inner edge of her lip and then dipped to find her own enticing tongue. They twined. They mingled. They gave completely of themselves. Hugh felt the heat of his need wash over him like crashing ocean waves. He needed Catherine. Her laughter. Her warmth. Her love.

"I love you." The words tore strong and absolute from his very soul. His love for her was more real than the stars overhead. More real than the very ground upon which they stood. In this moment there was no Adele. No obligations. No world of rules and rings and vows to be taken. There was only Catherine and his singular, total love for her.

"I love you." He whispered the words against her mouth, his breath coming in ragged gulps. He dug his fingers into her long, perfumed tresses and pressed her cheek against his chest. He closed his eyes and drew a deep draught of night air. "I love you." Hugh pressed a kiss on her soft, unfurrowed brow and held her close. *Forgive me, God.*

Fourteen

When Catherine and Hugh returned to the encampment, the men were engrossed in preparing the venison. Some carefully peeled away the hide, while others spitted meat for roasting over the fire. Everyone seemed extremely busy. Even Avril was nowhere to be found. Catherine went directly to her tent and, once safely inside the cloth walls, sat dazedly on the edge of her blankets trying to absorb all that had occurred in the last few minutes.

She felt both ecstasy and agony. Hugh loved her. The sound of those words rang in her ears. She closed her eyes and could feel his arms around her. The heat of his loins against her had seared to her very core. His kisses were like a molten elixir pouring fiery need through her. Need she had never believed existed before.

An hour ago she had believed she could love Hugh and live without him. Now she knew inexorably that such an existence would be little more than a living hell. She remembered the repulsive taste of Sir Jeffrey's kisses upon her mouth, how repugnant his touch had been. It would be the same for her with any man who was not Hugh. A vow of marriage would not change the way she felt.

In the space of a single hour Catherine had found and lost what she most desired. She had Hugh's love, but not Hugh. She had tasted need, desire, the driving power of love; but she knew the defeat of facing a life without it. Cupping her face in her hands, Catherine laughed aloud. What was she to do?

A cough outside her tent brought her attention to the present. "Yes?"

"The venison is ready, milady."

"I'll be right there, Avril." Another cough. "Yes?"

"Lady Catherine . . . er, we were wondering. I mean, I was wondering . . ."

"Avril," Catherine said impatiently as she pushed aside the tent opening and stepped outside. "What do you wish to say?" The page opened his mouth, shut it, then opened it again. "If it was summer, you might catch a fly that way," she warned. Then more gently she added, "Avril, we have known each other a long while. In these past days you have entertained me, cared for me, and saved my life. Ask me whatever you wish and I will do my best to answer you."

"You and Sir Hugh, is all well?"

Catherine bent her head. "Who's to say?" she asked softly. Then more loudly. "Of course. Hugh and I have been friends for many years.

A little tiff over dames will not ruin our friendship."

Avril pinned her with a remonstrative look. "I am not so silly as I look, milady. I know you are in love with him. Everyone knows. *That* is what we are concerned about. Gladmoore and Baston have watched you grow up, and Wesley du Fonte believes you are the most beautiful woman in all of France. They are worried that naught but harm can come of giving your heart to someone you will never marry."

"Hugh is an honorable man," Catherine told him.

"Yes, everyone agrees. But—"

Catherine reached out to squeeze Avril's hand. "All will turn out as it should. We trust in God for that." And so saying, Catherine headed toward the campfire, leaving Avril to shake his head in frustration as he tagged along behind her. "God and Hugh Vougnet," he added under his breath.

It was as if the entire entourage of men had taken it upon themselves to outdo each other in providing a meal that was appealing to Catherine. Grier carefully sliced the venison, which was juicy and tender, and had saved a small panful of drippings to sauce it. Baston had found a few handfuls of wild brambleberries which he sprinkled over Catherine's plate, adding a pungent sweetness to her meat. There was still a bite of cheese left from noon and Avril himself had plunged a mazer of perry into a nearby stream until it was cool and refreshing for her.

It was a delicious meal, and Catherine delighted over each morsel while she lavished praise on the various contributors. But in the pit of her stomach a seedling of dread and fear blossomed for Hugh did not appear at supper. The more pronounced his absence became, the more the men worked to make merry. But she knew, as they did, that all was not well.

At last she could pretend no longer. Thanking them once more for the succulent meal, she went to her tent. But she lay wide-eyed beneath the furs long hours after the camp had grown quiet and everyone else was long asleep.

Was everyone right? she wondered. Was she a fool to give her heart to the man she loved even though he was not the man she would marry? Catherine refused to believe that to be true. Somehow it would be made right. A love such as theirs would find a way to triumph. It had to be.

But in the midst of her conviction, tiny doubts continued to rise unbidden to the surface. Why hadn't Hugh realized that everyone in their entourage had been watching them and knew about their feelings for each other? And why hadn't he appeared for supper tonight? The vassals had considered his absence a bad sign, of that much she was certain.

Hugh had said that he loved her, but he spoke not at all of a solution. And each time he kissed her, when the kiss was over, he set her away from him. It was almost as though he could not help himself for desiring her, but he regretted every time he touched her.

While he held her, while he kissed her, Catherine could feel the depths of his emotions. But afterward there was always a certain distance that Hugh put between them.

And it was Catherine who fought that distance, not Hugh.

As she lay in the stillness of her tent, Catherine refused to listen to the small voices that seemed to whisper everywhere that much was amiss. Hugh had said he loved her, but all was not well.

A heavy covering of clouds lay overhead all the next day. The road on which they traveled was busier by far than any other time during their journey and the thoroughfare was transformed into a mire of sludge. Catherine's mare slipped and slid in the mud up to her fetlocks and Catherine was forced to ride in silence, concentrating on staying in her saddle above all else.

It was just as well that she did, for there was little conversation between anyone. Hugh had not given her so much as a word all day. He rode well ahead of the others and at noon sent Avril back to tell Catherine that they would not have time to stop for a respite.

"But we must be close to Paris," she commented to Avril when he gave her Hugh's message.

Avril made a face. "We are. Sir Grier says we are less than a league from the royal palace now, but Sir Hugh has changed our plans. We will not go to Paris, but straight on to Chantilly. It seems we must get you to the *abbaye* forthwith."

All Catherine could manage in response was a small "Oh."

Clearly irritated, Avril slapped his pony's reins against his thigh. "Is this how your knight sees to everything, milady? Last night he lured you out into the woods, then today he cannot get you to the *abbaye* quickly enough. I am sorely vexed at my master. Sorely vexed!" he declared.

"Nay, Avril, you are wrong to speak so of Hugh. He has done nothing to dishonor me and it is his duty to deliver me to the abbess at Chantilly. That is what my father asked of him."

The young page twisted his mouth in a gesture of displeasure. "I do not see how this is the right of it." Taking a deep breath, Avril squelched the other thoughts he would have expressed. "We will be at the *abbaye* well before sunset, milady, so prepare."

Avril rode back to the front, and as his pony's hoofbeats faded, Catherine's heart sank in misery. Before sunset. Before sunset she would say good-bye to Hugh forever. The rest of the afternoon Catherine spent on a single thought. *Let something happen, God. Let some miracle occur that we may have a chance.*

The *abbaye* stood atop the crest of a rolling hill. Halfway down the gentle slope, a dun-colored stone wall encircled neat squares of fields that now lay fallow in the winter light. Catherine watched it as though with each advancing step she came closer to her prison. She had looked forward to the nuns, the quiet of the cloister, an opportunity to teach visiting young noblewomen the rudiments of reading and writing. But now it held no appeal at all. It was the ending. As inevitable as the coming darkness.

The gate in the *abbaye* wall was open, as was always the case with a convent or monastery. Travelers were always welcome and the gates were only lowered in times of war, or to provide sanctuary for those who might enter. As they rode up the winding dirt road, Catherine saw the nuns, in their black gowns and veils and wearing a white wimple draped about their necks, working patiently in the fields. They would spend the winter hoeing the field stubble into the soil to refresh it and picking stones from the earth to make the fields better for growing.

The *abbaye* itself was charming and welcoming. The sand-colored stone walls formed a perfect square, and surrounding the *abbaye* itself were a series of workshops for spinning, weaving, dyeing and baking.

Long before they reached the *abbaye* door, the prioress was waiting for them. She was a woman possessed of an uncommon beauty that shone despite the stark simplicity of her habit. She stood with a straight back, her hands clasped calmly in front of her as the band of travelers approached. When they at last came to a halt before her, she paid no attention whatsoever to Hugh and the vassals who rode with him. Instead, she stepped up to Catherine's horse, clasped both her hands in her own, and smiled with warmth and generosity up at Catherine. "My child, it is so good to have you with us."

Catherine bowed her head respectfully. "I cannot tell you how pleased I am to be here," she replied.

Turning to Hugh, the prioress continued. "Welcome, Lord Vougnet. We heard of your coming in the last letter I received from the count and Countess de Tralle." Then, with a look of concern she added, "I must speak to you privately as soon as possible. But first I shall see to the needs of our honored guest."

Catherine dismounted, and the prioress gave gentle directions to a pair of nuns that they must see to the needs of the mare. Leaving the men to fend for themselves, she led Catherine into the covered passageway that formed a square around the center cloister. All was quiet and peaceful within the walls of the *abbaye*. In the center of the cloister a fountain splashed. The grass was still green here, for the *abbaye* kept it warm in the garden. At each corner, boxwood formed neat borders around carefully tended flower gardens. Fat rounded flowers in autumn yellows and rusts bloomed in profusion along

with medicinal herbs and plants that were culti-
vated beneath belljars all winter long.

Along the inner wall of the covered passageway were a series of alcoves which housed statues
of Christ and the Virgin as well as reliquaries of
saints. Small, plain doors stood closed and silent
along the outer wall and Catherine knew that
one of these opened to the cell which would be
her room for the next six months. The prioress
turned up a set of stairs that led to the second
story where another arching passageway looked
down over the cloister. There she turned to the
first cell door and opened it.

Catherine stepped into the simple, unadorned
room. It was narrow and not very long, with a
single small window that looked down over the
abbaye road. Inside, there was a small cot with a
straw-stuffed mattress, simple white linen sheet
which had been made at the *abbaye*, and a woolen
blanket tucked neatly into the mattress edges.
Catherine ran her hand over the oat colored
blanket. It was softer than any blanket she had
ever felt before.

As if reading her mind, the prioress nodded.
"It was made from the wool of our own sheep.
We often trade our blankets for other worldly
goods we cannot make here at the *abbaye*. Services from the blacksmith or shoes for the winter
months. I hope this will suffice for your needs."

Catherine nodded and smiled at the abbess.
"It will be perfect for me."

"I'm glad to know that. It has not been so for some of our other guests."

"You must have travelers pass by often," Catherine commented.

"Yes. Most stay only overnight. Occasionally we have an unexpected visitor who wishes to stay longer." Returning to the subject at hand, the prioress continued. "I believe you will find that our needs are few here, but they are the ones that are the most fulfilling to our soul. The refectory is just below your room and meals are served there at five, noon and five again. Masses are immediately prior to each meal. Matins at dawn, lauds at midnight. Devotions may be carried out at any time during the day. When you are not at prayer, it is best that you be at work, for idleness is the enemy of the soul."

"To labor is to pray," Catherine added, repeating the remonstrations of Father Gilbert.

The prioress nodded. "Yes. There is much you can busy yourself with. I understand from your mother that you are accomplished with herbals and medicinals."

Catherine nodded.

"We can always use help making pastes and brews for the sick. And you are welcome to use the library. We have a fine collection of illuminated manuscripts in the scriptorium as well."

"I will not be idle, milady," Catherine atoned.

"You may call me Sister Mary James, Lady Catherine."

Catherine nodded again.

"Now, I imagine you will wish to freshen yourself from your long journey. I will have a tub set for you and warm water brought."

"You are very kind, Reverend Mother."

Catherine was not alone in her room for very long. A series of short, quick knocks at the door came close on the heels of the prioress's departure. Opening the door, Catherine was confronted by two nuns who must surely be related, she thought. They were both short in stature and wide in girth. They sported twinkling blue eyes set behind plump, cherry-red cheeks and a pair of brilliant smiles.

"Good eventide, milady," chirped one as she bustled past Catherine and began to push the single nightstand in the room flush against the cot. "You'll excuse our presumptuousness, but the Reverend Mary James—"

"Our devoted abbess," chimed in the second nun.

"Yes," the first continued, "our devoted abbess. Whom," she added giving a clear, 'don't interrupt again' look at her companion, "you have already met, asked us to see to your bath."

"As well as the other thing," added the second.

"Yes, the other matter. . . . Now what was that?"

"It was the—"

"Well, bathe first. To all things there is a season, as our good Lord tells us. And after a long journey, a bath cannot wait."

"Well, give me a hand then," the second nun called from the passageway.

"Oh! Oh, yes. Edith, why didn't you ask for my assistance before!"

"Because you were talking, my dear, why else?"

"But of course. I shall have to double my devotions this evening. I'm such a chatterjay!"

"Now, now, dear. Don't be too hard on yourself. You know what Sister Mary James tells us. It's a joyous fault to have."

Edith, or the one Catherine supposed to be Edith, huffed loudly as the wooden tub came around the corner and slid into the room. "It's not copper, milady, but here at the abbey, we find our comforts in the spiritual and doing good."

"It is a treasure," Catherine asserted. "I have either been on horseback or in a tent for days now. And the one night I had use of a tub . . ." Catherine shuddered at the thought. "Well, I wouldn't trade that tub for this one ever."

The two nuns had come to stand at attention, hands folded before them while Catherine spoke. "I see," they said in unison, eyes blinking. Then noticing that Catherine was not continuing, they again began their bustling about.

"Now for the water! Gilbert," Sister Edith instructed. "We must get the buckets."

"They're in the passageway, dear."

"Well, can you get them?"

"I'll need help, dear," Gilbert called in a singsongy voice.

"Of course you do, and here I come," replied Edith. "Now, get yourself undressed," she admonished Catherine as she scooted out the door.

Catherine stripped off her tunic, kirtle, and boots as the two moon-faced nuns hauled in a set of horsehair buckets each.

"Climb in now, dearie. Don't be shy about it," Gilbert instructed. Sisters Gilbert and Edith took care of everything, and there was nothing to be done about it, so far as Catherine could see, but to give them their way. There was no pretense of relaxation in this bath, for it was all business. The first bucket was poured gently, but unceremoniously, over Catherine's head. Then the two nuns went to work in unison. One scrubbed every inch of her front to a bright pink state of clean, while the other duplicated the procedure on her backside. The second and third buckets were utilized for rinsing and the fourth recruited for washing her hair. By the time it was over, Catherine felt like a pair of hose scrubbed threadbare by overzealous washerwomen.

"No need for anything fancy here," Sister Gilbert told her as she and Edith rubbed her dry with rough linen towels. We've brought you something simple and comfortable from Sister Mary James. Edith trotted off on her stubby legs while Gilbert took to her hair with a horn comb.

"We're *so* delighted to have you here, my dear," she said talking faster than Catherine even thought possible. "I always enjoy the young women who come here for schooling. You're a bit older than they are, but I think I'll enjoy that even more. So nice to have a fresh young face about, and how romantic! The prioress has told us all that you are on your way to your wedding. A baron! How fortunate for you, my dear. I myself could not bear to be anywhere but here at my dear *abbaye* where I can dedicate every waking moment to our Lord, Jesus Christ. But if I was not myself, I can not think of anything I'd rather than to be marrying a baron. There," she said, defeating the last knot in Catherine's long tresses. "I think it will be best if you wear your hair pulled back. The more plainly we carry ourselves, the more pleased is the Lord with our meekness."

Edith returned carrying a soft linen blouse that gathered with a simple drawstring at the neck and wrists and a soft woolen kirtle the color of sand to wear over it. Catherine began to pull the blouse over her head, but the two nuns would have none of it. Gently batting away her hands, they donned the dress and shirt, helped her into a pair of thick woolen hose and a simple pair of leather slippers. They plaited her unruly red hair into a single thick braid that hung down her back, but when they reached for a wimple, Catherine put her foot down.

"Nay, Sisters," she protested gently. "I do not care to wear things on my head."

The two nuns looked at each other and frowned. "But—"

"I will not," Catherine told them simply. Turning to the simple nightstand beside her cot, Catherine picked up her pendant and put it on.

"How very lovely, dear," Gilbert commented carefully. "But adornments are things of pride. Perhaps your finery would best be laid with your other things for after you leave here."

Catherine pursed her lips and shook her head. "I do not wear it as an adornment, but as an endearment. It was given to me by my parents many years ago, and I wear it always." Sister Edith came close to examine the heavy gold of the pendant. "See," Catherine explained as she turned the bejeweled circlet over in her hand. "It is inscribed by my parents."

"I see, indeed," Edith agreed. "I think Sister Mary James will understand, Gilbert. We have but to explain it to her."

Gilbert nodded in acceptance.

Catherine smiled at them both. "I will double my devotions tonight as penance for not wearing a wimple and for instead wearing my necklace," she told them to lighten their concerns.

Edith's face brightened and dimpled and a chuckle escaped from Gilbert's plump breast. "As you will, Lady Catherine." She laughed. "We all have our vices. 'Tis all we can do to pray for forgiveness."

"Would that all our guests were so agreeable," Edith commented, rolling her eyes heavenward.

"*That* one would never be so humble as to admit her vices," Gilbert stated with a shake of her head that sent ripples of fat shivering across her overly generous bosom.

"Well, she'll be gone soon."

"And I shall have to spend all day tomorrow on my knees before the altar. I've had so many ungenerous thoughts about her," Sister Gilbert confessed.

"Well, we'll be there together, my dear, along with half the *abbaye*. But an evil presence is an evil presence. I don't think we are supposed to like her."

Catherine listened with interest to their conversation. Clearly there were other guests here and not all of them were as well received as others. Tower bells rang out in the evening air.

"Oh, my! Mass is about to begin!" Edith announced breathlessly. "How the time passes. You have been a dear child. Now you won't want to miss Mass before the evening meal. So hurry and get your things put away. We'll get the tub later."

The two nuns scurried for the door. "Edith, dear," Sister Gilbert cried distractedly. "You forgot that other thing!"

"What other thing is that, Gilbert?"

"The letter, of course. The one the Reverend Mother told us we must give to Catherine immediately."

"Oh, yes!" Reaching into the pocket of her habit, Sister Edith extracted an oilskin packet and held it out to Catherine. "I'm so glad I didn't forget."

"You did forget, dear," Gilbert reminded her gently.

"But with your help, I remembered," Edith explained simply. "Now don't be long reading it, for there is Mass to attend, Catherine dear." And with that the two nuns bustled down the corridor toward the ringing bells of the chapel.

Catherine quickly broke the wax seal on the oilskin. It was from her father, and she assumed it was just a letter of welcome and encouragement. She was anxious to read it, for she missed her family very much. She would read it once over quickly now, go to Mass, have a nice supper, and then read it again more carefully after the evening meal. She could savor the words more slowly at that time, imagining everyone at Avignon in her mind's eye.

Unrolling the fine parchment scroll, she began to read her father's fluid quill strokes.

My Dearest Catherine,

I hope you have arrived at Chantilly and into the Reverend Mary James's care in good health, and safety. I am indebted to Sir Hugh for seeing you safely delivered to the abbaye. *Your mother and I had hoped that you would spend half of the Lord's year in the nuns' care and then travel on to your wedding. However, just after your departure from Avignon, a messenger arrived from the Duchy of Strasbourg bearing sorrowful and difficult news. Hugh may be able to tell you more of this than we even know, for word of change travel slowly and these events are not new.*

In the same year that Hugh traveled to Jerusalem, King Conrad of Germany also rode with an army toward Constantinople. What happened there, we were told little of, except that a few days outside of the city, the German Army was routed by Saracen warriors. Thirty-five thousand men, women, and children were murdered by the Muslim butchers. Among them was Lord Gustav, your betrothed husband. . . .

The words on the parchment spun off into a meaningless fog before Catherine's eyes. Dazedly, she sat on the small cot and stared at the rough-plastered wall in front of her. A thousand thoughts crowded into her mind, spinning together and then apart. But slowly one concept repeated itself over and over again, growing stronger and brighter with each passing moment. Then suddenly she jumped to her feet. Out the door and down the passageway she ran. Down the stairs and into the cloister.

The *abbaye* was a world of silence. No one walked the halls, no sound came from any cell. In the distance she could hear the chanting Latin of the nuns at Mass. Catherine looked first one way, then the other. Where was Hugh? She must find Hugh. The guest house! She had seen the finely built lodging just outside the walls of the *abbaye* itself. It was built differently from the other buildings for it was meant to house passing nobility who patronized the *abbaye*. It would have all the amenities noblemen and women were accustomed to so that they might have comfortable lodgings while they traveled.

Running as fast as her feet would carry her, Catherine raced toward the building. Inside she could see the warm light of the hearth and the torches on the walls. Hugh was there indeed. Catherine crashed breathless through the portal, letting the thick oaken door thud loudly against the stone wall behind it.

In the diminutive center hall of the lodging, the men who were not at Mass relaxed by the firelight. "Where is Hugh?" Catherine asked breathlessly.

"Lady Catherine!" Gladmoore rose from his chair. "You should not be here!"

"I must see Hugh! It is of the utmost importance."

Grier and Baston came to stand beside Gladmoore, forming a solid wall in the center of the room. Catherine shook her head in confusion. "Why are you all acting so strangely?" she asked. "I need to see Hugh. Where is he?"

"What does it matter, Lady Catherine," Wesley du Fonte said gently. "You are delivered to the *abbaye*. Hugh has done as he promised, now your lives must go there separate ways."

Catherine turned as the sound of a door opening drew her attention.

All time seemed to stop for her. Her father's

letter still held aloft, Catherine watched Hugh emerge from a side room. As he stepped into the hall, he turned to take the hand of a woman. He led her through the doorway with all the courtesy one would afford a queen. And as she emerged from the room, he bent and pressed his forehead to the back of her jeweled hand. The woman looked directly at Catherine and a cold smile touched her mouth. Following the woman's gaze, Hugh turned and his eyes met Catherine's.

For one moment in time, their gazes locked. Then, slowly, silently, Catherine turned away as a coldness spread through her that was like ice on her soul. From somewhere far distant, she heard Hugh's voice. It was not speaking to her.

"Adele, forgive me, but I must—"

"Must what?" came the reply. "I have waited five years for you, and have even come far from home to greet you with loving arms. What could possibly be of such import that it should take us away from one another?"

She did not hear Hugh's response.

Catherine felt a strong set of arms about her shoulders. "Come with us, Lady Catherine. It's been a long hard day for you." She did not know how she got back to her cell. She had no memory of crossing the pebbled courtyard nor of the covered passage or the stairs. She only knew that she was in her cell and laying upon her narrow cot, that the two plump nuns were hovering over her with salts and thimblesful of strange-smell-ing liquids that they urged upon her. And upon the tiled roof overhead, she heard the sound of rain beating down on all the world.

Fifteen

The rain pounded down hour after hour as the night dragged on endlessly. Muffled conversations carried across the tiny cell and in the passageway just beyond her door, but Catherine heeded none of what was said or by whom. She saw the hulking shadows of Baston and Grier, Gladmoore and Wesley du Fonte pass back and forth in front of the single candle that lit her room and felt the soft excess of the little nuns who bent solicitously over her. She spoke to no one, but laid upon her cot half awake and half asleep letting the endless, silent stream of tears roll down her cheeks and soak the straw mattress upon which she set her head.

She listened to the rain, glad for its droning noise. Its presence was like a balm on her heart, replenishing the well from which her tears sprung, enabling her to cry away the hurt and loneliness and sorrow. She knew that Avril sat upon a three-legged stool at the foot of her cot, but she did not look at him. When he spoke her name softly once during the night, she rolled onto her side to face the whitewashed wall and did not move again. She did not want to talk to them. She didn't want to hear them say how sorry they were that they had been right. She didn't want to see their pained expressions or hear Avril talk about the wrongs Hugh had brought upon her. She only wished for the night to pass and with it the ache that throbbed through her soul.

She must have fallen into a deeper sleep then, one where she was not still aware of the coming and going of people, for when next she opened her eyes, the wall was awash in the clean white light of morning. Catherine rolled onto her back and ran the back of her hand across the tear-swollen lids of her eyes. In the far corner, Sister Gilbert set down the tapestry needle she plied and came to sit beside her on the cot, her ample behind taking a fair share of the narrow berth.

"I feel so ashamed of myself," she confessed, wringing the excess water from a cloth which had been set nearby with a pitcher and basin. "All those things I said last night about your baron and being married soon and how very fortunate you were." Gently, she pressed the cool, damp cloth to Catherine's face. "I had no idea the news that awaited you in your missive."

Catherine smiled wanly and shook her head. "It's not any fault of yours, Sister."

"We were all so terribly upset for you, my dear. You cried and cried and no one would say a word about what had upset you so. Men are so secretive sometimes!" she declared. "Then, thank the Lord, Sister Mary James took matters into her own hands and read the letter from your father. Oh, to have your whole life altered in the passing of a second or the writing of a simple message! But we must look to God's grace for the answers. Everything happens for a reason, and there is a reason for this, we can be assured of that. Prayer," she continued. "That is the answer. Prayer and work."

"Where is Avril?" Catherine inquired quietly.

"Avril? Oh, that sweet young page who sat at your feet like a pup! Why he's gone, my dear."

"Gone?"

"Yes. Early this morning. The minute the rain stopped."

"And Gladstone and Wesley? And Hugh?" she asked.

"Gone, all of them. They left together, of course. And that pinch-cheeked Lady Adele with them."

Catherine closed her eyes and drew a steadying breath. "Of course."

"The abbess has asked to see you as soon as you are feeling up to it, dear. May I tell her it will be soon?"

Catherine closed her eyes and sighed. "Yes. You may tell her that I will be ready very soon. I just need a few minutes to clear my head."

Less than an hour later, Catherine emerged from her cell into the damp noon. She had found a clean blouse and kirtle of the same color and style as the one she'd been given the day before lying across the stool on which she'd last seen Avril. She brushed her hair and replaited it, splashed water from the basin on her face, and with a deep, stabilizing breath stepped out into the world. She found Sister Mary James kneeling amid a patch of hyssop in the cloister. Bending to pluck a single leaf, Catherine crushed it with her fingers, releasing its subtle fragrance.

"Good morning, my child," the prioress said, climbing to her feet. "I feel in need of a walk. My legs tire much more easily than they did in my younger years, and I find a good walk refreshes them." Sister Mary James removed the gloves she'd worn to tend the garden and slipped her hands into the generous sleeves of her habit. Bowing her head, she led the way to the front entrance and from there down into the fields. Catherine followed in silence.

"I know your news is painful, Lady Catherine. Had I any idea of the news your letter bore, I would have made preparations. I am so sorry."

Catherine swallowed hard. It was better that the abbess and all the nuns believed it was the baron's death that had caused her such anguish. Better by far than for them to know she was in love with another man and that it had been the sight of him with his own affianced wife that had been the root of her pain. "There is nothing to be done for it, Reverend Mother."

"Perhaps not, Catherine. But there is healing to be done, and I cannot think of a better place for the healing of a wounded soul than here."

Catherine looked at her in surprise.

"I know that the initial intent of your visit was to prepare you for your married life. But there is much here that can assist you now. You need quiet and work. Lots of work to keep you busy and your hands active. You will find that filling your time with all there is to do at the *abbaye* will give your mind little time to remember. And you will be doing useful tasks as well."

Catherine did not know what to say. She had not thought of anything beyond the fact that Adele was alive and well and that Hugh had clearly sent for her to be here when he arrived. It was very clear to her now why he did not wish to stop in Paris but rather ride straight to Chantilly where Adele was waiting for him. The simple thought of Hugh sending for Adele caused such pain in her breast that for a moment Catherine could not find her breath.

"There are beekeeps to tend, jams and jellies to be made up for winter. And there are the herbs. Wormwood and mustard, sage and witch hazel. They all must be gathered and dried and applied to the correct salves and creams. And there are children to teach, Catherine. Your parents have written of your talents in this area. The young women who will live here this winter are to be taught the arts of needlework, spinning, and weaving. They will be taught music and how to play an instrument. But they could also be taught to read or how to blend herbs for the cure of ailments that will afflict their serfs . . ."

Sister Mary James came to a halt in the middle

of an open field and looked out over the valley. "It is peaceful here, Catherine. It's a good place to heal."

Catherine closed her eyes and breathed in the damp, misty air. She did not think she could bear going home just now. It would mean riding over the same road she had passed along with Hugh. And that thought alone was overwhelming to her. Opening her eyes, she smiled at the abbess. "I'll stay."

Sister Mary James patted her hand reassuringly. "I will send a message to your family."

Catherine leaned over the pot and nodded to Esseline, who sprinkled comfrey and dried feverfew into the boiling liquid. "Now you must stir it well and let it cool. It will thicken as it cools and you will be able to put it in the jars," she told her, nodding in the direction of the crockery jars they had set out earlier. The girl anxiously did as directed and Catherine moved to the open window where she looked out over the hillsides of Chantilly.

Two months had passed since she'd come to the *abbaye*. Her days were filled with the peace of this place. She had found many friends among the nuns, particularly Sisters Edith and Gilbert. As they had from the first, the two were inseparable and fussed over her like twin hens over a chick. And Catherine was valued as well. She knew that the new medicines of which she had brought knowledge to the *abbaye* were deeply appreciated. Already two barons from well on the other side of Paris had sent their daughters expressly to learn Catherine's skills. But she still had not forgotten.

A light dusting of snow lay over the countryside, and it reminded her of the night when Hugh had crawled into the brambles with her. Everything reminded her of Hugh and his betrayal. Leaning against the stone sill, she let her mind wander to happier times. She pictured Hugh riding through the forests of Avignon after boar and stags as they had when she was only twelve. How strong and invincible he had seemed to her then. Why hadn't she seen the truth of him? Why hadn't she seen that he only cared for her as someone to pass his time?

In her mind she heard Jeffrey Winfrey's angry voice sneering at her. Catherine tried to blot the sound out, but it would not go away. So often she heard his words. Over and over again. In her sleep. In her work. Vicious, pounding, painful words. And they hurt her so, because she had refused to believe them, but they had been the truth. *"We say we will reach for the goals of godliness and goodness, Catherine, but we are prisoners of our base needs. What is worse? To admit the truth or to hide it? To admit the truth or to hide it?"*

She had hated Jeffrey Winfrey. Despised everything he was. And yet, he had proven to be a more honest man than the man she thought she loved.

Esseline came up behind her. "Look! We shall have visitors for Christmas, Catherine!"

With a start, Catherine followed Esseline's fingertip to where it pointed to two riders galloping over the frozen winter ground. "Knights," she said with a sad smile. "They are just a pair of knights."

"Peace to you in this Christmas season!" Terrence called to the nuns approaching from the abbey doors. Dismounting, he bowed low, holding his bad arm against his waist.

"Good Christmastide to you also, sir," they called in unison.

"They look like a pair of plump partridge just waiting for the butcher's knife!" Jean whispered into his ear.

Terrence smiled broadly and nodded.

"May we offer you shelter on this cold and frosty night?" one nun inquired kindly.

"You may indeed," Terrence replied. "We do not require much. A simple bed of straw in your barn will suffice."

"Oh, my dear sir," the one that Terrence had determined was a hairbreadth taller than the other said, "we have a lovely guest lodging for your use, and your companion's as well. And you may partake of a fine hot supper there. 'Tis among our calling to offer such services to travelers, and 'tis the yuletide besides." Terrence bowed low and expressed his gratitude for such generosity on the part of the nuns. "Come with us, then," the shorter one said, marching off in the direction of the barns. We can offer you a warm bed and fresh food, but wayfarers must tend to their horses and personal attentions for themselves."

"We remain indebted to you, Sisters."

"Where are you bound?" one nun inquired. But Jean, impatient with their chatter, spoke before Terrence was able to reply.

"Is it possible for us to see the abbess tonight?" he inquired anxiously.

The two nuns nearly collided in their hurry to turn and eye the young man suspiciously. "I'm certain the abbess would be willing to meet with you tomorrow," one explained politely. "But at the moment she is at Mass and then the evening meal will be served, followed by devotions of the nuns which she will hear. Then there is the special yuletide prayer which she has been leading and then it will be far too late for her to speak with visitors."

"I'm afraid my friend is overanxious tonight," Terrence interjected as he gave Jean a warning look. "You see, we have reason to believe that his sister is here at the *abbaye*."

"Your sister!?" the shorter one exclaimed. "Oh, how wonderful! Now, who do you look like," she said, circling back around to have a closer look at Jean in the fading daylight.

"He looks like Sister Constance, dear," the other stated.

"No, no. You are quite mistaken. He has the features of Sister Delphine Marie."

"I'm sure you're wrong, dear," the first insisted, leading the way into the cloistered garden area.

"Neither is my sister," Jean declared in frustration. "Her name is Catherine. Catherine de Tralle, and she is not a nun but a visitor here."

"Catherine! You are our own dear Catherine's brother? How wonderful!" the shorter, and to Terrence's observations, the more talkative, declared. "We must make a surprise of this occasion. She does not know you are coming, does she?" she asked suddenly.

"Nay. There was no time to send a message." Jean explained.

"Oh, good! Then this is what we shall—"

"Terrence! Jean! Oh, Jean!" Catherine hung over the second-story balcony, waving her arms joyously.

"Catherine!" Jean called back.

"Wait!" she cried. "I will be right there." She disappeared from view, and a moment later was running full tilt toward the two men. Throwing her arms around her little brother's neck, she gave him a warm kiss on the cheek, then, turning to Terrence, did the same to him. "What are you doing here?" she demanded, both laughing and crying at once. "And why did you not send some message, so I might be *prepared*?"

Jean laughed good-naturedly and gave his sister's plaited hair a good ruffling. "You have been at this *abbaye* too long. You run off at the mouth as badly as the nuns!"

The two nuns jostled each other in mute accusation of the other, while Catherine smiled gleefully. "If that is true, it is because I have saved so many words over the past two months. Now, no more admonishments. Let me take you to your lodging where we may sit and talk."

They spent the evening merrily. Sitting before the hearth in the hall of the guest house, they shared stories of the past months as though it had been years they were apart. Sister Mary James came to offer welcome to Catherine's visitors and a sumptuous meal was brought for them by the nuns. Catherine wanted to hear about everyone. Her little sisters were fine, she learned, and it seemed that Terrance had learned to deal with the impairment of his arm very well. What about Amaranth? she asked. And was Thomas taking good care of her falcon? And did her mother wish for some special gift for Christmas?

It was getting late, and Jean had long since retired for the night before any word was said about Hugh. "Have you heard any word from my brother, Catherine?" Terrence asked as the two of them sat staring into the fire in amicable silence.

"Nay, Terrence," Catherine said quietly. "He left the morning after I arrived here, and I have never heard from him again."

"What really happened, Catherine."

"What do you mean?" she asked, not wishing

to bring up any details about their last hours together. "We arrived here, the men stopped long enough to eat and rest, and then they left."

"It could not have been that simple," he said with a sidelong glance. "Like you, I have not heard one thing from Hugh since he left Avignon. That is not like him, Catherine. When you left here, all was not well between you. Did something more happen during your travels?" Terrence let the silence draw out into a long void before he spoke again.

"I'm worried about him, Catherine. If you know something, you must tell me."

"I have not heard from him, Terrence. What I tell you is the truth. I have never seen or heard from him since he left here with Adele."

"Adele?" Terrence queried, a look of shocked surprise on his face. "What was Adele doing here?"

Catherine knit her fingers together in her lap as she tried to keep the pain in her at bay. "He sent for her, of course."

Terrence's eyebrows shot up. "Sent for her? Nay, Catherine," he told her with a definite shake of his head. "Hugh would never send for Adele."

"You're wrong, Terrence," Catherine asserted as she felt hot tears form behind her eyes. "Perhaps you don't really know Hugh. He is not the man many think him to be."

Terrence leaned forward in his chair, resting his elbows upon his knees as he stared intently into Catherine's face. "I know my brother well, and I know that sending for Adele is the last thing he would ever do. Especially because he was so deeply in love with you."

"In love with me?" Catherine's voice broke, and for a moment she was unable to continue. "No, Hugh was not in love with me."

"Then you must tell me why not," Terrence said quietly.

Slowly, Catherine began to unwind the story of their journey. She left nothing out, not even details of Sir Jeffrey Winfrey's death. When she had finished describing the scene she had witnessed in the very room where they now sat, Terrence sat for a long while in silence while Catherine went to splash water on her tear-stained face.

Returning, she lowered herself slowly into the chair. "He always spoke to me of honesty. Of duty and honor. He always seemed so driven to do what was right. I could not believe that he would take my affections so lightly. I thought that if he was still betrothed to Adele, he would have told me. He would not have kissed me. But he did, Terrence. He told me he loved me. And I believed him. Then, less than a day later, he was kissing Adele." She looked Terrence square in the eye and continued.

"Jeffrey Winfrey was right, and I despised him. Hugh was wrong, and I loved him. That is the worst part of it all."

"Sir Jeffrey was not a good man, Catherine.

Don't confuse Hugh's actions by believing that they made Jeffrey a good man. Did you know he sent his page back to Avignon?"

Catherine cocked her head toward Terrence in surprise. "I remember that his page was gone. Avril had complained about it because then Jeffrey made the other pages do the work for him as well as their own lords."

"He sent him back to Avignon with a message for your father. I believe the message was meant to anger Bernard, perhaps so that he would send someone to replace Hugh as your protector on your journey. But whatever the reason, his missive claimed that Hugh had mistreated you. But Bernard trusted Jeffrey Winfrey little and put his faith in Hugh."

"It was Jeffrey who mistreated me," Catherine said. "Not Hugh. It was never Hugh. I was lost in the forest the first night of our travels. I slid down an embankment and couldn't get up. Hugh came to find me."

"Then Bernard was right to trust him. And I think you were right to trust him as well."

"I trusted him deeply. So deeply that I thought it was all right that we should care about each other. I thought that if there was a reason why we shouldn't, Hugh would tell me. I had told him about the baron. He knew where I was on my way to, and why."

"And he would have known as well that yours was a relationship which could never be. Not really," Terrence added.

"As did I."

"Then what happened that hurt you so, Catherine? What happened that Hugh should never send word that he arrived safely at Pontoise?"

"Don't you see, Terrence? Hugh never told me Adele was still alive. Why did he kiss me? Why did he tell me he loved me?"

"Perhaps he could not stand *not* to tell you," he offered.

Catherine's lower lip quivered and she felt the hard knot of tears form in her throat. "Why did he send for her, Terrence? Why did she have to come to the *abbaye?* Couldn't we have had one last day? Hugh was so eager to see Adele, to put me aside that he had her meet him. Surely he must love her, Terrence. And just as surely it could not be me he loved."

"Catherine, there is much I don't understand about all you've told me. And I mean to find out so that I can answer your questions. Or better yet, so that Hugh can answer it for you. I will send you a message from Pontoise. I promise you."

Catherine sat quietly, her head bent in defeat, her hands folded and still in her lap.

"Can you wait for that?" he asked. "I promise you my message will arrive within a fortnight. Can you hold back judgment of my brother until then?"

For long minutes she made no reply while she saw it all happen again in her mind. How she had run, ecstatic and breathless into the room.

How she had called his name with a child's cry of delight. How the door had opened and he had come from the secluded room, leading Adele, kissing her hand. He had seen only Adele, never noticing Catherine until she had gasped in disbelief. And then, as Hugh stood there, not moving, not acknowledging her in any way, Catherine saw the look of triumph in Adele's eyes.

Catherine's head was pounding and her eyes glistened with unshed tears. Carefully, she took a ragged, steadying breath. "I will wait to hear from you," she told him at last. "I will believe in him until then, until you tell me otherwise."

"Good." Terrence leaned over and kissed her gently on the forehead.

"Terrence," she whispered in a choked tone. "He never even said good-bye to me."

"Perhaps because he could not say that and mean it. Perhaps that is why."

Catherine looked away, staring into the fire silently as a single tear traced a path across her cheek.

Sixteen

The ceremony was small. It was attended only by Hugh's elder brother and his wife, Adele's family, and the officiating priest. There were no revelries following the service as was expected when the lord of a castle married, especially one the size and influence of Pontoise. Adele had termed such things "pagan" and "sores unto the heart of the Lord" when mention was made of it. Instead, there was a private dinner to which neither the villeins of Pontoise nor the vassals whose allegiance was pledged to Hugh were invited. While the serfs and vassals dined as they did every night and speculated as to the strange wedding of the new duke, in the Great Hall Adele had arranged a feast for her family the likes of which none had ever seen or tasted before.

"Adele, or shall I say, Duchess?" Philip de Pisan laughed with delight as he plucked another pheasant leg off of a passing platter. "You have truly outshone yourself tonight."

"Are you pleased, Father?"

"Pleased!?" he snorted as he wiped his fingers on his sleeve. "I am thinking about moving in."

Adele made a face that she believed passed for a smile and made a mental note that the serving maid with the long blond tresses and narrow waist was far too slow. She would have her beaten with a willow switch tomorrow. A good lesson to her that sloth was the devil's work and vanity in one's looks could lead only to worse sin.

Giles's wife, Petra, leaned over to pat Adele solicitously on the hand. "We are so pleased to have you as part of the family," she assured her.

Adele carefully removed her hand from beneath that of her new sister-in-law and glanced at her through narrowed eyes. "It has turned out quite fortuitously, has it not?"

"Your pardon?" Petra Vougnet asked.

"That I should have to be betrothed since birth to a man who could only ply a trade, and now I am a duchess."

"It is hardly accurate to say that Hugh is a mere tradesman," Petra commented. "He has long been the most trusted vassal of our king, and has become equally valued by King Baldwin of Jerusalem. Such talents can hardly be called a 'trade.'"

"Call it what you will," Adele responded with a shrug. "If I had not implored Hugh to take up the cross, he would not now be sitting in the seat of the Duke of Pontoise. It was only through God's grace that everything we enjoy this evening came to be."

"Assuredly so," Petra agreed. "But some credit belongs with Hugh, I think."

Adele stared at her as though she had grown two heads. "All credit for all things belongs at the feet of the Lord."

Hugh pushed his chair back from the high table and stood. He could not bear to sit there one more moment.

"Hugh, where are you going?" Adele demanded as he turned to leave.

"For a walk through my duchy, Adele. Would you care to join me?"

Adele sniffed disdainfully at the mere thought of it. "Nay, you go if you must. I shall never understand a man's need to tromp through filth and sludge."

"It is not filth and sludge, Adele," Hugh said with a steely edge to his voice. "It is my land. The land upon which my serfs will toil to bring us food and flax for cloth and all our needs. You should treat it with more respect."

"Humph," Adele responded. "All I need comes to me through prayer. You would do well to remember that your needs are answered through prayer as well."

Hugh made no reply. He passed behind his brother's chair, and his sister-in-law's as well, and then crossed to the doorway. From a hook by the door, he took a long mantle which he slung over his shoulders for warmth on this hoary winter night. As he stepped out into the

cobbled courtyard of his bailey, he breathed
deeply and closed his eyes.

He was married. Married to Adele. This day
had been in his future for nearly twenty years
and *he* had been the one to set the date the moment he arrived at Pontoise. He had wanted the
marriage done. No more looming out in the future somewhere. He wanted it consecrated and
done. Why then did he feel dead inside? If this
was what God had wished for him, then why did
he feel as though his life had come to a final
and irrevocable end?

He opened his eyes and looked around the
bailey. Pontoise was a magnificent keep. Having
only been completed ten years before, it was
quite modern, with several large windows and a
more open feeling than most castles. The cobbled bailey alleviated the courtyard of mud, and
the roof was peaked with slate tiles set one over
another like the scales of a fish. There were
more rooms inside than in other castles. Besides
a Great Hall, there was a room specifically for
the serving of meals, and the kitchens were attached as part of the castle itself rather than a
separate building. Even the chapel was of stone
with a slate roof and a fine turret at each corner.
The only structure which was not of the gray
hewn stone was a small, ancient chapel which
had been there before the castle was built. But
it was tucked into a shadowed corner of the
bailey where it got little attention. He liked his
new home very much. He even liked the little

timber-and-dauber chapel, for its quaintness softened the expanses of gray in the cobbled courtyard.

"Congratulations, Lord Hugh. 'Tis a fine evening to be wed." Gladmoore strode toward him
from across the bailey, his hand extended in a
gesture of felicitation.

Hugh clasped the proffered hand and tried to
smile. "Thank you, Gladmoore."

"But what are you doing outside when you
should be celebrating with your bride!?"

"I tired of celebrating alone."

"Alone?" The vassal knit his brow and frowned.

Hugh gave a short snort. "Alone indeed. The
people seated at my tables inside my hall are not
celebrating my good fortune. They congratulate
Adele on *her* achievement. They compliment her
on Pontoise as though it was hers. They speak
of moving into *my* castle, yet they do not speak
of it to *me*. Only my brother and his wife were
invited to meet my desires. The other people I
would have to celebrate my wedding were not
invited."

"Who would that be, my lord?"

"Why, you! And my other vassals. Men who
have served me well and are deserving of a night
of good food and cheer. And my serfs. The fami-
lies who tend my land and depend upon my protection. They should have been there as well."

"*Oui,*" Gladmoore agreed quietly. "I am glad
to hear this from you."

Hugh looked at his vassal, his face darkened by concern. "Have you felt slighted?"

Gladmoore hesitated a moment. His hands clasped behind his back, he looked out into the darkness. "We are all concerned. It is not for us to say what you do with your life. But you have not been the same since—we arrived here." Hugh knew he had changed his words at the last minute. But Gladmoore's unspoken thought had mirrored his own. He had not been the same since they had left Chantilly. Since he had ridden toward Pontoise with Adele and left Catherine behind. "It's as though . . ." Gladmoore hesitated.

"Go on," Hugh told him. "Speak your mind. I am not one to punish a man for speaking a truth I do not like."

Gladmoore took a breath and continued. "It's as though you are no longer the one in charge. Everything is as Adele wishes it. And Hugh . . ." The vassal cleared his throat. "You must be the one to say yeah or nay. It is not good for the serfs to see you deferring so much of your power. You are the duke and they expect you to make the decisions. Even if it is just about hiring the steward."

Hugh's brow creased and the furrows around his mouth deepened. "And who says that I am not the one who will make such decisions. I have been here less than a month and mayhap I have been slow in looking into such things, but I fully intend to make such decisions myself."

Gladmoore turned to look at Hugh. "The new steward arrived today."

Hugh's voice was controlled and intense. "When?"

"Just before your wedding ceremony. And the villeins had a great deal to say about it, too. It appears he's well known and not well liked."

"What is his name?"

"Gaspar Corvey. Weaselish looking if you were to ask me. Shifty about the eyes. I tried to have a few words with him, to find out if the complaints about him might be true."

"And?"

"And he talks in circles, my lord. He never gave me an answer that was straight out. I can't say I liked him myself."

"And did you ask him who retained him?"

"Nay, Hugh. That was not my place. But the villeins . . ." He let the sentence trail off unfinished.

Hugh clenched his hands into fists. What was Adele doing now? Wasn't it enough that he had acquiesced to her wishes regarding this wedding? The people who were under his care had been excluded while her family feasted on a meal that would feed a hundred. And he had been angry about that, but because it was to be her wedding day, he had reluctantly agreed. Did she also intend to have her way with everything at Pontoise? Had *she* hired a steward without consulting him? And to what purpose? Of course she would think he was inept at such a thing.

She considered him nothing more than a warrior. A fighting instrument. All brawn and little brain.

The muscle in his right cheek jumped as anger rose like a hot spray of molten iron from his belly. He would see this steward, and he would see him gone from Pontoise before the sun was gone tomorrow. And he would give his villeins and vassals a feast. He would have them celebrate tonight. He did not care if Philip de Pisan didn't eat another bite. He didn't need food anyway. A few weeks without it would do him a world of good.

"Gladmoore," Hugh said with an icy calm in his voice. "Get the other men and have each meet me at the door to the kitchens."

"*Oui,* my lord," Gladmoore replied with a hint of satisfaction in his voice.

Hugh spun around and headed toward the back of the castle with strides that swallowed up the earth beneath him. He stepped through the open doorway into the first of the three rooms that comprised the castle's kitchens. The head cook turned, a large wooden spoon in his hand, about to reprimand a lazy boy. But when he saw the duke standing, arms locked across his chest and legs set akimbo, he began to stammer and bow and wave his cooking spoon around all at the same time. "My lord!" he sputtered. "How may I help you? Is there something that displeased you about the meal?"

"Yes," Hugh replied calmly. "It displeases me

to see so much food put to waste. What do you intend to do with so much food?"

The cook looked around uncomfortably. "Throw it away."

"What!?" Hugh burst out. "This is how you put my money and the animals from my forest to good use?"

"No, my lord! I would not do such a thing. Normally, I send what is left over to become something else tomorrow or I give it out to the serfs. But Lady Adele wanted nothing saved or given away. Everything must be destroyed. Those were her instructions."

"Well, here are *my* instructions," Hugh said with deadly calm. "All this food, everything except the bear haunch, pudding, and roasted roots is to be put in baskets. Give the baskets to my knights. The bear, pudding, and roots put in a basket for me. Then take two kegs of ale down to the stable. Another ten kegs are to be taken in a cart, and as the men distribute the baskets of food among the villeins, have your kitchen boy provide several measures of ale to each home."

The cook's look of worry slowly dissipated and was replaced with a broad grin as Hugh's meaning became clear. He wasted not a moment, but began calling orders to the kitchen help, sending boys racing for baskets and women to divide the food equally between each basket. Satisfied, Hugh turned to where Baston, Grier, Gladmoore, and the other knights stood at the ready.

"Each of you is to take a basket and deliver the food among the homes of the serfs. Be sure the kitchen boy is generous with the ale. Avril," he said, turning to his page, "You oversee the ale." Avril nodded, his face echoing the satisfied smiles of the knights. "Then, when you are done, come to the stable. We will celebrate together there."

An hour later, the men reported to the stable as Hugh had instructed. There they found the wide hall between sets of stalls transformed. Hugh had moved a trestle table and benches into the center where a huge keg of ale stood ready to be tapped. On the table, the succulent bear haunch sat upon a silver platter, the steam giving off a delicious aroma. With hearty cheers, the vassals sat down and Hugh took his seat at the head of the long table. When each of the men had a mazer of ale, he lifted his in salute. "To the best men I have ever ridden beside."

"To your wedding!" Gladmoore called out in reply.

"Here, here!" came the chorus of agreement.

Oui, Hugh said to himself as they drank to the toast. 'Tis done now.

Terrence and Jean crossed the drawbridge of Pontoise in time to hear the randy refrain of an ancient battle song being sung by a group of loud, deep voices none of which sounded any too sober. They gave each other a querulous look and then turned their horses toward the stables, which were aglow in light and from which the song issued.

Leading their horses behind them, the two were greeted by a rather strange sight, for a party was well underway within. "Hugh!" Terrence called to his brother, who sat atop an ale keg. "What goes on here that you must now eat and drink in the stable? Has the king disposed you from your castle and title? Or are you just so accustomed to the life of a knight that you aren't comfortable unless you can smell your horse?"

"Terrence!" Hugh roared. He jumped down from the keg and took a moment to steady himself before crushing his younger brother in a bruising embrace. "I thought it would be months before I would see you again! Let me look at you!"

"I recovered well. Bernard and Marguerite saw to my every need, as you would expect. And Jean helped me exercise so that I could build my strength back up. I do well with it," he continued, indicating the arm that hung useless at his side.

"Jean!" Hugh cried as though he had just now realized who accompanied Terrence. "Come, both of you. Join our celebration!"

"And what are you celebrating?" Terrence asked. "All of Pontoise seems to be reveling tonight, for there wasn't a darkened window in any of your villeins' homes as well."

"Oh!" Hugh cried with a carelessness born of too much spirits. "My marriage! We celebrate my marriage. All of Pontoise . . . my vassals, my serfs, my family all celebrate my wedding day."

For a moment neither of the new arrivals spoke, then Terrence nodded slowly. "Of course we will celebrate such a fine occasion with you, Hugh."

Hugh slapped his brother on the back and pulled him into another embrace. "Bring my brother and Jean a mazer of ale and prepare food for each of them."

He led them to the table where the vassals greeted their friends warmly and made room for them on the benches. Mazers were placed in their hands and steaming trenchers of meat and pudding were placed in front of them. The two joined in the celebration and soon the songs began again.

The sky was just beginning to be streaked with pinks and yellows when the men at last set down their mazers and headed unsteadily in the direction of their beds. Jean, tired from the long ride and unused to ale in any sizable quantity, lay in a mound of straw snoring unevenly. Only Terrence and Hugh remained at the table.

"Then you are happy, Hugh?" It was a question and it expressed all the questions that Terrence held in his mind. He had joined his brother in celebration, saddened because as he celebrated he knew he must send a message to Catherine that would break her heart even more thoroughly than it had been broken thus far by Hugh. But he needed to know if Hugh was indeed happy about his marriage. He seemed pleased enough, judging by the carefree demeanor he had greeted them with, but it was strange that he should be out here in the barn with his vassals. Why were they not all in the Great Hall as would have been expected? And why had Hugh spent his wedding night drinking when he should have been bedding his wife.

" 'Tis what was to be done," Hugh told him.

"And Catherine?" It was a blunt statement. But Terrence had to know. He had promised her, and he would keep that promise.

"Catherine?" Hugh looked away from his brother. His face was grim, but set as though all was behind him now. "Catherine is where she belongs. In another few months she'll be on her way to Strasbourg and her own wedding."

"Nay, Hugh. Jean and I stopped at the *abbaye* on our way here. Jean had messages from Bernard to deliver to your Catherine, but the baron is dead. He has been dead for four years, and Jean was sent to see how his sister fared."

"Dead?" Hugh stared at Terrence as though he did not believe his ears. "Dead, how?"

"He was with the German king, Conrad."

"When they took the land route from Constantinople and were slaughtered by the Saracens?"

Terrence nodded.

"Forty thousand people were killed before Conrad turned back. We told him to go by sea."

"I was there as well, Hugh."

"But we didn't know that Catherine's baron was there. Why not? We would have heard the names of the high-ranking men."

"Perhaps we heard the name and didn't know it was her baron."

Hugh stared at the stable's stone walls. "When did she find out this news?" Terrence didn't answer him, and his silence carried a heaviness with it, boding such import that Hugh felt his heart lurch in his breast. "When, Terrence?"

His brother's voice was very still when he spoke. "It was just after your arrival there. When she saw you with Adele," he waited for a moment and then finished. "She was coming to tell you when she saw you with Adele."

Hugh squeezed his eyes shut as if that would eradicate from reality the image of Catherine as she had stood staring at him in the guest house of the *abbaye*. There he had stood, his hand in Adele's. The pain, the betrayal in her eyes, had stabbed straight to his heart. Yet he had done nothing.

Hugh's mind came alive with the memory of that day. He hadn't known what to do when he had found Adele there at the *abbaye*. How had she gotten there? How had she known he was coming? To this very day, he did not know the answer to that question, though he had asked it.

Always, Adele would turn her gaze elsewhere and tell him that the Lord had spoken to her in prayer. He had told her to go to the *abbaye,* and so she had done.

The moment he had seen her, Hugh had felt his world being torn asunder. He had not been ready to return to Adele and all the heavy trappings of a life he had not wanted. He had known with each day that passed, as they rode closer and closer to Paris, that he was indeed going back. The last day, in fear of his feelings for Catherine, he had even told himself that he must hie himself back to that other life as quickly as he could or he would commit a sin—for he could not keep himself away from Catherine any longer. His need was too great, his love for her an abiding thing that would not go away, but would, instead, continue to grow until it was beyond his ability to resist or keep within the bounds of propriety.

But the moment he had seen Adele, Hugh had known with a surety which was final and absolute that he did not belong there. And yet there was naught to be done about it. No step he could take to prevent it. His future had been set so long ago. So many expected it, depended upon it, demanded it. It was a destiny which was not his to control. And so, at the moment Adele presented her cold cheek to accept his unoffered kiss, he had done the only thing he could. He had sealed his love for Catherine away. And it was at that same moment that Catherine was reading her father's message, learning that her world was irrevocably changed.

And when she had come to him, when she had needed him, he had been at the side of another woman.

"What will she do?" Hugh asked, rubbing the palms of his hands across his brow. "She has no future now. Where will she go? Will Bernard and Marguerite find her another husband?" Then, as though he had forgotten that Terrence was even there, he said to himself, "Of course she will find someone, easily. She is so beautiful. So kind. So full of life and spirit and joy. The men will be falling one over the other to win her hand."

Terrence watched his brother closely. "I believe she intends to stay at the *abbaye*."

Hugh looked at him for a minute as though he didn't understand, then his brows came down and he stared at his brother. "You cannot mean that she will take the vows?"

"She's in love with you, Hugh. That is one of the reasons I came here so quickly. It is you she wants, you she loves, and she says she cannot wed another man. It would be a lie, a sham which no man deserves to live with. Hugh, she told me about you sending for Adele at Chantilly. You hurt her deeply."

"I didn't send for Adele. I still don't know how she knew I was on my way to Chantilly or on which day I would arrive there. But she was there when we arrived. What other choice did I have?

I could not hurt Catherine any more. I left as soon as possible."

"Then you don't love Catherine?"

Hugh buried his head in his hands. "Love her?" he said, his voice cracked with emotion. "Terrence, I love her as I have never loved anything in my life. The sound of her voice is like sweet music to me. To look at her—to watch her on a sunlit day as we rode or to sit by the campfire and see the flames light her hair with red and gold, to see green eyes that sparkle with laughter—to look at her is to be at peace. And to kiss her. By God, Terrence, I kissed her, and my soul hungered not. Only with Catherine have I felt whole and accepted. Only then."

"Then at least you must tell her this yourself. I promised her I would talk to you. Promised her I would tell her what I found out. But I cannot tell her that you are married. If you love her, Hugh, you must go and tell her yourself."

Hugh took a ragged breath. "I'll leave today."

Seventeen

Adele did not bother to knock. Instead, she simply let herself into Hugh's apartments—still his apartments since she had made no effort to move into his rooms either before yesterday's wedding or this morning. "You have been summoned?" she inquired as though she'd just bitten into some foul fruit.

Hugh continued to pack the small leather bag that was always strapped to the back of Cepheus's saddle when he traveled. "I am riding south. Terrence brought some news which I must see to."

"Terrence!" Hugh watched the look on his wife's face sour even more. "Why did you not tell me that your younger brother had arrived? I would have greeted him sooner."

"I think not, Adele. You have little enough love for Terrence as it is, but now he will seem most distasteful to you."

"Why do you say that?" Adele queried warily.

"I told you he was injured during the Crusades." He is lame now, Adele. And I will not have any member of my household treating him ill because of it."

Adele turned to examine the tapestry hung on the closest wall and Hugh knew it was to hide her repugnance at his news. It was to her credit, Hugh thought, that she changed the topic of conversation. "I wanted to thank you for deferring from the customary taking of the wedding bed last night. It speaks well of the sensibilities you acquired as a Knight Templar that you did not stoop to such unnecessary vulgarities."

"Vulgarities?" Hugh let out a sharp laugh. "Do you not wish to breed children, Adele?"

"It is not written anywhere in the Bible that all women must bear squalling babes. God alone will see fit to bless us or not."

"Then God will decide if we are to share a bed?" Hugh asked with a wry shake of his head as he resumed packing. Adele de Vougnet. His wife. The truth was that his wife was as cold as a dungeon floor. And as dull. Her watery blue eyes held no spark. Her body was thin—too thin. Bones protruded at sharp angles that matched her chin and cheeks. Her hair was a dull, muddy brown that she wore plaited in a thin braid that was nary as thick as his little finger.

She did not want to share a bed with him, and she did not want to bear his children. For a moment the de Tralle family flashed before his eyes. A passel of children, all loved, all wanted. He pictured Catherine with a bevy of young villeins clinging to her skirts and the happy sound of her laughter as she played with them. He could still picture the sparkling emerald of her gaze. How alive she always seemed to him. How full of all good things. He stopped to look again at Adele who stood, arms across her chest, in the center of the room. His wife.

"How many days before I shall expect your return?" she asked. Hugh could not help thinking that she sounded not at all sad to know he was going.

"Three days at the most," he replied. "And Adele," he said, coming to a halt in front of her. "When I return, I shall hire a steward. You may tell Monsieur Corvey that an error was made and he is relieved of his duties here."

Startled, Adele sputtered as she cast about for a response. Then Hugh watched as indignation filled her, puffing her up like a trussed goose. "My lord, I regret to remind you that you are a vassal of the king and at his every beck and call. Evidence this very moment that you prepare to go to him," she declared. "You must admit that it is I who will run this fief, not you. And as such, I must have the steward I see as fit for the position, else he will not work well with me."

Hugh did not move, nor did he acquiesce to what she claimed.

"I had no intention of usurping a decision which is yours to make," she continued haughtily. "I merely acted upon what I know to be truth."

"I understand your reasons, Adele. But it matters not. You are mistaken if you believe I will be at war for Louis as I was when I went to Jerusalem. I have come home now to care for my fief and make it prosper. I intend to be here much. And I will select my steward as I will select every man who works for me. You will send Corvey away."

Adele looked away from him and pursed her lips. "He should be allowed to stay at least until you return. He deserves a chance to prove his capabilities."

"No. He will be gone by the time I return," he said.

"Then I will see you in a fortnight." Without waiting for Hugh's affirmation, she left the room. Hugh stared at the heavy door as it closed behind her, torn between the deception he was about to perpetrate and the need that raged within him. He had not lied outright to Adele, but neither had he told her the fact of his destination. His goal was not Paris, though he would stop there to see the king. It was Chantilly.

He could not let Catherine believe all that Terrence had said she believed. Once more he would see her, though he had meant never to set eyes upon her again. But his intentions had changed since last night. Catherine was left with no place to go. No future for which he could think she was destined. He had to see her once more. He would explain that he had not sent for Adele. And he would see to it that Catherine was all right.

He would convince her to return to Avignon.
Or perhaps go to court where Louis, who was
her father's cousin, would see to it that a suitable
husband was found. Hugh told himself that his
motives were for Catherine's sake. He would see
her once more, and then he would face his life
with Adele. A life which he saw quite clearly now
would be filled with harsh words, occasional
empty endearments, and long, lonely nights in
an empty bed.

Grabbing his satchel, Hugh strode from the
room. In the bailey, Avril stood at Cepheus's
head, a cross look on his face.

"What eats at you, boy?" Hugh demanded,
taking the reins.

"I think I should come with you, my lord."

"I think not."

"Who will look after Cepheus and see to your
tent?" he demanded indignantly.

"Avril, I spent many years caring for myself
and my horse without your fine services. I believe I can manage for a few days." The page
squared his jaw and silently expressed his dis-
agreement with his knight. "Besides," Hugh
added at last, "I need someone here in the event
that a message must be gotten to me. I put you
in charge of that."

"I don't know where you will be, my lord,"
Avril responded in a piqued voice.

Hugh mounted the stallion and then leaned
down, indicating that Avril step close. "I will be
in Chantilly."

A satisfied smile spread across the boy's face. " 'Tis well, my lord. I shall stay." Hugh shook his head. He was about to turn Cepheus to the portcullis when a lone rider approached through the open gate. He rode directly to Hugh, dismounted, and handed him an oiled skin containing a scrolled correspondence.

Hugh eyed the messenger carefully. "I know you," he said quietly, still holding the unopened packet in his hand.

The messenger nodded. "I serve the Duke de Neville, whose keep you recently passed a night in."

Hugh pursed his lips grimly. "And this correspondence is from his lordship?"

"Indeed, my lord."

Hugh was tempted to heave the packet into the moat unopened. The Duke de Neville could only be brewing trouble. Still, it might be foolhardy to ignore correspondence from a man Hugh deemed dangerous. At last he ripped the packet open and read the scroll within.

My Dear Vougnet,

    I thought you would like to know that Sir Jeffrey was found dead in my moat three days after you departed. How strange, do you not think, that the man who also found Lady Catherine a delectable morsel should be murdered? I travel to Paris to see Louis. I fear this matter of my dear friend's untimely demise must be brought to his attention. Unless, perhaps, you have a sugges-

tion for a different resolution? I shall journey to my beloved Pontoise before I visit the king. One way or another Pontoise is mine.

de Neville

Hugh crushed the inked parchment into a ball with the power of one fist. His face was deadly calm, and when he spoke his voice was as still as a glassy lake at dawn. Yet the messenger shook in his very boots at the piercing sword points that emanated from the ice-cold blue eyes of the Duke du Pontoise.

"Do you know where to find your master?" Hugh asked softly.

"*Oui,* my lord. He has told me where I might find him each night. He expects a reply."

"Good. Then take him my reply. Don't forget it, boy. Repeat it exactly as I tell it to you. Do you understand?" The messenger nodded, a lump of fear lodging in his throat. "Tell the duke that I spit upon his words. Tell him he may come to Pontoise with an army if he so wishes, and I will destroy his army. He may send the king and all his vassals to defeat me. This is *my* castle, and so it shall remain. And *nothing,* nothing at all, will cause me to relinquish it. Not even the king. It was given to me in good faith. And in good faith I will go to my death protecting it." Hugh did not wait for a response from the pale messenger. Wheeling Cepheus on his hind legs, he spurred the stallion into a gallop and rode out of the castle.

* * *

Sister Edith nudged Sister Gilbert and silently nodded toward the hen yard. Catherine stood in the midst of fifty hens, scattering seed on the frozen ground. She watched them peck away at the food with unseeing eyes as her hand scattered another fistful of seed. In the crisp morning light, her hair glistened like a red-gold river running down the back of her simple cloak. Though it was plaited, as always, all around her face unruly tendrils created a froth of curls that caught the sun's glistening light and turned it to spun fire.

"She's pale, you know."

Gilbert nodded in agreement. "Such a sad thing. She doesn't belong here."

"No, one can not use these walls to hide behind."

"What do you think it is?"

"Oh, a broken heart, dear. I'm quite certain of it."

"A troubadour should pen a song for her."

"Quite so."

Sister Gilbert sighed. "Isn't there something to be done for the child? I don't think my heart can bear to watch her day after day. It's too sad."

Edith nodded. "Well, let's have a talk with her."

"Indeed."

The two portly sisters crossed the yard of the *abbaye*, sending chickens scattering in all directions as they surrounded Catherine. "My dear," Sister Edith greeted her as she slipped an arm beneath Catherine's.

"Why good morning, Sisters," Catherine said with a soft smile. "Shouldn't you be at Matins?"

"You should be there also, dear," Gilbert reprimanded gently.

Catherine shook her head in an act of resignation. "I have prayed so much I fear the Lord grows tired of the sound of me," she explained. "I suspect it is better that He listen to the others today."

"Take a walk with us," Edith urged. She took the bucket of grain from Catherine and started toward the *abbaye* gates in her short-strided roll.

Catherine smiled affectionately at the two nuns and let them lead her through the gate and out along the road that wound through *the abbaye*'s fields. The two little nuns, had befriended her from the first day she'd arrived at the *abbaye* and they had remained so, cooing over her and concerning themselves with her welfare, or what they deemed her lack thereof. She was certain that today would be another tender discussion of her well-being.

"Are you feeling quite well, dear?" Sister Gilbert asked. She was always the one to take the less direct route. Edith, on the other hand, spared nothing in getting to her point.

"You cannot pine away here, Catherine, you know."

Catherine smiled at the pair and gently pressed

a kiss against Edith's soft forehead. "I promise you I shall not pine away. I spoke with Sister Mary James last night and have asked her to consider me as a candidate to be come a sister here."

Sister Gilbert's eyes popped wide in her head and Sister Edith gasped audibly. "The abbess did not agree to such a thing, did she?"

"Well, no," Catherine admitted as a chorus of sighs issued from the two nuns. "But she is considering it."

"Catherine, my dear," Edith said, squeezing her arm with motherly affection. "The *abbaye* is a wonderful place for people like Gilbert and me. We have always dreamed of coming to an *abbaye*. Hoped for the opportunity to serve the Lord in solitude and quiet. But you do not belong here."

Catherine gave a shrug of resignation. "It seems I belong no place."

"Oh, no!" Gilbert declared a bit too loudly. Meekly, she looked about to see if anyone had noticed her unseemly outburst. "We adore you, Catherine. But you aren't here because this is where you wish to be. You are here because you don't know where to go. There is an important difference."

"You are both so kind," Catherine said gently. "But I will be fine. I think I'll walk a bit by myself now. Would you mind?"

"No, no, dear!" the two chorused at once.

Catherine gave them each a pat on plump, mittened hands and struck off across a grassy knoll. Her pace was unhurried and thoughtful as she gazed out over the rolling hills, a wan smile touching her lips. It seemed a lifetime ago that she had been in Avignon. Not even three months had passed, yet she knew she could not go back there. She had changed. In Avignon, she had believed in silly things like the integrity of men, and faith in following your heart.

She felt so much older now. Now she knew much better than to believe such absurdities. There were no noble causes, only people pursuing their own needs. There was no chivalry. The songs they sung of love won, fair and true, were merely tales. There was no truth in them. She had believed in them. But she had learned much since then.

Her parents had done her a disservice, she thought sadly. She had grown up seeing love in their eyes when they looked at each other, and she had believed it was so with every couple. She hadn't known that love could grasp your heart and wrench it from your soul, leaving you bleeding and mortally wounded. She hadn't known that life was predetermined, that although you found love, you were not guaranteed to keep it. The cycle of time, the things set in motion years before, did not bend to accommodate love. Life went on. People went on. Except her.

She had thought that love would alter Hugh's life. She had believed that God would move his hand and make a place for them in the world—because she loved him. But Hugh's life went on.

Only hers had come to a screeching, soul-tearing halt.

She tried to remain confident in Terrence's words, tried to believe that there was some hope of Hugh telling his brother that he loved her and that his life, like hers, was changing because of that love. She closed her eyes and imagined him riding over the hillside. Coming to her free and clear.

But in her heart she did not believe that would ever come to pass. In her most secret place, she felt that Hugh was gone forever. She had thought, for the passage of a few short magical days, that he was there with her. But it had not really been so. He had always been gone. He had always belonged to Adele.

Hugh had spoken words of love which he never intended to turn into actions, and so, they had cost him little. Worse still, she, too, had spoken of a love that cost her little. She had still planned to go on to Strasbourg. She had thought that she would love him for a while, and go on with her life as it had been laid out for her. She had not planned to change anything. She, like Hugh, had spoken of love, but not understood what love required.

It required sacrifice. It required change. It required all that you had to give, in every way, at every moment, for all of your life. It required ripping your world and your soul apart, if necessary. And, Catherine acknowledged with a soft smile of understanding, it was always necessary.

Because to love someone truly, to love them as she loved Hugh, meant changing the mold of your life. It was impossible to simply *add* a love such as that to your life. Once love truly took hold of the fiber of your essence, your life became a joint existence.

Since the moment Hugh Vougnet had smiled up at her where she perched upon the portcullis when she was but twelve years old, she had been changed. Hugh had woven himself into the very weft of her being. She had believed that she could go on. Believed that she was not utterly changed by the knowledge that there existed in the world a person whose soul was made of the same stuff as her own. Whose eyes saw with a twin vision, whose heart beat an identical rhythm. But she had been so very wrong.

She had spoken of her love without understanding it, without knowing its true nature or the demand which it set upon her. She had spoken the words without understanding the price real love exacted. She had spoken her love to Hugh, but her words had been meaningless, meaningless until the moment when she had understood how utterly love had changed her. And how she must change her life because of that love.

Catherine would never have been able to go to Strausborg. She could not live such a lie, just as she could not live the lie of marrying any other man now. She would have been ostracized for her refusal, condemned and punished and shamed. But she would not have been able to go.

Nor could she go back to Avignon. Her love for Hugh had changed her too much. Avignon had been a place for dreams. Now she had only the reality that she loved and could not reap the harvest of her love. She would stay here. Here she would be safe from living a lie, and here she would have her love and still be able to exist. It was a sort of self-banishment. She would be safe from a world that would not understand.

Hugh would not be coming for her. Terrence, though his intentions were good, did not understand. Hugh had not understood love. So his love for her had not been real. If it *had* been real, he would have seen that his life must be rent apart and resewn with the thread of their love, fashioned into a new design the form of which was completely made from the weave of their unity. Until one understood love, one could not love completely.

No, Catherine thought sadly, Hugh would not come. He was going on with his life. Only hers was changed forever. Slowly, she turned and headed back toward the *abbaye*. She did not see the lone rider against the horizon who raced toward the hill.

Eighteen

But across the valley of Chantilly, the Duke de Neville *did* see the rider. Astride his charger, he motioned to a vassal. "Tell me, Lionel," he said, nodding toward the rider outlined by rays of the early-morning sun. "You can hit the mark at forty paces, can you make out the rider's herald?"

The knight didn't hesitate a moment. "My lord, it is clear to me from here. He wears a dove-gray tunic emblazoned with a red eagle-griffin and rides a black destrier."

"You know the herald?"

"*Oui*, my lord. 'Tis the same that took comfort at your castle, the king's most honored vassal. 'Tis Hugh Vougnet, now Duke du Pontoise."

The duke smiled. "Exactly as I thought."

Only the day before, his page had returned from Pontoise bearing the insolent reply of a knight who had far overstepped the boundaries of his place. That Vougnet would *dare* to send such a message infuriated him. What was more, he had spoken the words of impudence, not in private where his disdain for the message conveyed would have been delivered beyond the ken of others, but in public. In the bailey with the entire castle assembled for his leave-taking, that was where he chose to deliver his audacious response.

Lying awake all night, Bueil had created and discarded a thousand methods of revenge. Ridicule was not to be tolerated. His was an ancient family, and though its power had been much depleted since the time his father was duke, it was his own intention to restore the true rights and power of the family and himself.

The lands and title of Pontoise had been integral to the fruition of his plans. Vougnet had thwarted him once, and now he thought to obstruct him again. But Vougnet underestimated him. Underestimated him greatly. He was not, perhaps, of a size even close to the knight, nor was he possessed of fair face as was his adversary. But he was shrewd and cunning. And he had access to people and influence that an uninitiated fool such as Vougnet could not even imagine.

By dawn he had devised a scheme that was perfect. Over and over throughout the night, he had come back to the thing which he knew to be the knight's single point of vulnerability. And that was Catherine de Tralle.

Now he saw an even better opportunity. Why should he endanger himself when he could have someone else accomplish his end for him? He had met Adele de Pisan at court and she did not deceive him at all. She was of a nature similar to his own and her shield of piety did not hide from him her true disposition.

The duke turned to the vassal who sat on horseback beside him. "Lionel Martel," he said. "You will remain within sight of the *abbaye*." The vassal nodded. "If you see Vougnet depart, you are to ride as though Satan himself was chasing you. Come to the Castle at Pontoise, I will be there. If he does not come back through the gates, stay here at your post."

"*Oui,* my lord. But we do not know for certain that the duke rides for the *abbaye*."

"Oh, but we do, Lionel. We do."

He had seen her on the hillside just outside the *abbaye* walls. There could be no mistake that it was Catherine. The sun lit her flame tresses as she walked, and even from afar he had known it was she. Now Hugh galloped Cepheus through the *abbaye* gates and into the center of the walled compound. He was out of the saddle before the stallion had come to a complete halt. Thinking that he was a marauder come to harm them, frightened nuns ran for shelter, and Hugh was left standing alone.

Looking all around him, Hugh searched for Catherine. But if she had been here, she, too, had run for shelter. The prioress appeared through a doorway and came toward him, her stride unafraid and her face set with grim determination. Hugh smiled and bowed as she approached. "Sister Mary James."

"Your Grace," she responded, acknowledging his title as the duke.

Hugh grinned. "You are the first to recognize my title since my official investiture. I have just come from the king."

"Then I offer my congratulations," Sister Mary James added. "But I also add a reprove, for you have frightened the nuns terribly."

Hugh smiled and tipped his head in assent. "My apologies. I was only eager to make my arrival."

"Well, we are delighted to see you again, although I confess that I did not expect to see you so soon. Come, I shall show you to the stables and you may tell me what the nuns of Royaumont can do to assist you."

Hugh led Cepheus as he walked alongside the prioress. "I have come to see Catherine, if I may. There is a misunderstanding which I must correct."

Sister Mary James was a handsome woman, Hugh noted as they entered the stables. Tall and willowy, she must have been quite a beauty at one time. Yet she was formidable. Sure of herself and very determined to keep all aspects of the *abbaye* running smoothly. Hugh tied Cepheus and began to unsaddle him. As he worked, the prioress made no attempt to leave. Instead, she stood very calmly just a few strides away.

"There is no need for you to wait, Prioress. I

shall see to my steed's requirements and then come to your reception place."

"I was thinking that perhaps this is a better place to talk, Your Grace. It is quiet here and one may always speak their mind."

Hugh cocked a brow as he began to rub the sweaty hairs on Cepheus's back with a course sack. "I am hoping to see Catherine, as I said."

"You have had news of her circumstance?"

"*Oui*. I am concerned for her."

The prioress considered him for a long minute. "You know your way to the guest house?"

"Yes, thank you."

"I will send someone to fetch Catherine for you. I must warn you, my lord. I think there is some chance that she will not wish to see you."

Hugh stopped the circular motion of the sack against the steed's back. "Why do you suspect so, Sister?"

"She has borne a shock. It affects her deeply and as of yet, I have not seen her begin to recover.

Hugh looked sharply at the prioress. "Is she well? If she is ill, I must get her to Paris at once. The king's physician will look at her—"

"Nay, my lord. She is not sick of the body, but I fear that she is ill within her soul. Sometimes, that is the greater wound."

Hugh stared down at the packed mud floor of the small stable. He was to blame for Catherine's hurt, and he was here to hurt her further. Perhaps he had been wrong to come here. Perhaps things were best left as they were.

"If you feel it would do Catherine more harm than good, I will leave." He looked the prioress directly in the eye. "I shall defer to your judgment, for you have seen her, and not I."

For a long minute, Sister Mary James seemed to consider Hugh's offer. A soft smile at last touched her lips and she looked at Hugh and shook her head. "I think it is best if you see Catherine. Perhaps it will do her good."

Hugh smiled. He led Cepheus to a stall and filled a skin bucket with water. "Where will I find her?"

"She will be up in the medicinals room by now. She is quite talented with herbs and plants. In such a short time she has taught us so much. We shall miss her sorely when she leaves." Without another word, the prioress turned and left Hugh to the cleaning of his saddle.

He finished his work in a matter of minutes and made his way in the direction that Sister Mary James had indicated. The room was on the third floor of the lone turret in the *abbaye*. He should have stopped to bathe, but now that Catherine was so close at hand, he could not wait.

At the top of a long flight of winding stone steps, Hugh found the door the prioress had indicated. He knocked twice and waited. A moment later the door opened, and Hugh found himself looking into the wide-eyed face of a girl perhaps a dozen years old. The dark-haired child stood speechless with the door open but a crack and Hugh began to mumble an apology as he wondered how he could have ended up at the wrong room. Then he heard Catherine's voice come from inside the room.

"Esseline, what is it?"

Hugh reached out and gently pushed the door open. Esseline moved silently out of the way as Hugh stepped through it. The round tower room was warm despite the cold winter day. Along the walls stood tall cabinets lined with jars and crockery of all sizes and shapes. In the center of the room, a round table piled high with soft, finely made skeans of yarn served its mistress, and to one side a bench held more. The midmorning sun slanted through twin narrow windows where a breeze blew through to freshen the room. A kettle hung over the brightly burning fire in the hearth, and Catherine stood over it carefully dipping a skean into a dye the color of hyacinth in springtime.

Catherine. Her cheeks blushed with shades of peach blossoms that matched the hue of her simple woolen gown, and her coppery hair, though twined into a long plait, as always wreathed her face with loosely curling tendrils of fire. She was even more beautiful than he remembered. More petite, more finely wrought. From the gentle curve of her golden brows to the long, slender taper of her fingertips, she was perfect. There was nothing of her that was not the masterpiece of a sculptor's hand. And he wanted to touch her. He remembered the feel of her against him, the warmth of her lips upon his, the spring-fresh scent of her. And he hungered for it.

Time had suddenly frozen and stopped, like the stilled water that ran through the cloister on a winter's dawn. Catherine could not move. She stared at the man in the doorway, willing it not to be so. It could not be Hugh. Not here. Not now. Not when she'd healed so much. Just now, when she was beginning to be able to see life as it would be, she could not believe that he had come back to torture her.

She forced herself to straighten, pulling the yarn from the kettle of dye. With slow, measured steps she crossed to the drying rack and carefully laid the skean over a rod to dry. Every movement was a victory. Every step an accomplishment. Her heart pounded so against her chest she thought he must surely hear it. Her hands shook and she clasped them before her, twining her fingers together to make them still.

"Hugh," she said at last. She made the name sound like any other word, not letting her voice quaver or break. There could be no sign that it mattered to her at all that he was here.

"I must speak with you, Catherine."

His eyes were the same. Soft, warm eyes of a color unlike any other. His face, as well, was exactly as she knew it. But, she reminded herself, he was not as she knew him. He did not know the meaning of love. He did not understand that words spoken meant nothing without understanding. He was not hers. He would never, ever be hers. And she must keep him at arm's length. Even farther. She must send him away. Now, and in a way that he would know never to return.

"You should not have come, Hugh."

He stepped toward her and Catherine retreated an equal distance. Turning to Esseline, he nodded toward the doorway. "You must excuse us. I have need of a private moment with Lady Catherine."

"Stay!" Catherine cried as Esseline took a step toward the door. "Stay, Esseline. It is not fitting that we are left alone."

"Go, Esseline." It was a soft, yet undeniable command. "Sister Mary James knows I have come to see Catherine, and I have received her blessing to do so. Go, Esseline. And send no one to disturb us."

The girl noiselessly slipped through the door and Catherine listened to the softly receding patter of her slippers on the stone stairs with a sinking heart. Hugh took a single step backward and closed the door, letting the iron latch fall into place.

Catherine turned away and walked to one of the slitted windows. She brushed a wayward wisp of hair from her face and stared out over the barren fields below. She did not speak. She only felt the numbness that had encased her heart. Hearing Hugh's footfall behind her, Catherine turned abruptly, holding out a warning hand. "No, Hugh. Don't come near. 'Tis much better that you keep an arm's length between us. I don't know why you have come. It cannot bring us any good, whatever it is."

"Cay."

He spoke the pet name with a yearning that nearly split her heart in two, but she did not let it sway her. Shaking her head, she crossed to the hearth. Catherine crossed her arms before her, forming an unconscious shield against the power of Hugh's presence.

"Please go," she entreated him. "Don't you understand? Nothing can come of any of this."

Hugh hung his head in despair. "You are right, Catherine. So right. But I cannot go until I have made you understand."

"What am I to understand, Hugh?" Catherine asked, turning to face him. "That you love Adele? That I was merely a distraction? A secondary thing? A pastime? Nay, Lord Vougnet, save your words. I know that already. I admit that I did not understand it to be so until very recently. I thought . . ." Catherine stopped, unable to continue for the knot of tears that constricted her throat and lodged her words there. She struggled for control, determined that she not weaken now. Then, pursing her lips against her pain, she continued. "I thought it was a true love we spoke of to each other. But it was not."

Hugh's head jerked up, and he stared at her with piercing intensity, but Catherine continued on. She wanted it over. She wanted to destroy any hope that remained within her. And there *was* hope. Though her mind told her all that was sensible, though she knew with an intellectual certainty that she had nothing to hope for with Hugh, despite all that, a tiny blossom of hope still existed in her heart. She had felt it when she saw him standing in the doorway. She had felt it when the sound of his boots on the stone floor told her he stood only inches away from her. She felt it now as she told Hugh that there was nothing left of them. And it hurt. She wanted it gone, for it was a vain, silly thing. A thing of the past. A thing that the Catherine of old would have believed in, and nurtured. But there was no place for it in this new world of hers, and she was determined to obliterate it once and for all.

"Was it not real love we spoke of?" Hugh asked her. He shook his head. "I think you are wrong, Cay. 'Twas real love in my heart. Strong, and true, and more real than any emotion I have ever felt."

"Nay," Catherine replied with a determined shake of her head. "We each spoke words of love, but we did not grasp the true meaning. We played at affection, enjoying for the moment the bond we shared, yet not tempted to change the course set for us."

Hugh stepped toward her. "It is real love for me, Catherine. It comes from the best place within me."

"But you did not think to change your life for me," she accused. Her breath was short and her heart had begun to pound again. She clenched her hands at her sides, feeling the oval tips of her nails dig into the flesh of her palms.

Catherine did not want to hear his words. She did not want the pain that spread like a throbbing ache within her. "Did you come here to tell me that you love me?" she demanded as a growing panic seized her. "So that I should have your words as I watch you ride across the frozen plains on your way back to Adele? Is that why you are here? For if it is, you may spare yourself, Hugh. I do not want such a love. What service do you do me to tell me you love me truly, yet show me the measure of your love by returning to another's embrace?"

"Another's embrace?" Hugh spat the words from his mouth like some foul poison. "Do you think I come from another's embrace, or go away from you to the same? It is not so, Catherine." Hugh closed his eyes and drew a long breath. Catherine could feel the pain that pleated his brow as though it was her own, and it was all she could do to stop her hand from reaching out to brush away his hurt.

His mouth forming a bitter line, Hugh turned away from her. He ran his fingers through his blond locks and stared for a long minute out beyond the hills of France. Catherine waited with a growing dread. This morning she had been so certain that Hugh had betrayed her. She had believed that she understood with absolute clarity the inherent weakness in their need for each other. But now she had lost all of that. She only knew that she ached to touch him. That she loved him as she would never in her life love anyone else. That of all the people in all the world, there was no one who had been created as perfectly for her as Hugh. And as she waited for whatever was to come, she knew that the pain of losing him again would be unbearable.

When he turned to face her once more, the searing pain had spread until it changed the contours of every plane and angle of his face. His cheek jerked reflexively as he clenched his mouth into a thin line of pain. "I came here to tell you that I am married, Catherine."

Of all the words he might have spoken to her, they were the most painful, for they were irrevocable words. Absolute and unalterable. Catherine closed her eyes against the anguish that gripped her like a vise. "Thank you for telling me," she whispered. "It was important that I know."

"Terrence told me of the promise he had made to you." Hugh sighed. "I could not let him send you such news in a missive. I had to tell you myself."

Catherine nodded. "It was good of you to come so far. I am glad, Hugh, that I did not hear it from some messenger or passerby. It is far better that I know it from you." She was numb and unable to think. She heard herself saying words that sounded right to her ears but spoke not one sliver of the truth that lay in her heart. In her heart she was sick with grief. She felt the walls that she had so carefully constructed crumble beneath the onslaught of his words. She could not protect herself. The hurt was too great. She loved him. She loved him with an absoluteness that brooked all else. There was no reason, no sense, no logic to the total, consuming need that flowed through her.

"But there is more I must tell you, Cay."

She looked up at him in confusion. What more could he possibly say? What else of import existed? Dully, she nodded.

Hugh saw Catherine sway on her feet. He crossed the room in three long strides and took her gently by the elbow. "Sit down."

She did as he said and, miraculously, there was a leather stool beneath her. Her knees shook, and when she set her fingers upon them to quiet their quivering, she saw that they, too, trembled. Hugh bent onto one knee before her and placed his large hand over hers, steadying it.

"I married her, Catherine. It was my duty to do so. But you must know it is a marriage without love. Without even the smallest morsel of affection."

Catherine shook her head. "You must try to love her, Hugh. It is not fair to her—"

"Nay," he whispered softly. "You do not understand, Catherine. It is not me alone who feels nothing. It is Adele as well. We were betrothed when she was still a tiny babe as a means of uniting the properties of two adjoining fiefs. It is a common enough practice. But Adele has never looked at me and seen anything but a course, Godless man. She is pleased enough to be the Duchess du Pontoise, that is evident. She has already made it known to me, and to the entire fief, that she cares little for what I wish done and intends to run it as she pleases.

"She has not yet discovered that it will not be as she wishes." A wry smile touched his lips for a moment. Then it disappeared, replaced by thin lines of fatigue that marked either side of his mouth. "We will never share a bed. Even on our wedding night, we did not touch." Hugh shook his head quietly. "And she thanked me."

Hugh's hand on hers moved. His broad war-scarred fingers closed around hers and he stared solemnly into her eyes. Blue touched green. Need reached for need. Despair melded with despair. For long seconds, he held her eyes. But at last Catherine broke the spell of their gaze, and her stare dropped to where her hands rested beneath Hugh's.

"I love you, Catherine. Do you think I did not know the meaning of the words when I said them to you? Perhaps you are right. I did not know that I couldn't go on without you. I looked at Adele and saw duty. I am a warrior, Catherine, and duty to my king is all. It is a shallow excuse, I know. But it is the truth. I thought I could leave you behind. Believed I could put you from me. But it is impossible. Even as I rode here, I believed I could tell you of my marriage, see to your welfare and be done with it. What a fool I was!"

He took her hands in his, pulling them toward him as he searched her face. "Look at me, Catherine."

She did not want to. She wanted to turn and run, escape. Some way, any way, she needed to put a shield back between them.

"Catherine." It was a voice she knew so well. Hugh's voice. The deep, gentle tone she loved. Slowly, she lifted her eyes to meet his. "Forgive me. Forgive me for fulfilling my duty. But more than that, forgive me for loving you. I have no right, but neither can I help what I feel. I ask for nothing more. But I kneel before you, and beg your forgiveness for a love that burns like a bonfire in my soul. I have no right to your affections. No right to your heart. Only say you forgive me."

Like the first drops of rain that portent a torrent of water held in rain-heavy clouds, Catherine felt her love for Hugh seep from the vessel in which she had attempted to hold it and quench her soul. Her fingers curled around his strong hands, speaking in a language without words. Gently, she broke the grasp and her fingers reached for his face. She touched his brow as though memorizing it—each crease, each line, its texture and contour. And where her fingers moved, her eyes followed. She touched the lids of his eyes and the strong, straight ridge of his nose. The flat planes of his cheeks sported the fine nub of a day's growth of beard and she traced along the line of his jaw to the place where he bore a battle scar that had not been there when she had first met him. She let her fingers run across his mouth and felt the warmth of his breath against her flesh.

Her eyes moved back to his, and her lips parted in a soft sigh of surrender. "I love you, Hugh. I will love you for all time."

The world beyond the circle of their souls melted away. There was only the two of them. Only a love stronger than the forces of time or duty or tomorrow. There was only now. Only their overwhelming need for each other. Hugh's lips pressed against her fingertips, his kiss was like the golden warmth of sunlight reaching to her soul.

Catherine leaned forward and let her fingers slip down to his chest as her lips replaced fingers against his mouth. Her eyes closed as his lips moved against hers. He pressed gentle kisses against her mouth. Kisses that grew and deepened as they released the need that had been held so tightly in check. She felt the tip of his tongue run along the crease of her mouth and she gave entrance there, feeling it caress the soft inner wall of her mouth. And Catherine returned in kind. Her tongue touched his, exploring, discovering and learning.

She felt his arms close around her as he drew her from the stool and onto his bent knee. Her arms twined about his neck and he drew her

closer still. Her breasts pressed against the broad
expanse of his chest as she buried her fingers
deep in his golden blond hair and their kisses
grew strident. A moan escaped from deep within
Hugh. He kissed her mouth and her cheeks, her
forehead and the tip of her nose. He pressed
kisses into the tendrilled curls about her face and
sighed against them.

"I love you, Catherine. As God is my witness,
I love you."

"And I you," she whispered back. Pulling herself back from their embrace she cupped her
hand along the strong curve of his jaw and
looked into his eyes. "Love me, Hugh. That I
might know what it is."

Hugh opened his mouth to speak, but Catherine placed one finger against his lips. "What
else have I? I will not marry another man. Let
me have once, what will never be mine."

Hugh searched her gaze. She was here at the
abbaye. And Adele had made much of telling him
she had no interest in sharing his bed now or
ever. He and Catherine, each of them separately,
would be alone. What wrong could there be in
giving themselves to each other? They gave what
no one else wanted from them.

Hugh pulled Catherine against him, holding
her tight in his encompassing embrace. She
pressed a kiss against his neck and then another.
He bent his head to hers and their gazes locked.

"Love me," she whispered again. With a final
groan of surrender, Hugh dipped his mouth to

TEMPTED

hers. Her tongue flicked along one corner of his mouth and he met it full with his own. White-hot embers seared through him as though a fired sword blade had been thrust to his heart. He crushed her against him and his hand ran down the length of her back, curving around the soft-ness of her buttocks. His desire was beyond de-sire. It was beyond need.

Catherine. In all of his life, only Catherine reached to his soul. Only she saw him as he was, loved him as he was. All his life he had been but half. And Catherine was the other half, the thing he had searched for relentlessly and without fruition the world over. Hugh stroked her golden-red tresses and kissed her gently. "Wait." Stand-ing, he crossed to the table and scooped up the pile of undyed skeans that lay there. He carried them to where Catherine sat before the hearth and let them drop to the ground, covering the hard stone floor. He repeated the same with the skeans that lay upon the bench and, when he was done, the floor before the crackling fire was transformed into a bed of soft lamb's wool.

Coming back to her, he drew her up from the stool and pulled her into his arms. She came willingly. He turned her face up to his and once more searched there for fear or doubt, but he saw only the soft curve of her smile and a sure, loving gaze that spoke volumes to him. Hugh slid his arm beneath her legs and lifted her in his arms. Gently, he lowered her onto the makeshift bed and stretched out beside her. He reached for the ribbon at the end of her plaited hair and untied it with a single movement. He drew her hair from its prison and spread it across the soft skeans like coppery strands of the same.

It was his turn now to trace the contours that were Catherine. He began at her face, lingering at the soft rise of her cheekbone and tracing the curves of her ear. Catherine felt his fingers trail from the lobe of her ear along the length of her neck, blazing a searing path across her skin. Hugh showered her with kisses as his fingers pulled the string that gathered her dress and loosened the top that he might explore further. His hand dipped within the confines of her gown and she gasped at the warmth of his palm cupping her breast. As the pad of his thumb rubbed across her nipple, she felt it harden under his touch.

He rained kisses along her neck. Following with his lips the path his hand had forged. As his fingers gently caressed the fullness of her breast, he laid open the neck of her gown further and dipped his head to where his hand now played. Catherine felt warm, sweet pleasure course through her as his mouth closed over the pink peak of her breast. His tongue encircled it, his teeth nipped ever so softly at it, and then, as she thrust it higher, wanting more from him at the very time she did not know what more there was, he suckled at her breast. Catherine pushed her fingers through his thick golden hair, pressing his mouth more fully onto her breast. With a moan of pleasure, she rolled to her side and molded her hips against his in a movement as ancient and natural as life.

Hugh released her nipple from his tongue's ministrations and brushed his lips across hers. His kiss demanded more, his tongue plunging deep within the recesses of her mouth and then running across the pearly fronts of her teeth before dipping again to the soft inner part of her mouth. His hand moved to her buttocks and he cupped them, pulling her closer against his hips, fitting her intimately to him. Catherine felt the hard maleness of him thrusting against her. But she was not afraid, for it was the manifestation of his need for her. And she felt it, too. Her own undeniable need for him. It scored her heart, branding it as his for all eternity. It reached deep within her and demanded satiety. It called for her to follow where she had never journeyed before.

Following Hugh's lead, Catherine set her fingers to exploration as well. She caressed the soft folds of his shirt beneath his gray tunic and felt the hard curve of his chest. He was as solid as an oak and yet pliant. Rough and yet smooth. As she explored and became bolder, Hugh reached over his shoulder to pull the tunic and shirt off. She knew his body, for hadn't she seen it twice when she'd bathed him at Avignon? But it was as if she saw it now for the first time. She reached out, running her fingers through the furred hairs of his chest. She encircled his nipple with her finger as he had done to her and felt a surge of pleasure when he moaned against her ear at her action. Remembering her own delight, Catherine dropped her mouth to his nipple and licked the tip until it stood hard and sharp against her tongue.

Unable to bear it, Hugh pulled her against him, drawing her mouth back to his, searing her lips with an onslaught of kisses. As he held her close with one hand, the other sought entrance beneath the heavy folds of her gown. Gently, Catherine brushed away his fingers. She sat up and, reaching for the hem, drew the kirtle over her head and lay back against the heavy wool. She was more beautiful than he could ever have imagined. Her skin was as pale as cream and as perfect, and she was formed as though God himself had taken a hand to the suppleness of her body.

Hugh ran a single finger down the length of her leg as he sat up and began to loosen the drawstrings of his hose. A moment later he was beside her again. Together they touched and traced. Admiring each other. Seeking to give as each received. The fire was warm and the skeans of yarn soft, and for Hugh and Catherine the world beyond each other had ceased to exist. Hugh caressed the flat plane of her stomach and nibbled at her hip. He traced the soft, sensitive inner part of her thigh and Catherine was filled with desire that raged and grew and consumed. When her breathing became short he brushed his fingertips across the soft mound between her legs, gently stroking as she pressed against him.

Hugh's touch was sweet beyond her wildest imaginings. Never in her life had Catherine believe that sensations such as those that swept over her in cascade upon cascade could be. When he touched her, she felt the need within her grow to bursting. Higher and higher she flew, like Amaranth in flight. She soared and swooped, and yet as she did, she also searched. She arched toward Hugh, and he covered her body with his. Poised above her, he pressed a kiss to her ear and whispered softly, "It will hurt, Catherine. But just for a moment."

Catherine opened her eyes and looked into Hugh's with a trust so deep it cut to the core of his heart. "Nay, my love. It cannot hurt," she told him gently. "I have felt hurts, and there is nothing painful in my becoming a part of you."

Hot tears formed at the corners of Hugh's eyes as he bent to press a tender kiss against her mouth. "I love you more than life itself, Catherine. I will forever."

She arched toward him, her gaze locked with his, and he slid inside her. The pain was quick and sharp, but it was obliterated by the sensation of Hugh within her. Skin against skin, heart against heart, they formed their union. Their eyes never parted as they began to move in unison with each other. The desire that had built within her drove Catherine onward. Her arms around Hugh's shoulders, she rose with his rising, retreated with his retreat. Hugh held himself taut, moving within Catherine yet denying his need. But with every movement, she pulled him deeper within her, creating a fire inside him that raged and consumed and seeped through every fiber of his being. He watched Catherine's desire grow and then, just as he knew he must satiate his own need, she drew him against her with an urgency that brooked no refusal. Together they soared. Together they mounted the sky and flew. As Catherine felt the falcon within her crest its flight, Hugh convulsed against her, pouring himself within her. They were united. One. No longer separate, but joined for all eternity through the sacred rite of love.

Hugh rolled onto the soft skeans of wool and drew her against his chest. Her head was tucked beneath his chin, and he stroked her fiery hair as he watched the flames in the hearth consume the enormous logs set there. Until he had seen her today, he had not known. Catherine had been right. Until he walked into this room and saw her standing here, he had not understood the depths of his love for her. He had not known because he had never felt such a need before. He had not understood that there could be a person without whom life was not worth living. But he had learned. He had understood the very moment he had set eyes on her again. There was no compromise. There was no duty. There was only Catherine and his abiding love for her. Against his chest he heard her soft, even breathing. Reaching across her, he pulled her gown over her, to warm her as she slept. And so he held her as the light faded beyond the tower room and far into the night.

Matins had ended, and as the nuns returned to their cells for the night, Sister Mary James stood quietly in the cloistered garden. The dim light that issued from the medicinals room in the *abbaye* tower told her the fire still burned brightly, stoked by some hands that remained in the room. She was thinking of her own youth and of the man she had loved beyond all reason. But it was not to be, and she had come here to seek solace and shelter for her heartache.

How many years ago was that? she wondered. So very long ago that her arrival here was nothing but a dim memory. But the love she had felt for her own knight remained as sharp as the first light of dawn on the horizon each day. Perhaps if she would have fought. Perhaps if she knew all the things she knew now, she would have done it differently. *Forgive me, my Lord, if I have sinned this day. Forgive me if it is wrong of me to wish for young Catherine that she not hide behind these walls. There is solace here and much joy. But I believe our Catherine is destined for other things. If I have done wrong to aid that, then I profoundly beg your forgiveness.*

Touching her fingers to her forehead, breast, and each shoulder, the prioress retired for the night to her cell.

Nineteen

It was still dark when Hugh kissed Catherine awake. The bells had not yet tolled for Mass, though the first brightness of dawn would soon begin to touch the sky. "Come, Cay," he whispered in her ear. I will take you to your room. The *abbaye* will soon be stirring."

Catherine opened sleepy eyes and looked up at him. Her smile was sweet and warm, and she reached up to caress his cheek unconcerned that the world around them was about to come alive. Hugh leaned down to catch her lips in a kiss and gave her rump a gentle pat. "We cannot be here, Catherine. 'Tis asking too much."

Nodding in understanding, Catherine pulled her kirtle over her head and slid her feet into her soft kid slippers. Hugh dressed quickly as well and together they carried the skeans of yarn back to the table and bench. They made their way in silence, and when they reached the door to Catherine's cell, Hugh pulled her once more into his arms.

"I love you, Catherine. And I say those words understanding, at last, their impact. I do not know what will happen now. I only know I cannot live without you. I ride for Paris again, where I shall speak in private to the king. I don't know what he can do, but I trust him. Mayhap he will have an answer."

Catherine leaned up to kiss him. "I love you, Hugh. And I will be here, even if you cannot return."

Terrence held his stallion in check behind the copse of pine trees as he watched the scene before him. In the yard of a villein's home, the new steward of Pontoise leaned over a serf who held one crying babe on her hip as two more clung silently to her skirt folds.

"Monsieur Corvey," she entreated with a sob. "How can I pay? My husband is dead nine month ago from the flux and I've four children to feed and clothe. My Denys works a full day in the fields though he's not yet ten. And I work at the castle with the other laundresses. 'Tis all I can do! There is no time for me to plow my small plot, how am I to give you the grain and seed you require?"

"That is not my concern!" the steward told her as his lip curled in contempt. Shaking a long parchment in her face, he sneered at her. "My job is to collect what is owed to the duke. What excuse should I give, eh?! Should I have my position threatened because of you? Gaspar Corvey took the woman's free arm and pulled her face close to his. "You have three days to get me the grain and seed required. Otherwise, I'm afraid you'll have to be whipped." The woman whimpered in fear, but Corvey merely shrugged. "I need an example. So the other villeins won't think that excuses are acceptable. And I'm afraid it will have to be you."

As he turned to leave, the toe of Corvey's boot caught on the pants of one of the young children at her feet. With a curse, he boxed the child's ears and sent him reeling, then strode to his horse and was soon galloping up the road to the castle.

His lips pursed in anger, Terrence urged his stallion out from their hiding place. He rode into the small yard and dismounted. The woman was busy quieting her child's wails of pain and did not see Terrence until he was nearly upon her. Gasping with fear, she fell to her knees and pulled her children close against her ample breasts. "Do not hurt them!" she cried.

Before he could speak, two villeins appeared from behind the house, each carrying a sickle. They came to a stop when they had put themselves between the mother and Terrence. "Leave her be, now," the first said quietly.

"I intend this woman no harm." Terrence told them. "I am the duke's brother, Terrence Vougnet."

"Then fie to you and a hex on the new duke, say I," the second affirmed.

"What has my brother done to deserve your contempt?" Terrence demanded.

The two men looked at each other and laughed. "Tell us what he has *not* done! A nastier lord we've never heard of in all our days. The old duke was a good man, and if we lose our heads for our words, then 'tis better that we suffer quickly than suffer slowly under this man's torturous rule."

"You still don't tell me the things he has done to you," Terrence repeated calmly.

"Then let me tell you now!" said the taller man. He set the end of his sickle on the ground and leaned forward on it with both hands about the wooden handle. "Before he was even back from the Crusades, he ordered a tax of every serf. Two bushels of wheat, another of flax, a cow, two hens, and a pig! 'Twas his greeting to us that he pauper his own people before he has even made Pontoise his home!"

"Oui!" the second man agreed with a rapid nod. "When it was learned he would wed, notice was given that the villeins would not be included in the celebration." He shrugged. "We have heard of lords like that. Men who did not include the serfs in their personal celebrations. The old duke would have, but we thought but a little of his choice."

"And?" Terrence prompted.

"And then, the night of the marriage, his knights come knocking on every door. They pass out food and ale and tell us the duke wishes us to celebrate as well."

"In his cups that night he was," the woman

piped in as her fear lessened and she began to nod in agreement with the men. "That's why he sent the food."

"Mayhap," the tall man agreed. "But the very next night, the knocking comes on our doors again. Only this time, 'tis the new steward. He says someone stole all the food and ale from the castle! Wherever he finds remnants of the food, the man is given ten lashes."

"My own son was whipped because he said the duke sent the food and drink himself and Corvey accused him of lying!" added the second man.

"I do not believe these were Hugh's doings," Terrence told them with an angry shake of his head.

"Who else then?" the two men asked in unison. "No one else has such power!"

"And he hired Corvey, did he not?" added one. "His reputation is known for miles in all directions. 'Tis said he lives to hurt the innocent. He rapes the women, whips the men, maims the children. What kind of man would hire someone like Corvey? We have done nothing but attempt to serve this new lord of ours well."

"It won't be tolerated," warned the second. "People here know they work hard. They will not stand for treatment such as this."

Terrence stood in silence, listening to the men as he nodded. He knew Hugh would not do these things, and he also knew whom he believed would. He had never cared for Adele. He had decided that he would try to make peace with her now that she was Hugh's wife, but if she was responsible for the villeins' growing hatred for his brother and the problems rebellion would create for him, Terrence would do whatever was necessary to protect Hugh's interests.

He turned to the woman in whose yard he stood. "What was the duty Monsieur Corvey required of you?"

The villein put her head in her hands and once more began to weep. "He wants the tax! The wheat and flax, hens and cow and pig! Look!" she cried, holding out her arm to indicate her house and tiny yard. "Where will I get those things? I will be whipped and then I will not be able to work at the castle. I'll earn no wages and then my babes will starve!"

Terrence shook his head gently. "Nay, mistress. I shall get the tax required and bring it to you tomorrow. Then you may pay Corvey and he will not hound you any further."

The widowed woman looked at him in wonder. "Milord, I could never repay you."

"I have not asked for repayment, have I?" The woman shook her head mutely.

"What is your name?"

"Herta, milord," she replied, curtsying.

"Herta, your tax shall be here before Corvey comes to collect it." He turned to the two men who listened to the exchange with sharp interest. "My brother has not done this. As a sign of goodwill from you, I ask that you hold your judgment until he returns from Paris and I can speak to him of all this. And if another such incident occurs, one of you must come and tell me. I am staying at the castle."

The two men nodded in agreement. "Not all brothers are alike," replied the tall one. "But until another incident occurs, we will put some faith in you, for you have proven yourself with this kindness to our friend."

Terrence held out his good arm and in turn each man grasped his hand in friendship. The woman named Herta curtsied again and Terrence left them, riding thoughtfully in the direction of Pontoise Keep.

Adele sat on the stool in her solar, spine straight as a broomstick as she listened to the Duke de Neville.

"Unfortunately," he continued in a sympathetic voice, "it is common. You know that a man's eye is often turned away from his wife by a fair maiden. But because I consider myself your friend, I could not in good conscience let you go on unsuspecting of his infidelity." He paused for a moment and then continued. "And to discover that you are wed less than a fortnight! My dear, I am appalled at your husband's lack of control."

"Hugh has never had control," Adele averred. "Satan has a hold on his soul and his mind, I have always known that. But now his command of my husband has reached into his body." Her

thin hands were balled into tight, unyielding fists
which she shoved into the lap of her kirtle. "He
breaks the Lord's commandments and does it
within the walls of a sanctified abbey! Always he
has shamed himself with his Godless ways. But
now, he has shamed *me* as well. Now the taint of
his sin touches me!"

Her head jerked up sharply and she stared at
Lord Bueil with sharply narrowed eyes. "He will
never touch me! Thanks to the good Lord that
I did not let him in my bed on our wedding
night. I am still virginal and pure in the Lord's
eyes. Hugh will never set the stain of his adul-
terous hands upon my body. Never."

The duke nodded in understanding support.
"I fear, though, my dear Lady Adele, that he will
go back. Probably they were lovers before you
were even able to reach him at the Abbaye de
Royaumont."

Adele turned to him and clasped his hand in
hers. "Thank you so much for your warning,
Lord Bueil. I saw the whore there and it was
clear she thought she had possession of him. Of
a certainty they sinned even then. I tried to save
him. I rode a full day to reach that place, which
surely God has now forsaken, just to save his
soul! But for naught! His sin was already upon
him. And now he has doubled that sin by making
it adultery against our marriage."

"The question now," Bueil stressed as he gave
her hand a pat and let it drop, "is what you shall
do about it. Is it enough simply to keep Hugh

from your bed? Do you not care that he returns again and again to the red-haired wench? Perhaps she will stay at the *abbaye*. It is a convenient place. Nearby, but secluded. He can be with her there whenever he chooses."

"Nay!" Adele cried out in anger. "He will not continue to vilify a place of God's. He will not continue to breach our marriage vows. It will not be!"

"Then if you confront him, his respect for you is such that he will stop seeing the woman?"

Adele stared unseeing at the rushes by her feet. No, Hugh would not respect her enough to leave the she-devil.

Child of Satan. That was what the red-haired woman was. Temptation. Lust. Greed. Voluptuous and pagan. In Adele's mind, Catherine was the embodiment of all evil. Hugh was weak. From her earliest recollections she had known he was weak. He sought pleasure. He never cared to toil and do penance, gaining favor in the eyes of God. He attended Mass, he said the words of piety, but he did not *live* piety. He rode out on his hulking black horse, full of pride. She sent him to the Crusades to do God's work and what did he do? He returned with the spoils of war and his pride was even greater for he did not say, "God gave me these things." He said, "Men gave me these things. The king gave me these things." He was blind and deaf to the Lord God. And now he spent his body upon the devil. A body that, by rights of God's law, was *hers*, to use or not, as she pleased.

He spent it with a whore. A woman who would hide behind the walls of an abbey and think nothing of vilifying it with her adultery. He spilled his seed upon her. Filled her body with his power. And who knew when that seed would take root and a child, a bastard son, grow in her belly.

NO! Adele's mind screamed out. The whore woman would *not* drag her husband into her den of iniquity. Adele would save Hugh and wreak God's vengeance upon the woman who dared to defy his law.

Lord Bueil, Duke de Neville, smiled as he watched Adele Vougnet's fury and fervor rise. Lionel Martel had arrived at Pontoise yesterday with the news that Vougnet had spent the night at the *abbaye* and ridden for Paris at dawn. The choices were numerous. He could threaten Vougnet with blackmail, accuse him of murdering Jeffrey Winfrey, or put him in doubt of Catherine de Tralle's welfare.

One way or another, he would get what he wanted from the knight. But first, he thought, he would make Vougnet squirm like a worm on the hook.

Avril worked his cloth through another ring in Hugh's mail as Terrence entered the armorer's shed at the back of the stables. "Lord Terrence!"

the armorer called over his hammering. "I have your mail for you to try."

"Good," said Terrence with a grin. "I'm anxious to see if your idea works." Terrence had approached the armorer with a unique problem. Ever since his arm had shrunken, he could not fit his mail properly. Perhaps there would be little use for it in the future, but he wanted to be ready should the need be there. Despite his injury, he was still strong and skilled with a battle-ax which he could wield well with his good left hand. He glanced over at Avril and laughed. "You are going to wear Hugh's mail down to nothing, lad. The thing shines so already that I can barely stand to look at it without shielding my eyes!"

Avril said nothing, but attacked the steel links with renewed ardor.

The armorer tossed his head in Avril's direction and smiled. "He pines for his master, I think."

"He should have taken me with him," the boy pouted without looking up.

"Avril, Hugh asked you to stay behind for a reason. I heard him say so myself," Terrence said. "Have you been doing as he asked?"

"No message has come that I must take to him."

"How do you know that? Have you been watching for signs that Hugh should be called back to Pontoise?"

Avril's head came up at last and he eyed first

the armorer and then Terrence. "Perhaps you are right and the mail is clean enough." Avril carefully set the mail on its hooks, put his rag away, and headed for the door. As he passed Terrence, he gave him a hard stare and a short jerk of his head.

Terrence followed the page outside with a wry smile. "What is it?"

"Strange things are going on here, Lord Terrence."

Terrence pursed his lips, saying nothing until they had passed through the bailey's portcullis and were beyond the hearing of interested ears. "Tell me what you have seen."

"It is everything!" the boy told him with a wave of his arm. "The knights grumble that Lady Adele sets rules which His Grace would never agree with. The armorer, the cooks, the workers in the fields. They all talk of unfair treatment and grumble that they shall not serve a lord who abuses them. But my master would not do such things as they describe."

"I know," Terrence agreed.

"It is that woman."

"That woman is your master's wife," Terrence warned. Avril clamped his mouth shut, stuffed his hands into his belt and walked faster. Terrence reached out to grasp his shoulder and slow him down. "I agree with all you have said, lad. It is just a warning that it is dangerous to speak ill of someone with as much power as Adele."

Avril stopped and turned to face Terrence. "I

cannot stand by and watch it, so I polish his mail and Cepheus's saddles or have the cook sharpen his ax. But it is not good. Lord Hugh needs to return to Pontoise and set things right."

"He is not due back for several more days, but I think perhaps you are right. He should come back before something more happens that sends the villeins into revolt. But I don't know where he is. He could be in Chantilly or Paris."

"I will go to both and find him," Avril declared.

Terrence looked the boy square in the eye. "I will send you with Wesley du Fonte to Chantilly. I will take Grier and Gladmoore and head for court in Paris."

Avril nodded, his eyes sharp and serious beyond his years.

"You know the message you must take?"

"*Oui!* I shall not come back without him if he is there."

"Good." The two turned and walked back to the keep in silence. When they reached the bailey, Terrence clamped his hand on Avril's shoulder. "He is lucky to have you, lad."

The boy's face lit with pride. "I hope I serve him well."

The four men left at dawn the next day. Two headed south and west toward Chantilly, the others south and east to Paris.

* * *

Despite his agitation, Hugh forced himself to sit perfectly still and listen to the king's lecture. "You have created a very uncomfortable situation for me, Hugh! What am I to do? Ignore the pope? Fly in the face of the church of Rome? I have no idea why you went through with the marriage. You sit here now," Louis declared as he paced across the room. "Telling me your troubles. Why could you not do so before? Why didn't you come and tell me that you did not wish to marry Adele de Pisan?" The king shook his fist in frustration at his favorite vassal, the man he had invested as a duke not three days before. "Then I could have done something. Without the blink of an eye, I could have declared the betrothal nullified.

"But a marriage! Hugh, a marriage is a different thing."

"I thought it was my duty," Hugh replied simply. "I didn't know there were other alternatives."

"Unfortunately," Louis stated flatly, "now there are not."

Hugh leaned his elbows on his knees and clasped his hands together, pressing them against his forehead. There had to be a way.

The king crossed to Hugh and rested his hand upon the knight's shoulder. "I am sorry, Hugh."

" 'Tis my own fault," Hugh replied. "But thank you, Your Majesty, for hearing my case."

"I am always concerned for your welfare. I must, after all," he added with a grin, "see to it that my prize war horse is happy."

Hugh smiled and nodded.

"You may go now, Hugh. I have too much yet to do. I will call for you in a few weeks and we will discuss how you are dealing with your new wife. Until then."

Dismissed, Hugh stood and let himself out of the king's private chamber. The palace was alive with activity, but Hugh wanted only to get to his rooms. He needed to think. Reaching his destination, he entered his apartments and closed the door behind him.

"Did you know that most of France seems to be looking for you?"

Hugh spun around to find Terrence lounging in the lone chair by the hearth.

"Other than you?"

"I am, indeed, looking for you. But Lord Bueil is also in Paris and looking for you."

"Bueil wants Pontoise," Hugh explained.

"Then he is a dangerous man."

"More dangerous because I told him he'd never have it. But what could he want with me in Paris?"

"The same thing he wanted when he was in Pontoise," Terrence replied.

Hugh turned to his brother in surprise. "When was the Duke de Neville in Pontoise?" he demanded.

"Not more than two days ago, Hugh. He came unexpectedly and stayed but a day. Adele said he was an old acquaintance of hers. They visited, and the next day he left."

Hugh leaned one arm against the stone wall and furrowed his brow. It was important that he understand why Bueil would go to Pontoise. Did he mean to threaten him again? The messenger who had spoken to Hugh as he prepared to depart for Chantilly had said nothing about the duke coming to Pontoise. It was out of the way for him. Farther north than Paris. He would only have gone there for a specific reason. And the fact that Hugh could not discern that reason concerned him greatly.

"You still have not told me your reason for coming to Paris to find me," he told Terrence as he turned his thoughts momentarily away from Lord Bueil.

"You need to return to your fief, Hugh. There is trouble and the villeins do not know you well enough to see that it is not you who wishes to hurt them."

"Hurt them? Who is hurting them?"

"Corvey, your steward."

Hugh smashed his fist against the unyielding stone wall. "Damn her!" Hugh bit the words out with a venom that took his brother by surprise.

"You know what Adele is doing then?"

"I know she hired that man behind my back. And I know I told her he was to be gone from my property. Now you are telling me that she has defied me outright and because of that defiance, my tenants are suffering."

"He is a brutal fool with little brain and too big a head. I don't know if he takes his orders from Adele or if he decides that these taxes should be collected in your name, but either way—"

"What taxes?" It was a question spoken with deadly calm. Hugh stood before Terrence, every muscle in his body tense and ready to spring.

"Two bushels of grain, one of flax, a cow, a pig, a passel of chickens."

"To whom has this tax gone?"

"To your coffers."

"Then the tax collector will answer to me." Hugh threw open the chest that stood at the foot of the bed and pulled his clothes from it, stuffing them into the leather bag he took everywhere he went. "I will be ready to leave with the hour. If you are up to the trip back, I would like you to come with me."

Terrence stood up, a broad smile on his face. "I am only too pleased to help you send Gaspar Corvey to the devil!"

Catherine straightened her back, listening again for the faint sound that had caught her ear. No, she thought, 'twas just her imagination. It had been giving her a great deal of trouble the past few days, for she always thought that she saw Hugh in the distance. With a shake of her head, Catherine returned to her raking. The small plot Sister Mary James had designated for conversion to a dyes garden was still months away from planting. But Catherine knew that there was much to do in preparation for spring and she worked doggedly on her small parcel of ground. Just this morning the carefully marked packets of seeds had arrived from her mother and Catherine's excitement for her project had been redoubled. As she worked, she imagined the beautiful colors that could be created for the wool the nuns spun into beautiful yarns.

The sound came again. Knitting her brow, Catherine set down her hoe and walked toward the entrance to the *abbaye*. She strained her ears, waiting for the sound to repeat itself again. There! She heard it a third time. It was a child's voice, calling out in the fading light. Catherine walked more quickly as she realized that the sound issued from the direction of the river that ran around the north wall of the *abbaye*. Just two weeks ago a group of pauper orphans had been brought to the *abbaye*. They were an unruly crew. One boy in particular was prone to get himself in trouble. Already he had twice been fished out of the hog pens, and Catherine pursed her mouth in concern, for the small river was cold as ice and in places fast running.

Her worst fears were confirmed a moment later when she heard the sound for a third time. She was closer now, and the panicked child's cry for help came clearly to her ears. Lifting her skirts, Catherine began to run, though the going was slow over the uneven fields. When the cry issued for a fourth time, Catherine raced faster, tripping on clumps of soil and the stubble left by the sickle's sweeping arm. Rounding the *ab-baye* wall, she saw the small boy waist-deep in the rushing water as he clung to a low-hanging branch.

"Here I come!" she called in a tone meant to send encouragement. The boy wept and cried out to her. "Milady, help! My foot is wedged beneath the rocks!"

Catherine plunged down the sloping bank of the river and raced to him. "Here, take my hand," she directed, taking hold of a nearby pine branch and leaning with an outstretched hand over the icy waters. The boy ceased his cries, but he did not reach for her hand. Instead, a grim look of pity filled his face. Catherine felt a blinding pain explode in her head and then she felt nothing at all.

Twenty

Catherine woke to pitch blackness. Her hands were bound behind her back by a thin hemp that chafed her wrists. A heavy sack had been pulled over her head and she choked on the rough knot of cloth that had been stuffed into her mouth. Where was she? Shaking her head, Catherine tried to clear her brain but got only a splitting pain at the base of her skull for her troubles.

She lay very still and tried to recall what had happened. She remembered the beggar boy in the stream and wondering in the instant before pain had exploded all around her why he looked at her so strangely. There were wisps of memories after that, times when she must have drifted in and out of consciousness because she remembered the incredible aching of her head as it had banged repeatedly against a horse's haunch.

Who had thrown her over the back of a horse bound and gagged? And where was she now? Through the sack, she could feel rushes or grass. Rushes, she decided, for beneath that was the cold hardness of a stone floor. A shiver ran through her, and Catherine tried to pull her legs up against her chest for warmth. Something heavy held one leg down like iron fingers around her ankle. She shivered again and tried to swallow, needing to wet her throat. The gag made it impossible. She lifted her head again, but lights exploded behind her eyes. Slowly, she laid her cheek against the floor. Every inch of her body ached, every movement was excruciatingly painful. She felt herself drifting back into darkness and she didn't know how to prevent it. Where was she?

A toe nudged her in the ribs. "Wake up."

Catherine's eyes fluttered open, but she saw only the black interior of the sack. The toe nudged her again, hitting her sharply in the ribs.

"Wake up, wench. I didn't hit you so hard."

Catherine moved one leg the slightest bit so her captor would know that she was awake. Even that slight movement was painful. She was cold. Cold to the center of her soul. And in need of water. Her mouth was dry beyond description. It was too hard to think, or feel. She was so cold.

Rough hands grasped her by the shoulders and hauled her to a sitting position and let her head bang against a hard wall behind her. The sack was hauled over her head and the gag pulled out of her mouth. Catherine leaned back against something solid and hard behind her and gulped in cold, sweet air. Her tongue was swollen to nearly twice its normal size and it

filled her mouth like some strange slab of meat.
She tried to swallow, but there was no moisture
in her mouth. A hand pinched her jaw on either
side of her chin and rocked her head back and
forth. Catherine opened her eyes and looked
into the face of her captor. He was swarthy-com-
plected with flat features and small black eyes
that were cold and cruel. She did not know him.

"Here," he said, holding a mazer of water to
her lips. The water ran out of both sides of her
mouth and soaked the front of her kirtle as Catherine drank eagerly. The strange man gave a
hard, cold laugh. "So you're a fighter, eh? I
wouldn't have thought it. Not hiding out in that
abbey." He stood back and looked at her as if
assessing her. "I can see why he wanted you for
his whore," he said with a sly grin. "I'd have
locked you up in an abbey, too. Wouldn't want
any other hands touching a prize like you."

"Who are you?" Catherine asked. The words
came out in a strangely jumbled slur, her water-
starved tongue making her speech slow and swollen.

"That is none of your concern," he told her
nonchalantly. "And instead of questions, you
might be thanking me for giving you some water.
But women like you never do." Without another
word, her captor turned and left.

When he was gone, Catherine looked around
her. She was in a chapel of sorts, though it was
an ancient one to be sure. One leg was clamped
in an iron and chain, the other end of which

connected to an iron peg that had been pounded into the stone altar. A single candle lit the chapel, its meager light revealing little of the building that was her prison. It was cold and Catherine's teeth began to chatter uncontrollably. She tested the rope that bound her hands, but it was tight. For a long while, she sat there waiting for the man to come back, but he never did. The cold and damp penetrated her meager kirtle and soon her entire body began to shake. Catherine curled into a tight ball huddled against the altar as she tried to warm herself.

She didn't know how many hours passed. Time began to blur as exhaustion and cold numbed her mind and she drifted in and out of sleep. She did not know where she was or what this man meant to do. But somehow he was tied to Hugh. Perhaps Hugh had gone to the king and found Louis furious at his admission of their love for each other. Perhaps this was some henchman carrying out the king's own orders. She tried to think of another answer, but her mind would not respond. And so Catherine sat huddled in the rushes at the foot of the ancient altar, trying to keep away the cold, and pain, and fear.

Hugh, Terrence, Grier, and Gladmoore rode into the bailey just as the dusk disappeared and was replaced by night. Two meager torches lit the courtyard, although the glazed windows of the keep blazed with light. A stableboy scurried out to take the horses and Hugh strode to the door of his home expecting to find his vassals awaiting dinner and the place alive with activity. Terrence was close behind him and Hugh turned to give his brother a puzzled look as he entered. The hall stood empty. There was not a person to be seen, yet two dozen torches blazed in their holders on the walls.

Hugh turned to Terrence. "Find Baston. He has been here and may know what goes on. Bring Grier and Gladmoore as well. They will be hungry, as I am, and the cook can give them some supper."

"Nothing goes on here, Hugh. Adele gave instructions that all torches be lit in the keep every night."

"And the evening meal?"

"The men are to fend for themselves. Of late they have taken to eating in the kitchens."

"Adele has not had food made for them?"

"Food aplenty," Terrence replied. "But not for them."

"Then for whom?"

"Adele and her family. Her parents and two brothers are still here."

Hugh shot Terrence a look of fury, and without a word crossed the Great Hall, headed for the kitchens. He entered just as a cook took a cleaver to a fully dressed roast swan. "Stop!" Hugh ordered as the cook raised the cleaver to hack at the swan again. "What are you doing?"

The cook turned to Hugh and lowered the

cleaver to his side. "I am only following the instructions I was given, Your Grace."

"Which were?"

"I was told that this swan was unacceptable," he replied. "And instructed to feed it to the pigs."

"The duchess gave you these instructions?"

"Oui," the cook replied angrily.

Hugh's eyes narrowed as he looked at the cook. "You are not the same man who I spoke to on my wedding night. Where is he?"

"Sent away, milord. Sent away for the crime he committed against you."

"What crime do you speak of? I gave no indication of such orders."

"Monsieur Corvey accused him of stealing the food from your wedding feast and giving it to the serfs. He was accused of stealing ale as well."

"Where did he go?" Hugh asked.

The cook shrugged and turned away from Hugh's questions.

Hugh turned to a boy about Avril's age who sat frozen on a stool in the corner. "Go and get Monsieur Corvey," he ordered. The boy's eyes grew enormous. He edged off the stool but made no attempt to do as Hugh ordered. "Go!" Hugh barked.

"Your lordship," the boy stuttered. "Monsieur Corvey will have me beaten for disturbing him."

Hugh turned an icy countenance on the boy. "You tell Monsieur Corvey that the duke wishes to see him in the Great Hall immediately. You will not be punished, now or ever, for obeying the command of your duke. Do you understand?" The boy nodded, and without another word dashed to do his master's bidding. Hugh turned back to the cook. "My vassals are coming at any moment. Feed them. Feed them well. And if you know where the man who was cook here last week has gone, see to it that he is told I wish to speak to him. He has done nothing wrong in my eyes, and I was very fond of his bear." Without waiting for the cook's reply, Hugh turned and headed back toward the Great Hall.

Minutes later, Gaspar Corvey appeared. Hugh was seated in a chair by the blazing hearth, a mazer of ale in his hand and his feet propped upon a small, leather-covered stool.

"Your Grace," Corvey said with an elaborate bow.

Hugh remained where he sat and let the steward stand in awkward silence as he drained his cup. At last Hugh set the mazer on the arm of his chair and looked Corvey straight in the eye. "Get off of my land, Corvey. And if you ever set foot within sight of my home again, I will come after you with my broadsword." The steward opened his mouth to speak, but Hugh spoke first. "Two of my men will accompany you to your rooms to pack. Then they will escort you to the border of my lands. Is that clear?" The steward nodded in silence. "Oh," Hugh added as he untied the money pouch that hung from his belt. "Here are your wages. Now go."

It was a command as cold and absolute as anything Gaspar Corvey had ever heard. For a moment, he considered the idea of telling the duke about his red-haired whore. There was a possibility that he could ingratiate himself with the duke by divulging everything he knew about the plot. But he did not. He was being sent away, and shamed by his sudden banishment from the property of an important knight and duke, he owed him nothing. Corvey bowed to the duke and left. Let him find his whore for himself, he thought.

Adele stood upon the gallery that circled the Great Hall listening to every word Hugh said to Gaspar Corvey. Her long, thin fingers grasped the railing until her knuckles were encircled in white and the hard edges of her bones formed sharp lines against the back of her hand. Terrence stood beside Hugh's chair, a look of satisfaction upon his face. She should have known Terrence would do something as foolhardy as bringing Hugh back from Paris. He was like a shadow that never left Hugh. She had always despised him, but the crippled hand that hung useless at his side sickened her even more. It was God's punishment. A sign for all the world to see that Terrence Vougnet was not fit for the religious life his father and mother had prepared him for. She had told Hugh he must go to the Holy Wars alone, but Terrence, as always, had Hugh's ear when she did not. A thin smile touched her lips. But Terrence had gotten his repayment. The Lord always knew.

Below her, Hugh tossed a coin purse to her steward. He was going. But Adele was no longer thinking about him. The old chapel! Silent as a wraith, Adele slipped down the stairs and into the entrance of the keep. She slid her mantle off the peg by the door and put it over her shoulders. Pressing herself against the stone wall, she waited until Corvey had headed for his quarters beyond the kitchens. She heard Hugh's vassals enter the hall, and their loud voices filled the hall with noise. Under the safety of their loud discussion, Adele opened the front door and slid out.

She crossed the bailey in long, fluid steps, never hesitating in her direction. She passed the stables and the round, windowless buildings that kept their grain dry. She crossed the long row of workshops where villeins plied their trades. Walking along the high stone wall of the keep, she left them behind. It was dark in this portion of the bailey. On either side of her, high stone walls—one for the keep, the other for the outer wall—rose, blotting out what little light there was. But Adele moved swiftly and surely toward her destination.

She reached the entrance to the old chapel without detection. It did not matter if someone spotted her. It was a common sight to see her head for the old timbered structure several times a day. She preferred using the tiny chapel to wor-

shiping with the villeins in the church that stood
at the head of their hovel of huts or the elegant
chapel which had been set in one of the castle's
turrets.

Praying in the old chapel allowed Adele to abject herself fully before God. Hour after hour
she knelt in the rushes before the stone altar so
that the Lord might see her devotion, her piety,
and her faith. So even if she had been seen, no
one would have given her even a thought. Reaching the front door, Adele opened it and entered.
The leather hinges of the door creaked as it
closed behind her. For a moment she stood very
still at the back of the little chapel. Corvey had
lit a single candle, and in the darkness, Adele
wasn't certain if the whore was even there. But
then she saw her, huddled like a beggar in the
straw. A tattered horse blanket was wrapped
carelessly around her and she shook in her sleep
as though she had the fever.

Slowly, Adele approached the woman until the
toes of her slippers were only inches from the
whore's face. She did not move except to shake
and shiver in her fitful sleep. Not far from the
woman, Adele spotted the wadding which
Corvey had used to keep her from screaming as
he transported her back to Pontoise. Adele
reached for the cloth, picking it up with one
hand while the other grasped the flame-red hair
of the whore and yanked her head back.

Catherine's eyes flew open as she was abruptly
dragged from her fitful sleep. Before she knew

where she was, her head was pulled back and the wadding that she had been relieved of stuffed back into her mouth. She stared into the sharp, unyielding face of a woman, and her visage frightened Catherine far more than that of the strange man, for there was a light of victory in the woman's eyes.

Without a word, the woman let her head drop back to the floor. She went to the altar and ran her fingers over the elaborate box that had been built into it in adoration. Catherine realized it must hold a holy relic—the hair of a saint or perhaps a sliver of the Cross. She bent close to it, pressing a fervent kiss upon the box. Crossing herself, she turned back to Catherine. "What is this?"

Bending beside her, the woman reached out to finger the gold chain of her pendant. Catherine stared at her. She had seen this woman before. She examined Catherine's necklace, turning it over in her hand. Staring at the lettering on the back, she moved her lips as if trying to sound out the words there. "Humph," she said at last. "You have no need of finery. You must abject yourself before God." She lifted Catherine's pendant over her head and placed it in the purse that hung from her own belt. "Finery is braggartry. You have sinned greatly. You must show God your worthlessness before him." The woman stared down at her for a long minute. "But you won't. You are too prideful, aren't you?" Turning, she walked away leaving

Catherine as she was and taking her pendant with her.

Hugh did not see Adele slip back into the keep as he and the others finished their meal. The roast swan had been served to the famished men, as well as several other courses. Nowhere in France was higher praise of the chef sung than at the table of Pontoise that night. The men were tired and hungry, and glad to be home.

The night seemed to offer a sort of confessional for the men as one by one they told Hugh of the things they had seen, heard and experienced these past few weeks. Hugh listened and asked questions, but for the most part he simply pursed his lips into a grim line of anger. The way his fief had been run in his absence had nothing to do with what Hugh believed was proper. Nor fair. He had been deeply proud to return to France a duke. As a second son, Hugh had never thought about having his own keep with serfs to oversee and property to protect. As a boy, he had occasionally daydreamed that *he* was Giles and would someday become the Count d' Anet. In those moments, he had organized a fief that was run fairly and with good results.

In his dreams, he had singlehandedly swept reform through the land. Every villein was treated fairly, all cases were heard with an ear to justice. The land prospered, the people respected him. His wife supported him. When Louis had awarded

Pontoise to him and with it the title of duke, Hugh had envisioned those same dreams. The dreams of a boy. He had thought that his fief would be all those things simply because he wished it to be so. It was not a task so easily done.

In less than a fortnight his fief had nearly been brought to its knees. And it was not locusts that came so close to destroying it, nor the ravages of drought or flood or wind. It had been caused by the will of one person. His wife.

Hugh sat before the hearth and listened to the stories told not only by the men who served him and who knew him well, but by the cook and those who worked for him. The house staff came forward once they saw that Hugh would not have them beaten for speaking their mind and talked of ridiculous requests made by Adele and her family. And with each story his anger grew.

He was angry because Adele had taken so much into her own hands without consulting him. Angry because the way she treated his villeins could only be described as mean-hearted. Angry as well because with each tale he became more fully aware that he could not afford to leave Pontoise. Louis expected him to be at his beck and call. But to do so required being away from home for weeks or months at a time. Pontoise needed his attention, and Hugh was eager to give it. After only eight days of traversing the countryside between Pontoise, Paris, and Chantilly, he was tired of it. He wanted to stay here. There was so much to learn, so many places where he might apply his hand and knowledge in order to improve the fief. But to remain in Pontoise day upon day left one enormous void in his life. There was no Catherine.

Although the king had not offered him a solution, Hugh would not abandon his hopes. He could no longer resign himself to a life he did not wish to live. Just as he knew that he would change the course of things at Pontoise after today, he also knew that somehow he must find a way to be with Catherine.

Draining his mazer of its ale, Hugh stood up and stretched. "I cannot sit all night long talking of war and drinking," he declared to Grier beside him. "My body craves sleep and it will not be denied."

Grier laughed and slapped Hugh heartily on the shoulder. "Then you have aged overnight, Your Grace. Because just this past autumn I recall you as the man who, when we could not keep our eyes open, was still playing games with Lady Catherine or riding out at dawn after a late night of merriment to hawk with her! 'Tis a sad day to see you resigned to pouring over account books and measuring the fullness of the grain houses." Grier smiled and gave Hugh's back another hearty slap. "Truth be told, we're all jealous of you. Every one."

Hugh smiled in appreciation of the vassal's comment. "I am well pleased. I only hope I can make it strong. I hope my serfs learn to trust me and be proud that they are of Pontoise." He ran his fingers through his thick blond hair and sighed. "But there is much to undo here."

"It has waited this long, it will wait until tomorrow," Grier said.

"*Oui*," Hugh agreed. "It can wait one more day."

The next day dawned gray and wet. Hugh awoke just as the sun rose to the sound of a heavy rain beating against the thick-paned windows of his room. A damp chill permeated the castle's thick walls that no amount of tapestry or furs could dispel. Hugh rose, bathed, and dressed in moss-green hose and a matching long-sleeved shirt over which he donned a soft leather tunic.

A serving boy knocked at his door to ask if he would break fast in the great dining room or the privacy of his own apartments. "I shall eat in the hall," Hugh informed the lad. Then he added, "Where is Avril?"

"They have not yet returned from their journey, Your Grace."

Hugh cocked a brow in surprise. "Who is they and where did 'they' go?" he asked.

"Your page and Sir du Font, and I don't know where they went, milord."

Hugh contemplated this for a moment. "Is Lord Terrence up?"

The boy nodded. "*Oui*. He is already in the dining room."

Without another word, Hugh pulled on leather boots and headed for the castle's eating room.

He found his brother seated with Gladmoore as the pair devoured a breakfast of aged cheese, freshly baked bread, and rabbit. Hugh took a seat on the bench next to the pair. "Terrence, where did Avril go?"

Terrence cut another wedge of cheese which he laid over his bread. "I sent Avril and Wesley to Chantilly. We didn't know where you were, and this afforded us the best opportunity of locating you. Since you weren't there, I assume that the two returned the day before we did."

"They haven't returned."

Terrence looked at Hugh as though he had not heard correctly, then he turned to Baston. "Did Wesley and Avril return?" he asked.

Baston shook his head. "Not yet. But any number of things might have befallen them. I don't worry about them. Wesley is a very skillful fighter and they didn't travel far."

"If they went to Chantilly, then they should have returned by now," Hugh asserted.

Terrence nodded. "I agree. But perhaps after they found that you were not at the *abbaye,* they decided to head for Paris, believing that they would find all of us there. I'm sure they will be here by tomorrow."

"I will send a message to the king, just in case. If they are there, he can tell them that we are in Pontoise."

Terrence nodded.

Temporarily satisfied, Hugh devoured breakfast. There was much to be done today, despite the weather. He must go to the villeins and present himself to them, something he should have done the moment he arrived at Pontoise. He must see to it that Gaspar Corvey was indeed gone. And he must talk to Adele.

Consulting with Terrence, Hugh planned a meeting with three or four villein leaders. Terrence suggested the two men who had come to Herta's defense and Hugh agreed. He would let them select two additional men with whom Hugh could establish a plan for seeing that the needs of the serfs were met. As the two brothers discussed their ideas, Hugh periodically looked up to see if Adele was ready to start her day. At last, as the morning grew old, Hugh asked a serving girl to inquire after Lady Adele.

The girl returned a few minutes later to inform him that the duchess had just recently risen. She intended to breakfast in her rooms and then retire to the solar.

Hugh listened dispassionately. "Tell Lady Adele that I shall plan to meet with her in the solar in one hour's time." With a nod, the girl disappeared to do his bidding.

"The villeins will want to know that Adele is not the one running this fief, Hugh."

Hugh directed an angry scowl at Terrence. "And they shall have my assurance that I am, indeed, the one to whom they must answer. Adele must understand as well. Of the two, I'm certain she will be the harder one to convince."

Terrence nodded. "I don't envy your discussion with Adele today."

Hugh agreed. "And it is best that I get it done now." Rising, he bade good day to his vassals and headed for his rooms. Once there, Hugh took a parchment and quill from the coffer at the end of his bed. Sitting at the small table set before the hearth, he dipped the sharpened quill into a small vial of ink. He would use this hour before he spoke with Adele to write a missive to Catherine. The letter was not long. Despite the things Hugh wanted to tell her, he did not know how to say that Louis had suggested the dilemma was not correctable, and so he filled the page with inane bits of information that had little to do with anything. He had just scattered sand on the sheet to dry the ink when a knock sounded at his door.

"Hugh! Are you there?" Terrence's voice sounded from the hallway.

"Come in!" Hugh called out. A moment later Terrence burst into the room. With him was a very wet page. "Avril!" Hugh greeted him. "So you could not wait for me. You had to go and have an adventure on your own, eh?"

"Nay!" the boy exclaimed. "It's just that . . ."

Hugh held up a single hand. "There is no need to explain. You did as Terrence instructed you. And I am well pleased for that." Avril nodded distractedly. "I would have thought you might be more pleased with my comment."

"I am, milord. But Wesley and I discovered a problem when we returned to the *abbaye*."

"And?" It was not Avril's words that concerned Hugh so much. It was the fact that he was so distracted.

Avril wrung his hands. "Lady Catherine has disappeared."

Twenty-one

"What do you mean?" Hugh asked with an icy calm that made Avril's heart thud like a drum in his chest.

Standing behind Terrence and Avril in the doorway of Hugh's apartments, Wesley du Fonte explained. "We arrived just after nightfall. The nuns offered us shelter and food and we asked if you were there."

"We were told that you had left two days before," Avril continued, and Hugh nodded in agreement. "I wished to see Lady Catherine." He ducked his head and looked at Hugh through worried eyes. "I thought you would not mind since she and I were—"

"Friends," Hugh finished for him. "I have no concerns regarding you, Avril."

The page sighed in relief. "The nuns said they would tell her we were here. But an hour later, neither they nor Lady Catherine had returned. I waited another hour, but could not wait any longer after that."

"We went to find her for ourselves," Wesley explained, relieving Avril. "But we were no farther than the door of the guest house when the prioress appeared. No one could find Lady Catherine. Every nun turned out with torches and candles and every corner of the *abbaye* was searched, but she was not there."

"By this time, it was dark and there was no moon, so we could not look for her that night. But the moment dawn arrived, we began to search the field and gardens of the *abbaye*, every outbuilding and shed. We found several things that might have given us a clue as to her disappearance, including a hoe that had been abandoned on a plot just inside the *abbaye* walls," he continued. "But it was not until much later that anyone connected the two. We took the nuns to the place where the hoe was found, and it was then that the prioress saw a connection. She had just told Catherine that she could turn the small tract into a garden of plants to be used in making dyes for the *abbaye*'s wool. Although Catherine had not told anyone that she intended to work on it that day, it was the only thing we could think of."

"Why would she leave the hoe and disappear?" Hugh asked.

"That is the problem," Wesley said, shaking his head in frustration. "We don't know. But it indicates that she did not leave of her own accord."

"Her clothes were all still in her cell," Avril explained. "She did not even take her warm wolf-fur boots or mantle. If she had planned to leave, she would have taken these things. Lady Catherine is not a fool. She would have planned well."

"But you do not know where she is." It was a statement to which Avril could only give a guilt-ridden shake of his head. Hugh stared silently at the flames in the hearth as they devoured the fagots that fed them. Fear gripped his heart like a mighty hand, for nothing sounded right. Everything Wesley and Avril described stank of foul play. She would not simply walk away one day leaving everything behind. Avril was right, she was far too smart for that.

He thought of his conversation with the king. Had Louis taken fate into his own hands and removed Catherine from Hugh's reach? Hugh quickly discarded that possibility. The king was always reasonable when it came to personal comforts. He would have understood that she had belongings which were prized to her, and he would have allowed her to collect them. Not wishing to elicit the wrath of the pope, he would also have informed sister Mary James. Rubbing his fingers back and forth across his brow, Hugh tried to think of who else might have a reason to harm Catherine. For long minutes he could think of no one. Everyone loved Catherine. She was sweet and warm and a full measure of all good things.

He closed his eyes, willing himself not to think the worst. He could not lose her now. Images of Catherine filled his mind. Catherine hunting with him and sitting across the table as he ate supper. Catherine asleep in the chair by Terrence's bed or laughing with Avril as they rode across the white, snow-covered landscape. Her eyes shining with pride over his accomplishments and her honest acceptance of him as he was. And then he visualized her as she had been when last he saw her, laying naked beside him upon the soft woolen skeans. How beautiful she had been then, her hair spread about her like red-gold ribbons of silk as long, spiked lashes rested like soft crescents against her skin. Her lips, gently parted, had curved into the slightest smile of serenity as she lay curled against him in sleep.

Never before had Hugh known contentment such as that. He had not slept that night, but instead had lain awake to watch her—and watch over her. In those long, quiet hours he had learned the price of love. Learned that it cannot be put into a convenient coffer and taken out when desired. He closed his eyes and sighed deeply. *Don't take her away from me, Lord. Not now that I finally understand.*

"We'll leave for Chantilly as soon as you can have horses saddled," he said to Wesley and Avril. "Perhaps the nuns have found something else. Perhaps," he said with a desperate hope, "she is there now."

Wesley excused himself, saying that he would see to fresh mounts for himself and Avril and ask if any of the other vassals wished to come along.

Avril stood where he was, his young face drawn tight by fear. "We must find her," he said to Hugh.

Hugh turned to him and nodded. "We will not rest until we do. Now go and see to the preparations."

When he was gone, Hugh leaned forward in his chair, putting his elbows on his knees and burying his face in the palms of his hands. Terrence crossed to the hearth, drumming the fingers of his good hand upon the stone mantel. "Have you thought of Bueil?" he asked.

Hugh nodded, his head still in his hands. After a moment he looked up, meeting his brother's measured gaze. "*Oui*, he threatened her outright when I was preparing to leave his keep. But he was in Paris when she disappeared."

"He would have hired someone to carry out his wishes."

"But it would do him little good to kill her. Only if she is alive can he use her to get Pontoise."

"Then she may yet be alive."

"Perhaps I should go to Paris first," Hugh contended. "If Bueil has her, he will be ready to negotiate."

"What will you use to bargain with?"

"With what he wants, of course."

"You would give him Pontoise? Louis will be furious. You will never receive a title and holdings from him again. You will be back to where you were—simply a warrior for the king. Worse, if you are able to get him to agree somehow, he will despise you for weakening him. You will fall out of favor with our king."

Hugh looked at his brother with a calm that took Terrence by surprise. "What have I to lose that is greater than losing Catherine? This place has no value to me if each day in it I am reminded that I chose stone and dirt over her. I want nothing if I can't have her."

"You are married to Adele," Terrence reminded him. "Despite your love for Catherine and hers for you, you cannot change that."

"At least I can be certain she is safe. Whatever the cost, I must see to that."

Terrence pursed his lips into a grim line. "Well, the first thing is to find her. If you go to Paris and I go with the others to Chantilly to search further, then we are not leaving any stone unturned."

Hugh agreed. "I shall see you in the bailey soon."

When Terrence had left, Hugh sat back in his chair and set out a plan. He would speak to Bueil. Once he was assured that Catherine was safe, he would have the papers prepared. The issuing of a title required the signature and seal of the king of France, but Louis would not do such a thing knowingly. Hugh would have to fill him with wine and have the documents at hand. When Louis was well drunk, he would get the signature. Hugh smiled in wry disbelief of what he planned to do. Louis would surely banish him for it, or worse, he would have him hung. But at least Catherine would be safe. He would have Terrence and Avril take her back to Avignon where she would have the substantial protection of her family.

Whatever happened, he realized sadly, he and Catherine would never be together again. He might never touch her again. Never set eyes upon her. Hugh's heart broke at the very thought of the time he had wasted. So many hours that he could have spent with Catherine if only he had stopped resisting the need that drove him to her. He had taken so long to understand that their love was a thing born of God. Given like a fine gift to those whom he chose to bless.

And now it was too late. Hugh knew that he would willingly give up everything he had to save her. Those things mattered little. What life did he look forward to without her? Adele's recriminations and distaste? Day upon day and month upon month of battling foes whose faces he might never see wherever Louis sent him? Nay, he thought with a sad shake of his head. Such a life was no life at all, so it was of no account that he would miss it.

Rising, Hugh left his rooms and followed the hallway to Adele's rooms. He knocked and then knocked again when there was no reply. He rapped a third time, and was about to look for her elsewhere when he a response came from the room.

"Be gone!" came the sharp command.

Irritation flashed through him, and Hugh opened the door to her chambers and stepped inside. "I would have a word with you, Adele. It is unfortunate that you don't see fit to inquire as to who is at your door."

Adele was seated on a stool before her small table, her back turned toward the door. At the sound of his voice, she jumped and seemed to quickly put something back into the box on the table. "Hugh, I did not know you were here," she lied. "Else I would have come to open the door myself."

Hugh stayed where he was, just inside the door. He had no desire to go closer to her. She was dressed in a fine velvet gown and kirtle trimmed with fur. It should have been a beautiful dress, for clearly it had cost a fair number of gold pieces, but she had selected a dull brown color that washed out her features and reminded Hugh of nothing so much as dead leaves in winter. Though she tried to smile at him, her eyes remained dull, and her features hard. And suddenly Hugh wondered what things made the sharpness leave, for he could not remember ever seeing her any other way.

"I am leaving again for a day or two. But before I go, there are a few things I must discuss with you." He watched Adele's face turn shadowy as she tried to determine what it was he wanted. "Listen carefully, Adele. There is no discussion in what I tell you." Though Adele remained silent, her eyes narrowed into slits and the skin drew tight across her sharp cheekbones. "I have paid Gaspar Corvey a fortnight's wages and banished him from my lands. I have called a meeting with the best men among the serfs and will return to every villein their livestock and grain, for it was taken in winter when they need these things to survive the fallow season."

"We will have nothing to eat!" Adele protested angrily.

"You should have been more frugal with the things we had. It is wrongful to order twice the food needed for us and our guests and then have whatever remains thrown away unused."

"Old food spoils and one may become sickened from it. I will not eat sullied food. 'Tis not safe!"

"Nay, Adele. I think you will not eat such food because you wish to impress your family." Adele opened her mouth to protest, but Hugh held up a warning hand. "Do not interrupt me again. I have much to say and I doubt you will like any part of it. But that is not for you to say. *I* am master of Pontoise. This is *my* keep and my land. My serfs and vassals. My grain and livestock and food. You may be mistress here, but that position requires obedience to your lord, and that, Adele, is *me*.

"Mayhap I have been gone so long that you have become accustomed to handling the affairs of life on your own. I would apologize, except you were the one who urged me so strongly to go to Jerusalem. Perhaps it is unfortunate that I came back," Hugh told her. "Then you would have all this and not have to take a place behind me." He stared at her for long seconds. For the first time in his life he evaluated her true nature without feeling his own guilt. He had always looked first at her self-proclaimed piety. But her words were merely that, he realized. Utterances to disguise the true nature of her heart. He looked around her rooms as if seeing them for the first time. In truth, he had barely been in her apartments. Her bed was draped in rich tapestry lined with fine Belgium wool. The coverlet was thick and overlaid with throws of ermine. Her fingers were heavy with rings he had sent back from Jerusalem. Rings given to him in return for his bravery and protection. He had thought little of them, for they were the spoils of a needless war. But Adele had clearly sifted through them all to find the finest and take it for herself without asking his permission.

"You are too proud, Adele," he told her bluntly. At his words, she rose from her stool in protest, but he silenced her again. "Before I left I told you that the steward you had hired was to be dismissed, but you disobeyed me. You abused my serfs and my belongings, you helped yourself to whatever you wished, never consulting me. Never asking my approval. 'Twas not yours to take, Adele.

"I am leaving Gladmoore and Grier here while I am gone. I am setting them as your overseers. Whatever you do, they shall report to me.

Do not cross me, Adele, else you may find yourself in your serving girl's cell with nary a fur or
tapestry to keep you warm."

Adele glared at him. "You would not do such
a thing. I am your wife and as such command
your finest treatment."

"Only if you are an obedient wife, Adele. Remember that."

Without another word, Hugh turned and left
his wife's apartments. As the door closed behind
him, Adele began to shake with the indignation
that she had held in check all through his
speech. How *dare* he talk to her thus? If not for
her, Hugh Vougnet would be nothing. Hadn't
she been the one to urge him to take up the
Cross? And in doing so, hadn't Hugh won everything he owned? The keep, the land, the serfs,
the jewels and finery. Everything. And yet he had
the gall to tell her that she was disobedient! To
threaten her! Take her to the servant's cell?
Never. Turning back to her dressing table, Adele
leaned her hands on the surface, staring down
at the assortment of jewels scattered there. Her
gaze fell on the sapphire pendant she had taken
from the whore. Of all the jewels she had, none
was so fine as that single piece. Her long, thin
fingers closed around the pendant, and with all
the power in her thin body, Adele threw it at the
thick oak door that Hugh had just closed behind
him.

The jewel hit the door and fell to the stone
floor. "You have shamed me twice now, Hugh

Vougnet. Once with your whore and now with your disrespect. But vengeance is mine, sayeth the Lord. You think to have everything you desire and leave me to pick up your leavings. Nay," she warned. "It will not be." Grabbing her cloak, Adele threw open the door and headed for the old chapel.

In the bailey, Wesley, Baston, Terrence, and Avril sat astride their horses ready to depart. Cepheus was saddled and pawed impatiently at the cobbles as if he sensed the urgency of their mission. Hugh carried his broadsword at his side as he walked up to the men. If Bueil had harmed Catherine in any way, if he had set one finger upon her, Hugh knew he would kill him. Mounting, Hugh signaled for the men to follow him. The portcullis gate was lifted and the five men rode out through its opening. Just beyond the drawbridge, Hugh pulled Cepheus to a halt. The men followed suit and Hugh turned to them, issuing instructions.

"Terrence, you take Wesley and Baston to Chantilly. Search everywhere for Catherine. Talk to every person there. Avril, you will come with me." Hugh expected some response from his page but got none. "Avril!" he repeated sharply. The boy twisted his head to look at Hugh. "Pay attention!" Hugh growled.

"My lord," Avril interrupted. "Look!" Hugh followed the line of Avril's pointing finger to two small riders in the distance. One rode Catherine's roan mare and both were dressed in black habits and wimples. " 'Tis the two plump nuns from the *abbaye!*"

"Oui!" Agreed Wesley du Fonte. "The two who cannot stop talking." But Hugh did not hear the vassal's comment. He was already galloping Cepheus toward the approaching women.

Catherine shifted uncomfortably against the hard stone altar, trying to tuck her feet further under her dress. Since late last night she had been alone, without food or water or warmth. The thin blanket the man had tossed over her had long ago been overpowered by the damp and cold, and sleep had been nearly impossible. She did not know what time of day it was, but what little daylight filtered through cracks in the timber and daub walls had been there for several hours.

Catherine knew she was weakening. As she leaned against the altar, she could feel herself go from freezing to burning hot and back again. She drifted in and out of sleep that was peppered with strange dreams, and it was becoming increasingly difficult for her to recall which things had really occurred and which she had dreamed. She was fairly certain that the man had been real, although if that was so, why hadn't he returned? But she was less sure that Adele's had been anything but a strange apparition. Her wrists were raw from the hemp that bound them behind her and the iron cuff around her ankle had cut into her flesh, leaving bloodstains on the brittle rushes.

But Catherine did not want to think about those things. Acknowledging them only made the pain worse. Instead, she chose to concentrate on Hugh. He would be in Paris now. Talking to the king, perhaps. It was a useless endeavor, though she loved him all the more for going. Catherine had known before he had even ridden out of the *abbaye* that no one could undo what had been done. Hugh had married Adele, and there could be no turning back. But now, at least, she understood what had driven him to the marriage. She could well understand the obedience to duty that had been ingrained in Hugh from a young age. It was not love that had taken Hugh away from her and pressed him into marriage with Adele, but duty. And although she could not be with him, Catherine's heart was soothed by that knowledge. In the darkness of the chapel, she found the strength to smile. He loved her. This much she knew without question.

Closing her eyes, she tried to recall everything about him. Hugh was the hard and the pliant twined together. A warrior without equal and a man of gentle heart. Strong and determined with a will of iron in battle, he was also quiet and possessed of self-doubts that hounded his every thought. He led with power and self-confidence, and some, she knew, would describe him as intimidating and hard. Yet there was another side of Hugh which was comprised of easy laughter and warm companionship. She loved all the parts. One was no better than the other, for they were all things which made Hugh the man he was.

She closed her eyes and saw his face against the backs of her lids. The strong, straight nose and well-sculpted jawline. She remembered touching the furrows that creased his forehead and running her fingertips across the rough stubble of his chin. She recalled the hard, sinewy feel of his shoulders under the palms of her hands and the soft tickle of his furred chest against her bare breasts, and for a moment her bonds and prison melted away, replaced by the warmth of the fire as they lay together in the *abbaye* tower. She had wanted so badly to know that feeling, to be united with Hugh in all ways. Perhaps she had intuitively understood that they had only one chance. Catherine had no illusions that she would ever see the sun or the blueness of the sky again. This chapel would be her dungeon. Her coffin. Her death.

As she sat shivering in the cold, she heard the sound of rattling against the door. Hot despair poured into her breast as the door opened and a woman's form was outlined against the gray sky. Adele had not been a specter. The door shut again and Adele, shrouded in a warm woolen mantle, walked toward the altar. She carried an enormous basket laden with goods and she walked past Cath erine as if she did not exist, placing the basket on the altar. She stood less than a foot away from Catherine's huddled body, but never looked at her or acknowledged her presence.

My God, Catherine thought. *Have I become invisible to all the world? Less than a mite upon the rushes?* Catherine could not see what Adele busied herself with, but as the chapel began to fill with the soft glow of light, she realized that she must be lighting tapers. The scent of warm wax wafted through the cold, stale air. It was as tantalizing as the smell of any food to Catherine, for it was the first sign of light or heat she had seen in days. She closed her eyes and breathed it in, willing it to warm her.

Adele lit more and more candles, and as she did, she began to chant in a high-pitched voice that quivered unsteadily. Her chanting grew louder, and Catherine now began to smell scented oils in the air.

"What are you doing?" she asked suddenly. She was tired of being treated like the vilest and least noticeable of things.

Adele turned and stared down at her as though she had not known she was there. There was a strange look in her eyes. As though she was not really seeing Catherine at all. Without a word, she returned to whatever she was concocting upon the altar.

But Catherine would not give up so easily. "I know a great deal about oils and herbals," she told Adele. "Perhaps I can assist you in your preparations."

A strange smile spread across Adele's lips, but she did not answer her. Her candles filled the entire altar and she began to set thick tapers among the rushes. Catherine leaned close to those she set near her, letting their heat thaw her frozen limbs. The chanting, which had stopped for a moment as Adele set out more candles, began again and Catherine realized with horror that it was a funeral incantation that Adele sang. But something was wrong with the tune and she realized that Adele did not sing it in the long, sorrowful tones that Catherine had always heard it sung. Instead, she sung it with a joyful anticipation, as though a funeral was a wonderful event.

"Is there to be a funeral?" Catherine asked lightly.

Adele looked down again, and this time she seemed to see Catherine. She smiled at her, a cold smile that was a mere movement upon her lips and held nothing but evil in it. "Oh, yes. A wonderful funeral."

"How is a funeral a wonderful thing?" Catherine asked.

"Any death is fine that cleanses the world of an evil being, don't you agree?"

"Who is to say if something is evil or good?" she replied.

"Why, God tells us," Adele responded simply.

"Does he speak to you, Adele?"

She smiled again and nodded. "He comes to me in my dreams. He fills me with him. He speaks to me and guides me. I do nothing that He has not directed of me."

"This then?" Catherine asked quickly. "He has told you to come here and light candles?"

"Prepare a sacred devotion," Adele corrected. "Cleanse the world of evil."

"What evil?"

Adele gave her a startled looked. "Why you, of course."

Catherine took a deep breath. "Am I evil?"

Adele shook her head. "That is what is so hard to believe. You are the vessel of Satan's evil and yet you do not even know it. You are so filled with his sinfulness that you cannot see it. That is why this is a blessing for you as well. You will be cleansed of Satan's evil. That is why death will hurt you. If you were pure, death would come painlessly. It will be the terrible wickedness in you that will make you writhe with pain as it seeps out of you. But it will be better for you."

"God does not want death, Adele," Catherine said softly. "What you hear cannot possibly be God speaking to you. He would never speak of destruction and murder. Our Lord God is goodness and light. He has not told you to kill me."

"Stop!" Adele screamed at her. Her calm and composure crumbled and the mask of reason she had worn fell away, leaving the face of madness in its place. "How dare you speak His name! You defile it upon your tongue. The tongue of a whore!"

The word was like a slap and it hit Catherine square and hard. So this was her punishment. She loved Hugh and she had chosen to make that love a real thing. And for that sin, she would die at the hands of a madwoman. What was worse, though, was that Hugh would live with this madwoman for the rest of his life.

Adele grabbed her by the shoulder of her kirtle, hauling her to her feet with an amazing strength. Catherine stumbled upon numb legs and nearly cried out at the pain of being thrust upon her frozen feet. "Kneel!" she commanded, and Catherine found herself forced to back into the rushes. "Now," Adele said as her frenzy calmed. "First we must anoint you with holy oils, and then we shall burn the devil out of your soul."

Twenty-two

Hugh reached out to take the peach-colored ribbon that fluttered from Sister Edith's fingers. He turned to Sister Gilbert and, squatting, looked carefully at the beggar boy who hid behind her ample skirts. He was gaunt from lack of food and had the wily look of someone who had seen too much at far too young an age. Though he was clean and free of fleas since coming to the *abbaye*, he had lost none of his fear of drunken beatings or cold nights without a roof over his head. Hugh had seen boys like this one often with groups of pilgrims. They traveled with the Crusaders because their mothers were camp followers. Sometimes they were women who believed that a pilgrimage to the Holy Land would save their souls, other times they followed the Crusaders hoping to find a protector for a few months.

He did not want to scare the boy, so he spoke softly, looking him squarely in the eye. "It is a beautiful ribbon you have." The boy eyed him warily, saying nothing. "The lady who wore it is very beautiful, too. This color looks so pretty in her hair. It's hair the color of flame." Slowly, the boy nodded. "Someone has taken the lady and that person means to hurt her."

Hugh waited to see if his words were taking hold, but he couldn't tell. Taking a deep breath, he went on. "You know what it's like to be beaten, don't you? To be hungry and cold and never to feel safe?" The boy's eyes filled with tears and again he nodded. "The Sisters have been good to you, haven't they? The lady is their friend, and mine, too. She is cold now and hungry and she is not safe. Whatever you can tell us, however strange it may seem, may help us find her. Please," he urged the boy, "Please tell us whatever you know."

The boy looked up at Sister Gilbert, and the nun nodded. Licking his lips nervously, he looked back at Hugh. "I found it on the ground after they were gone," he said in a tone that was barely above a whisper.

"Who besides Lady Catherine?" Hugh asked quietly.

"The man. The man who hit me."

Sister Edith came around behind the boy and taking his hand, gave it a gentle pat. "Start at the beginning, child. You are safe with us."

"I was playing outside the *abbaye* walls. There had been more of us, but the others complained that it was getting cold and went inside. I don't know where he came from, but he grabbed me by the neck and shook me hard. I tried to bite him, and he boxed me ears for it. So I was quiet

He took me down to the water and dropped me in it! I never been in water before. There was a tree fallen in the water and I grabbed it. And then I started shouting for help.

"The lady must have heard me, because she came running from the *abbaye*. I'd seen her there, so I knew she was a good person who would help me. The man had disappeared, I don't know where he went, but all I cared about was getting out of the river. The lady came fast. She was not afraid at all!" he exclaimed, the amazement still in his voice. "Just as she reached out for me, I saw the man. He was behind her and he had a bludgeon held over his head. I didn't have time to warn her," he said, dropping his chin to his chest. "He hit her hard and caught her just in time to keep her from falling in the water. I called for him to help me out, but he just laughed. He put the lady over the back of his horse and rode away. He left me to die there!" the boy continued angrily.

"But I wasn't gonna die. I remembered the lady, how she came running across the field to save me, and I pulled myself out. I found the pretty ribbon on the ground just near the gate to the *abbaye*. It reminded me of the pretty lady who tried to save me."

"What did the man look like?"

The boy made a face. "He was small for a man, not at all like you. His hair was black and he had mean eyes."

"Black eyes?" Hugh asked.

The boy thought for a moment and then nodded. "He rode a fine steed." Nodding to Cepheus, he added. "With a saddle like yours, milord."

Hugh's head jerked up and he stared at the boy. "Like mine?"

Nodding, the boy let go of Sister Gilbert's skirts and walked to the giant black stallion. "With this," he said pointing to the eagle-griffin bearing the *P* of Pontoise on its chest.

Hugh's gaze shot to Terrence's and back to the boy. He reached out to pat the boy on his shoulder. "You have helped me much," he said. Then turning to the nuns he added, "Take him to my home, Sisters. The cook will feed you well and you can rest."

Hugh turned back to his brother and neither needed to speak the common thought in their minds. The saddle had come from Pontoise. The man could only have been Corvey.

"I don't know if we can find him, Hugh," Terrence said.

Hugh gave him a measured look. "But Adele would know that Corvey went to Chantilly." Without another word, Hugh leapt onto Cepheus's back. He wheeled the stallion around, and a moment later they were racing back to the keep.

Hugh threw the door wide and took the stairs two at a time. He did not bother to knock, but burst into Adele's rooms like a Saracen assassin coming over the walls of a fortress.

The room was empty. Hugh crossed to the

maid-in-waiting's cell and threw open the door. That, too, was vacant. Angrily, Hugh slammed his fist against the stone wall. The solar! She would be there. He crossed back to the door, and as he reached it, his boot landed on some hard object among the rushes. He kicked at the rock in vexation, and, as he did, a glint of gold caught his eye.

Hugh bent over and reached through the straw for the metal object, but before his fingers touched it, he knew what it was. The soft blue sapphire cabochon was cracked, and one of the pearls that framed it had loosened from its setting, but it was Catherine's. Slowly, he turned the pendant over in his hand. Someone had taken the tip of a knife to the inscription, digging deep scratches through the finely etched script. It didn't matter, though. Hugh knew the words by heart. If only he had heeded their meaning from the first time he heard them. They had been a portent of all that was to be between Catherine and himself.

Vous estes ma ioy mondeine.

You are my earthly joy. Don't be gone, Catherine, he prayed. *Wherever you are, be alive. Let me find you. Let me save you. Let me know that you are safe.*

Closing his fingers around the pendant, Hugh ran in the direction of the solar. Just as he had in her bedroom, though, he found the solar deserted. Hugh raced back down the hallway and down the stairs. He leapt down the last dozen steps, sending frightened housekeepers scattering for protection behind timbers and stone pillars. Among them he recognized the maiden who served Adele personally. He took her by the arm and drew her out from the corner she cowered in. "Where is your lady?" he asked, ignoring the wide-eyed fear that patterned her face.

"I—I don't know," she stuttered. Then, seeing that this was the worst possible answer, she added, "Perhaps in the chapel. She goes there often at this time of day."

Hugh nodded, released her arm, and started in the direction of the chapel that had been built for the duke's family in the far wing of the castle.

"Nay, Your Grace," the woman called out.

Hugh turned to stare at her, his brow knit into a deep furrow. The woman wrung her hands self-consciously. "Not that chapel. She goes to the old one."

"The old one?" Hugh repeated in disbelief.

She nodded. "It is holier," she explained. "Because of the relic, the bit of the shroud Christ's body was wrapped in. A knight from the first Crusade brought it back and had it enshrined in the altar of the old chapel."

It was all the explanation Hugh needed. Hugh changed direction and raced for the door just as Terrence burst through it. "Hugh," he said, his urgency adding an edge to his words. "The old chapel."

"I know," Hugh replied. Together they raced for the forgotten structure that stood in the shadows of the keep.

* * *

Catherine knelt before the altar, her eyes never leaving the jeweled dagger in Adele's hands. The candles that had warmed her frozen body and filled her with hope an hour ago, now putrefied the still chapel air with acrid smoke that hung like a cloud among the rafters and against the thatched roof. It stung her eyes and made her throat ache. But it did not cloud her vision of the needle-sharp dudgeon Adele held above the flames on the altar.

"This dagger came from the vaults of the king of Jerusalem," Adele said in her singsongy voice. "It was found upon the very soil where Christ walked. It is holy indeed." She held the blade closer to the flame letting the heat blacken it, purging it of any evil. Carefully, she poured a scented oil on it, making the flame leap higher. Then she grasped it by its jeweled haft and held it aloft before the altar. Throwing back her head, she mumbled fervent words of prayer that Catherine could not make out, and then she lowered the blade, holding it at arm's length as she dipped the fingertips of her free hand into the scented oil again.

Now Adele came around to Catherine. She reached out with a single, oil-coated finger and drew the sign of the cross upon her forehead. Catherine looked up at her, hoping against hope that she would see some sign of sanity in Adele's eyes. But all she saw was a glassy stare. Adele had gone slack-jawed; her eyes were dilated and her face flushed. Catherine closed her eyes and sighed.

Adele moved to stand beside her. She grasped a handful of Catherine's hair and put the dagger against it, sawing back and forth until a foot's length of the red-gold tresses lay in her hand. Walking to the altar, she held the shorn locks to the flames. Catherine watched her hair burn. The foul smell assaulted her nostrils, mixing with the candle smoke and ancient dust. Adele dropped the burning hair on the altar and returned for more. She reached for another lock as the door to the chapel flew open.

Hugh stopped dead in the doorway staring at the scene before him. The chapel was filled with the smoke of over a hundred candles that burned everywhere around the sacrarium. They covered the altar and stood amid the rushes on the floor. In the center of the altar knelt Catherine, her hair streaming in a wild froth of red-gold curls to the place at the base of her back where her hands were bound with rope. Beside her stood Adele, a long thin-bladed dagger held in her hand.

Behind him, Hugh heard Terrence utter his disbelief. "My God," his brother whispered. "She is insane."

Adele looked up, her fingers still coiled around Catherine's hair. "You see, Hugh?" she called to him, her voice strong and strangely high-pitched. "There is no escape from your sins."

Turning her attention back to Catherine, she began sawing off another handful of the flame-
colored tresses.

Hugh stepped forward, intent on stopping the
vile abuse, but Adele was quick. She hacked off
the locks with a single stroke and then turned
to face Hugh, the glistening blade of her weapon
pointed directly at his heart.

"Do not come closer!" she warned. " 'Tis
God's work done here. And you shall not stop
it!" She looked him up and down and a sneer
of distaste curled her lips. "You are an abomi-
nation before God! You and your whore have
defiled a sacred abbey, you have broken the laws
of the Lord with your adultery."

Hugh watched Adele's every move with sharply
focused intent. She was too close to Catherine
for Hugh to try to take the dudgeon from her
yet, and the fanatical glint in her eyes made him
wary of every move she made. Both he and Terrence had seen the light of fanaticism in the eyes
of Saracens and they knew enough to give it an
absolute respect. Men with such a glint in their
eyes were always the worse opponents. Wild and
undisciplined, anything might happen when you
faced such a man—and Hugh knew that Adele
could be just as unpredictable.

As he listened to Adele, watching her every
move for an opportunity to strike, he also kept
watch over Catherine. Something was very amiss
with her. Although Adele had said his name and
his voice echoed through the rafters, Catherine

had not moved. She knelt with her head bowed, mindless of the locks that Adele sheared from her. Mindless of anything that went on around her. Hugh saw her sway every so sightly on her knees and realized that she was close to swooning. How long had she been forced to kneel there? And when had Adele last fed her or given her water?

Anger consumed Hugh. Catherine had done nothing. Nothing but love him. Nothing but need him. She had given him everything she had, and for such a gift she deserved to be sheltered and loved, not punished. Not called names and made to atone for her sins. He stood watching the horrid scene before him and his fury mounted with each passing second that Catherine was made to kneel before the pagan altar Adele had created.

Who was the evil one? he asked himself. The woman who knelt meekly before the altar, or the knife-wielding demon who had forced her there? Because Adele dressed her actions and her words in the name of God, did that make the horrors she perpetrated here acceptable in the eyes of God? In his heart, Hugh knew this was not so. Catherine had faced her sin with admission and prayers for absolution. But Adele denied hers and glorified them in the name of the Lord.

Adele!" he called out sharply as she reached for a third handful of hair. "This is not sanctioned by God! Let Catherine go before you mire your immortal soul in such sin as can never be washed clean."

Adele turned to stare at him. She set her back rod-straight and narrowed her eyes to two tiny slits in the hawkish planes of her face. "Do not think to tell *me* of God, *husband!*" She spat the word like some loathsome bile she must rid herself of. "I have purified myself while you have defiled yourself and our marriage. How *dare* you speak to me of holiness! Get out of this place before you stain it as you befouled the abbey. Have you no Godliness in you at all that you would come here? I have prepared an altar for the sacred cleansing of this woman's soul. It is her only chance of attaining everlasting life," she explained. "At least I will have saved her eternal soul while you destroyed it."

"You are deranged, Adele. You have taken God and used him, and that is the worst of all sins. No one who would kill another in the name of God is truly meek."

"You know nothing about it!" she screamed at him. Hugh stared at her in fury, his face alive with his anger. "I know so much more about it than you could imagine. What do you think the Knights Templar were? Simply men who justified their riches and lust for blood by claiming it in God's name. I know *everything* of it, and I know it is evil."

"*She* is evil!" Adele swept her arm around, pointing at Catherine. But as she did, the long sleeves of her gown swept across the altar sending a handful of candles tumbling into the rushes. Immediately the rushes burst into tiny pockets of flame. Adele stared down at the minute bonfires all around her in fascination. Then, with a feverish cackle, she turned to Hugh and smiled.

"There is no more sacred rite of purification than that of fire, is there? How fitting that these sins be washed away with heat and flame." Without another word, she reached across the altar and swept every candle onto the floor.

Terrence jumped forward beside Hugh as the flames spread quickly across the floor. "The building will be engulfed in moments!" he whispered urgently.

Hugh watched Adele ignore the flames that spread like a pox. Already the fire licked the base of the timbers, and he knew that Terrence was right, in less than a handful of minutes, the entire chapel would be engulfed in flames. But Adele seemed not to care in the least. She turned toward her victim, the dagger held aloft. "You will not defile my world any further," she cried out to Catherine. "You will not!"

Hugh was upon Adele long before the blade could find its mark. He ripped the dagger from her hand, letting it clatter to the floor. "Run, Catherine!" he cried. "You must run!"

Catherine looked up as though seeing Hugh for the first time. She struggled up from her knees, and it was then that Hugh saw the iron manacle that cut into her leg and bound her to the altar. Filled with disgust at Adele's dementia and her cruelty, Hugh turned her loose. "Save yourself, Adele," he told her with revulsion. Turning his attention to Catherine, Hugh drew his broadsword from its scabbard. He grasped it with both hands and in a single stroke, cleaved in half one of the iron links that tethered Catherine to the altar. But Adele was determined that her work not be undone.

Lunging forward, she grabbed the vessel of oil she had used earlier. With a lightning-quick motion, she threw the oil at Catherine, soaking her kirtle. Then she grabbed a candle from the floor and tossed it onto the hem of Catherine's dress. The single flame multiplied and grew, and in seconds her dress was aflame. Sudden fear startled Catherine from the stupor of illness that had fogged her brain only moments ago. With a scream, she bent to beat at the flames, but her sleeves had been soaked in the sacred oil Adele brought and they, too, were soon aflame.

Hugh grabbed Catherine and threw her to the floor, covering her with his own body to extinguish the flames. All around them the building was engulfed in the blaze. The ancient timbers were like tinder, and the flames used them like wisps of straw. The air was alive with cracking and popping wood and the smell of burning grasses. The flames of Catherine's dress put out, Hugh jumped back onto his feet and gathered her into his arms. Across the chapel, Terrence

called to Hugh. "Hurry! The roof will give way
any time."

Hugh ran to the chapel door where Terrence
waited with the door held wide. They stepped
out into the bailey to find the staff and serfs
frantically forming a line to pass buckets of water
to put out the fire. Turning to Terrence, Hugh
handed Catherine to his brother. "I have to go
back in."

Terrence's head jerked up in disbelief. But before he could say a word, Hugh had disappeared
into the inferno.

As he stepped inside the chapel, one far corner of the roof gave way. Its flaming timbers
crashed onto the floor, carrying part of the wall
with it and creating a barrier between him and
where Adele stood. She had climbed onto the
altar, and clawed at the crude crucifix that hung
from the wall.

"Adele!" Hugh cried above the roar of the fire.
"You must get out! The building is going to col-
lapse at any moment."

Adele either did not hear him or chose not
to. She continued to attempt to climb onto the
cross. Hugh stepped forward just as another
huge beam crashed to the ground. Jumping
back, he found himself completely cut off from
Adele.

"Adele!" he called again. "Come out!"

Turning, Adele gave him the ugly glare she
would have bestowed upon a leper. "I will not

let the relic be lost to fire! 'Tis the cloth from Christ's burial! It must be saved!"

Hugh stared in disbelief as Adele turned back to the cross and attempted to scale its smooth, well-oiled surface. The fire had surrounded the altar, and flames leapt up to lick at the hem of her skirts. "Adele!" he cried once more.

"Go away!" came the reply. Hugh could barely see now so thick was the smoke that filled the ancient place. Then there was another crash of timbers falling and a single scream. Hugh felt a heavy hand clamp down on his shoulder.

"Come out or you shall be the next one." It was Gladmoore firmly directing him out of the chapel. "Ye have someone here who's in need of your care," he added.

Hugh stepped out into the bright sunlight. The serfs had stopped their bucket line, for the structure was nothing more than a tinder box now. He walked over to where Terrence stood holding Catherine in his arms. She did not move, and he would have thought her asleep if sleep in such a ruckus was possible.

"She is ill, Hugh," Terrence told him. "I'm not certain she even knows where she is or what has just happened."

"It is just as well that she doesn't," Hugh said as he gathered her into his own arms.

"Adele?" Terrence asked quietly.

"Dead."

Terrence shook his head. "You could not reach her?"

"No," Hugh said. "She would not come out. She wouldn't listen. She wanted the relic, and nothing else mattered."

Terrence pressed his mouth into a grim line. "She has always been like that, caring only about what she wants and needs. Still, no one deserves to die in such a way."

Hugh looked down at Catherine. He did not want to hear about Adele anymore. She had lied to him, gone behind his back, ridiculed him, and attempted to murder the woman he loved No, he thought. He'd had enough of death and destruction in his life. Now all he wanted was to be with the woman who lay in his arms and see to her care. She was light as a feather as he held her. Her skin was pale and translucent except for the dark smudges that lay like smokey crescents beneath her eyes. A thick streak of black soot darkened one side of her face and her lips were dry and cracked from lack of water. Hugh wrapped his arms gently around her and, as he did, he instantly understood Terrence's concerns, for she raged with fever. Touching her skin was like laying a hand upon the sands of the Holy Land at midday. Her breathing was shallow and came in short, uneven pants, and a thin film of perspiration coated her face. He held her close, burying his face in her hair. Someday, he swore, he would find Corvey and kill him for bringing her here and subjecting her to such horror.

Holding her as though he carried the most precious object in all the world, Hugh carried Catherine away from the smoke and fire and destruction. He did not once look back, but walked straight ahead. Ready for a new day.

Twenty-three

Catherine sat at the table raised above the two hundred wedding guests and tried valiantly to suppress the smile that had begun to make her cheeks ache. It was no use, however, for the grin seemed permanently etched upon her face and today, of all days, she saw little point in trying to suppress it.

She was quite certain that there had never been as fine a wedding in all of France. Upon hearing that his cousin's eldest daughter and his favorite vassal were to be married, the king had insisted that the wedding and celebration take place at his palace. Golden platters of food flowed in a never-ending stream from the kitchens while minstrels and jugglers dotted the room, plying amusements for the guests. Along the large wedding table was assembled her entire family. Her mother and father glowed with pride and pleasure, for they had made it eminently clear that they could not have chosen a son-in-law whom they would prefer to Hugh. Her brothers and sisters created a long line of heads down one side of the table, and beside her brother Jean sat Avril, proudly discussing the assorted adventures which afflicted a page. Terrence also sat at the long table, and Hugh's older brother, Giles, too, whom Catherine thought she would come to like very well indeed. But best of all was the large, warm hand that rested gently over hers upon the table. It was Hugh's hand, and it was the hand of her husband.

The other assembled guests comprised the highest ranks of the French nobility, and although Catherine could not hear it, their conversations this day leaned heavily toward the unusual story of the wedding couple, who, it was rumored, were deeply in love. They drew not only a good deal of conversation about their unusual affection for each other but in regard to the striking pair they made. And as many comments were made about the Duke of Pontoise's broad shoulders and long blond mane as about the stunning beauty of the bride. But Catherine did not concern herself with the kind and, surreptitiously envious, discussions of her guests. She concentrated all her attentions on her husband.

Her husband.

Not even two months ago, she had thought she would never see Hugh again much less find herself wed to him. Watching him as he carried on a conversation with her father, Catherine was filled with an overwhelming joy. There was no finer man in all of France, or the world for that matter. And that they were about to embark upon a life intertwined was a miracle as absolute as the miracles of the Bible. A gentle tap upon her shoulder drew Catherine's attention away from her husband. Turning, she found Sister Edith smiling down at her.

" 'Tis getting late, my dear!" she said with a happy smile. "Gilbert and I have made all the preparations. And I must say, I have had one of the best times of my life! I should like to make a habit of it, but I don't believe Sister Mary James would think preparation of the wedding bed an appropriate hobby for us!"

Catherine laughed and placed a gentle kiss on Edith's soft, round cheek. "I shall miss you and Gilbert so much," she said softly. "And Sister Mary James and everyone. You have become like my family to me."

Sister Edith huffed and made much of flicking away a wayward tear. "You have given us the very best thing, my dear. You have given us the joy of seeing you happy. You know, you were never destined for the *abbaye*. This has always been where you belonged. Gilbert and I knew that from the first day you arrived here. It's just that the way is not always clear at first. We must always have faith, you know."

Catherine nodded.

"Now, no more dawdling, my dear. Your husband must be anxious to quit this place and have you to himself."

"Edith!" Sister Gilbert exclaimed from behind

her as she noticed Catherine's blush. "You'll frighten our poor Catherine."

Catherine laughed. "But she is right, Gilbert. It is time to quit this place." Rising, Catherine leaned over to kiss Hugh gently on the cheek.

Hugh turned to her in surprise. "Cay, where are you going?"

"Where we can be alone," she told him with a warm smile.

Hugh smiled in return. "Then I shall make haste to end my conversation with your father and the pleasantries of thanking the king, for there is nothing I desire more than to hold you in my arms this night."

Giving his hand a tight squeeze, Catherine took leave of her wedding guests and followed Edith and Gilbert to the apartments the king had given over to them. An hour later Catherine sat in a chair before the hearth, letting the flames warm her as she waited for her husband's arrival. There was a short knock and Catherine rose to greet Hugh as he came into the room.

The sight that greeted Hugh took his breath away. The chamber was lit only by a single torch and the light of the fire burning brightly in the hearth as he entered. Lit from behind, Catherine's diaphanous nightgown was like a sheer veil that accentuated, rather than hid, her shapely form. Beneath its flowing lines he could see the clear silhouette of her slender waist and gently rounded hips as well as the full curve of her young breasts. Her hair was like a red-gold cloud that billowed about her face and shoulders. And, best of all, upon her lips he saw a smile that was warm and welcoming.

Slowly, Hugh crossed the room until he stood mere inches away from her. "Are you certain you are ready?" he asked.

Catherine smiled. "My love, I have awaited this day for so long. I am not afraid. I am eager."

Hugh smiled. "I, too, am eager." Reaching out, he cupped her chin in the palm of his hand and she turned her face up to his in earnest desire. Hugh looked down at her and the softest of moans escaped his lips as he lost himself in the sea-green depths of her gaze. She filled a void in his soul that no one, and nothing, had ever been able to fill before or since. And since the day he had met her, he had thirsted for more and yet more of her sweet fulfillment.

Catherine reached up onto her toes drawing him to her, and his mouth closed over hers with ardent need. She met his kiss with her own urgency, parting her lips so that his tongue might gain entrance to deep recesses of her mouth. Hugh plunged his tongue into the soft warmth that awaited him there. Flicking the tip of his tongue against smooth white teeth, he gently dipped into the warmest place within, drinking in the warmth of her. His hands splayed across her back and then dropped lower to cup her buttocks in his palm. Hugh drew her closer against him as his need raged stronger with each passing moment.

Catherine matched him passion for passion and need for need. Almost of their own volition, she felt her arms twine around his neck. Her fingers knit their way into his thick blond hair. Caressing. Exploring. Memorizing. She felt the hardness of his broad chest against her breasts as her nipples grew taut and peaked as her desire grew. Hugh's fingers traced a tantalizing trail along the crevice between her buttocks until Catherine could not prevent herself from instinctively pressing her hips more strongly against his. She felt the hardness of him against her, and felt a wave of heat rush through her loins in response.

His lips never leaving hers, Hugh slipped an arm beneath her legs and lifted her into his arms. He carried her to the elaborately dressed bed that Edith and Gilbert had prepared for them, and laid her upon it. Never taking his gaze from hers, he drew off his tunic and hose, leaving them where they fell. Then he, too, stretched out across the fine linen sheets so that their bodies molded against each other, limb to limb and rib to rib. He could not leave her, even for a moment and so, still holding her, Hugh sketched a path from her shoulder to the very tip of her nipple with his thumb. Reaching for the ribbon that gathered the gown at her neck, he pulled the bow until it gave way. Spreading its gossamer cloth, he dipped his head to her breast, teasing each nipple in turn with his tongue and teeth until she moaned with desire.

Catherine pulled his mouth harder over the sensitive peaks of her breasts, thrilling at the heat that coursed through every limb and pooled itself deep within her belly. Her hips began to move in rhythmic circles, reaching for some ecstasy she did not fully understand. She knew only that she would not be complete until Hugh had buried himself deep within her and satisfied her aching need for their union. She felt his hand move gently across her belly, sending streaks of fire burning through her. His fingers moved lower, and lower still, until they touched her most intimate place at the warm triangle between her legs. She felt his hand spread her legs and his fingers gently seek access there. And then, as his mouth moved over hers, and his chest pressed against the fullness of her breasts, she knew a sensation that was more sweet than any nectar she'd ever sipped.

It began small and tantalizing, seeking venue through every part of her from her fingertips to her very soul. And it grew. Stronger and stronger still until she writhed with the power of its heat. Knowing she was close to finding satiety, Hugh moved between her legs. Their eyes met. Gazes locked. Green reached for blue and blue found green. Catherine arched to meet Hugh as he buried the length of him deep within her—their eyes never parting, their love fully met, their union reaching to the very heart of their being.

Slowly, Hugh began to move within her. First with long, full strokes that rekindled the fire in her belly and brought it further aflame until it drew her to a new height that was beyond bearing. Catherine arched higher, meeting him thrust for thrust and need for need. She felt the muscles of Hugh's stomach tighten and his breath shorten. She wrapped her arms around his shoulders, moving with his movement, clinging to him, reaching for him. And then, when she thought her need was too great, that she would break and crumble for want of all of him, she felt a molten fire pour through her. Gasping, she wrapped her legs around him clasping him within her, and suddenly Hugh shuddered. His mouth against hers, he drove deep within her, pouring himself into her. Filling her even as she filled his need.

Locked together, Catherine and Hugh lay entwined upon their marriage bed. There was no ending of one or beginning of the other. All that existed was the oneness of their being, the presence which was them together. Catherine reached out to gently trace along the fine straight line of Hugh's nose and across his brow. Hugh turned to meet her gaze and a gentle smile played across his mouth.

"Hugh," she said as tears of joy filled her eyes. "I love you so."

"And I love you, Catherine."

She smiled softly. "What shall you call me now?"

Hugh knit his brow and shook his head. "What shall I call you?"

"*Oui.* Ever since I have known you, you have called me by a pet name. Mite. Cay. And I am just wondering, now that we are wed, what name will you call me by? Catherine? Wife?"

Hugh reached for her hand and drew it to his lips. Locking his gaze with hers, he kissed her fingers. "What shall I call you? I shall call you what you are.

"I shall call you my Life."